THE WAR BEGINS IN PARIS

ALSO BY THEODORE WHEELER

Bad Faith

Kings of Broken Things

In Our Other Lives

THE WAR BEGINS IN PARIS

A NOVEL

THEODORE WHEELER

LITTLE, BROWN AND COMPANY
NEW YORK   BOSTON   LONDON

Little, Brown and Company
Hachette Book Group
1290 Avenue of the Americas, New York, NY 10104
littlebrown.com

First Edition: November 2023

Little, Brown and Company is a division of Hachette Book Group, Inc. The Little, Brown name and logo are trademarks of Hachette Book Group, Inc.

The publisher is not responsible for websites (or their content) that are not owned by the publisher.

The Hachette Speakers Bureau provides a wide range of authors for speaking events. To find out more, go to hachettespeakersbureau.com or email hachettespeakers@hbgusa.com.

Little, Brown and Company books may be purchased in bulk for business, educational, or promotional use. For information, please contact your local bookseller or the Hachette Book Group Special Markets Department at special.markets@hbgusa.com.

ISBN 9780316563673
LCCN 2023935067

Printing 1, 2023

LSC-C

Printed in the United States of America

No one is a Nazi. No one ever was.

—*Martha Gellhorn*

CONTENTS

PROLOGUE 1

A Story of Two Women – The Sudetenland

PART ONE 9

PARIS 11

Sunrise in Capoulade – About Us, Without Us – Meet Me at Maxim's
Prevailing Winds – Out of Order in Saint-Martin – Café Not Always
The Party – A Formerly Lovely Creature – Herschel Grynszpan
Night of Broken Glass – The Spree – Suspended Sentence

PART TWO 119

BAD NAUHEIM 121

Paris Postscript – Coughlin Compatriot Lands in Berlin
A Date Which Will Live in Infamy – Express Train to the Third Reich
The Grand Hotel – On the Balcony – Christmas Day
To Be Remembered – Lady Haw-Haw: A Royal Pain – xoxo Jane
The Living Martyr – Invitation to Gomorrah
Last Night at the Grand Hotel

CONTENTS

BERLIN 185

The Georgia Peach – The Adlon Gala – The Comic Opera
Between Grief and Nothing – Radio Zeesen – The Audition
Persil Bleibt Persil – Bombs over Berlin – Sweets and Cookies

STUTTGART 249

Like Clockwork – Station Platform in Nuremberg – Palace Solitude
The Scales – Only an Animal – Hotel Silber – One Step, Then Another
The Sword – The Cauldron – Two Sisters

SALZBURG 317

A Flood of Displaced Persons – For Most of It I Have No Words
Let It Die – The Trial

ACKNOWLEDGMENTS 342

PROLOGUE

A STORY OF TWO WOMEN

One was famous for her audacity, her beauty, her appetite for headlines. The things that made people love her were the same things that made people hate her.

The other woman, nobody ever noticed her.

They met in Paris in 1938, working as foreign correspondents. Jane Anderson spent most of that year on a speaking tour to rally support for the nationalist side of the Spanish Civil War. She had a way of putting herself at the center of a story, so it was no surprise that she was one of many journalists who took up a cause célèbre. Hemingway and Dos Passos and Gellhorn advocated for the elected republic: the socialists, the peasant soldiers who fought with birding guns and conspired to blow up bridges. Jane, on the other hand, sided with Franco and the clerical Fascists. She was a strict Catholic (ardent, anyway; Jane was strict about nothing) and she took it personal how the Republicans burned cathedrals and wanted to nationalize all the lucre owned by the Church. Jane loved the Church. All its pompous glory. The glittering robes and golden crosses and the little chime a burning censer made swinging from its chain with incense smoke trailing behind. Much the same as she loved the pomposity of Fascists and their claims to empire. That kind of ambition was addictive to some—aspiring to rule the world as the Romans did, as Charlemagne did, to make themselves a link in the chain of history. Not to say the Church and the Fascistas were the same thing, but in Spain that decade, in Jane's heart, they were close enough.

But there was more to her than her politics. Some facts about Jane Anderson, largely undisputed:

She was born in Atlanta in 1888. This made her fifty when she met the other woman, though Jane always claimed to be younger than she was. Thirty-six, at the most. Her mother came from a good family. Luckie Street in Atlanta is named for her grandfather. She was given his first name, Foster, though she took on Jane as an alias when she attended Piedmont College, and by the end of her life she responded only if addressed as Doña Juana. Her childhood was split between Georgia and Arizona, where her father was a lawman and a confidant of the showman Buffalo Bill Cody. (Jane knew him as Uncle Buffalo.) She was five foot nine, with deep-set green eyes and tawny-red hair she wore long, curled at the bottom. She was partial to chichi hats, dangling peacock feathers, pert silk bows, long jackets with epaulets on the shoulders. At one point she laid claim to being the most beautiful woman in the world. In those days she seduced Joseph Conrad (a national hero in Britain) and made a ludicrous bid to usurp his fortune. Her only defect, it was said, was her nose. Her nose was broad, the nostrils too prominent, and it made her look common to those who knew what a nose should look like. A phrenologist claimed, because of the shape of her nose, that she was prone to sociopathy; that she was a born liar; that it would be a crime if she ever reproduced. She never did.

Jane reported for the *Daily Mail* from both Allied and German trenches during the First War as the personal protégée of publisher Lord Northcliffe. She began carrying a Red Cross uniform to pose as a nurse to sneak in where journalists weren't supposed to go, then kept up the habit her entire life. After the war, she was an alcoholic, a failed actress. Her star fell. It became known that her life was a complete mess, as she wrote about her exploits in the news, in three novels. She stalked H. G. Wells. She hatched a scheme to assassinate Lenin. She accepted marriage proposals from at least two dozen men but was married only twice: once to a famous composer and once to a Spanish count who finagled a royal wedding at the Gothic cathedral in Seville as a bridal gift. Despite the honest commissions she made as a correspondent and that she was typically surrounded by rich men, she was almost always broke. She spent her whole life chasing money, as people do when they grow up teased with affluence that isn't really theirs.

Jane Anderson was one of the most baffling, provocative women of her generation, and she knew it. Most people struggled to resist her field of gravity.

The other woman (the one who had a talent for going unnoticed) was only twenty-four when the Second War started. She had been in Paris less than a year when she met Jane. This was her first time more than fifty miles away from the Mennonite assembly in Iowa where she was born. It was a remarkable thing to make a jump like that, though by all appearances she was an unremarkable woman.

As a girl, she was raised to value simplicity, sobriety, pacifism, and patriarchy. She and her siblings were educated at a public country school with children from neighboring farms, and she made regular trips to the town library to read its clothbound editions of German poetry and the collected works of Friedrich Schiller, which instilled in her an appreciation for personal freedom. At home she spoke a dialect of Pennsylvania Dutch. She was also fluent in Iowa-inflected English and could speak German with a low accent. She was a dour child. That was a strange trait for children in her assembly, where kids were typically mischievous and genial and overcome by boisterous laughter at any provocation. When she left home at age sixteen, the librarian in Kalona arranged for her to attend Coe College in Cedar Rapids. Once she left, according to the law of her commune, she could never return. She belonged to the rest of the world thereafter, if it would have her.

This young woman was tall and had dark hair, a square jaw, long, swinging arms. She moved like a stork stuck in mud because her legs had suffered severe nerve damage when she fell from an oak tree as a child. The muscles of her calves could not untense. In college, she spent most of her free time reading magazines in the school library, which was her way of learning about the world that existed outside Mennonite farms. She discovered a few women journalists who reported on war and politics. In back issues, she read firsthand accounts by Rebecca West and Jane Anderson. (Yes, Jane.) Saw Jane's stories about life and death in the trenches of Flanders. These were women who made their own way in the world (whose intelligence and appetites apparently weren't held against them). She wondered if Rebecca or Jane had ever been promised in marriage to a fifty-year-old bachelor farmer named Yoder. She was certain they had not.

Once she arrived in Paris, in the spring of 1938, she took a furnished room in a hotel in Montmartre. This woman could read and understand French but was hopeless when it came to speaking. Iowa was too heavy on her tongue. She wore tan shirts and slacks and a long canvas jacket that resembled a butcher's smock. She wandered the city alone at night. She was tall and glum and limped. Nobody bothered her. Nobody talked to her at all until she discovered the community of war journalists and bohemian poets and trust-fund novelists who then lived in Paris. They were everywhere, once she learned how to spot them.

Really, the story is about this woman. Her real name was Marthe Hess, but they all called her Mielle. Jane gave her that name.

She and Jane would meet in Paris. Jane would be a corrupting influence, as was her custom. They would spend every evening together for a torrid month to waylay the cabarets of Montmartre and observe a flash of violence during the November Pogrom firsthand, then Jane would vanish from Mielle's life just as quickly as she appeared.

Mielle would feel so lit up inside to have a wild friend like Jane Anderson. How unexpected it was that someone like herself, with her limp and her simple country manners, could be an intimate of someone like Jane. Someone like this young woman, who was raised on a religious commune to be the exact opposite of women like Jane.

How strange, then, how fitting, that Mielle would be plagued by visions and would one day cross the border into Germany with the intention of killing her friend Jane.

But that's not where the story starts.

THE SUDETENLAND

(William L. Shirer)
As reported on September 24, 1938

There was some confusion among us all at Godesberg this morning...but tonight, as seen from Berlin, the position is this: Hitler has demanded that Czechoslovakia not later than Saturday, October 1, agree to the handing over of Sudetenland to Germany. Mr. Chamberlain has agreed to convey this demand to the Czechoslovak Government. The very fact that he, with all the authority of a man who is political leader of the British Empire, has taken upon himself this task is accepted here, and I believe elsewhere, as meaning that Mr. Chamberlain backs Hitler up.

That's why the German people I talked with in the streets of Cologne this morning, and in Berlin this evening, believe there'll be peace. As a matter of fact, what do you think the new slogan in Berlin is tonight? It's in the evening papers. It's this: "With Hitler and Chamberlain for peace."

PART ONE

PARIS

October–November 1938

SUNRISE IN CAPOULADE

What she would remember most was waiting in the cafés early in the morning. Before sunrise with the light sluggish behind the terra-cotta facades, that sensuous curve of sandstone from the lips and hips of art deco that were lined up in rows of gray like the wool jumpers the schoolgirls wore that season, with just an occasional gabardine pink or lavender. Mielle never stayed in a hotel that was garish enough to be painted in bright colors, the same as she never, as a girl, wore a coat that was anything but black. Only white blouses and bonnets, black coats. Even those days in Paris, two years before the invasion, she dressed plain. Photographs from this time show her in a black canvas jacket cut past her waist, with tan trousers in wool, and a pair of unlaced men's brogans on her feet. A handsome young woman with a worried face, dressed in men's work clothes. She would be pretty now, what we consider pretty, in an androgynous way. But from the desperate look in her eyes in photographs, you can tell she was used to being ignored.

She lived downhill from Sacré-Coeur de Montmartre and caught the first morning train at Abbesses Station. She always left early, even on a Saturday, like this one, with the shops closed behind their gates as she limped to the station. Her dark hair was combed straight back with a perfumed oil she bought at the Ornano flea market. It smelled of rosemary and thyme and, vaguely, camphor. Her jacket, also bought at the flea market, reminded her of the smock her father wore when he butchered animals. It had a pronounced collar that flopped with the stiff way she walked. She could move smooth only with great concentration; without it, she devolved to a halting gait. Her hotel was halfway up the hill on rue Gabrielle. Most of the time, when she returned home, she zagged up narrow side streets to avoid the steepest inclines. It was impossible to avoid the hill altogether.

There was a certain pride Mielle felt, being up first. Sliding into a subterranean coach that was empty except for a flower woman with white hair pinned to her temples or a broom salesman with big ears, his pack of sticks and bristles blocking the aisle. All of them with jacket collars over the backs of their necks. That contentedness showed in her face when she climbed from her stop in the Latin Quarter, hair falling in her eyes, with the Dôme still lit green from sodium lights embedded in the ground. The first peach blush of dawn was on the horizon.

She felt, deep inside her, that something special was going to happen that day. It was her twenty-fourth birthday.

Her whole life, she had visions that made her worry it was the devil inside her and not God. When she was a girl, her visions scared her so much, they were so grisly, so vivid, that she couldn't describe what she saw to anyone. She saw over and over, when she was sixteen, that a stranger would come live on her family's farm, and, because of what this stranger would do to her, she would be forced to leave the collective forever. Bad things had happened to her in Iowa—things she didn't ever talk about, that had spoiled what her life was supposed to become. She learned the hard way to believe her visions, because they always came true. The same would happen this time, during the war.

But what she felt that morning in the Latin Quarter wasn't her second sight, which always left her with a stabbing pain behind her eyes. This was just a feeling, just a hope, that her life could be extraordinary because of who she was inside. This sort of thing is easy to understand. She was young.

Mielle was the first to arrive at Café Capoulade. The terrace hadn't yet been watered off and was still dusted with ashes from the all-night smokers who had leaned forward in wicker chairs to argue until closing time. Inside, it smelled of spilled wine, but the bread was being delivered and that smelled better. The cook wiped sleep from his eyes and lit the gas burners. The waiters polished the dishes and preened one another's costumes. And in the corner, smiling to herself, Mielle was getting settled. She pulled a small notebook and a pencil from inside her jacket, then ordered a soft-boiled egg and a café au lait, three sugars, and a basket with half a baguette and strawberry jam. Mielle didn't have to order the bread and jam, as that came complimentary, but she worried the waiter would forget. She was very hungry.

She drank two cups of coffee, slowly, and watched how the sun rose lazily, then all at once. The density of the light appeared to lessen by the minute outside the window until she could see all the way down boulevard Saint-Michel to the Luxembourg Gardens. The color of the city bloomed from gray to its marble and sandstone, those pinks, as the light came up.

Before long, other reporters milled along the walkway, hungover, with surreptitious glances to keep an eye out for the door of Capoulade. Foreign correspondents were like somnambulists. Their mornings were different than Mielle's. The walkways swept and watered by nine o'clock. The gates of shops raised to expose the florists and flowers, the butchers and plucked geese. The terraces arranged neatly. The cafés warm and buttery with breakfast.

All sorts of writers, famous and otherwise, revolutionary or otherwise, stopped by Café Capoulade when they weren't trying to be seen at Les Deux Magots or chatting with Sylvia Beach on the ratty sofas inside Shakespeare and Company. If it was fame and glamour and celebrity thinkers you wanted, sipping espresso at Les Deux Magots made more sense. If you wanted to meet Gertrude Stein (charging into late middle age with her hair butched) or James Joyce (frail and white-haired with a black patch over his left eye),

Shakespeare and Company was the spot. If it was coffee and ham and eggs and talk about transit permits, Capoulade was the place to be.

That day (maybe at breakfast, maybe at the Anglo-American press briefing), Mielle was supposed to meet William Shirer. They had both graduated from Coe College, in different decades, and that year Shirer would become a star correspondent for CBS Radio because of his broadcasts from Germany. Mielle supposed meeting Shirer was what her earlier feeling was about, that he might change her life. He was coming with his boss, Edward Murrow, who was bureau chief for CBS in Europe. Both men would be famous in a general way soon, not solely among other reporters, like Sigrid Schultz or Howard Smith or Virginia Cowles was famous. Mielle had dressed up as much as she could to impress them. A silk blouse, tan, with a borrowed silk scarf, white. She ironed a crease into her slacks, also tan. These were her best clothes. She bathed that morning, in icy water, because the boiler was still cold before sunrise. Her skin was pearly, chilled and scrubbed. She felt translucent. Mielle was so self-conscious, dolled up, that she pulled on her long canvas jacket to cover her body. She told herself that she could unbutton or remove the jacket later, when she was to meet Shirer and Murrow, but she would forget. That jacket was like a second skin.

Mielle was supposed to give Shirer a packet of postcards from Iowa. Her old dean at Coe had sent them, as a way to thank Shirer for the letter of reference he'd written that got Mielle a job reporting from Paris. Someone at Coe probably noticed that Shirer had earned a little notoriety and hoped he had some money to spare. They sent Mielle these postcards in a manila envelope via transatlantic post. Scenes around campus with little notes from professors scratched on the backs.

On top of that, Mielle hoped that Murrow might need to hire more correspondents to report on the situation in Europe. Mielle was so green, so quiet, she didn't really stand a chance of getting a job like that. But still, atoms bounced around inside her gut that told her such a thing was possible. If the sound of her voice was just right, if those men thought she was clever enough, if they liked her, then why couldn't Mielle become one of them?

That morning there were ten of them at the big table. Not yet Shirer and Murrow, but a few names. Dorothy Thompson, who was loud, who acted like she was old money, and who was the first American journalist Hitler expelled from Germany, in 1934, something she was very proud of. And Jean-Gérard Dreyfus, with his spectacles and his bald head, tweed suits, and British sweaters. He didn't write all that eloquent but was very good at the important parts of the job. He used the nom de guerre *J-G* and was claimed by both French and American writers because his childhood had been split between Paris and Washington. Virginia Cowles of the *London Daily Telegraph* was there too. A. J. Liebling of *The New Yorker*. A few green correspondents fresh from Eastern colleges in navy blazers and striped ties, the same style they wore in prep school.

These people were fairly cruel to Mielle. Uncaring, at least. They were self-involved and gauche. Successful, but pretentious. Mielle felt like the most unlikely member of this fraternity, like an amphibious creature among witty pros with their Ivy Leagues and family estates and their fathers' notorious suicides. How glamorous they were capable of being. And she was not. She was quiet and blended in with the wallpaper. She wrapped her chest flat with the lapels of her jacket and avoided looking anyone in the eye. A rumor had gone around that she was a virgin. Not many of them seemed to even remember her name, but she became an acquaintance, a familiar face at the table. "The tall one," they might call her. "The young one." "Her."

This was generally acceptable to the young woman. Even when the others did remember her real name—Marthe Hess— they tended to say it wrong. (She pronounced it "Mah-tah," the way they'd said it in her assembly, not how some French said it, "Mahr-*teh,*" with the aspiration exaggerated, or the atonal American way, "Marth," or, worse, something closer to "Marf," like she had been subjected to by her composition professor in college.) She dreaded hearing her real name spoken by anyone those first months in Paris—mostly because it was forbidden for her family back home to mention her name. She had left that person behind in Iowa, she believed. If it came down to being Marthe Hess or being invisible, she preferred to be invisible.

It was Alden Linden Elder who first invited her to join them at Capoulade. He'd spotted Mielle while they both covered the annual *Harper's Bazaar* spring fashion broadcast. Very often since then, he arrived not long after her in the morning, so they had a few moments alone.

They were nearly the same age; he was twenty-six. Neither of them was experienced enough to belong there. That early October in Capoulade, Alden sat next to her at the table, said, "Bonjour," not at all ironically, then reached across her plate to snatch a piece of bread from her basket. Capoulade was both home and office for Alden. Most of his stories were broadcast over shortwave radio just around the corner at a state-run studio in the Sorbonne. If Alden kept an apartment, he went there only to change clothes and collect his mail.

It was well known among them that Alden had his heart broken when he was at Yale. The Vassar girl he'd planned to marry hadn't even returned the engagement ring when she ran off with a French boxer, one who was knocked out by Joe Louis at Madison Square Garden in 1935, dispatched back to Dijon after three rounds with Alden's sweetheart in tow. It was in the hope of impressing this woman with his own Continental bona fides that Alden arranged for a post in France with International News Service. His father was old friends with William Randolph Hearst.

In Mielle's eyes, Alden Linden Elder was a hopeless case. He was tall, with a pronounced stoop to compensate for his endowment. He wasn't yet bald but would soon be bald. He had a soft tenor and wooden way of speaking. But Alden was fascinated with her, and she often liked the attention, whether she would admit it or not. He'd never met someone like Mielle, who didn't seem to belong anywhere. "You know so little about anything," he sometimes told her. "No offense." With that long sloping brow, his small nose, his skin pale like a child's, it was easy to forgive him.

"Tell me again," he said to her that morning, the two of them in the packed corner. "Tell me what it's like to live in an agrarian cult."

"*A cult?*" she objected. Her voice quiet and contralto. "The Anabaptists? They are Christians, but they believe in a more focused way."

"Now, that. Why do you say 'they' instead of 'we'? Are you not one of them?"

She didn't want to tell Alden again how it was with the Mennonites in the assembly. But he wouldn't let it drop unless she explained.

"Once I left, I can't ever go back."

"Never? Now—"

"Take this down so you'll remember." She plucked his notepad from his front pocket and slapped it on the table. "It's the last time I'll explain."

But she didn't tell him any more about her people, or why she'd stepped off the commune only to attend school or ride in a buggy to raid the Kalona library until a professor whisked her away when she was sixteen. She didn't want to think about the looks on her parents' and little sister's faces as she drove away—that moment when she was forced to give up her family and all their scrupulous traditions by stepping into a shiny Hudson Model T. She wanted only to be present in Café Capoulade on the Left Bank of Paris. What did she need Iowa for in that moment?

In that moment, in fact, Mielle looked across the café and noticed someone standing at the bar who looked like Jane Anderson. Tall, with tawny-red hair, in a wide-brimmed hat and a black silk dress and an overlarge scarf. She had never met Jane; she didn't even presume that she would. Before that year, Mielle hadn't thought of Jane Anderson since those lonely days in college when she read back-issue magazines and first learned that a young woman could travel the world, that she could write about war and politics and sex and whatever she wanted. Jane had done all that as a young woman. So how strange for Mielle to spot a woman who looked like Jane Anderson sitting across the room in a crowded café. The woman sipped a brandy at the bar with two men, both of them doting on her. She didn't acknowledge the correspondents at the table, even though the café was to the gills with writers that morning. Not yet Shirer and Murrow, but others who had spent the past week holding fast to the fender of a truck that belonged to the Czech army, flying along country roads in the borderland to see if war would break out, only to have their stories ignored or cut down to filler because Chamberlain had been compelled to give half of Czechoslovakia to Hitler for nothing. The reporters were exhausted and buzzing, disoriented, like honeybees are punch-drunk in October once the temperature drops.

"There's nothing to stop war from coming now," Dorothy Thompson said, orating, her graying hair combed back wet over the shape of her head. She was very erect and expecting in her posture, her eyebrows arched in contemplation. She was square, a large, capable woman, and her voice was surprisingly feminine, high, and a bit stiff because of her breeding. She smelled nice, like a finicky flower that grew only on Tahiti or some remote island you had heard of but couldn't find on a map. Thompson stared out onto the boulevard, in that moment, where life went on as normal. The boxy black taxis racing around one another, the walkway crowded with weekenders and students and housekeepers who rushed to pick up a few things from a market during their half-Saturday on the clock, these last few hours of the French workweek.

"The war has already started," Thompson observed. "But look at the people here. They can't believe it, they won't. Running around with bunches of flowers in their arms."

"An old gentleman told me last night, over there," Alden said, pointing to the bar, "that there is no possibility France could ever lose a war. And do you know why? Because la culture. The Germans know nothing of how to cook and eat and enjoy life, he claimed, so Germany is a very poor nation."

"Is that so?"

"And France is a very rich nation, by his definition."

"They do have that going for them. I won't argue."

"He had all sorts of things to say about the French race," Alden said.

"That's how they always put it. But French isn't a race."

"French is a fine race," J-G said definitively, laying on his accent. He leaned back, slid his glasses to the top of his nose. "Anyone who says different is a dog."

He glanced around the table to see if anyone disagreed. It was impossible to tell if he was joking or not.

Mielle began to deflate with disappointment, listening to them banter. She brushed crumbs off her lap, noticed a spot of jam on her borrowed scarf. She should have been exhilarated to sit in the middle of these people who had just seen how close the world was to slipping over an artificial edge into war. But Mielle couldn't get out of her own head. She'd had a feeling that today would be special. No one here even remembered her birthday.

She glanced across the café, but the woman who looked like Jane Anderson was gone. "Did you see that woman at the bar?" she asked Alden.

"Who?"

"The redhead. I think she was Jane Anderson. Do you know her?"

Alden paused mid-bite to look Mielle in the eye. "You mean the *propagandist* Jane Anderson? The Marquesa Cienfuegos? Francisco Franco's lackey? That one?"

Mielle had heard all that, but she didn't care. The Jane she remembered was the one from old magazines who flew in biplanes upside down over Hyde Park, who jotted down the life stories of Tommy soldiers just before they crawled over the top of a trench into no-man's-land.

"I used to love her work," Mielle said. "I read her all the time in college. Her old stuff."

"It must have been very old."

Alden tried to turn back to the table, but Mielle pestered him. "Do you think it was her?"

"I didn't see the woman," Alden said. "But Jane Cienfuegos is in Paris. I do know that. It could have been her. Though, honestly, I hope it wasn't."

"Na, deevil," Mielle teased him. "Nearly every reporter in Europe is here today, right? Except for William Shirer."

"Bill? He will show. It's a long train ride from Munich to Paris. He's probably sleeping late."

Dorothy Thompson stepped up to the bar, then a moment later the headwaiter followed her back with a dozen little snifters of Chartreuse on a cork tray, the Martian-green booze lit up by the sunlight that now flooded Capoulade.

"He wants to drink a toast with us," Thompson explained, "to the end of the war." Her voice was so clipped and restrained that her lips hardly moved when she spoke. "But just one, I told him, since it's breakfast."

All the waiters rushed around jubilant that morning. They were drinking toasts at all the tables to celebrate how wonderful it was that war had been avoided. "I fought in one war," the head-waiter told them, "and that's enough. Tant mieux."

Once the snifters were passed around, Thompson did the honors.

"To the Munich Agreement and stepping backward off a cliff. What the difference is between them, I don't claim to know."

They downed the Chartreuse, handed the snifters to the head-waiter, and tried their best not to make sour faces at the taste.

ABOUT US, WITHOUT US

That morning there was a press briefing about the Jewish refugee situation in Czechoslovakia. At a quarter to eleven, the correspondents rushed out the door to file into taxis. All except Dorothy Thompson, who was going to London to see the reaction there.

Mielle was the last to leave the table. She glanced around in disappointment and shoved the final crust in her mouth before she flagged down the waiter. Shirer and Murrow hadn't shown.

"Deevil, na," she said to herself. "Time to get going."

Alden grabbed her arm outside the café. With how the numbers worked out, with how she'd drifted to the back of the queue, she had to either squeeze into a full car or pay for one herself. "Come on," Alden said. He pulled her into a black Renault, as boxy and severe as a coffin. Given how tall they both were, they had to hunch over in the car with their noses practically touching, her legs crossed over his.

"I apologize," Alden said, blushing. "We can get our own. If you—if this is too much, we can—"

"Shut up," she said to him. Then, to the driver, *"Allez!"*

Their boasting about the disaster in Munich continued in the taxi. All the young ones had crowded together, she and Alden and three others. (If she didn't have a name they could remember, they don't deserve names in her story.) They shouted over one another, cut loose from their mentors and bosses.

"What was the point of it all except theater? That nervous tic the dictator had, the rally at the Sportpalast, dragging in Premier Daladier when the French weren't even part of the negotiations.

Everyone knew Chamberlain would sell out the Czechos for a nickel."

"He didn't even get that!"

"What was it the Czech president said?"

"Beneš?"

" 'Decided for us, without us.' "

"That's your headline! Why waste the weekend going to Munich for a photo op?"

"Munich is a fun town. Or don't you like beer halls?"

"Oompah music makes my teeth grind."

"Well, I'm glad I went," Alden said. "I had not yet seen the little dictator with my own eyes."

"Yeah? What did you think of him?"

"I thought he would be taller." Their guffaws filled the car like a burst balloon. "All the men were short except Chamberlain. You imagine they are ten feet tall until you bump into one in the hallway."

Their voices were like the blaring Renaults and Peugeots that choked the boulevard. One of them lit a cigarette. Five of them practically lying on top of one another, and the one in the middle couldn't stop shaking ash into his lap (and on all their legs) with the rattling of the taxi.

"You really must go to a rally," Alden told Mielle. "Think what a shame it would be to report on all this and never see Hitler for yourself. Who would believe you were even here?"

"What are you working on anyway?" the smoker asked her. He was already laughing in anticipation of what Mielle would say.

"I go to Milan and Rome in two weeks," she told him. "If that holds now. It's been planned for months."

"Italy? Is that what you mean?"

Earlier in the summer she'd made the mistake of showing them a list of the magazines and weekly rags that ran her little columns on fashion and society. Mielle mostly wrote brief dispatches on Continental culture and the fashions of married women for a syndicate of ladies' journals in the Great Plains. Hokey stuff. Color pieces. Not exactly shrewd feature spots about Elsa Schiaparelli or Coco Chanel. She wrote the sort of thing that took up one column of a Sunday insert and could be surrounded by four columns of ads. Almost all of it was uncredited. She was still trying to find her way. Everyone at Capoulade knew that. In the meantime, the provincial burgs where her columns were printed had become a running joke.

"Why," one of the green reporters said, joining in the gag, "our lady reports for all the great cosmopolitan cities. Where did you say her columns run?"

"I heard Milan? Is that Milan, Missouri?"

"Well, then, Cairo?"

"Cairo, Illinois!"

"London?"

"The one in Kentucky!"

"Oh, yes. How cosmopolitan!"

"Ease up, fellas," Alden told them. "Even Hem had to cut his teeth at the *Kansas Star,* didn't he?"

"Ha. Did he say Hem?"

"'You're an expatriate. You've lost touch with the soil.'"

They'd all seen Hemingway once at Shakespeare and Company—that tilt of his prodigious jaw, like he'd ridden through the door on a gilded mustang—when he was up from Madrid for the weekend. Afterward, there was an awful lot of talk about sending off cables and popping into the *Herald Tribune* and meeting up for an aperitif in the afternoon. By the way a junior reporter carried himself, you could tell if he would quote *The Sun Also Rises* as if it were scripture.

"'You get precious. Fake European standards have ruined you. You drink yourself to death. You become obsessed by sex.'"

"How do you suppose she got this job anyway?" the one at the other end of the taxi asked. "Usually a gal requires highly special-ized *experience* of one kind or another to get a plum job like she's got. From what I hear—"

"Well, you don't mean to impugn anyone's integrity, do you?"

"Quite the opposite!" the one smoking said, whirling his cig-arette like a baton. "That's the mystery. When a young gal comes into a position like this in Paris without any qualifications, she has some skill that convinced an editor to stash her overseas. I don't imagine this young gal has *that* skill set, but with how she dresses, nobody knows for certain."

He touched her leg as he said *skill set,* dragging his middle and index fingers from her knee to her ankle along the fabric of her trousers. Mielle could feel her face turn red. She tried to grab one of his fingers and twist it into two pieces, but he pulled away.

"Stop it!" Alden tried again to cut them off. "It is not like her audience consists of the Duke and Duchess of Windsor. She writes for country people. She speaks to the uneducated farm- and house-wives between the coasts. There are people out there, remember."

"Alden, quit," Mielle said. "You're not helping."

She rolled the window down and craned her head out of the taxi, as if she were an ostrich, to plug her ears with wind and the rattling of tailpipes. They sped across the Île de la Cité by Notre-Dame and then along the Right Bank of the Seine.

She never understood how men could jab at each other nonstop. Maybe they had seen enough of the Tuileries with its spouting fountains, where that summer gardeners planted palm trees and tropical flowers that grew ten feet tall, or the puppet shows in brightly colored tents, or the mobs of children around a carousel.

The drive with the green correspondents took only ten min-utes, but that was ten minutes too long, as far as Mielle was con-cerned. Today was supposed to be an important day. At that moment she felt like she had no time to waste.

MEET ME AT MAXIM'S

The briefing at the Hôtel Continental was nothing, but at least there was food.

Knowing there would be a spread in the press room, Mielle had limited herself to only one soft-boiled egg and coffee and most of a baguette at Capoulade. She felt like she was teetering on the edge of starvation when she stepped into that rococo ballroom, the most beautiful room she had ever seen (its plaster scrollwork, its crystal chandeliers), which the French Ministry of Information had commandeered to meet daily with Anglo and American journalists.

By the time she finished one cup of coffee and was filling her second, a little French official in a military uniform and egg-shaped wire-frame glasses was behind the podium. Every day at eleven and six, this man (he was named Gazal-Salomon) emerged to discuss the day's events from his government's point of view. That day he spoke about a French intention to help the refugees who were streaming out of Czechoslovakia, though he was vague about what form that help would take. The Allies were nervous about resettling eighty thousand Jews within their own borders because it might anger Hitler. The hope was that the United States would take all the Jews if Britain provided the boats and France could guarantee safe passage over land. No one would commit to anything—just as they had refused to commit to helping refugees at the conference at Evian earlier that year after Hitler took Austria in the Anschluss coup.

Mielle knew what would happen if the refugees were abandoned in Czechoslovakia. On a stopover that summer on her way back from Munich (for she *had* been to Munich, not to cover a so-called peace conference but for an exposition put on by a manufacturer who had dirndl and lederhosen concerns in Texas and Wisconsin), she wandered away from the train station in Karlsruhe during the hour before her connecting train arrived. About fifty people and ten dogs gathered to watch a gang of Brownshirt thugs round up "enemy criminals" at the medieval fountain. Entire Jewish families wore their finest wool coats and carried suitcases and cherrywood dining-room chairs. They were herded into the backs of open trucks, then driven away to who knew where on who knew what pretext. All of them—those on the trucks, those watching—had been neighbors before. After, the square was littered with suitcases and pieces of furniture the Brownshirts hadn't allowed on the trucks. Anything of value was stacked up and taken away by the townspeople. The dogs rooted in what remained.

Mielle had turned to a man next to her and, speaking in her Low German dialect, asked how long these spectacles had been going on.

"Drei Jahre," the man told her. Three years. He pulled his hat down to hide his face. Seeing the panicked look in his eyes, Mielle suddenly remembered that Hitler liked to give speeches here. Karlsruhe was tucked just behind Germany's Westwall fortifications and was within artillery range of France's celebrated Maginot Line. Jews and Communists and any resisters were being arrested en masse and sent to camps. That such purges went on was common knowledge among correspondents.

"They are Jews?" she asked, breathless.

"Yes, these were Jews," the man had said. "Last month, they took my sister."

"She's a—"

"An epileptic. They said it was to have a hysterectomy. But I know what they will do."

"She will come back."

"No. She will never come back."

Mielle's bad leg ached as she hurried to the station. But she took deep breaths. She composed herself. She wouldn't let the Brownshirts see her limp.

She knew it was nonsense what Gazal-Salomon, the French official, said about a multinational coalition that would ensure the safety of refugees. All promises they had heard before that nobody believed. It was a sales job, really, to convince people that France hadn't blown its best chance to stand up to Germany.

About two dozen reporters milled, incredulous, in that gorgeous ballroom, nibbling at bananas while Gazal-Salomon answered questions from the gaggle for a half hour. Mielle drank orange juice, ate another roll, kept an eye out for Shirer and Murrow. She was getting annoyed with herself, the way she kept looking for them over her shoulder. She spent more time watching the other reporters than she did taking notes, studying how the veteran correspondents stood, how they focused on certain points to follow up with questions later. How they styled their hair and what kinds of hats they wore. She looked for the woman she had thought was Jane Anderson on the off chance the woman might be here too. She was not. It was Jane who had inspired Mielle to be a reporter, not that long before. Seven years. Mielle fingered her press credentials as she snuck glances at the others. The white string hung awkwardly around her neck. Her press pass wasn't yet a second skin like it was for the veterans. She kept pinching the little ink-stamped card, kept checking the print to make sure her name was spelled correctly. And there it was. *Marthe Hess*. She was a credentialed journalist. She had a card that said so.

When she looked up, Shirer and Murrow had joined the gaggle. Murrow, black-haired and tall in a fedora and a three-piece suit; Shirer hatless, his sandy hair floating in wisps over his scalp, sucking on a pipe, wearing a frumpy sweater under his sports coat. Mielle began to work up the nerve to talk to them. Her stomach turned. She'd had the feeling earlier that her life would change forever that day. Meeting these men, she presumed, would be the start of that change. But first she had to sit there and pretend to take notes.

The little French official announced that there was to be a conference of the Allied nations in two weeks in Lausanne. Nobody knew if the Allies would accept any Jews—perhaps they'd take a small percentage who had extraordinary talents, like Einstein, if there were any Einsteins left.

"What will you tell them, these refugees?"

It was Shirer who elbowed his way to the front, tripping over his own feet because he was blind in one eye from a skiing accident, until he stood face to face with the undersecretary.

"How will you justify yourself to the refugee mother when you tell her and her miserable children to stay out?"

"Monsieur Shirer." The undersecretary grinned and sucked his thin mustache into his mouth. "How nice to see you again."

They smoked outside after, in a dark corridor blocked in on both sides by luxury hotels. The passageway was littered with puddles. Toward the light, where the corridor opened, Mielle could see the bright Place Vendôme square with the sparkling glass of its shops and the forty-meter-high column that immortalized Napoleon's triumph at Austerlitz. Each corner was occupied by groups of gendarmes with heavy capes and tall hats and carbine rifles. Because of the situation in the Sudetenland, the French military made itself conspicuous.

Mielle was last out again, so she had to search for Shirer and Murrow in the blue clouds of smoke. The two of them, in black wool overcoats and white scarves, chatted with J-G Dreyfus.

Shirer and J-G were both soft in the chin, bald on top, and appeared ten years older than they actually were. This was a common condition for correspondents. Chronically underslept; abusers of caffeine, alcohol, tobacco, amphetamines; consumers of fatty meats and packaged sweets eaten in the middle of the night. Shirer wore glasses and had a fuzzy mustache. Other than the fuzzy mustache, J-G could have been his French twin. Both dressed in thick wool sweaters with diminutive bow ties pressed into the soft undersides of their chins. Both were small in stature and had soft voices. It was hard to imagine two men like them holding a dictator to account. But they were powerhouses. Shirer always pushed to the front of a line, like he had in the ballroom. The trick was in his elbows. It took a lot of guts to stand up to Hitler and Mussolini, or anyone.

"So that is you," Shirer said, turning to face Mielle.

He sounded just like he did on the radio. His voice on the nasal side, an earnest heldentenor with flat, measured speech, like he was from Iowa. The edge of his mustache was discolored white with the milk from his coffee.

"Do you like it here?" he asked her. "It's a far sight better than Cedar Rapids, I hope."

"I like Paris. It's beautiful. There's a lot to write about." Mielle could feel herself shrinking as she spoke, like she was going to curtsy. She ought to give him the postcards, she told herself, instead of pinching them inside the pocket of her jacket. She ought to thank him for his letter of reference, but the men kept talking over one another and she couldn't break in.

"I got her a job with American Plains Wire," Shirer said to the other men.

Murrow raised his eyebrows in response, trying to humor her. He seemed to find her amusing. The way she looked in her black canvas jacket. That they were about the same height. She met his eyes without having to look up. He reached out to stroke the back of her elbow. "Is that canvas?"

She nodded vigorously, then pulled the bundle of postcards from her pocket and handed them to Shirer.

"What on earth could this be?"

She felt ridiculous, handing him the cards. All those fellating notes in chicken scratch. The droll photos of sights around campus, the white columns, the square brick buildings squatting on a flat terrain.

"Look, boys," Shirer said. "From my alma mater. Would you look at that. Cedar Rapids. As if I weren't depressed enough." The men all laughed.

"Probably fishing for a donation," J-G said, peeking over Shirer's shoulder.

"The worst years of my life were wasted there. And that's saying something." He turned to Murrow. "Did I ever tell you—"

"You told me a million times."

"That place. Two years of Bible study but no courses in philosophy. None in foreign literature, and nothing modern. I thought it was a wasteland, all the smiling people aside. But I did learn to drink there. Got my fraternity house suspended a whole year, we drank so well."

"You told me."

"They did make me editor of the school rag and let me write whatever I wanted without censor. That's more than I can say for the Germans or, for that matter, CBS Radio."

Shirer flipped through the postcards one more time, ordered them into a stack, then handed them back to Mielle. "Thanks for showing me," he said. "Very cute."

Mielle was confused. She tried to reverse the exchange, told him, "They're for you, for keeps," but Shirer wouldn't take them. He shoved his hands into his coat pockets.

"Paris is a frightful place right now, isn't it?" he said. Mielle didn't know what he meant. She asked him to explain. "They have misinterpreted this as victory. The French people have no inkling of what has actually just happened."

"You're so gloomy," Murrow said. "I am too."

"Popping champagne bottles might help."

"It might."

Murrow was only thirty years old then. He looked older, but in a way different than Shirer and J-G looked older. Murrow was more dignified. His hands in the pockets of his overcoat, his shoulders forward, pensive, tilted toward the street. He carried a lot of weight; it was obvious. His eyebrows arched when he was thinking. His cologne was sweet, vaguely grassy, with a hint of black pepper. "We should get our own shortwave transmitter set up in Poland," he said. "That would be better. And a staff of American radio reporters. That would be best. If only I had a head for business, we could make it happen."

Perhaps it should have been obvious to Mielle by then that this wasn't going to work out. She felt like she was being steam-rolled, still clutching the stack of postcards in her hands, but there remained that hope inside her. This was to be an important day.

Dozens of questions raced through her head. Was Shirer staying in Paris long? Had he brought his wife? Where was he going next? Did they have any advice for her? Did they have any leads on a better job she might get in Europe? Her mind was too slow to butt in. Every thought she had was too dull, too obvious. She might as well ask them how they felt about the weather.

But she had to say something, didn't she?

"Mr. Shirer," she said, too loud. Shirer startled. They all turned to hear what she needed to say. "Mr. Shirer"—her voice lower—"do you have plans for lunch? All of you are welcome. I have so many things to ask you, if you're willing."

Shirer grabbed her arm and laughed, relieved that this was all she had to tell him.

"Lunch isn't going to work," he said, still smiling. "There's a friend Ed and I have to meet for drinks. A champagne lunch, which, I'm afraid, is a private affair."

She felt herself shrink again. She took a step back, felt the word "Oh" escape her lips. The three men watched her reaction. She wasn't the type to cry, and she wouldn't. But her chin trembled. She looked like she forgot to breathe. All the hope from earlier escaped her.

"But there's dinner," Shirer said, trying to revive her. He never liked to disappoint a woman. "Where are you eating tonight? We have a table at Maxim's. Have you been there?"

Mielle shook her head. She had heard of Maxim's, of course; it was the most famous restaurant in the world. But she hadn't eaten there, hadn't even lingered on the sidewalk to steal a glance through the window because she was afraid of the maître d'. Most nights she ate terrine at a café or omelets in the room of one of the widows she lived with so they could teach her how to speak French and she could teach them how to speak like an American.

Murrow took off his hat, looked at Mielle like she was his little sister. "So you will come?"

She nodded.

"Well, good," Shirer said, pleased again. "We will see you then."

When Shirer released her arm, Mielle took a step back, but she hesitated to go. Shirer was looking her over because her jacket had fallen open; she felt like he could inspect her legs inside of her tan slacks, her navel and chest under her blouse. She felt the borrowed scarf, stained with jam, slide over her neck like he was pulling it over her skin.

"And if it isn't too much trouble," he said, "put on something nice. It is Maxim's, after all."

Mielle slumped, walking away, deflated by that last jab. *Put on something nice.* She thought she already had.

That day felt like something special, it had since sunrise, like something grand would happen and change her life forever. She'd expected that meeting these men would be that bright instigation, but it wasn't. Bumping into them changed nothing, not in the way she felt.

She was adrift, tripping over a curb, limping around the hotel like a wounded bird. She stumbled out where it was loud and bright on the Seine side of the hotel.

Alden grabbed her arm.

"Here you are," he said, out of breath, his face ruddy. "Will you share a taxi back to Capoulade?"

"I don't—"

"Just the two of us this time, I promise. Our legs will have their own hemispheres." He flashed his blue eyes at her, swept back a swell of his thinning hair with his hand. "I feel bad about today. Everyone seems to be treating you poorly."

"Well, that's not true." She spoke without thinking about it.

"I want to take you out for lunch. That is, if you still have an appetite after raiding the buffet at the briefing."

Mielle had never met a man like Alden before, the kind who posed for department-store catalogs to sell toothpaste and wood-paneled radios and snowshoes, a New England dream of what life should be. His light hair and square jaw, his degree from Yale, his father's connections. There was nothing wrong with Alden. On three previous occasions he had tried to kiss her, slid a hand to her chin, but each time she turned away. Mielle knew it would never work out with Alden, not like that. He might stay in her life a long time, their whole lives, as long as her life lasted, but never like that. She was certain.

"I'm sorry, but no," she said. "I will see you tomorrow."

"You are coming to dinner tonight, are you not? Ed told me you were invited."

"You're going?" she asked. "To Maxim's?"

"Yes, of course. It wouldn't be the same without you. You are coming?"

"I told them I would come."

Alden looked into her eyes, perhaps wondering why she hadn't yet pulled away. He held her by the elbow. He still didn't let go.

"Will you at least share the taxi?" he asked.

"No. What I need is to go for a walk."

"But your bad leg."

She took a deep breath and pulled together all the muscles in her body until she could move without limping. She could control her limp when she wanted to. She just had to breathe and focus and ignore the rest of the wide world.

"Alden, don't you ever worry about my legs."

PREVAILING WINDS: CONTINENTAL TRENDS AND FASHIONS

(American Plains Wire)
As reported on October 15, 1938

Let there be no doubt—Paris is best for the rich.

Though the budget travelers among you need neither despair nor avoid the City of Light. If you can get to Europe, relatively easy these days with a one-to-thirty exchange rate, there are plenty of ways to make the most of your trip to remember.

Sightseeing, for one. There's no charge to stand outside and gawk at the architecture. There's a reason the Tour Eiffel, as called by the locals, is the favorite tourist destination in France. You can see the tower from almost anywhere in town, and it's free to look at!

But if you absolutely must venture inside some of these world wonders, here's a tip: go to the Catholic churches.

All for the price of a candle, these churches are filled with high-art sculptures and paintings and are the best-built buildings anywhere.

Don't tell your reverend at home, but a girl can find a week's worth of edification by observing Mass in this great Catholic metropolis.

Notre-Dame de Paris, Sacré-Coeur de Montmartre, and l'église de la Madeleine are the big ones and not to be missed!

The pipe organ at Madeleine is said to be the most angelic in the world.

Sacré-Coeur has the best views of Paris.

And what more needs said about Notre-Dame? It's among the most famous churches in the world, where kings and queens used to be wed, until the beheadings.

Every neighborhood in Paris has an attractive church with its own story. Go inside and the old mother on duty will tell you all about it, whether you speak the language or not. Thank her with a fifty-centime donation to the abbey.

Then reward yourself for the money you've saved by splurging on steak tartare, red wine, and chocolate éclairs!

OUT OF ORDER IN SAINT-MARTIN

It began to rain.

Mielle stayed north of the river and wandered in the general direction of home. She had no obligations for the rest of the afternoon except to dismantle her armoire in search of a skirt and jacket that might pass as dinner clothes. She had only one skirt, a calf-length midi she bought out of a Sears and Roebuck catalog, made of a stiff green fabric that was most often used to upholster furniture. Whether it passed for *something nice* or not, it would have to do.

She wasn't sure if she should join the men for dinner, she was so embarrassed, or if she even wanted to go. Maxim's was impossible to get into if you weren't a celebrity (as Murrow and Shirer were) or a vivacious beauty (as she was not). And on Saturday night, no less, its dining room studded with actors and noted chanteuses and high-priced escorts. All that sounded horrible to Mielle. She didn't feel capable of downing champagne on some adventure in Vendôme, even if it was her birthday. Her legs hurt quite a lot by then. Her calf muscles stiffened and seized, and her knee joints ached from her brogans slapping on cobblestones. She should stop walking, hail a taxi, and go home to dress. But she didn't want to go home. She wanted to walk alone on streets where she could allow herself to limp without being teased.

Her heavy jacket kept her dry in the rain. Only her hair and face were wet. She merged into the fog and falling drops until nothing existed of her except the sound of her shoes on the cobblestones and the cold rain that dropped from the tips of her hair.

Across from Canal Saint-Martin, a crowd of schoolgirls filed onto the sidewalk. Mielle followed them from behind like a governess. The cloud of their bare legs pale against the gray of an autumn rain. They were loud; they were singing. Slapping each other on the arms. Kicking puddles. Girls with brown eyes who wore gray sports jackets, navy blue skirts and hats with brown gym shoes.

It wasn't so long before that Mielle was a schoolgirl walking home with her own sister. They cradled their books in their arms as they walked in the gravel alongside a highway. It was a familiar sight in that part of Iowa. Horses and buggies and Anabaptist kids walking everywhere. She and her sister made the two-mile walk to school each morning and back after lunch to help with the milking. At that moment, at home, it would have been the first weeks of the harvest. She thought about what each member of her family would be doing. Canning beets and carrots. The boys tying horse traces to the thresher machine and making sure the red-brick corncribs were ready to be filled with golden kernels. Her father knocking into things in the barn. Thinking of harvest made her homesick for that joyous feeling of exhaustion. Corn husks tumbling across the fields in a cool autumn wind. The soil black with manure. The sound of buggies up on the road. The clopping of hooves.

Nothing back home would be changed by her absence.

She thought of her family a lot but never said their names, not even to herself. They weren't allowed to mention *her* name back on the farm or in the little wood-sided church up on the hill above the English River. That was against her people's law—since she left. And if the Ordnung prohibited even her mother, even her sister, from mentioning her name, she wondered, did that mean they would stop remembering her? Would she be erased from the minds of her family?

Once a week that summer, she woke early and took the Métro

to witness Mass at l'église de la Madeleine. She loved the churches, these bulwarks to the great French god of war. Sacré-Coeur and Notre-Dame. The squatty, red-brick parish churches tucked around Montmartre like bunkers. She hadn't been in a church for years until she got to Paris. She'd meant to give all that up. She told herself that she didn't believe in God, that He didn't exist, at least not inside of her. Otherwise, she wouldn't have been pried away from home. But she still sang some of the old songs on Sundays, out of habit. "Holy, Holy, Holy" and "I Sought the Lord" and "Beneath the Shadow of the Cross." She couldn't help but feel some movement in her heart when she said the Lord's Prayer (the Unse Vader, the way she learned it) and hope there was a bit of God left inside her after all.

That day, if she were home for her birthday, her mother and sister would have been baking a big vanilla cake. They would have been whipping the cream. Her father would have traded a round of cheese at the grocer's for a can of pineapple. Pineapple cake was her favorite. It made Mielle sad to think that her mother wasn't making her a birthday cake that day. She felt a little guilty to deprive her mother of that joy and that her father had no reason to drive a buggy to the grocer's to trade for a can of pineapple. Mielle shouldn't have started thinking about her family, or the farm with its meadows of clover and sunshine, or the bend on the river where she waded through the water to the dry shoals in the middle to build fires with her sister, where they caught small gray toads in the sand. Her religion, her family, the old homeplace, even the old neighbors, the Yoders and Schwartenzdrubers—all that was lost to her now, forever.

Her second sight had warned her about the stranger for months before he arrived. She saw it so clearly, sixteen years old, the grind of the dry hinges when the door opened behind her, how he would find her alone in the milking barn. He was not an elder, only thirty, but he would seem old to her. He would have a neat little beard along his jaw, dark eyes, thick hair that curved in waves over his head. He would be stocky, have small but sturdy hands. He would say nothing when he found her except in whispers: "Quiet, lamb." She saw it so clearly, with that pain behind her eyes, with that ache in her stomach, before the stranger came to Kalona to find their assembly, but she ignored the vision of what he would do to her.

The first time she saw him in the flesh, she thought he was just another vision because her physical reaction was overwhelming. Her head spun, her weak legs weakened, as a familiar stocky man loped up the hill from the country road and was greeted outside the butcher barn by her father. Her father stood stiff at first, as if resisting what the stranger said to him, but then he laid his hand on the stranger's shoulder to listen. Mielle pinched the skin of her forearms, watching them, to wake herself up out of it, to make everything stop spinning. Her father shook his head to whatever the stranger asked him. And Mielle whispered along. "Bitt, Daadi. Nee, Daadi." But her father softened; such a trusting man. He nodded. He and the stranger shook hands and walked together to the porch steps, where Mielle stood trembling with her arms crossed over her chest, still praying. *No, Daadi. Not this one.* That familiar face and toothy smile only a few feet away from her.

"This is Joubert," her father said. "He is one of us. He will work here until he decides if he wants to stay."

So many times after Joubert arrived, she wanted to tell her mother what her second sight had warned her about, that this man was evil. But when she'd told her mother before that someone tried to touch her, her mother had always told her to squeeze her thighs tight and the man would go away. So many times she prayed that her father would ask Joubert to leave the farm without her having to tell him that she had seen what would happen. But she worried her father would laugh if she told him she had a second sight, that her father would tell her to have more faith in God, to put more trust in her fellow Mennonites. She never mentioned her vision to either of her parents. And so it happened how her second sight said it would happen. Joubert caught her twice in the milking barn, just that way.

Even a child knew how it went, that a girl would be blamed, that it would be the girl who would have to leave home. It didn't have to be this way for Mielle. Her father caught Joubert in the act that second time, when he heard her struggling. If she and her parents had agreed to forget and forgive and stay quiet about what happened, she could have stayed and lived the rest of her life in Iowa the way she had always planned to live the rest of her life. Her parents would forgive her; they would believe her. They would even stay quiet; her father would never tell a soul what he saw in the milking barn. But they couldn't forget. That's why she had to leave.

Mielle didn't understand when she was sixteen, or even at twenty-four, but it didn't matter if she understood. She still had to leave.

She was lost, wandering somewhere north of the Gare de l'Est, she thought, because she could hear the steam whistles of passenger trains. This was still Saint-Martin. She found her way back to the canals to watch the water dimple in the gentle rain. She pulled the postcards from her pocket and dropped them in the canal. The postcards floated atop the water, showing those little Iowan scenes. They didn't float away. They didn't even sink.

Life couldn't go on like this forever, she knew.

Mielle wondered if the men would miss her if she didn't come to dinner at Maxim's. She didn't like being flirted with, teased, demeaned, but she would have to learn to enjoy sparring with boorish men the same way Dorothy Thompson and Martha Gellhorn liked to spar. Not that Shirer and Murrow were necessarily boorish. But there would be champagne and whiskey and red meat. That was enough to make any man a boor. The men wouldn't miss her. They were probably so drunk on champagne by then, in the middle of the afternoon, that they'd forgotten all about her. Still, she had waited months for that dinner invitation. She'd had that feeling about this day, her birthday. She wasn't in a position to ignore such feelings, she believed. Whether she felt like it or not, she should go to dinner. If she didn't show her face at Maxim's, she might never receive an invitation like that again.

This is how disordered her days were. The echoes of her feet shuffling on the cobblestones, the waves of echoes washing over each other in only more waves of echoes, until all she could hear was the knocking of her shoe bottoms against stone in a halting rhythm, that painful rhythm of her legs at that moment.

At that moment, a hand reached to grab her shoulder. This time it wasn't Alden Linden Elder. This time it was a woman.

"It *is* you, isn't it? What are you doing over on this side?" the woman asked. "I could ask myself the same thing, right? Both of us must be lost."

Mielle turned to see who had her by the arm. It was Jane Anderson. Mielle had to look again. She *had* seen Jane across Capoulade that morning. And here she was again. Jane. Her face with its narrow eyes, wide brow, and high cheekbones. She wore a man's hat that her hair tumbled out from under. She had tawny hair with a pattern of chestnut and red flashes, like the feathers of a rare owl.

Jane leaned close, pressed her lips to Mielle's ear. "Paris is better by yourself," she whispered, "even if it's lonely. These streets are made for us orphans."

They stared at each other a moment, breathless, their damp faces only inches apart. Mielle tried to speak but could say nothing, Jane still holding her by the arm. "Come with me," Jane said. She pulled Mielle into a café on the corner. The place was empty except for the two of them and the man behind the bar.

Jane was already set up at a zinc table by the window. That

weekend's copy of *Candide,* a biweekly reactionary rag, was folded on the bench seat.

Two squat glasses containing brandied plums were brought from the bar.

"You look like you're all edges," Jane said. Her voice was low-pitched, contralto, and penetrating. She spoke effortlessly, it seemed, her lips pursed but her voice gentle, clear, seductive. "This is mellow. That's what you need."

They ate the brandied plums without another word, then Jane waved to the barman and asked him to bring them a rosé Rhône wine. "This is mellow too."

Mielle sat perfectly straight in the chair, a puddle on the floor underneath her where her clothes dripped. She felt like a child fresh out of the bath, waiting to be dried off, with her hair stuck wet to her forehead.

She only glanced at Jane. Jane wore a dress with wide sleeves that were lined with black silk so her pearly arms gleamed in the shadow and an overlarge tasseled plaid scarf that covered her shoulders and neck. It was her. Mielle couldn't quite believe she was sitting across from Jane Anderson in a Paris café and that it was Jane who had brought her in out of the cold. But there she was, sipping from a squatty glass. Jane was bigger than Mielle thought she would be, with a well-cut jaw and dissecting green eyes. She looked expectant, waiting for her chance to blurt out a thousand words on any subject. Jane reached to the table where she had rolled half a dozen cigarettes and offered one to Mielle. "No?"

Mielle wondered if Jane knew who she was and, if so, how, or if Jane had the habit of grabbing strangers off the street for an afternoon drink. That phrase (*It is you, isn't it?*) could be attached to anyone.

There was something about Jane, as her eyes desperately tried to hold Mielle's eyes, that made it clear she couldn't stand to be alone.

"Are you really an orphan?" Mielle asked. "Like you said. *Us orphans.*"

"Not now, not anymore. I'm thirty-six years old! But my mother did die when I was a girl. So, in a way, I was an orphan. That sounds more pathetic than it was. A judge forced me to take a train all the way to Arizona to live with my father. I was a poor little animal living out under only God's eye like that. Dad was a lawman and a gunslinger. Can you imagine? How awful."

Jane explained that she didn't have a happy family growing up. Her father left after she was born…her mother died when she was ten…her maternal grandparents, the Luckies, tried to bring her up as a debutante, with mixed results…so she moved out to Yuma, where her father was a U.S. marshal…he was named Red because of the color of his hair…and he killed twenty-eight men during his time as a marshal in Arizona.

Mielle didn't know why Jane was telling her all this right off the bat. She assumed Jane was lying about everything. Jane overenunciated her words. She slipped in and out of accents from sentence to sentence, from cowpoke to society Londoner to Southern belle, then back around, her eyes wide to emphasize her points. Everything she said sounded like a tall tale. But what Jane said was true, at least as far as the record shows.

Jane kept asking, "Can you imagine?" Mielle didn't know what to say. Her own father was such a gentle man; he would waver in the breeze if it weren't for his heavy coat holding him to the earth, but he kept all of them alive, smiling, resting his hand on the back of her neck to express that life was okay, that they were okay. She couldn't imagine what it would have been like to be fourteen in a frontier town like Yuma, a girl alone with her father, a man whom she'd really just met, a man who shot drunkards and scoundrels dead in the street.

"Twenty-eight men," Mielle repeated. "Twenty-eight," as if that were the largest sum there could be.

The barman refilled their glasses and brought another decanter of water. The plums had gone straight to Mielle's head. She had started drinking only that year, and any amount of booze was enough to knock her a little sideways.

She wondered again how Jane had recognized her outside. So she asked.

"You're part of the correspondents crowd," Jane explained. "We were never introduced, but I've seen you at Capoulade. You're there every single day."

Mielle had trouble believing this—that Jane remembered her. "You saw me?"

Jane nodded. "Is it true you're Amish? From Iowa?"

"I'm from Iowa, yes. But not Amish. Not exactly."

"I've never seen one before, an Amish, or whatever you are. When I saw you at Capoulade, I knew there was something very different about you."

Jane brushed a strand of still-wet hair behind Mielle's left ear, then kept her hand there with her fingertips grazing Mielle's cheek. Mielle felt herself blush, could see herself reflected in how Jane's green eyes lit up across the table. There was a spark between the two of them, Mielle felt it, something more than the warmth of the liquor. There was a glow to Jane's face, Jane's skin. In Mielle's eyes, Jane looked just like she had in the old magazines, back when she was the most beautiful, the most charming, or at least could claim to be the most *something* with a straight face. Mielle wasn't seeing things clearly—this wasn't really how Jane looked by then, not exactly—but Mielle didn't care.

"I asked Dorothy about you after I saw you sitting at her table this morning," Jane said. "Is it true what she said? That you're a virgin?"

Mielle pulled back, then turned her whole body away so she didn't have to look at Jane. The way Jane asked that made the freckles on Mielle's nose come out. "I don't know what to say."

"Tell me the truth. That's easy."

"No, it's *not* that easy to talk about that kind of thing."

"Ha! Well, that says everything right there."

Mielle filled her water glass and tilted her head to drink it all. "Is that really what Ms. Thompson said?"

"Don't worry about her. If the others didn't think you were a virgin, all they'd talk about was what a colossal slut you were."

If Mielle's jaw hadn't yet dropped, it dropped then. She snapped it shut and snorted out her nose. She couldn't look at Jane, though what Jane said must surely have been the truth. She stared at the tin ceiling tiles and tried to breathe, panicked that the spark between them had started to fade. Mielle could feel the situation slipping away. To have met Jane Anderson, inexplicably, only to have Jane tease her about being "the Virgin." She couldn't believe her poor luck. She wished she could float up out of the room, out of Paris, and explode in the sky.

"Honey." Jane grabbed Mielle's elbow to pull her from the ceiling. "It's just a joke."

This was the first time cracks appeared in the facade of Jane Anderson—or at least the facade as seen by Mielle. The look on Jane's face as she laughed about her joke, opened her bag, made a few passes at her face as she looked in a little mirror, redefined her lips with the lipstick, straightened her hair. For a moment—a flash in Mielle's eyes—Jane's skin loosened on her face, her jaw, and her neck; there were bags under her prominent eyes. In a flash, Jane's face marbled with deep wrinkles; dust surrounded her as the makeup was loosened, her face thick in middle age, at fifty, her fleshy under-chin, her hair a dull orange like a pumpkin still on the vine in the middle of winter, not tawny, not vivacious or mysterious.

But then Jane's face changed back in Mielle's eyes just as quick. Jane looked young again, like she could pass for thirty-six.

Mielle never saw Jane quite clearly those days in Paris, not for who she was. That's worth pointing out, one of the odd things about Mielle. She saw the world differently than everyone around her. Mielle knew she shouldn't trust herself, since Jane was so amorphous: a woman fed by attention, adoration, false love, one who was crippled by alcoholism and abuse and loneliness, but only to those who had the right eyes to see this.

"Hey," Jane called to the barman. She paid their bill, then looked at Mielle and winked toward the door.

CAFÉ NOT ALWAYS

The rain had stopped and the light was changing again. The fronts of the buildings regilded as dusk neared. The air was clean. Bugs flew out from heaps of leaves to dry their wings.

Jane grabbed Mielle's elbow and pulled her to boulevard de Magenta, then toward Montmartre. The two of them were a spectacle on the walkway. Mielle, tall in her slim wool trousers and the simple cut of her butcher's jacket, her broad shoulders, her uncovered hair turning to frizz as it dried. She *was* all edges. Stiff as she walked, her joints rusty. When the two stopped at a corner, it looked like Jane waited next to a lamppost. Jane was not much shorter—she was five foot nine, very tall for a woman in France. Jane with her flowing silk sleeves, a wide-brimmed Spanish hat perched on her mess of hair. Her dress was cut to accentuate her hips; her cleavage swelled under her scarf as she moved. Jane's legs didn't hurry. She walked in a distracted way, stopping in the middle of boulevard de Rochechouart, a pale hand emerging from its decadent sleeve to point at the street sign on the corner—*Ah, yes*—like she couldn't believe a car could hit her.

It was almost five and the noise of the evening was picking up. The early starts of traffic. Sidewalks full of housewives and maids, all the dusky working people trudging to a seat at a bar on the other side of the hill, to Ornano, with bloody knuckles and bowed shoulders.

Mielle couldn't stop thinking about the others calling her the Virgin. She couldn't explain to anyone how complicated the truth was for her. She had agonized over whether she was a virgin or not, if what Joubert did to her counted or not. She was desperate to become a new person in Paris. Not a damaged woman, confounded that all the people she knew had found a spot in the world where they fit, but she would never fit. She didn't want to be Marthe Hess, a woman who had no control over her life, with little to offer. If the other correspondents wanted to make her a virgin again, she would let them. She had been touched many times, starting when she was ten. Almost always on the outside of her clothes. Almost always with fingers. That's just the way it was. Her brothers, the bachelor farmers, a church deacon. She'd wondered too, at that age, if being touched meant she wasn't a virgin. She was so simple because she had been told nothing about the mechanics of intercourse. She didn't even learn the word for penis or vagina or testicle or anus until she went to college and had the bright idea to take human anatomy. Those animal words. Mielle still blushed when she remembered anatomy class and its diagrams; she still became nauseated when she remembered Joubert. Being seen as a virgin was fine, it was good. What did it matter if the others called her the Virgin? If they could believe this, so could she. And if she could believe, then it was true.

But how was she supposed to say this to anyone? How could she explain her past in a way that wouldn't sour things?

"I don't care a row of beans that they tease me," Mielle blurted out. "I'm inadequate to sit at a table in Capoulade, I know that. What can I say back to anyone?"

Jane looked up at the buildings, the four- and five-story Second Empire houses where women were hanging wet laundry on the balconies. Jane looked distracted. She unclasped her purse and plucked out a single white pill that she swallowed. She wasn't listening. Mielle kept talking anyway.

"I was asked to dinner at Maxim's tonight. Going would be a mistake, I know, to sit between Shirer and Murrow and spend the whole night trying to think of something smart to say. I'm not too good at impressing people. Especially not men as accomplished as them."

The color in Jane's cheeks rose to a bright red. The flesh of her face perked up again, her eyes brightened, with the pill.

"Why on earth *wouldn't* you eat supper with those lugs?" Jane asked. "Don't you think they started somewhere too? And had people doing them favors along the way?" With Jane's mouth moving, her legs started going. "When they put me in a trench in Flanders, it was a joke to the old men who covered the World War. But I got the story better than anyone, didn't I?"

"Yes. I've read your stories," Mielle confessed. "You're very good."

"All the cynics can go to hell. Nobody climbs a wall without a little boost. If you get an advantage, make the most of it. Trust me, you'll never hear a man complain about someone doing him a favor. That's because he thinks he deserves everything he gets and more."

"Yes," Mielle said. "You're right."

"Go eat at Maxim's. I won't stop you. If you want to hob-nob and eat oysters on someone else's dime, go ahead. But those men, I'll tell you, personally, we don't get along. I try to avoid that Capoulade set as much as I can."

Jane was awake again, her arms pumping, those big sleeves of hers flapping like flags in the wind.

"Writers make the worst companions. Present company excepted. They drink too much, and it makes them boring. Impotent. Pompous. Boring! Sure, I drink on occasion, from necessity. But writers talk about alcohol like it takes talent to booze. They think they're charming when drunk. At least I know better. My charm comes from my training. As a girl, I was a *deb-u-tante.*" Jane said the word slow, with Georgia allure in her mouth. "The reporters who moonlight as novelists are the worst," she went on, faster, like someone might make her stop. "It's torture to be wrapped up in popularity contests, to be rewarded for sharing the tragic details of their grotesque lives. Sure, there's some money in it sometimes, as long as you have a mental dysfunction the public finds entertaining. There are a few writers who seem to be decent people—who are content in faithful marriages, who love their children, who work hard because they believe in the work. But nobody reads them."

Mielle stared at Jane a moment, slowing her stride.

She wondered where Jane fit within her own description of a writer. Much of Jane's career was propelled by sensationalism and gossip. Mrs. Foster Jane Anderson Cienfuegos was a character herself, in full command of her voice on the page, a fast woman with the erudition and dramatic timing of a charlatan. Then Mielle wondered if she herself fit in with the *decent people,* as Jane called them. She aspired to be read. And if being decent excluded her from that, she didn't know which she would choose.

"Here it is," Jane said. She had Mielle by the elbow again, pulling her into another café. This one was called Pas Toujours.

Two men waited for Jane at a table, the same two who'd drunk with her that morning. One, in his forties, had thin dark hair combed back to make his hairline cloven. The other, younger, wore a purple velvet vest and bow tie. He examined himself in the mirror behind the bar.

The older one stood and helped Jane into a chair, then bent so their cheeks touched.

"This is my husband," Jane said.

He took Mielle's hand and kissed her on her knuckles to formally introduce himself. "Marqués Eduardo Álvarez de Cienfuegos," he said, and "Enchanted," and "Sit here," helping Mielle into a chair next to Jane. He wasn't surprised at all that his wife had made a friend.

Cienfuegos was good-looking, though much shorter than Jane. (In the only surviving photograph of Jane with her second husband, they are both seated. Jane made a point to avoid standing next to Cienfuegos in public—she apparently more embarrassed of his height than he.) Cienfuegos had very pale skin, a soft chin, and a prominent mole under his left eye. He kissed Jane on the lips before he sat. Jane tilted her head and flung her coat back with a flip of her wrist to expose its silk lining and the elegant beige of her dress.

"That one," Jane whispered. She nodded at the younger man. "He's a gigolo. Not professionally, but just because. If you like him, he's very available."

The gigolo still stared in the mirror. Mielle had never seen a real gigolo, so she didn't know if Jane was joking about this too. In any case, he was beautiful. A strong jaw and a body with perfect proportions, slightly built. With short, manicured hair; shaved smooth, without a nick or pimple on his dark tan skin; expressive hazel eyes, what were called aurelian eyes those days. He smiled just slightly when introduced. He had nothing at all to say.

Pas Toujours was a modern café, though not as large as Capoulade or what you would find over in Montparnasse. Here they served food cooked in the Marseillaise tradition. They had olive tartine and rouget, a fish with red skin. Jane ordered two plates of it at once.

A jukebox in the corner played "I'm Looking Over a Four Leaf Clover," an old standard, the version with Bix Beiderbecke's trumpet solo. Beiderbecke was from Mielle's part of Iowa and she said so. "That's Davenport he came from, but not so far away."

Cienfuegos stopped her. "What is a Davenport?"

Jane laughed and explained it to him. "She means a dinky little city in Iowa, love. A straight shot west from Chicago, or thereabouts."

"Ah, Chicago! I have been to Chicago. You and this Bix come from a great city. The City of Proud Shoulders, yes?"

"It's the City of *Big* Shoulders," Mielle said.

"Like you!"

"Yes. Like me."

It was easy to laugh along with Cienfuegos. He and the gigolo were pretentious, but they followed Jane's lead. They were nice to Mielle and it made her giddy.

The four of them sat over glasses of cheap marc brandy, and, once she told a little about herself, Mielle sketched out how she ended up in Paris, hired as a women's culture correspondent on the recommendation of William Shirer. "I'm meeting him for dinner this evening," she said, to remind herself as much as to tell the others.

Neither Cienfuegos nor the gigolo had heard of this radioman Shirer.

"Bill says lots of nasty things on the radio," Jane said. "He's very unfair."

"We both graduated from the same college in Iowa," Mielle went on. "That's why Mr. Shirer recommended me. Otherwise, me and him met only a few hours ago."

The gigolo sat up from his trance. "You talk a lot about Iowa. I never heard of it."

He had a North African accent, some Mediterranean lip in his pronunciation. They were all speaking English, for Mielle's benefit.

"She's homesick," Jane said. "That's all there is to it."

"No, I'm not really."

"She's being haunted. That's how bad she's got it."

They all looked at Mielle like they felt sorry for her.

"If you're homesick," Cienfuegos said, "why don't you go back to Chicago to be with your people?"

"I can't. A decision had to be made and it can't be undone now. They wouldn't even let me come back."

They sat still, in confusion, like she was an alien in their midst and they had only then realized she was an alien.

"Oh my Lord, honey. You're too sweet. My little saccharine *Mielle*." Jane put an arm around her. "None of us want to go home again anyway. That's why we're all such pals over here."

That was the first time Jane called her Mielle, naming her anew with a pun, part in a sort of French way and part in drawl, its two syllables set apart with a pert rise and descent, the Georgia patois back in Jane's voice. *Mee-ell.* Dignified and sweet, condescending. *Mielle, Mielle.* The words like candied mint from her lips.

Mielle said nothing to Jane, just smiled. Smiled so wide her teeth showed, the color back up in her cheeks. She was so grateful to be renamed—to no longer be Marthe from Iowa, as she had been christened by her father, but Mielle from Paris. Jane gave her this.

The hook Jane set would stay in Mielle a long time. In some ways she would never shake the feeling of her unchristening.

"That's a good name for you, isn't it? Mielle?" Jane showed her own glistening teeth. "So much better than the Virgin."

THE PARTY

Cienfuegos and Jane had a place at 40 rue des Abbesses, on the middle floor of a five-story building with an elevator. This was south of Sacré-Coeur, about halfway to the Montmartre Cemetery, not far from Pas Toujours.

Jane kicked off her shoes as soon as she stepped in the door—said, "Those damn things"—then showed Mielle to what must have been the parlor, an enormous space that was empty except for a Louis XIV sofa, an absurdly large white velvet divan covered in pillows, and a liquor cart near the windows that was made entirely of clear Lucite so the bottles should appear to be floating. There were eight rooms in the apartment, most of them bare, with paint peeling off the walls and hardly any furniture. On windowsills were crude pieces of art Jane collected that were made by soldiers during the First War. "They were gifts," she explained, "made by boys in the trenches." (Mielle didn't know this yet, of course, but Jane and her husband had little except this art, their clothes, and a thousand hectares of arid Spanish hillocks in Extremadura that were treed with cork oak and home to two hundred Merino sheep Cienfuegos had inherited. Jane had spent her whole life moving and owned almost nothing.) In her collection of trench art were spent nine-centimeter brass artillery shells with poppies and roses engraved on the exteriors. One had a large vine holding a bunch of grapes. One read VERDUN with starbursts around the word.

"These are real bombs?" Mielle asked.

"Look for yourself," Jane said. She flipped one to show the

factory imprint. RHMF DUSSELDORF—NOV 1908. "This once belonged to Kaiser Willy's army. Maybe they tried to drop it on my head during the war." She said, "Plop!" with a pop of her lips, then dropped the shell back on its base.

More littered the other rooms. Cigarette lighters, candlesticks, a crucifix—all made from bullets. A cast-iron effigy of Emperor Franz Joseph. A pickelhaube battle helmet with a shrapnel hole the diameter of Mielle's thumb punched through the top. A dozen pieces in all.

Only one painting hung on the wall—the typical watercolor of Montmartre in spring you saw all over—and it probably belonged to the landlady. A few impressionistic paintings leaned in a corner, shepherd girls in bucolic scenes that Jane had bought that summer but hadn't bothered to hang. Without them, discolored spots on the parlor walls showed.

It would have been a very dreary place if it weren't for all the noise when the neighbors arrived.

"We don't usually entertain," Jane said.

That was clearly a lie. As soon as the door was open and the lights switched on, a stream of oddballs stopped in for a drink. Some of them brought their own stools to sit on.

There was a woman in a black beret and a white boa; plump, pert, and hippy, like a starlet in a silent movie. Her man—Mielle thought he was a man, though with cabaret people, it was sometimes hard to guess—he had a slight build, neat hair, and pink lips. Following them was a thin woman in a black pillbox hat and a black blazer who cupped her hand over a match when she lit a cigarette, even indoors. And a professional drinker who looked old, though he was probably younger than Jane, who had a shabby coat and a white beard and hair to his shoulders like Walt Whitman. And two or three nondescript men of the kind who linger at the back of every party waiting for a woman to get drunk, their hair slicked with pomade, their big French noses like inverted rhinoceros horns. They smoked cheap Greek cigarettes and palmed wedding rings into their pants pockets.

One of them was a man in a green bow tie with a snakish shape to his head. He walked around with a bottle of marc and peered over everyone's shoulders to ensure there wasn't an empty glass in the room. "A toast! A toast!" he kept shouting as an excuse to keep pouring. Cienfuegos rushed back and forth with a magnum bottle of champagne, which was much more popular than the marc. He accepted tips, then folded the cash and stuffed it into a shirt pocket so the rose-colored five-franc notes looked like the rumpled petals of a hibiscus flower.

All formality vanished after this crowd took over. They draped their arms over each other. One snuck into the kitchen to steal a hunk of cheese and a piece of fruit. Jane enjoyed all of this on the divan with her legs folded to the side. She talked non-stop, her contralto floating like a fog around their bodies as she answered questions about the places she had traveled, the battles she had seen, the famous men she had met and where they liked to be scratched.

Cienfuegos had a nervous look in his eyes always, but especially when Jane got their guests hot with stories about her exploits.

"You leeches," he called them. "You will ruin me!" Desperation stretched his voice higher but he kept pouring until the bottle was empty.

The snakish man with the bottle of marc got to Cienfuegos then. "A toast! A toast!"

"Fine, fine." Cienfuegos laughed. "I know one toast. Arriba, abajo, al centro—"

Jane stood from the divan and put a stop to it before they could drink.

"You slob." She pushed Cienfuegos out of the way. "What kind of toast is that?"

"Then toast us, scribe!" Cienfuegos said. "Incandesce us!"

"Fine," Jane said. She held out her empty glass until the marc man filled it, then she stared into the ceiling a moment to think.

All of them shuffled the leather soles of their shoes on the wood floor to egg her on, but she ignored them. Girlish, she balanced on one leg as a bare foot rubbed along the calf of the other leg. She smiled, her not-so-subtle *Who me?* smirk, the high arches of her eyebrows, those piercing green eyes that had made her irresistible to men like Conrad and H. G. Wells and the French diplomatic corps. Everyone who couldn't help themselves. She was conning them because they begged to be conned. She looked down from the ceiling when they wanted it enough and caught each one's eye in turn.

"To those who wish to see me fall on my face," she said. " 'Do not let us quarrel any more. Bear with me for once: Sit down and all shall happen as you wish. You turn your face, but does it bring your heart? I am grown peaceful as old age tonight. I regret little, I would change still less. Since there my past life lies, why alter it?' So, again, to those who wish to see me fall on my face—"

Jane downed her drink, then twisted and collapsed onto the divan in a single swoon, her ass straight up in the air.

"Brava! Brava!" her people shouted. They all cheered, pleased mostly because she had made this speech before, it seemed.

Jane sat the rest of the night cross-legged on the divan, the dirty bottoms of her feet exposed like a child's, surrounded by large cushions. She invited Mielle to take her shoes off and come laze in the pillows too.

"Isn't that better?"

"Yes," Mielle agreed. The fabric of the divan was tufted and soft. She sank half a foot when she sat down. "Is that Browning you recited? For the toast?"

"Yes, that's good," Jane said. "The one about the painter Andrea del Sarto and his loose wife! Do you read Robert Browning?"

"In college. They made us."

Jane laughed. "At least you remembered."

"I can't help it," Mielle said. "It's true what they say: A Mennonite never forgets."

"Ha! I've never heard that." Jane stared at Mielle over the rim of her glass as she sipped. "What a strange disorder for a race of people to have. Being unable to forget. It sounds very ominous."

"Not really. They're just sober people. Teetotalers never forget either."

"That's true!"

Mielle sat with Jane in the pillows a long time. A brass bowl with water in its bottom tilted on a cushion where Jane dropped smoked cigarettes to end them with a *tssh*. She stayed occupied with one cigarette after another—rolling one, slowly, contemplatively, as soon as its predecessor was extinguished.

"These keep my hands busy so I don't drink too much," she explained, eyebrows raised, one eye closing. She drank plenty. As soon as she finished one drink, she'd raise her glass to have it filled by her husband, or the man with the marc, and they obliged.

Somehow Mielle trusted Jane and all these misfits. They told secrets from past lives that had been revealed by hypnotists. They debated the finer points of their birth charts. They gossiped about Lilian Harvey and Louis Armstrong and Django Reinhardt and Josephine Baker.

Mielle never made it to Maxim's. That should be obvious.

Bill and Ed and J-G and Alden would get along fine without her. Now, she could say the same about them. She found a birthday party for herself after all.

"I met Piaf once," Mielle said, trying to butt into the gossip. She raised her glass in the air until it was filled. "I stood next to her outside a brothel in Pigalle, by accident. I was just walking by, and there was Piaf. She's very small."

"Yes." Jane laughed. "That's why she is called Sparrow."

The two of them floated on the divan, barefoot like a pair

of girls from the low country. Jane's feet were swollen, her nails pink and unpainted. She had high arches and delicate toes, but red marks spotted her ankles. White scars raised in thin, straight swipes between her toes, the lines of which intersected on the soles of her feet.

Jane noticed Mielle staring. "Do you want to know what happened to my feet?"

Mielle nodded.

"I used to have the most beautiful feet. Used to be the most beautiful woman—"

"Still is!" Cienfuegos shouted above them.

"—until the Communists took me prisoner."

"In Madrid?"

Mielle had read Jane's entire account of her experiences during the Spanish Revolution when the story was syndicated in the spring of 1937. Dozens of papers across America published the saga in a six-part series of full-page spreads in Sunday ladies' sections with the byline *Jane Anderson, the Marquesa de Cienfuegos*. It was melodramatic, sensationalist, but Catholic mothers in all forty-eight states ate it up. That was the whole point.

"Only the Spaniards could conceive of the torture I suffered for forty-three days in a Madrid jail," she said. "Six weeks in the Checa de Mujeres. A secret prison. Every night one of us would die. They would line us up in front of a firing squad, dozens of us blindfolded, but only one would be shot. You never knew if it was you or not, even that moment when the shot rang out. These marks on my ankles? Rat bites. These scars on my toes? From an inquisitor's razor. I could barely walk when Uncle Sam got me out. The Reds had sentenced me to death, and if it wasn't for the U.S. State Department, the Communists would have hanged me that day. I will hate them forever. I will never forget."

"I'm sorry," Mielle said. She didn't know what else to say. It was horrible to hear about someone being tortured—and twice as bad to hear the details from the victim herself. It was overwhelming to hear Jane describe what happened to her with a practiced tone in her voice. No wonder her lectures stateside were so effective. The look in her eyes. Those horrid scars.

"You will never forget," Mielle said. "Just like a Mennonite."

Jane broke out of her state. She asked, "What do you mean?"

"You called it the *ominous* affliction of my people, having too vivid a memory. You will never forget what happened to you, just like a Mennonite never forgets."

"Yes." Jane laughed. They both laughed. Mielle hadn't meant it as a joke, but she'd lightened the mood.

Mielle took Jane's foot in her hand, suddenly, inexplicably, and pulled it into her lap. As a Mennonite, Mielle had washed other people's feet her whole life. Mennonites had a thing for feet because of Mary Magdalene. She inspected Jane's foot, top to bottom. With a fingertip, she felt along the ridge of the white razor scars between Jane's toes. She had to stop. It was too intimate—holding the sole of another's foot against the palm of her hand, the blue vein under Jane's skin that crossed the ridge of her metatarsal bones—and Mielle, blushing, had no idea why she was moved to do such a thing without asking permission.

From across the room, the creeps watched, lips parted. They wouldn't miss one woman holding another's foot or what it could lead to.

"Will you ever go back there? To Spain?"

"Yes, of course," Jane said. She pulled both her feet toward her body and pressed them into the fluff of the pillows. "In about a month. General Franco has invited me to give a tour of nationalist cities in the south. It's for Americans, if you're interested. I can get you a good rate."

Mielle knew all the things Jane had been saying stateside. Jane had come to Paris to convalesce after she spent eight months on a speaking tour with engagements in Catholic enclaves from Baltimore, Boston, and the Bronx to Montreal, Chicago, St. Louis, and San Francisco, with biweekly spots on Father Coughlin's *Golden Hour of the Shrine of the Little Flower* radio show. (A pro-Fascist program broadcast out of Detroit that had thirty million coast-to-coast listeners each week.) Jane's mandate was to build support for Generalissimo Franco and his army of nationalists.

"Are you really friends with Franco?"

"Of course! He's El Jefe. What's not to love?"

"And you met Hitler?"

"Not yet, but someday soon."

"Are you serious? You *want* to meet him? Hitler?"

"For enough money, I'd do just about anything." Then, only to Mielle, behind the back of her hand: "Have you heard what Nazis pay for good propaganda?" Her eyebrows shot up. "You might not know it, Mielle, but there's a lot of scum in the world. Coming up like you did, with only your own folks around to make sure you kept yourself pure—most people in the world aren't so lucky. The Fascists represent the law. They will restore the rightful order of tradition. History is on their side, Mielle. All of history. And I'm not going to get left behind."

It wasn't so strange to hear people talk like this. Mielle had heard plenty of this logic in Iowa. The German American Bund had a chapter in Cedar Rapids—a small one, nothing like the notorious hordes in New Jersey and Long Island and Los Angeles that drew thousands to their raucous, hateful rallies, those societies for the preservation of...those so-called clubs where everyone dressed in militia gear. Mielle had seen plenty from them. There were beer halls in towns all over where it was no surprise to see a swastika (as unsurprising as it could be to sit down at a table and see hanging above the mantel that red flag with all its right angles and sharp points) or, as happened to Mielle once, to have a familiar-looking young man lean close as he passed her on campus and whisper in her ear, *"Heil Hitler."*

But those vulgar young men seemed predisposed to authoritarianism. If it wasn't Fascism, it would be D. W. Griffith or Fielding Yost. It was a little more shocking to hear those words come from a woman like Jane Anderson, whom Mielle now considered a friend.

There was such sturdy desperation in Jane's face. When Mielle looked closely, she saw it. The way Jane posed, using her hands to frame her jaw, her lips. Her eyes flashed constantly. It must have taken so much energy to maintain that composition, that imperceptible upturn of her lips. Mielle tried to look inside Jane, in through those brief cracks in the facade, but she didn't see anything. Just Jane's hair tangled and unbrushed, falling around her face and down her neck. She looked so tired all of a sudden, like she actually was fifty years old, not thirty-six like she claimed.

Jane went to speak but no noise came out because she kept yawning. It was almost Sunday morning.

"I should go," Mielle said. "I need to be at the briefing in a few hours."

Jane waved a hand, cigarette ash dropping on her legs, to stop Mielle. Then she leaned close. "A little secret," Jane whispered. "I'm afraid of being alone. I can't sleep unless it's in a crowded room."

Jane offered her hand and they shook, barely at all, Jane's hand on Mielle's fingertips. Then Jane turned and was talking to the gigolo, still dapper, who had brought Jane more tobacco in a tin.

The scene would repeat itself many times that October. Mielle would find herself in the same place as Jane nearly every night and end up in her party, with each night almost feeling like it was an accident.

A FORMERLY LOVELY CREATURE

All the shutters had been painted blue.

That's when Mielle started to worry there might be a war. The national anthem was on the radio. Posters on the sides of buildings urged people to prepare a defense POUR SAUVEGARDER LA PATRIE. Every fixture was painted horizon blue, that bright bleu de France.

The weather was surprisingly dry for several weeks. A perfect time to paint.

The night air was so pleasant, warm and invigorating, not at all what Mielle expected in Paris that time of year. Every night she went out with Jane, Cienfuegos, and the gigolo either to Café Pas Toujours or some small club close to her place on the Montmartre hill where four-piece acoustic combos played clip-clopping old jazz. In her head all day she heard racing piano and banjo and strutting gypsy guitar riffs. Mielle barely got her little articles written living this way, but teetering on the edge of deadlines was worth it to have friends. Not just acquaintances like So-and-So from the *Post* and Whoever-Whomever from the *Chronicle,* like at Capoulade, all those people who never even bothered to learn her name. Jane was different. She *gave* Mielle a name. There was real affection between them.

Mielle skipped out on breakfast at Capoulade that morning. She slept in, then walked toward the Hôtel Continental for the press briefing. Down the two hundred seventy steps from the Sacré-Coeur summit, past plane trees with seedpods like tan pom-poms, their white trunks like smooth Doric columns along the stone steps. She stopped for a single coffee with no bread at a table near the Abbesses Station (she could eat at the briefing), then wandered the rest of that hour, past the Opéra to Vendôme.

She was to leave Paris the next day. The syndicate she wrote for was sending her to Italy for two weeks. She was sad to leave at that moment, but she needed the money. With what she could make off a series of articles, she could pay her rent two months ahead. Plus, she had never seen Rome. Mielle had barely left Paris since she arrived.

The ballroom at the Continental was half empty. She was glad to avoid the familiar faces from Capoulade. She was hungover and happy, tired but not exhausted, wearing a black hat she'd borrowed from Jane—an old-fashioned felt cap that made her feel more than a little ridiculous. (In fact, Mielle didn't even own a hat. After spending her first sixteen years in a bonnet, she preferred to let her hair breathe.) Mielle was starving when she arrived, so she stuck to the back of the ballroom next to the food. There were better pickings this time. Croissants filled with chocolate and marzipan, kettles of very good black coffee, hard-boiled eggs, ham cold cuts, a large bowl of overripe butter pears that looked like hearts when halved. The French must have been getting desperate for friendly reporting if the foreign ministry decided to feed them this well.

There wasn't much to report that wasn't already in the news. Germany's Wehrmacht army was demobilizing after they'd been allowed to take Sudetenland without a fight. Charles Lindbergh had accepted the Service Cross of the German Eagle from his friend Hermann Göring at a ceremony in Berlin. (That was a big one back home, as the medal Lindy wore displayed a grand total of four swastikas, which was four too many as far as some people were concerned.) At the briefing, now that the war had been averted, the undersecretary Gazal-Salomon was again tasked with updating the press on the refugee situation. This was a week after the conference in Lausanne where a mechanism to save the condemned Jews was to be devised. The little Frenchman with wire-frame glasses took his spot behind the podium to explain that the Allied powers had committed to another conference, in 1939, at which they would review the refugee issue again. No solution had been found.

"This is settled for now," he said with that clipped, decelerating speech the French use to cut off a conversation, as if he had tied a bow around a package.

"What do you mean, *settled*?" Dorothy Thompson was in the front row of seats. Mielle hadn't noticed her sitting there with Alden and a woman who could be English author Rebecca West. The three of them acted chummy; Alden was like a grown boy being hugged between two middle-aged aunts. All three with legs crossed, little notebooks balanced on their knees.

Dorothy was square-shouldered and big-hipped with graying hair tied in Dutch braids. For a society woman, she looked an awful lot like a farmer to Mielle. That is, she looked useful. Most men were afraid of Dorothy, and she knew it. She viewed them with impatience, amusement. She had a big mouth and wasn't afraid of what might come out if she opened it. As a journalist, she was prodigious in the extreme, known for her late-night Dexedrine-fueled writing sessions. The syndicated column she wrote for the *New York Tribune* was highbrowed and principled and was read by ten million people every week. Dorothy Thompson cut a staggering figure in any gaggle.

"Two months yet remain in 1938," she said. She had a way of speaking: loud, clear, but never shouting. "So you put off 'the refugee issue,' as you call it. In the meantime, winter is coming and all the displaced Jews will be left to blow in the wind. Is that the general idea?"

"Good day, Mrs. Lewis."

"It is Ms. Thompson, thank you."

Nearly everyone knew by then that her marriage to Sinclair Lewis was on the rocks. She had seduced a traveling companion to follow her back and forth between New York and Europe. Her husband—the moody, often inebriated Nobel laureate—was on an extended tour with his newest play and the eighteen-year-old actress for whom he'd written the lead role.

"Ms. Thompson, then." The undersecretary tried to stand tall behind his wooden lectern. "I must beg you to recall that it takes time to build consensus. The French are not being cruel. Our cities are already full. And it is *your* country that has space for every Jew with room to spare. If Roosevelt gave the word to abolish *your* Johnson-Reed Act, there would be ships setting sail for the U.S. within the week filled stern to bow with new American citizens. You don't agree?"

"No, I don't agree. You're only half right. There's such a thing as safe passage. That's part of the problem too. How do you expect a million men, women, and children to get from Czecho and Austria to these ships in French ports? Will the French guarantee safe passage across Germany?"

"We cannot. France makes no promises for the Germans. Not if we can help it."

"Fine. Will the French guarantee that any refugee who makes it across the Reich will be allowed over the border?"

"At this time, no. We cannot."

"Because you're afraid of Hitler?"

"No, madame. Because we abide by our treaties. At this time, it is not possible."

"Then, sir, by the sound of it, you're making us late for our lunch dates today for very little reason."

That got a laugh.

The undersecretary seemed to like this game. His chest puffed out, the epaulets of his uniform trim and ordered, the same as his mustache, trying to show that nothing could touch his nobility.

Mielle liked the man. Gazal-Salomon had an impossible job, and he did it with good humor. Years later, during the Occupation, he would disappear. Mielle would sometimes, then, think back with affection to the mornings she spent listening to him relay French propaganda.

When the briefing was over, Alden found Mielle at the refreshments table. They hadn't seen much of each other for weeks, since Mielle was spending most of her time with Jane and the Cienfuegos legion. She had heard, though, that Alden was offered a job to broadcast the news for CBS from Stockholm. Ed Murrow made the offer that night at Maxim's when Mielle skipped out on dinner and ended up swilling brandy on Jane Anderson's divan instead. Her hope had been correct—that being in the right place at the right time would lead to good things—it was just that it worked out for Alden instead of her. The other green correspondents were baffled by the offer. Alden was wooden on the air and wasn't known as a very competent reporter. But he was seated at the table the moment Murrow wanted to hire someone; there was champagne and rich food to grease the skids. What was even more baffling was that Alden turned down the job. "No, thank you," he'd said, right there at a back table in Maxim's. Murrow was shocked to laughter; Bill and J-G cheered Alden on for being his own man, toasted his gumption, his freedom to throw away his future if that's what he preferred to do. The only thing Alden would say in explanation later was that he already had a job reading the news for Hearst, and he preferred to stay in Paris. He had his reasons.

Mielle didn't know what to think of Alden. So that morning at the briefing, when he grabbed her elbow and told her to follow, she shrugged him off.

"Fine," he said. "Stay here." Alden dashed across the Continental ballroom and pulled Thompson and the other woman over to where Mielle stood.

"Have you met Rebecca West?" He was obviously pleased with himself.

Mielle hadn't met Rebecca West but was happy to shake the woman's hand and hear her voice in person. Like Dorothy Thompson, West was very famous back in the days when a person could become famous for her biting literary criticism. She was a novelist too, known for her advocacy of the sexual and economic liberation of British women, and she was heavy into politics those days, committed to stopping the Nazis before they really got started.

She wore the sort of white blouse a Girl Scout or big sister would wear, a silk scarf tied in a bow over her chest, and a limp felt hat. Just then she was passing through Paris (staying a week, she said, to see people) on her way home from Yugoslavia. For years, she'd been writing a book about the history of the Balkans.

"Don't take this the wrong way," Alden told Mielle. "I have asked these two women to speak to you about someone. Someone who is a rotten egg, I believe."

"Don't beat around the bush," West said.

"It's Jane Anderson who he means," Thompson said.

"That *is* who I mean," Alden agreed, glancing at the women, vexed. "Both Rebecca and Dorothy have known Jane a long time. They have seen what she has become."

"Jane and myself ran together during the World War," West said. She spoke a bit mumbling, in the English version of a drawl, all her words running together in a charming way. "Jane was very beautiful, with orange hair that I am sure was natural. She had a slender figure, a ravishing complexion, and great charm of manner. She was extremely kind to me—we were friends—but as everyone knows, she could not write at all. She was about as bad as bad could be. The things she wrote were silly and melodramatic. She was more novelty than anything."

"I don't understand," Mielle said. "What are you saying? That Jane is a bad writer?"

"If she were here, I would say the same to her face."

"The point is," Alden said, cutting in, "we think you should avoid Jane, for your own good. With the company she keeps, she's a bad element."

"And she used to be such a lovely creature," Thompson said. "Everyone who mentions Jane is very sad about what sort of hysterical beast she has become, running around with the America First crowd. How awful."

Hired propagandists like Jane Anderson were grotesque clowns as far as the legitimate correspondents were concerned. Odd-looking, flamboyant, shameless. Their visions for a greater America dovetailed perfectly with their personal financial ambitions. The old woman Mielle boarded with in Cedar Rapids listened to radio evangelists nonstop. Maybe it was strange for someone like Mielle, who had been raised in a separatist religious sect, to realize only then that people could be made to believe anything if it was shouted loud enough, if you were called a coward for not believing, if the rest of your family was already bought and sold. Even if the other correspondents mocked *eccentrics* like Jane Anderson, it wasn't them Jane was trying to convince. Jane was playing a different kind of game. Mielle herself didn't really understand at that point. None of them did. They couldn't get over the hokeyness, the hackneyed delivery, the low-class mudslinging, to see that there was an audience for this kind of political entertainment.

Mielle kept putting food on her plate, then returning it to the platter. She disliked conversations about the politics of other journalists. If anything could make her lose her appetite, it was this. But she couldn't just walk away, not from these two exalted women.

"What's worse," Thompson continued, her shoulders back, "Jane and that man of hers are broke. She has asked half the paper editors in London for loans. Have you seen her around, Rebecca? Two nights ago, she was in Les Deux Magots."

They were backing up the line at the refreshments table, chatting instead of filling their plates. Hearing the grumbles, Alden shuffled them off to the side, their hands occupied with coffee cups and saucers.

"No, I haven't seen Jane in years," West said, louder, as Alden moved her. "Jane never comes to London, that I'm aware. Not since she became mixed up with the Falangists in Spain. From what I hear, she's in a bad way. Too many pills. And she's fat. Everyone says that first, because she used to be such a beauty."

Mielle took exception to that. She felt like she'd stepped into a wall. The woman they described wasn't the woman Mielle saw. When she looked at Jane Anderson, she saw a lithe tawny-haired beauty still in the prime of her life, dramatic and clever and charming. Mielle would defend her friend Jane.

"Who says she's fat?" Mielle's voice rose too, nearly cracking in its uncomfortable, reedy way. "Is she supposed to stay twenty years old forever? Of course she's put just a little flesh on her cheeks."

"Just a little?" Thompson said.

"Never mind that. That's beside the point," West said. She was much smaller than the other three and had to step closer and closer to catch their eyes. "The things that woman has been through. It makes a person psychotic. The condition of being at war, not with one's self but with one's environment. The desire to enjoy life spiced by danger and reckless pleasure without having to pay the tab. It destroys a person. No wonder she's fallen for a dictator."

Mielle knew she should listen, but she had heard all these stories before she even met Jane. Jane was incapable of saving a dime; she was promiscuous in the extreme; her man Cienfuegos wasn't really titled and maybe wasn't even Spanish but Cuban; that Jane ruined herself because of the wild life she lived.

Mielle didn't really believe all the stories, or she didn't care.

If she wanted to follow a woman who had aged into her prime, who had great depth of character, who had nobility of spirit and aristocratic airs, she could do no better than either of the two women standing in front of her. Rebecca West and Dorothy Thompson were the best of the best. But Mielle wasn't looking for a role model.

She wasn't homesick when she was around Jane. She felt accepted into a family of misfits and orphans. She felt like she belonged. When she was with the others, she didn't feel like she belonged. It was simple.

West and Thompson carried on about how Jane had gotten herself trapped in the Paris underworld ten years ago, caught with mobsters and prostitutes while researching a novel, and had to be rescued by an order of Carmelite nuns.

"Did she really work as a whore?" Thompson asked. The whole room was listening by then. "Just so she could see what it was like?"

"That's not the issue now. She's a drunk. A drug addict."

"She's in with that German American Bund crowd. All of them rabid, raving thugs. American Fascists—there's nothing worse. Except maybe the German, French, and Italian ones."

"You shouldn't trust Jane," Alden said to Mielle. He grabbed her arm, but she shook him off. "That's what they're getting at. We're all fond of you—"

"We've just met," West objected, "but Alden swears you're nice."

"—we're very fond of you and would hate to see a person like Jane lead you astray."

"But astray from what?" Mielle asked. They were exhausting her.

"Well. From the right path," he said. "The American way."

West and Thompson erupted with laughter and couldn't stop.

"We tried, son," Thompson said. "You're on your own."

Once Mielle was alone with Alden, she asked what he was really thinking. "Am I a Fascist? Is that what you're asking me?"

"I do not think you're a Fascist," he said, "but it would be nice to hear you say so. To see you associate with a known Fascist like Jane Anderson—it can't help matters."

Mielle nearly dropped her coffee cup because her hands started shaking. "I will tell you one more time about where I come from and what I believe. My people are pacifists. My people are collectivists. We live and let live. We are *anti*-Fascists."

"That may be. But you left the commune."

"Only because I had to!" She was shouting, she realized. She hadn't ever shouted before, because that, too, was forbidden in the assembly where she was born. The others in the room—West, Thompson, Gazal-Salomon—eyed her and Alden with amusement. Mielle took a breath. Put a hand on her chest. "I left because that was my only option. But I still am what I am. Who else could I be?"

"Good," Alden said. "I'm glad to hear that."

He looked pleased. His hands were deep in his pockets. He'd stopped slouching.

"I know about the things Jane says," Mielle admitted. "I will not defend her remarks or anything the Fascists do. They're despicable, as far as I'm concerned. But Jane is still an American. She will come around to what's right. When push comes to shove, she's an American first and a Fascist second. I know this. She wouldn't betray our ideals."

Alden winced when she said this. He spun away, then quickly back, as if Mielle had jabbed a needle in his gut.

"Be careful. That is all I ask. Jane Anderson has shown her spots. Trust what your eyes are telling you."

The others had gone by then, either to the corridor behind the hotel to smoke or out front to catch a taxi.

"Of all the things going on right now," Mielle said, "why try to bait me into defending Jane? Because I skipped out on Maxim's?"

"No. I told you. Associating with Jane Anderson is a bad idea.

People will think you share her politics. I am convinced nothing good will come your way as long as she is your friend."

"Get off your high horse. I've had enough popularity contests for a lifetime, hanging out with all you broadcasters." Mielle felt bold saying these things—like she had someone else's words in her mouth. These were exactly the sorts of things Jane said. "It's very boring to hear you all argue about whose life is more grotesque."

Alden seemed to take all this in stride, though the muscles of his jaw were in contortions.

"My high horse? After the way you ignore everyone who wants to be your friend? Maybe you don't understand this, but most of those *grotesque* reporters you speak of are just like you. They could help you if you'd let them. They struggle. Their ideas get rejected more often than not. Most of them are middle class of some sort."

"But listen to them now. They're horrible elitists, at least to me."

"For God's sake, Murrow went to college at something he calls Wazzu State. What about that screams *elitist?*"

Alden went on and on about it, his voice never rising. Who was born and raised in the Midwest (Gellhorn, Shirer). Who got their start covering a gossip beat and writing obituaries (pretty much all the women). Who were Jews coming to Europe at the exact time they should have been fleeing in the other direction (Liebling, Dreyfus, Gellhorn—who was half—and Alden himself; he slipped that in). Almost none of these people had been born to success like Mielle thought they had. Reporting was a rough, sometimes dangerous job, and it certainly didn't pay all that well unless you were at the very top. It wasn't a job for someone who was born elite but for someone who wanted to rise. Mielle wanted to refute his points, but she had nothing to say. She saw that Alden was right. She became a correspondent too because she thought it might make her better, freer, a fully emancipated woman. Those things she'd dreamed of while reading old magazines in her college library.

"Why do you think *you* got this job?" Alden asked her. He didn't sound so wooden all of a sudden, his hair flopping loose. "Because of luck? Based solely on talent? No, it's because you took it! You paid your own way here and you work for peanuts, so you get a shot, just like everyone else. You could see yourself as one of us. But you don't, somehow. It's quite unfortunate."

She didn't know what to say once Alden stopped. She'd never been lectured like this before. Even when she was a child, an elder might smack the back of her head, but he'd never tell her off. Mielle felt honored, actually, that she'd inspired someone to read her the riot act.

"How do you know all this?" Mielle asked. "Do you keep dossiers on every reporter in Europe and their politics?"

"Dossiers?" Alden smiled and raised an eyebrow mysteriously. "A dossier is unnecessary," he joked. "You know what they say: A Jew never forgets."

Mielle was sure Alden had not mentioned he was a Jew before. Now he'd said it twice.

She really looked at him then, Alden slouching with his stomach out, his chin tucked down. He could have been handsome, tall and young and square in the right places; he was just so earnest that it made him sexless. Mielle had written him off before because he came from the kind of privilege that made her uncomfortable, but he was different than the other green reporters, she realized, those hyphenates of New England who fell into jobs easily and failed upward thereafter. (No matter what Alden said, there were plenty of them around too.) But Alden wasn't exactly like them. *He's a Jew,* she said to herself.

"Why didn't you tell me before?"

"That I'm a Jew? Why should I have to? That's the point I'm trying to make." He handed his dishes to a busboy who was trying to shuffle the two of them out of the ballroom. "And, honestly, my real last name is Cohn. Didn't you know that?"

"Cohn is a Jewish name?"

He laughed, warming up to her again. "No, you wouldn't know about things like that. Did they not have any Cohns out in Iowa? Not on the commune, I bet."

Mielle didn't like to be teased, and Alden was starting. She told him that she was leaving Paris soon. "Tomorrow on the night train to Lyon, then along to Milan and Rome."

"You are leaving? What on earth for? On holiday?"

"It's for work! There's the winter season and I'm being paid to cover the shows."

"Now? With everything going on, all they want is coverage for the fashion page?"

Mielle wrapped a croissant in a napkin to slip in her pocket, then started to walk away.

"I will think over what you all told me about Jane," she said. "But only because it means so much to you." Then, after hesitating: "I do respect what you think. Maybe I shouldn't trust what you say either, Alden Cohn. But you're my friend too. I realize that."

Mielle did think it over. She thought a lot about the people she knew in Paris during her two-week trip along the Ligurian and Tyrrhenian coasts. She got it from both sides—Jane's perspective on why the Capoulade crowd were such boors, and Alden's exhortations on why people like Jane should be kept at arm's length.

But the thing that stuck in her mind was that Alden didn't fit into either group. The closer Mielle got to him, the more it seemed like Alden wasn't a reporter at all. He was, of course, in the sense that he read the news on radio broadcasts. But Alden acted different. He always pushed some mysterious angle, fished for information that had nothing to do with a story. He was more interested in the reporters themselves than in the drama they witnessed. And that alias!

She would think about Alden Cohn. One day she'd find out what he was really up to.

HERSCHEL GRYNSZPAN

(Dorothy Thompson)
As reported on November 14, 1938

A week ago today an anaemic-looking boy with brooding black eyes walked quietly into the German embassy
in the rue de Lille in Paris, asked to see the ambassador,
was shown into the outer office of the third secretary,
Herr vom Rath, and shot him. Herr vom Rath died on
Wednesday.

I want to talk about that boy. I feel as though I knew
him, for in the past five years I have met so many whose
story is the same—the same except for this unique desperate act. Herschel Grynszpan was one of the hundreds of
thousands of refugees whom the terror east of the Rhine
has turned loose in the world. His permit to stay in Paris
had expired. He could not work because no country would
give him a work permit. So he moved about, hoping he
would not be picked up and deported, only to be deported
again, and yet again. Sometimes he found a bed with
another refugee. Sometimes he huddled away from the
wind under the bridges of the Seine. He got letters from his
father, who was in Hanover, in Germany. His father was all
right. He had a little tailoring shop and managed honorably
to earn enough for food and shelter. Maybe he would have
sent his son money, but he was not allowed to send any out
of Germany. Herschel read the newspapers, and all that he
could read filled him with dark anxiety and wild despair.
He read how men, women and children, driven out of the

Sudetenland by a conquering army—conquering with the consent of Great Britain and France—had been forced to cross the border into Czechoslovakia on their hands and knees—and then had been ordered out of that dismembered country, that, shorn of her richest lands and factories, did not know how to feed the mouths that were left.

He read that Jewish children had been stood on platforms in front of classes of German children and had had their features pointed to and described by the teacher as marks of a criminal race. He read that men and women of his race, amongst them scholars and a general decorated for his bravery, had been forced to wash the streets, while the mob laughed. There were men of his race whom he had been taught to venerate—scientists and educators and scholars who once had been honored by their country. He read that they had been driven from their posts. He heard that the Nazi government had started all this because they said the Jews had made them lose the World War. But Herschel had not even been born when the World War ended. He was seventeen years old.

Herschel had a pistol. I don't know why he had it. Maybe he had bought it somewhere thinking to use it on himself, if the worse came to the worst. Thousands of men and women of his race had killed themselves in the last years, rather than live like hunted animals. Still, he lived on. Then, a few days ago, he got a letter from his father. His father told him that he had been summoned from his bed, and herded with thousands of others into a train of box cars, and shipped over the border, into Poland. He had not been allowed to take any of his meager savings with him. Just fifty cents. "I am penniless," he wrote to his son.

This was the end. Herschel fingered his pistol and thought: "Why doesn't someone *do* something!" Why must we be chased around the world like this. In every country there are societies for the prevention of cruelty to animals. But there are none for the prevention of cruelty to people. Herschel thought of the people responsible for this terror. Right in Paris were some, who were the official representatives of these responsible people. Maybe he thought that assassination is an honorable profession these days. He knew, no doubt, that the youths who murdered Austrian Chancellor Dollfuss are heroes in Nazi Germany, as are the murderers of Rathenau. Maybe he remembered that only four years ago the Nazi leader himself had caused scores of men to be assassinated without a trial, and had justified it simply by saying that he was the law. And so Herschel walked into the German embassy and shot Herr vom Rath. Herschel made no attempt to escape. Escape was out of the question anyhow.

Herr vom Rath died on Wednesday. And on Thursday every Jew in Germany was held responsible for this boy's deed. In every city an organized and methodical mob was turned loose on the Jewish population. Synagogues were burned; shops were gutted and sometimes looted. At least four people were done to death. Many, many more were beaten. Scores killed themselves. In cold blood, the German government imposed a fine of four hundred million dollars on the entire Jewish community, and followed in by decrees which mean total ruin for all of them. A horrified world was stunned. In the United States nearly every newspaper protested. A former governor, Alfred Smith, and the recent Republican candidate for New York State governor, Thomas Dewey, protested with unusual eloquence.

But in Paris, a boy who had hoped to make some gesture of protest which would call attention to the wrongs done his race burst into hysterical sobs. Up to then he had been apathetic. He had been prepared to pay for his deed with his own life. Now he realized that half a million of his fellows had been sentenced to extinction on the excuse of his deed.

NIGHT OF BROKEN GLASS

She was gone two weeks.

It felt like she was on trains the entire time. To Lyon, then Turin and Milan and Rome, where the Italians burned with fever about their victories in Abyssinia. Designers annexed that energy for the fashions that season. Little imperial flourishes, gaudy beads and earrings, dresses with boxy militaristic shoulders that Mielle doubted any of her readers on the Great and western plains would ever actually have the gumption to wear, not even as a joke. Not that this was the point of her reporting. It was fantasy. She wrote with pencil on loose pages in a second-class berth while the porter brought her sandwiches and milk from the dining car. The aisles were filled with refugees, desperate-looking people who wore multiple sets of clothes at once and grasped the overhead bin whenever the train snapped into motion. Middle-class Italian Jews were barreling toward France en masse on the slim hope that a border official at Ventimiglia would let them out. After the November Pogrom (*Kristallnacht* was the Nazi term; Goebbels dreamed it up to make the arrest of thirty thousand people sound like the antics of some looters), every inch of space on a train was sold and ticketed, even if some passengers had to stand in the aisles with their suitcases between their feet the whole trip.

From a telegraph booth at Gare de Lyon, Mielle filed six stories she'd scratched out aboard trains—four about Milanese footwear, rearranged for regional specification, and two broader features about the transmogrified national spirit of the Italians under Mussolini. His promises to restore the dominance of ancient Rome made for easy headlines. Il Duce was a newspaperman himself, after all. He understood these things.

Mielle knew Paris would be in a fever when she returned. The whole continent was. A Jewish boy had killed a Nazi official in Paris and nationalists everywhere were frothing. It was accepted as fact that the consequences would be bad. The only dispute was what amount of retribution was justified. Even up on the Montmartre hill, things felt different that evening. Thousands of nationalists flooded in from the countryside and suburbs to demonstrate in support of the slain foreign secretary vom Rath. Farm boys in green shirts and overalls. Young men and women from Saint-Denis, the industrial suburb where the Blueshirt Fascist movement burned the hottest. Dozens of groups pulled on colored shirts to unite the right wing of France. Herschel Grynszpan had shot the German secretary on Monday. This was Thursday, and the assassin hadn't yet been executed. To the right-wingers, that was proof that the French prefecture had been infiltrated by Jews. These boys stomped around in unison and waved the flags of their militias alongside the bleu, blanc, et rouge.

Mielle had no time to rest once she made it home to rue Gabrielle. She didn't unpack, just bathed after she stopped a moment to tell the old women who guarded the entry what she saw in Italy, then she was out the door, headed for the Left Bank. She needed to get to Capoulade as soon as possible to find out what was going on with the demonstrations. France was a democracy, of course, but had its own anti-Semitic streak. Mielle was scared there might be a pogrom in Paris too.

When Mielle arrived at Capoulade, it was obvious Jane was not well. She and her husband sat in the corner with the other correspondents. Jane looked out of place, and deranged. She slouched in a wicker chair, pushed back from that table where she hardly ever sat, and stared at the floor as she listened to the others. With how low she sat, her chin doubled, she looked older than Mielle remembered. She was wearing a lot of makeup. Too much. Jane almost resembled the degraded woman whom Dorothy Thompson and Rebecca West had described two weeks before.

Alden was at the table, of course. It was his twenty-seventh birthday. He sat in the middle, his back straight, on the edge of a chair, trying to smile as the others sang to him. Only half of them sang, though, because the week had been so depressing. With the demonstrations, they didn't want to look like they were chanting a slogan, even if that slogan was *Happy birthday to you, happy birthday to you.* Alden stopped them after the second languid line, said, "Thank you, thank you. No song is necessary. This is a rather sad occasion to have a birthday. So, please, forget it."

Their number was smaller than normal anyway. Dorothy Thompson had gone to Los Angeles to deliver a rousing anti–Fascist screed to a crowd of thousands at the Hollywood Bowl. Rebecca West and Ed Murrow were back in London. Shirer had gone to a ski resort outside Geneva with his wife and daughter. The big party of them from October had mostly broken up and scattered to the wind.

Virginia Cowles was still there, and Jean-Gérard Dreyfus. They were eating an early dinner, chicken fricassee and potato purée, since most of them planned to work through the night. They were all fairly certain something dramatic was going to happen. The weather was mild, warm with no wind, though they all brought along wool coats, just in case.

In the corner, Jane looked even more bitter because of the aborted birthday song. Her face frozen, lips tight, her shoulders pushed forward. Neither she nor Cienfuegos was speaking.

Jane didn't even notice when Mielle walked in. Only Alden acknowledged her, with his eyes, so she sat next to him.

"Happy birthday," she said, elbowing him in the ribs when he put his arm around her. "What did I miss?"

"Nothing, nothing. Just a pogrom. Thirty thousand Jews arrested and headed to concentration camps."

"I heard about that. It's the worst news yet."

Mielle hadn't wanted to believe something like this was possible. Even with the land grabs, the seizing of Jewish assets, the packing of Jews and Communists off to concentration camps in groups of ten to twenty; even with Hitler's murderous purges of his own party; even with the mobilizing of the Wehrmacht, the mobilizing of street thugs across Europe. Even with all that, Mielle, like so many, still hoped that the most recent outrage would satisfy the nationalists and restore normalcy. *When the lion is full,* they all said, *he stops eating.* But it couldn't work that way. Mielle wasn't shocked. She was disgusted. They had all seen this coming, yet nobody had stepped into the road to put a stop to it. To her, it felt like nobody in Europe had even tried.

"What are the French going to do about this?" she asked Alden. "What did Gazal-Salomon say at the briefing today?"

"*Do?* Ha. What they did was lock the doors at the Continental. No briefings. The French are more concerned with keeping their own windows intact over the weekend. You saw that there will be demonstrations?"

She nodded. It was too easy to feel dumbfounded, powerless. She didn't want to feel that way.

"Where do all those boys come from?" she asked. "You never think about how many angry young men there are in the world until you see them bunched together in the street."

"Well, you should think about it." Alden composed himself, combed his thinning hair back with the tips of his fingers. "Those angry young men have been filling stadiums across Europe for a decade now."

Around the table they were trying to decipher how the pogrom was being treated back home. Both Al Smith (a Democrat who ran for president and lost in 1928) and Thomas Dewey (a Republican who would run and lose to Roosevelt in '44 and to Truman in '48) gave big speeches against the nationalists. There were marches in New York and Chicago. These stories would get a lot of ink. But, of course, it didn't matter all that much what anyone thought if the president and Congress didn't agree.

Virginia Cowles was at the center of the table that evening. She took off her bracelet and ran the pearls over her fingers like a rosary. She was delicate, fashionable, and had a soft aristocratic accent with a little bourgeois overbite that was endearing. Appearances aside, Cowles had a reputation for finding herself at the spot where trouble was about to break out—to the point that some correspondents were nervous about even sharing a car with her. If she had something to say about a crisis, everybody stopped to listen.

"Something is changing," she said, the pearl bracelet going back on her slender wrist. "You can feel it in the air. If bosses are asking for articles and politicians are fighting to be first in line, I'd say America is finally starting to pay attention. Now: Is that good or bad news for the rest of the world?"

"It's good for business," Alden said. Then: "You know what I mean. We're needed."

"Who do we know that's in Germany now?" Cowles asked.

"Max Jordan?" "Edward Kennedy?" The green reporters answered uncertainly, like they were still being called on in a lecture hall. "What about Shirer?"

"Bill is stuck on a train in Switzerland."

"Max Jordan will get on the air first, no doubt. But does Jordan ever say anything that isn't rewritten by Goebbels?"

"He might tell something good off the record. Point us in the right direction."

"Sigrid Schultz went back to Berlin last week," Cowles said, tired of waiting for them to come up with the right answer. "She's writing it up for the *Chicago Tribune* as we speak. They promised her a spot above the fold for this. I can try to get her on the horn."

Cowles went to place a call. If she got anything good from Berlin, she'd share what she heard. There was no hope for a scoop from Paris anyway. They all just wanted to know what was happening.

"If this is the turning point for the United States, I think it's good news in the long run," Alden said. His eyes were lit, but his voice remained calm, the muscles of his face fixed with poise. "I do believe this is the thing that will demonstrate what kind of mania Germany is in and that these crimes need to be dealt with."

From the corner, Jane began laughing in contralto. Her laugh was the kind of noise that carried a long way.

"All last year I spoke at rallies in the States. Let me tell you, whole bunches of Americans are well aware of Adolf Hitler and the *German mania* without your condescending to tell them about it. Four hundred events, more than that, from Montreal to Monterrey, and at every one of them, more than half the room already knew the score."

Jane's body took on better proportions as she sat up tall and pulled herself to the table.

"Hasn't there been a murder here in Paris?" she asked. "Will you tell the American public that news too? Or is that where your fairness ends?"

Cienfuegos tried to stop her, but Jane waved him off with a frantic movement of her arm.

"What happened was a necessity. There will be law and order for this Grynszpan," she started again. By then it was too late. The table had heard enough.

J-G Dreyfus dragged his chair across the floor to Jane's end of the table. Right then he was working for the Paris edition of the *Herald Tribune* and writing incendiary columns for *Le Temps*. He was very much opposed to the Fascist movement and Hitler in particular—as a Jew, as a Frenchman, as an intellectual—and wasn't shy about saying so in print. Everyone knew who J-G was. They published a portrait with his columns, with his rounded shoulders and weathered boulder of a bald head, his suave mustache, thin and curving into his nostrils.

His face turned red with indignation as he pulled his chair next to Jane's. "Madame, to even compare the crime and the response, I do not think you are seeing things clearly. This kind of terror cannot be tolerated."

"Which terror do you refer to?"

"You know very well. The terror evoked by the German dictator. The same terror that befell the people of Guernica. If you recall, fifteen hundred innocents died there because of bombs dropped by Nazi airplanes."

"Oh, don't bring up the battle of Guernica."

"It was not a *battle*. That implies two sides fighting, not a massacre. Not a war crime."

Cienfuegos spotted Mielle then. He pulled her to the bar.

"Where have you been?"

Like most of them, he was hysterical. His thin hair out of shape, his tie undone.

"Madame is not well," he told her. "What has happened has been very bad for my wife, professionally. She has new troubles. A telegram from London this morning. You must speak to her, please. Tell her she will make it through this bad time. We have land. We have friends."

Mielle asked Cienfuegos to slow down and explain what he meant that Jane had new troubles, but he kept ranting.

"Please tell her. Take her outside. Oh, Madame is not pleased. Madame n'est pas heureuse," he said, as if saying it in French made it so. "You must make her stop talking."

Mielle wanted Jane to stop talking too, but what could she do about it?

Jane argued with half the table at once and kept rising halfway out of her seat so they could hear, though her voice carried even when she didn't shout. "But the Jews brought it on themselves. Tit for tat, tit for tat!"

"Come with me," Mielle said, lowering her voice to sound stern as she pulled Jane outside. "What's the matter with you?" she asked then. "Why would you say those things?"

They were out on the terrace, beyond the skinny café tables and wicker chairs, near boulevard Saint-Michel and all its blaring cars. The density of the light appeared to intensify from where the sodium lights lit up the Dôme green to where the color drained from the buildings. The pink and peach tones disappeared and it was all grays, as if the buildings were camouflaged in the dark. Headlights blinked on two by two up and down the boulevard.

"Eduardo told me you're in some trouble," Mielle said.

"He doesn't know everything. It's just how our business works. They always put bad news in a telegram. They're firing me, that's all."

"*Firing you?* Who? The Catholics?"

"No, honey. The *London Mail*. They still had me on retainer for updates on the situation inside Spain, but I haven't been to Spain for two years. I've been in Paris all autumn."

"I know that."

"It isn't a big deal. They didn't want anything about Paris or Munich or the United States, not from me, so I got the ax. You don't get paid for doing nothing. Marqués Eduardo comes from royalty. He doesn't understand that. The kicker, though, is this stuff in the Reich reminded them I was still on the payroll." Jane puffed up her cheeks and let her lips flap as the air escaped her. She looked dissatisfied by her own explanation and began to pace back and forth.

"Have you ever been to England?" Jane asked. "Do you know many English? They have too much gall. Englishmen can never just tell you something straight. They always have to add some nasty remark to make out like they're better than you."

Jane drank red wine from a stubby glass as she spoke, then held the glass between biceps and breast to light a cigarette. Her hair looked darker, more chestnut than tawny, like it had been dyed, and it was tied back in the Spanish fashion with a golden brooch in the shape of an arrow. Under normal circumstances Jane would have looked elegant in her navy blouse with large brass buttons down its front, with her dark hair, the shape of her eyebrows, so she resembled the Spanish aristocrat she claimed to be. But Jane looked unwell. There was an intensity in her eyes, the green flashing. She paced the sidewalk. Her bangles rattled on her wrist when she raised her cigarette. The clouds behind her were all orange and purple, inching to black.

There was a lot of noise all of a sudden. Honking horns and flashing headlights a block away. A dozen gendarmes in full capes and tall hats were closing off the boulevard. Mielle looked that way but couldn't see what was going on.

Jane asked her, "What's your birthday?"

"Today is Alden's birthday," Mielle replied. She still looked the other way to see what was coming.

"Sure, but what's yours?" Jane stepped in front of Mielle. "I want to know your sign."

Mielle told her: October 8.

"Ah, why didn't you say so before? Wasn't that the day we met?"

"It was."

"I would have said happy birthday."

"You didn't have to say that—you were so nice to me. And you did throw a party. Remember?"

"We did have a party! That's right. Well, then, happy birthday.

Cheers!" Jane finished her wine, then set the glass on the pavement. "You're a Libra. That means you're the scales of justice, just like my father was the scales. He was a Libra."

Jane took a small notebook from her clutch and scratched out the Libra symbol so Mielle could see it. The two lines intersecting at an odd angle so that one side of the scales pushed the other higher. Or was it one side forcing the other down?

"See? That's the sign for Libra. It's in the stars."

"You mean astrology?"

"You are a simple creature, aren't you?" Jane had flipped a switch and was charming again. "Libras are avant-garde and have very good luck in life. And don't forget the scales. You are the scales." She went on about it, saying how reading the stars helped calm her down and that she had seen every star in the known universe when she and Cienfuegos lived in the hills of Extremadura before the Spanish Revolution broke out. Jane was a Capricorn. "My symbol is a goat, of all things. Capricorns are demanding, independent, and always show good judgment, though they have rotten luck with friends. This describes me to a T."

Mielle heard the demonstrators chanting before she saw them. *France for the French!* The flickers of their torches. Their dark hair. Their pale faces made paler in the dark. About a hundred of them marched in the middle of boulevard Saint-Michel as the sun set. Young men with short hair and acne scars wearing tight shirts to show off their chests. They were members of Mouvement Franciste. They called themselves les Chemises Bleues, the Blueshirts. They wore light blue military button-downs and dark blue trousers, plus berets and armbands that featured their emblem. Just like the nationalists in Germany, who preferred brown shirts, and their comrades in Italy, who preferred black, they gave each other the straight-armed Roman salute.

They were right in front of Mielle now, marching north along the black gates of the Luxembourg Gardens. She could see their faces, red and shaved quick, the fanatical look in their eyes. All that pent-up electricity in their muscles. All the rumors, all the conspiracy theories about Jews and global cabals and secret assassins and race wars. And this the moment when they could let loose every popping bit of lightning trapped inside their bodies.

Mielle tried to pull back from the demonstration, but Jane grabbed her by the arms and held her to the spot.

"Don't run," Jane said, her voice shaking in ecstasy. "This is what we came to see."

Mielle let herself be held. She had come to see this demonstration, to see a horde of nationalists marching through Paris. Now, there they were. She could hardly breathe, she was so scared and angry and somehow surprised. This wasn't a voice on the radio, wasn't a newsreel, wasn't an isolated creep. There they were. She was finally face to face with them as they marched in the streets.

A few of the correspondents rushed outside. Alden and Cowles, who couldn't believe she wasn't there first, that she had to stare around Jane Anderson's backside to see all the shouting. Some other young ones who considered themselves sportswriters.

"No, not here!" J-G couldn't help himself. He knifed between Mielle and Jane. "Go back to the gutter, Fascistes!"

They shouted slogans back and forth.

"France for the French!" the Blueshirts chanted.

"Paris for the Parisians!" J-G shouted.

"*Blood and soil!*" the Blueshirts replied, louder. "*Droit du sang! Justice for vom Roth!*"

In minutes, the demonstration moved down the boulevard to the Seine.

Mielle, again, heard them without seeing them.

It was almost unbelievable to Mielle, to have seen something like this. Demonstrations were a tradition in Paris, part of the

French character. But to be stuck in one herself, and a Fascist one at that. To see the hundreds of them stream in from the countryside like they held pitchforks, like they were building a guillotine scaffold at Place de la Revolution. It was overwhelming. Her body was shaking, her hands, her knees. All of her. She had never even seen two people scream at each other until she was sixteen, in college, because raised voices were forbidden in the assembly where she grew up. Only meekness was allowed. Only the opposite of the current that ran through these belligerents.

Mielle tried to back away, to go somewhere quiet, but Jane held her. Jane was shaking too. Mielle could feel Jane's heart race through her clothes, could feel the brass buttons on Jane's taffeta blouse rattle. And in Jane's eyes, sincere exhilaration.

"What happened?" Mielle whispered in Jane's ear.

"Yes, yes," Jane whispered back. "They are here."

The correspondents lingered outside the terrace to share cigarettes and watch as police allowed cars onto the boulevard again. The cars rushed into the open space.

J-G stood with his back to them. His toes hung over the curb. He stared into the street at the spot where the marchers had stomped by as if he too couldn't swallow that this had happened here, right in front of the Sorbonne. The top of his bald head blushed with what could have been anger or fear or disgust or all of these things and none of these things. Mielle had no idea what J-G could be thinking. He'd spent that decade warning his readers about something like this happening, and now Jews were being trucked away by the dozens, by the hundreds, by the thousands, by the ten thousands. Now he was supposed to write something about this mess that would make people care. Mielle wanted to say something that would make both him and herself feel better. But there was nothing to say, nothing to write, that could make things better.

Mielle stood with Jane's arms on her and her arms on Jane. J-G stood at the curb, the cars again rushing by.

Two of the Blueshirts sprinted past Mielle toward the street. They pushed J-G in the back into traffic, in front of a truck.

The two boys in blue shirts gathered themselves on their feet. They shouted, *"Vom Rath! Sang et terre!"*

A couple reporters tried to grab the boys. Alden with his arms wide, shuffling to one side, then the other. He leaped at one but couldn't grab hold. The boys were younger, stronger. They had no objection to elbowing Alden in the chest. No objection to grabbing him by his jacket and trying to fling him into the street too if he fought them.

Mielle froze until the two boys sprinted by her, their long hair on top flopping in the wind.

She woke to the sound their shoes made stomping. She turned and chased after them for half a block, shouting for them to stop, but it was useless to pit her legs against their legs. Her legs didn't know how to run. There was no point stumbling down the block after the Blueshirts. The two boys disappeared into the crowd, were just two of many in the same uniform with the same haircut, shaved up the sides of their heads, shouting the same hateful words.

When Mielle came back, she saw a crowd around J-G. All their friends. The waiters from Capoulade wrung their hands in long white aprons.

"Is he dead?" Mielle asked. "Is that J-G?"

His body lay limp on the pavement. His legs were collapsed underneath him, his arms out. J-G looked dead. But then his chest heaved. He spit up blood.

Alden moved at once. He hailed a taxi and two of the others grabbed J-G by his belt and arms to load him into the back.

"We are going to the American Hospital," Alden said, hanging out the window. He looked to Mielle. "Are you coming? Get in!"

She had a hand on the taxi door, which was why he asked her, because she looked like she wanted to jump in. But she just stood there. She shook her head, said, "No." She backed away.

"Fine!" Alden shouted. "Someone tell the police what happened!"

Then they were off.

In the café, the headwaiter argued with two of the green reporters over who would pay J-G's bill along with the tab Alden had run up that day. The young men tried to convince the waiter to keep the tabs open until the men returned. The reporters had to rush to the office to write about what they'd seen before somebody else did. "But monsieurs," the headwaiter said, "what if your friends don't return?" Jane butted in to suggest the debt be added to Dorothy Thompson's tab, but the waiter wouldn't be tricked. "Madame Dorothy has no tab. She pays cash."

"Fine, put it on mine," Jane conceded.

"No, no, Madame Comtesse. We insist you especially pay cash as well. His receipts are not insubstantial."

The waiter passed a receipt to Jane. She glanced at J-G's tab, then immediately dropped it to the floor. "Two thousand francs? Why in the world did you let him keep charging?"

"We liked him," the waiter said.

The correspondents took up a collection to put a down payment on J-G's tab. The headwaiter would have to get the other four-fifths himself or accept the loss as an act of God, or an act of war. Alden's bill was more reasonable, so Mielle paid that herself.

"Is it true, mademoiselle?" the headwaiter asked, counting back her change. "Did they assassinate Monsieur Jean-Gérard?"

"I don't know."

"But it was Blueshirts that did it?"

"Yes. Two of them pushed him in front of a truck."

The waiter moaned. "How terrible. He was a nice man. He could have been important in a different life. I will never understand you journalists. What good does it do to make enemies all the time? And then to sign your name at the top! How terrible."

THE SPREE

The three of them skipped out to drink elsewhere. Jane and Cienfuegos insisted.

Jane had this big idea. If they could get a few quotes from American luminaries about the pogrom or J-G, she could sell them to Hearst for a response piece. She claimed to know WRH's personal number at La Cuesta Encantada, so the trio ran to the regular haunts to look for famous Americans.

To Les Deux Magots...to see if anyone there had heard something new about J-G's condition. Nobody there was famous. The few poets and philosophers scattered under the awning didn't even know J-G had been hurt. But Jane earned a round of middling cognac to sip on while she told the news.

To Shakespeare and Company...where there were always Americans with gossip. But the owner locked the door when she saw Jane coming. Sylvia Beach hated Jane. A tiny woman in an old-fashioned dress with short, curly hair, Beach shook her finger behind the glass when Jane knocked. "I heard already what happened," the bookseller said. "Don't bring your trouble here, Jane. My door is open to every American, but you no longer qualify."

To La Closerie des Lilas...but there were only tourists here, tucked behind potted plants, and not many. The place was half empty.

"Are we actually working this story?" Jane asked Mielle. They had collapsed at the bar to drink cold beer in slender half-pint glasses. All the running from place to place made them morose and thirsty. "Do we have anywhere to publish a story even if we did write it? Then why pretend? There were plenty of reporters, ones with jobs, who saw what happened. Let them get the scoop."

The attack on J-G had filled Jane with a dark energy. Mielle didn't like the look of it. Jane laughed alone in a way that filled the dimly lit bar with echoes. Her eyes big. Her fingers twisting the brass buttons of her blouse. Cienfuegos tried to sit next to Jane, to whisper some sense into her ear. Every time he sat, Jane hopped up and moved to a different chair. The man looked exhausted. His face wan and pale. His eyes bloodshot. He gave up, squared his shoulders to the bar, and pulled a cigar from inside his jacket. He asked the barman, "Are you married?" Then, when the barman shook his head, "Ah, bien. I'm jealous."

Mielle excused herself, not that Cienfuegos or Jane was listening.

She stumbled down the stairs to the washroom. She was drinking on an empty stomach and already she'd had too much. She needed a minute of quiet without Jane pulling her along.

Though she felt bad about it, Mielle was jealous of the reporters who jumped in the taxi with J-G. She'd had the chance but declined. They were there to help, surely, but also to be in the car or outside the operating room peeking in through a window in the door if a prominent political columnist like J-G died. The story lines must have rushed through their heads like threads flew through a spindle. *Dateline: Paris.* Mielle didn't believe she had the ability to do justice to a story like that, a story that might be a five-bell bulletin over the wire in France. It took special talent to be both first and right. Mielle didn't even know how she'd ended up in a race like that. And now, on top of it all, she was too drunk to even think coherent. She was stuck in a tourist bar with Jane and Cienfuegos. She wasn't going to write any story. She hadn't even helped take care of her friend. *God,* she thought. *What if J-G dies?*

She should go home to rue Gabrielle. That's what she told

herself. The old woman next door would have a bowl of soupe au vin for her. If the bathtub at the end of the hall was free, she would soak a second time that day. Or just collapse in bed and sleep until Monday, until Wednesday, until it was safe for her to show her face at Capoulade again after the things Jane had said and after Mielle had left with Jane. How embarrassing it was that Mielle had defended Jane at the press briefing weeks before. How devastating that Mielle had stood with Jane when the demonstrations came, and when J-G was shoved into traffic. Alden had warned her. She should have been careful of hitching so close to Jane. And now, she feared, it was too late to free herself.

Mielle splashed cold water on her face. She took deep breaths to calm down. She felt betrayed by Jane. Embarrassed. Fed up. Misled. She could never again defend Jane. Though, really, Jane hadn't betrayed Mielle, had she? Mielle realized this. It was Mielle who struggled to see Jane as she really was; it was Mielle who let Jane rename her. Jane was only being herself, and Mielle wasn't sure who she was. She felt herself sink, realizing all this at once.

Mielle had to get out of there. She had to get away from Jane. One more drink and she would be lost for the whole night. She could feel this. Her head spinning. Her heart racing. She splashed water on her face again, then looked herself in the eye in the mirror, water dripping from her cheeks. She made herself promise. She would say that Jane was despicable, loathsome. She would say this to Jane's face. Then she would walk out and take a train home. That would be that. She would be done with Jane Anderson.

None of what she told herself mattered. Mielle wouldn't make it out of La Closerie des Lilas without Jane sinking in her hook even deeper.

Someone was rattling the lock on the door. Then the lock popped open. Jane pushed her way inside and closed the door behind her.

"I was worried we'd lost you, Mielle." Jane's drawl was thick, which meant she was very drunk. "You wouldn't abandon me, would you? We need each other, yeah? Two ladies like us."

"I want to go home," Mielle said, trying to stand up straight. They were packed into the washroom hip to hip, chin to chin. "I'm going to be sick if I don't get out of here."

"No," Jane objected. "Listen, wait."

Jane fumbled with her clutch, her fingers slick on the clasp. Finally she got it. "Have you ever seen something as absolutely gorgeous as this?"

She pulled out an orange and blue tube filled with white powdery tablets.

"What is it?" Mielle asked.

"A package of miracles. I got them sent from Berlin. For clarity of mind and intellectual endurance. Pure energy in powdered form." Jane's eyes closed in ecstasy. "Take one."

Mielle tried to back away but there wasn't space for even half a step. They were boxed up. Jane slipped one of the pills past Mielle's lips. Jane ran the faucet and cupped her hands in the stream and brought water to Mielle's mouth to wash the pill down. Mielle's lips on Jane's fingers as she swallowed without thinking.

The pill was bitter and floury. Within seconds, Mielle's heart knocked against her ribs. Her eyes grew until they bulged from their sockets.

"Do you hear it?" Jane asked, as dramatic as a preacher. She was nose to nose with Mielle, searching for something in Mielle's eyes. "Do you see the light? Is it God?"

Mielle felt her back and neck and legs straighten until all her faults snapped off and fell to the floor. Their bodies, Jane's laughter, filled every inch of the washroom. Mielle smacked her head against the toilet tank. She jerked back to see Jane's face. Jane smiling at her. Jane's childish face, her sweet smile, perfectly round in all directions. Her beautiful brass buttons. The dark knot of her hair held by an arrow of gold.

To Mielle, it felt like they shared the same body. She couldn't resist.

She felt her chest open. She didn't know what was happening to her body, like her soul was breaking loose, like she was wanted by the world. Her whole life, she had never once felt this way, that the sun shined on her. She had never felt God inside her, not like this. This poor, crippled young woman. This dull, prudish woman. "I see it!" she shouted. She felt it all change with that pill on her tongue, choked down with water cupped from a washroom faucet. Cheek to cheek with Jane.

The lights flickered. Blinked three times. Mielle heard a chime with each blink.

Jane appeared in a strange light in the blinks. When the light came back, cracks showed in Jane's face, deep lines. Her skin began to loosen. She was different. There was no glamour in her. All Jane's softness vanished. The shape of her jaw was gone. All at once. There were bags under her eyes, her eyes lifeless. Her face was thick in middle age, her hair dull orange.

Mielle felt her body dropping, like the washroom was descending to the Catacombs below. Looking Jane in the face, Jane laughing alone, as Jane's skin sagged like she was a corpse. Her hair lost its gleam. The irises of her eyes turned black.

This was the first time Mielle had the feeling that she would one day kill Jane Anderson.

The vision came to her with a stabbing pain behind her eyes, as her visions always did. Her body stopped dropping. The room stopped spinning. Mielle merely stared at Jane, unglamorous Jane, horse-laughing Jane, and she felt something important: One day Jane would be killed and Mielle would be the killer.

Just as fast as it came, the prophecy dissolved.

The door became unlatched. Cienfuegos was pulling them out of the washroom and up to the street.

"One more for the road," Jane shouted. Jane was back to herself, as Mielle saw her before—her cut jaw, her green eyes and tawny hair. But "No, no," Cienfuegos requested; "No, no," the waiter demanded. Jane and Mielle had made big trouble. They must leave La Closerie des Lilas before the gendarmes had to be called. There had been a lot of shouting in the washroom. Mielle had ripped the washroom sink from the wall. The floor was flooding.

Mielle's head spun again as she was rushed out to the boulevard du Montparnasse. Her head still throbbed from her second sight. Even in the state she was in, Mielle knew this vision was real, because it hurt her. Her second sight, the pain, made it hard to think of anything except what she had seen. A sword in her hands. The point of the blade over Jane's heart.

The three got in a taxi, then they were crossing the river, the Seine all lit up with torches along its banks, along the quais, as they crossed an ancient bridge. Then they were on the Right Bank. The gigolo was at the taxi window staring in at them, saying, "God, Eduardo, you were right. Look at them. What do we do?"

Their hair and clothes were turned over. Jane's blouse had fallen off one shoulder to reveal the strap of her brassiere. Mielle, still bug-eyed, licked her lips like they were covered in a sweet sticky film. The two of them pressed to the middle of the seat, arms locked, one of Jane's legs crossed over Mielle's.

"One more," Jane insisted, ordering the gigolo into the back seat. She said an address and *"Allez!"* and they were blasting along the canals of Saint-Martin, cutting back and forth to find a cross street where there weren't demonstrators, and then they were inside, up to the bar, to order champagne.

To Noir et Blanc...a basement bar where they had to duck inside the door quick because groups of demonstrators clashed outside. Greenshirts from the countryside, Blueshirts from the industrial suburbs, and a group of student Reds. It was a free-for-all. The factions smacked one another with posters and pickets. Fist-fighting in the street. Where Mielle scanned the faces of the

Blueshirts to find the ones who pushed J-G in front of that truck, to have those two arrested, but the apple-cheeked boys all looked the same to her. Watching those boys, she felt it inevitable that there would be war. The masses marching in the street, the synagogues in the new Reich all burning. Austria and Czechoslovakia already fallen. Within weeks, months, by spring, the war would arrive here in Paris. (This feeling was wrong, of course; almost two years would pass before France was invaded, two years of the drôle de guerre, followed by the three-week collapse of the Third Republic.) That November evening, you could forgive Mielle if she thought the war was already here—that the war had begun in Paris—the streets filled, the sound of their singing like the sound of two iron pipes ringing together. The cruel look in their eyes. The close shave up the sides of the heads. The windows of half the businesses covered with brown paper. Cienfuegos pulled Mielle down through the door before she got hurt and pulled her up to the bar. In Noir et Blanc, where Mielle felt Métro trains rumble under the stone floor. Where a friend of the gigolo mixed whiskey cocktails and played imperial waltzes on 45 rpm records. They sat at a booth in the back and glanced around to see if anyone famous was there just to amuse themselves. This was apparently the favorite dive of Marlene Dietrich. But Noir et Blanc was empty because of the demonstrations. So they left.

To Le Rat Mort…where Jane peeled off her high heels and threw them over the awning. Where Jane shouted in jest at her flying shoes, "To the end of tyranny!" Where Jane's rosy cheeks swelled to their fullest, and her narrow eyes closed tight when she laughed. Where Alden spotted them through the window and rushed in to tell them the news. He was walking back from the American Hospital.

"What is the matter with you?" Alden said. He had Mielle by the shoulders.

"You owe me money," she said back.

"Money?"

"I paid your tab at Capoo...Capoo...lad."

Mielle's state reflected in Alden's face. The exasperated glare at how she was acting. Her speech slurred. Her hair, her clothes, her gesticulating limbs all so sloppy. He wouldn't stay long.

But he told them: J-G was dead.

Mielle screamed when she heard, a high-pitched sound. "It isn't true!" Then she turned red because she'd never before heard a lament like that in her own mouth.

"This is exactly what I feared would happen," Alden said, "and you were warned. You should take better care of yourself. It isn't good to get so tight."

"Oh, deevil," Mielle shrieked. "Leave us alone."

To Le Tourneur de Page...where a sudden gust of mistral wind on the terrace blew away all the men's hats. They were all Black men on the terrace. Where Cienfuegos complained that it made him nervous when he saw groups of Africans, as he called them, together at a café or outside a train station or selling trinkets on the steps below Sacré-Coeur. Where he said, "Why do they have to travel in packs?" And Mielle wondered out loud what would become of the Algerians, the Martinicans, the everyone, if the Nazis came to Paris. "I don't want to talk about that," the gigolo said. But Jane picked up on that bit of chaos and didn't want to let go.

There was a Black man at Le Tourneur de Page, alone at the table farthest from the door.

"Where are you from?" Jane asked him.

"Chicago," he said.

"I thought you looked American," Jane said. "We're American. That's obvious. But she's from Iowa, not far from Chicago. Don't get her started on Iowa."

"I lived here almost twenty years," the man said. "I stayed after the last war."

"Aren't you afraid to stay now?" Jane asked. "My friends and I were just talking about this. What will you do when the Germans come?"

"I'm not afraid," he said. "The whole point of staying in France was to not be afraid."

He had spots of gray in his hair and wore glasses. He sat straight and still, his fingers wrapped around the front of a wineglass. He looked Jane up and down, this broad made up like a Spanish girl, like she couldn't see how stupid she looked, barefoot inside.

He said, "Paris used to be a town where I didn't have to worry about bullshit like this."

Mielle could have left right then to go home. She could have apologized to the man for bothering him. She could have told Jane to shut up, but she said nothing.

To Knickerbocker...where a shooting gallery was attached at the side street, a sort of sibling operation where they served American beer in big glass jars and burned-to-black hamburgers covered in Düsseldorf mustard. It was very strange. Cienfuegos wanted to see Mielle shoot; that's why they stopped in. The marqués had the idea that Mielle would be a great shot, since she grew up on a farm, but she'd never even held a gun. "Nonsense." He wouldn't listen to reason. "Country people and guns go together like peas and onions." He bought great big jars of beer and pulled them over to the gallery. It was elbow to elbow on that side, every inch filled with -Shirts of one color or another, taking a break from the demonstrations. The racket poured out their mouths, eyes, and ears. All their shouting and the pinging BBs and the chimes from the sets, the barkers handing out prizes. Stuffed animals. Novelty field-marshal caps. These were the country people Cienfuegos wanted to see. Tall, their round cheeks stuffed with charred meat, lined up for their turn to shoot pellet guns. In Knickerbocker there were a number of diorama sets to pelt with BBs: A Western scene with cowboys and Indians. One at sea with pirates. An alpine tableau with mountain goats and short white-haired elves that looked like Santa Clauses to Mielle. The biggest one took up a third of the room: a French village with a town hall and a school and a tavern and a church, where a wedding party was coming out the door. The -Shirts really liked that one. They shot the mayor. They shot the bride and groom. Mielle started to lose it, her head spinning, watching this. All the shooting. The *ping-ping-ping*. The bride's tin body covered in divots.

Things were even worse for Jane. Even though she yearned for this chaos, this crowded room, she couldn't handle it—not with the shooting. She rattled so easily, without warning, after what was done to her in Spain. She jumped when a car backfired. She looked to the sky if she heard a factory whistle, which she said reminded her of the whistles the kaiser put on his mortars in the First War and the whistles the Germans put on their bombs when they strafed Madrid.

"Eduardo, dear. Don't you think we might be too old for this crowd?" Jane held her left hand to the side of her head to keep herself from shaking. "How do you expect us to breathe with all these children raising a din?"

They set their beers on the floor and left.

To Le Chat Noir…where indeed a black cat lazed in the front window, licking its paws. Where Mielle wondered what kind of woman she was becoming. What if her father could see her? Her little sister? Her brain tight as a tremoring wire drawn taut above the city. She was drunk. She was more than drunk. She attracted the leers of strange men, strange women, and liked it. For half an hour she grasped and rubbed the velvet inner thigh of the gigolo. She would do far worse things than this before the war ended, it hadn't even begun, but this was the start of it all, swallowing that tablet Jane had given her, letting her hand rub the gigolo's velvet thigh.

To Pas Toujours…where it was a very bad idea to end a night

like this, a place where they were regulars, where the waiters were already stacking the tables outside. The café was full of students with bloody lips, with swollen eyes that were red from crying all day, their voices hoarse and halting, because what was there to say that they hadn't already shouted? And still the streets outside echoed with demonstrations and fistfights and opposite slogans that sounded like identical slogans if you didn't understand the words. At Pas Toujours, where the headwaiter was so indignant—even for a Frenchman—that his face turned purple when he saw the four of them at the end of a spree, barely able to stand, Jane Anderson collapsing into the bar, her skirt slipping up over her ass, her bare feet in the air, to order one more marc, on credit. No place should have let them in that night. They were too drunk, too manic. They looked deranged. They were deranged. Even Jane's flawless Parisienne French, such as it was by that point, couldn't charm open this door. Not after the headwaiter saw her filthy toes sticking out.

"What a disgrace," the headwaiter said. "You come into my place barefoot, but not only that, then you ask to drink on credit? No. You are refused service. I am respectable." On and on, in the fittingly named Pas Toujours, where a headwaiter might still be muttering in disgust.

"It's time for bed," Cienfuegos told them. "Look at you, cariño. Look at your feets. They are bleeding."

SUSPENDED SENTENCE

The marqués and the gigolo were wrecked by the time they got up the stairs to the apartment. They kicked around Jane's collection of trench art in the parlor. The old brass artillery shells rolled around with such a racket on the floor. The two of them kept running into the walls, into the liquor cart, into each other. They hugged their chests together to stay upright.

The rooms were just as much of a mess. Empty bottles everywhere. Broken glass in the parlor. A burgundy-red stain dried on the white divan. Not that the stain stopped Jane. Once she changed into a black silk kimono and filled her glass, she spread herself across the divan.

"What happened here?" Mielle asked.

"One week of fetes, then the maid quit. Then another week of fetes. You were gone from our lives such a long, long time."

"Two weeks was all. Why did the maid quit?"

"Ha. Maids do that when you stop paying them."

Mielle swayed, felt the room turn upside down, then she too was lying on the divan.

"Do you think J-G is really dead?" She pictured J-G being pushed into the boulevard, his falling into the headlights.

"Yes," Jane said. "I wish he were up on his feet dancing with us right now. He didn't care for me, but I liked him all right. I like everybody."

"But if Alden got him to the hospital, they would have done something."

"Alden told you, dear. You screamed." Jane paused a beat for Mielle to remember. "I've seen too many people die not to know a dying man when I see one. You can tell from the look in their eyes, the rhythm of their breathing. In Madrid," Jane said, hesitating, needing another breath herself, "I saw forty-seven people die at once, in the same minute. Children, sixteen-year-old girls, little boys. No, Mielle. Ol' J-G did not make it. That I guarantee."

Mielle wanted so much to fall asleep at that moment. To not recall the look in J-G's eyes or how he fought to breathe. To not feel with such certainty that J-G was in fact dead, as he was, lying on a slab at the American Hospital over in Neuilly, just as Jane said, as Alden said.

Mielle had never drunk so much. Never stayed out so late. It was three in the morning, but still her heart raced, her body stirred. That pill Jane slipped her would not let her stop.

She sat up, despite herself, to rub her legs in the spots where her calves always hurt. But they didn't hurt that night. She felt light. She had no pain.

"What was in that tablet?"

Jane sat cross-legged, both arms raised and bent at the elbow to hold her drink and smoke. She smiled so big that her eyes closed.

"They call it Pervitin. Pure extract of solar radiation. With a dash of double lightning bolt." She laughed alone, the sound echoing off the walls. "Are you still on edge from it? A little wine, just a spot, will help with that. But no cigarettes for you, Mielle. Those make it worse."

When Jane tried to get up, her legs were stuck in the shape of a pretzel, flashing out between the bottom edges of her kimono from foot to thigh. She couldn't unfold enough to stand.

"What jokes God plays on us. Thirty-six years old and I'm as arthritic as a mule."

Mielle helped Jane back down to the pillows, then got herself a glass of red wine from the liquor cart. There was only one bottle left and it was almost empty.

Cienfuegos and the gigolo had passed out, since they didn't take any Pervitin. They slept together on the parlor floor, head to toe, back to back, like dogs.

Jane had her legs stretched out when Mielle returned to the pillows. Jane's feet hung off the edge in the lamplight. The bottoms of her feet were black where she wasn't bleeding. Grains of sand and grit she'd picked up on the street were lodged in her cuts.

"Don't those hurt you?"

"Nothing can hurt me," Jane said.

"You're bleeding."

"Nothing can make me abide the tyranny of having to wear shoes."

"Na, taunte. Sit tight."

Mielle set her glass on the floor and went to the kitchen. She got a rag and filled a mixing bowl with warm water, its surface sprinkled with flakes of dish soap.

She set both of Jane's feet to soak in the water, lathered the rag, then washed from Jane's ankle to her toes. Jane squirmed, ticklish around her pinkie toe, but she didn't pull back. Jane didn't tell Mielle to stop touching her where it tickled. She nodded at Mielle to keep going.

"You're good at this," she said.

"Feet are important. What would you do without them?"

Jane laughed. "That's true," she said. "You picked up a lot of sayings out on the farm, didn't you? I guess that happens when your people make up their own language."

Mielle smiled and kept her eyes on her work. She cupped Jane's heels to wash the bottoms and made them pink again. She ran her fingers over the scars between Jane's toes where the Republican guards razored her in Madrid. She felt the bumps from rat bites on Jane's ankles.

"We had to wash the men's feet in church fairly often. That

was peculiar to our assembly," Mielle said. "Like Christ and Mary Magdalene, they said. Like Christ washing the feet of Judas."

"I know the tune of that song," Jane said. "Both of those."

Mielle was almost finished when Jane reached down to sweep the hair from her face, to tuck the hair behind her ear. "Look it here," Jane said, smiling, but with her eyes open this time, her green eyes with flecks of ivory. The cut of her jaw. The dark red of her lips. Jane had once been the most beautiful woman in the world, Mielle remembered. Not that long ago. And Jane was still beautiful that night when she leaned down and pressed her lips to Mielle's lips.

The kiss lasted a long time, the kisses. The puzzling of their noses. Jane's high, wide nose, her one fault, and the feel of her hands on Mielle's shoulders, then her long fingers spreading across Mielle's back.

Mielle was the one who pulled away. This was her first kiss, her very first. In pulling back, she upset the bowl of water onto her lap.

"My," Jane said, feeling her own swelling lips with her fingertips. "Look what we did."

Mielle slept until after noon.

When she opened her eyes, all she could see was white light. Her head was pounding. She didn't know where she was. She had the feeling that she had done something very wrong, that she had disappointed someone, though she couldn't say exactly why. Her eyes ached. Her mouth tasted like garbage. She remembered that she'd wanted to tell Jane off, had wanted to take a stand, before their spree got started, but she hadn't done that.

She had slept in her clothes on the Louis XIV sofa. The gigolo lay naked on the other side of the parlor, afloat on the pillows of the divan that puffed like a white summer cloud around his immaculate Moorish body. They must have crossed paths in the middle of the night. The gigolo was muscular and long, practically hairless except for his armpits and on his pubic bone. His lazing member lay asleep, twisted upside down atop one of his thighs.

Mielle lay on the sofa a long time with her eyes open and dry. She sensed Jane had gone. Her ears ached, her eyes and nose, trying to capture a trace of Jane. The room was quiet except for the gigolo's delicate snoring and the rattle of bicycle wheels on the cobblestones outside and church bell tolls that rippled through the shutters, the sound of bronze *clungs* warped in refraction.

Mielle stood after a while, went to the bathroom to urinate, then checked each room to confirm Jane's absence. Her bed empty, the armoire in disarray. Somehow Jane had sneaked away. She and Cienfuegos had packed a suitcase and fled Paris to return to Spain, to Seville, a city where it was comfortable for nationalists like them. In a week, Jane would send for the rest of her possessions. The apartment on rue des Abbesses would be scrubbed down, aired out, and opened up to be rented to someone new.

Life felt so pitiful. Mielle was hungover and one of her few friends in the world had left without saying goodbye.

It was just as well, she realized. She remembered the vision that came to her the night before in the Lilas washroom, that pain behind her eyes. Mielle should stay away from Jane, she knew, or she would do something bad. She should have been relieved that Jane had left that morning, like she had avoided a great calamity. But she wasn't. She wanted to stay close to her friend, to keep the party going. And she knew in her heart, she feared, that it wasn't up to her to choose whether a vision came true or not. They always came true.

Mielle sighed. She wandered from room to room. The rooms felt otherworldly without Jane in them. Most of Jane's clothes were scattered across the floor. Jane's cigarette ashes still crumbled in the ashtray; her notebooks rested open on their bindings across the desk; empty bottles of champagne lined the bottom of the liquor cart; paintings leaned against the wall unhung. Mielle picked up an artillery shell with a grapevine and leaves carved into its side, from Jane's collection of trench art, and set it by the door to keep for herself.

On the dresser was a telegram from the paper in London that had fired Jane.

The last straw for us STOP For you too if you have a heart STOP

No wonder Jane had fled to Franco. She had burned just about every bridge she had. Even with the terror of the November Pogrom, even with J-G, Jane would stick with the Fascists. Mielle, realizing this, felt sick to her stomach. What she had told Alden two weeks before was wrong. Jane was not an American first and a Fascist second—not anymore. Jane had cast her lot. There could be no illusion about that.

In the kitchen, the pantry was still somewhat stocked. There were eggs, cream, half a stale baguette, a basket of soft fruit. When Mielle turned a knob on the stove, she expected the gas to be shut off, but the burner hissed and the flame caught when she struck a match. Mielle grabbed a tomato from the basket and sliced it on the counter. She fried two eggs and spread the tomatoes over the top like playing cards.

The gigolo, in a robe by then, found his way to breakfast. He sat at the little table. Mielle glanced at the gigolo only once before she handed him the eggs, then she turned to the stove to make another plate of the same for herself.

When they were done eating, the gigolo asked her, "Who are you? What's your name?"

She said, "Shut up."

She was learning how strange life could be.

It would be three years before she saw Jane again, in Berlin.

PART TWO

BAD NAUHEIM

December 1941–March 1942

PARIS POSTSCRIPT

Their ranks in Paris thinned.

Dorothy Thompson and Edward Murrow stopped coming from New York and London. William Shirer stayed in Berlin. Hemingway, Gellhorn, Dos Passos—they all returned stateside. J-G was dead. Virginia Cowles held on until the invasion, then rushed south with the refugees before the Blitzkrieg arrived, then she ended up in London. Novelists Gertrude Stein and Henry Miller moved south, to what became Vichy. James Joyce was headed for Switzerland. When war came to France in the summer of 1940, suddenly the nervous mothers of all the green correspondents wanted their sons back on the safe side of the ocean. Of course, Mielle's family didn't urge her to come home. Her parents had no idea she was in Europe, no idea if she was even alive. How ridiculous it would have been to them that a woman like her—who'd left the farm only eight years earlier—would be living in Paris.

Her life followed the same patterns as before. She wrote her articles for the women's page. She wandered the streets. She ate terrine and potato pancakes with the old widows in her hotel. She went to press briefings at the Hôtel Continental. She sat at café tables haunted by the American correspondents who remained and listened to their tall tales, though she spent less time at Café Capoulade than she had before J-G was murdered. If anything, she only went to see Alden. Mielle liked him more after she learned his real name, even though they both still referred to each other by their aliases. There was something dignified about Alden Cohn. The name opened and shut when she said it. That leafy nom de guerre he took on to disguise himself—Alden Linden Elder—was unpalatable once she found out that he'd made it up.

The last two days before the Occupation were strange.

Mielle felt guilty walking the streets because she knew the world was about to end. At least this gilded corner of the world. Notre-Dame was stripped of its stained glass. The vast halls of the Louvre were even vaster because the walls were bare, all the treasure hidden from the Hun in advance. Garbage trucks lined the middle of boulevards to stop the Luftwaffe from landing planes. All foreign press were given safe-conduct passes in case they left Paris. Most fled immediately, as they suspected the French government wasn't prepared for a fight, but Mielle decided to stay. She walked the canals, those last days, and saw the sun filter through the chestnut trees. They had lived such enchanted lives, she realized. Now the cafés were half empty, the Métro stations closed. The shops were nearly cleared of canned and paper goods, but there were still flowers and produce to be had. Thousands of refugees arrived by rail every afternoon at Gare du Nord. The roads south were jammed with cars loaded heavy with furniture. There were three suicides on Mielle's block. In the courtyard of her building, a woman shot her dog before she fled because she wouldn't leave her teckel behind for the Germans. Yet, with all this, trucks rumbled into the city each morning from the countryside with flowers and meat and exquisite bunches of green vegetables. There was a young housewife Mielle saw on rue Custine who filled her bags with leeks, with the bluish greens poking out. People stopped to stare at this young bride whose black hair was trimmed with neat, unswaying bangs. Her delicate white cheeks, the stubborn French jut of her chin, her skin so smooth and soft that if you touched her, your fingerprints would leave a mark like in dough. She held up her chin and marched down rue Custine with a bag of leeks and herbs. If she carried on, if the widows in

Mielle's hotel could still find flowers to buy, then why couldn't the rest of them believe in French victory?

On June 14 the Germans were there. The Wehrmacht put up giant red flags everywhere. By the afternoon they had rebranded the Arc de Triomphe, Ritz-Carlton, Hotel de Ville, and Eiffel Tower as monuments to nationalism. Jeeps carried movie cameras everywhere, the second spear of the invasion. The Nazis were always fighting a PR war. Weeks later, all the newsreels showed Hitler at the Eiffel Tower, giddy, unsure how to pose for his big scene under his new monument.

Mielle sat with the old women in her building that morning. Tears streamed down their faces. Then Mielle went out to cover the story. She heard for herself the sound of jackboots stomping everywhere in the City of Light.

Almost the entire corps of American correspondents had fled along with the French government. There were only a dozen left, mostly sportswriter types who would hitch rides on the siderails of transport trucks the next five years, looking for the front of some battle or another. Mielle stayed in Paris. Alden stayed. (Unflappable Alden carried around in his pocket two letters: one from U.S. ambassador William Bullitt and one signed only *WRH*, both of which vouched for Alden Linden Elder's importance to the American civilian delegation.) Under orders from Berlin, no American or American property was to be harmed during the Occupation. The Nazis still hoped they could be great friends with America, and many Americans still in Paris (not the Blacks, not the gays, certainly not the Jews) were invited to Nazi fetes. They had conquered Paris and wanted to enjoy the city that they too had read about in novels and seen in Impressionist paintings. They wanted to visit cabarets. They wanted real champagne. Business went on as normal, even for most of the French who remained in Paris. (Not les Noirs, not les Uraniens, certainly not les Juifs.)

White Americans weren't required to register with the police—it wasn't the same for Black Americans, who had to register with the Gestapo and were banned, on a personal order from Hitler, from playing music in public. Mielle was given a red seal to put on her door that verified she was American. The Gestapo was to leave her alone.

Mielle did nothing to slow the march of nationalism. Life went on. All she wanted was to start every morning with coffee and bread while staring out on a grand imperial boulevard, then waste her days getting lost amid the winding back streets of Montmartre. She kept her apartment. The Germans allowed her to work. The widows in her building suffered more than her, so she helped ease their malaise. She waited in breadlines with them. She bombproofed their windows with wool blankets and armoires. Helped them hide whole hams in the attic. The widows were happy to have an American journalist living with them. That bought them all space. None of the women on her block were dragged out onto the cobblestones and strip-searched. That happened on many blocks, to many women. The widows believed Mielle held sway with the barbarians. She was going along to get along. This was in her spirit as a Mennonite too. To let the world flash by. To let the outsiders kill each other if they wished. The world was full of evil. This was no surprise. What mattered was what little gem of God you kept in your heart. What simple song you hummed behind your lips.

Even by 1941, Mielle still hoped this would blow over. London was burning, but Paris was not.

Those years she received a dozen letters from Jane Anderson. Postcards from Baltimore, Valencia, Madrid. Mielle read them but didn't reply to a single one. They were goading letters. Jane wrote that Hitler was the savior of Christianity in Europe. *But no,* Mielle thought. *Christ is the savior of Christianity. Only Christ.*

Mielle wanted to forget everything about Jane except that Jane was once kind to her. Because it hurt to remember the other stuff about Jane: how she tended to embarrass everyone around her, all her drinking and the pills she swallowed, that she was a Fascist, that she had pulled Mielle down under her current that November night during the demonstrations when J-G was murdered. And Mielle had still run off with Jane and Cienfuegos to hop bars while the rest of the city was shouting in the street.

Sometimes it was easy to think about Jane and all her charms, her generosity. Even as the Nazis invaded Poland, a card arrived with a Madrid postmark on Mielle's birthday. *Happy birthday, Mielle, my woman, my little Libra. Don't forget—you are the scales. You fight for justice! Forever yours, Jane.* Jane was the only person who marked Mielle's birthday. Mielle became sick, sometimes, thinking about Jane's other face, that look of joy on Jane's face when the Chemises Bleues marched down boulevard Saint-Michel. Mielle could have told Jane off, could have said that to turn your back on killing is to condone evil. But Mielle had said none of this to Jane. And so Mielle condoned the execution of thousands with her silence. With her going along to get along.

Jane moved from Paris to Valencia, then to Madrid, to serve as Franco's publicist. Before long, Jane would be angling for a promotion to Berlin.

For a while, it seemed to Mielle that her second sight had left her. For over a year before the Blitzkrieg, she had no visions at all. But as Jane got deeper in the throes of Fascism, Mielle's second sight returned. Every goading letter from Jane, every postcard, would trigger a deep ache behind Mielle's eyes. The grisly vision Mielle saw while crammed into that washroom with Jane came back to her again and again. Mielle's hand gripped around the hilt of a sword. And at the end of the sword was Jane.

COUGHLIN COMPATRIOT LANDS IN BERLIN

(Marthe Hess)

As reported on February 23, 1941

The Countess of Cienfuegos, erstwhile known as Atlanta-born journalist Jane Anderson, has found a new home in the Germany of Adolf Hitler. A frequent guest on the *Golden Hour of the Shrine of the Little Flower* radio program of Father Charles Coughlin and a much-in-demand speaker on Catholic circuits, Anderson achieved new heights of notoriety in her home country in recent years.

Thanks to the Father Coughlin megaphone, Anderson reached millions of listeners with her dire warnings about the march of radical Communism and the existential threat posed by Jewish bankers.

The countess has written to friends in Europe numerous times in the last year about the deleterious effect that Communist and Zionist politics had by inflicting the Spanish Revolution on the people of Iberia. Her "stump speech" on the matter reveals her travails of facing torture and execution at the hands of the deposed Republic. That was back in the first time she lived in Madrid, in 1935.

She and her husband resided the last two years in the Madrid of Generalissimo Franco. Her task? To let the world know that Fascist Spain was open for business. The Communists are vanquished. American tourists, and dollars, are welcome.

Between speaking fees paid by Catholic dioceses and

her job with the Spanish ministry of propaganda, she claimed a high salary.

These days Cienfuegos is taking a well-deserved rest in Berlin.

With Father Coughlin having his cord cut by the bishop of his diocese and his access to the airwaves blocked by Roosevelt's brand-new Federal Communications Commission, right-wing raconteurs across the nation had their wings clipped.

America never saw a man rise to power in such a manner as Father Coughlin. A big-mouthed man in a white collar, he used radio waves to spread his political message from sea to shining sea. Coughlin attracted over thirty million listeners for his weekly show. In the tough times last decade, he helped push through Roosevelt's New Deal and warned about the threat of the Ku Klux Klan.

But Coughlin turned against the president by mid-decade. The "Radio Priest" found that he had more in common with strongmen like Hitler and Mussolini. If you've ever heard Coughlin shriek, you have heard the resemblance.

He tried to fend off criticism that he is an anti-Semite. But copies of his weekly magazine painted their own picture. Last year Coughlin printed the entire *Protocols of the Elders of Zion.*

The government said free speech has its limits. The Vatican wanted him gone years ago. Bishops around the country protested that this is not the time to be on the wrong side of the Jewish question. So the *Golden Hour of the Shrine of the Little Flower* is no more.

Robbed of her far-right loudspeaker in the States, Countess Cienfuegos returned to Europe to convalesce.

After years of touring Catholic cities and bouncing

between New York, Paris, and Spain, Anderson built her own following. An energetic orator with tales akin to a penny-dreadful, Mrs. Cienfuegos is a good match for Franco and Hitler.

Her critics say she misrepresents her experience as a prisoner in Spain. They say she embellishes, fictionalizes. They say she isn't a real countess. They call her nutty. Hysterical. A threat to democracy itself.

With the support of the Catholic Church now dried up after the victory in Spain, Jane is ready to turn the page.

She has accepted a position with the German propaganda machine. They formed something called the U.S.A. Zone at the powerful radio transmitter at Zeesen that was built to broadcast the Berlin Olympics around the globe. Fascism is now on the menu.

According to friends, the Marquesa will start this spring.

In the meantime, she's resting before she picks up her struggle to "show the American people the light."

A DATE WHICH WILL LIVE IN INFAMY

(Delivered by Franklin D. Roosevelt)
As reported on December 8, 1941

The attack yesterday on the Hawaiian Islands has caused severe damage to American naval and military forces. I regret to tell you that very many American lives have been lost. In addition American ships have been reported torpedoed on the high seas between San Francisco and Honolulu.

Yesterday the Japanese Government also launched an attack against Malaya. Last night Japanese forces attacked Hong Kong. Last night Japanese forces attacked Guam. Last night Japanese forces attacked the Philippine Islands. Last night the Japanese attacked Wake Island. And this morning the Japanese attacked Midway Island.

EXPRESS TRAIN TO
THE THIRD REICH

Things moved fast, all at once. President Roosevelt spoke before Congress on December 8. The correspondents listened to his address replayed on the radio. He sounded very American to Mielle. She'd been in Paris four years by then and couldn't help noticing his calm Yankee way of speaking, each syllable slow, to let the gravity of what happened set in. *Last night Japanese forces attacked Wake Island. And this morning the Japanese attacked Midway Island.* That great Capitol chamber silent. Not a single footstep echoing in the background. Not one fountain pen rolling and falling from the edge of a senator's desk.

Three days later, Hitler addressed the Reichstag. The correspondents listened to this on the radio too, packed around the Capoulade bar as Mielle translated the German for those who didn't understand. *I will let pass the insulting attacks made by this so-called president against me. That he calls me a gangster is tedious. After all, this expression was not coined in Europe but in America, no doubt because such gangsters are lacking here.* The address reeked of a petty politics of grievance. Hitler was in one of his manias. His voice stretched into a higher register to make his point. *Präsident Roosevelt has wanted this war. Now he has it!*

He had done it, they realized. Hitler had declared war first.

The correspondents knew it was over for them in Paris. They'd waited years for this moment, when Roosevelt and the Congress had no choice but to abandon American neutrality; or, as Hitler framed it, they made a play for American world domination. The mindset was new to those Americans who still lived on American soil, but it had been tortured so often in the correspondents' minds that they could hardly believe it had finally happened.

None of them knew what to expect. Prison? Expulsion? A concentration camp? Already hundreds of Americans—jazz musicians, socialists, men who wore too much lavender, anyone whose skin was too dark—had been sent off to the camp at Saint-Denis, then to Poland, to Auschwitz. For what purpose, nobody knew.

Being an American could no longer save Mielle. She would have to leave Paris.

"I won't go," she said in Capoulade after Hitler's speech. "I've stayed this long. I bend to every one of their rules. I will ride out the rest of the war here."

"They will not let you," Alden said. His voice typically wooden, so it took all the air out of her assertion. "None of us can stay. We are the enemy now too."

Mielle was guilty of thinking that some combination of her Americanness and her Germanness would save her. She was guilty sometimes of slipping into the pernicious thinking that a Jew is only a Jew, a socialist only a socialist, a homosexual only a homosexual. She had to remember, most of the people who had already been sent away to camps—Jews, sozis, homosexuals—were Germans, and most of them citizens to boot. All those shot point-blank in the purges were more German than Mielle was. All it would take was an SS or gestapo to see her limping, to have it out for journalists, anything, and she would disappear before she knew why she was disappeared. That was a fact, and she had to admit it.

Only five of them remained in Paris by then. Mielle, Alden, Philip Whitcomb of the Associated Press, Louis Harl of the International News Service, and Edward Haffell of *New York Herald Tribune*. Two of them were much older and had connections that made being expelled unpalatable. Louis Harl was wide-hipped but scrawny with thin silver hair and a small black mustache. He'd married a Frenchwoman after he was a soldier here in the First War and they had lived together in Paris for two decades, had five kids together, all of whom were French citizens. Harl even owned a farm in Brittany. Philip Whitcomb wore bow ties and was forty-eight—old enough to cover parts of both wars from Paris—and had five kids of his own between two marriages. Maybe they could have gotten out with their families a year or two before, but that wasn't possible anymore.

It was Haffell who bought the first round and toasted their looming departure from Paris. Haffell was thirty-six, clean-shaven, with slicked-back black hair. He was a bachelor.

"To being put out of business just as the war is getting good," he said with amusement, glass raised. All they had to toast with was marc brandy dressed up with a few drops of bitters. That's all that was left at Capoulade. The Nazis were busy sucking up every French delicacy they could, especially champagne, truffles, beef-steak, ham. Haffell wanted champagne. He begged the headwaiter to dig up a bottle that must be hidden under the floorboards, but there wasn't any. Every fatty bottle of bubbly had either been con-fiscated or was buried somewhere in the provinces, only a vintner knew where.

The two married men didn't want to toast, but Haffell bad-gered them into it.

"Okay, then, fine. To being an American in Paris," he said. "Who wouldn't drink to something like that? There's nothing better."

Alden bought the second round. Marc with grenadine, soda water, and whole Montmorency cherries, pits and all. "That we will stick together and remember the virtues of our Founding Fathers, wherever the Germans send us." A very judicious toast.

When it was Mielle's turn, she came back to the table with five shots on a cork tray.

"I will return," she said, deadly serious. "Wherever they send me, I will return." The men looked at one another sideways, choked down the marc, then smiled at her.

"Honey, someday soon," Haffell said, "I'm really going to miss you."

The order to leave didn't come for two weeks. The Nazis decided to send them to Bad Nauheim, a spa town outside Frankfurt am Main, only six hours from Paris. In normal times, Bad Nauheim was a destination for heart patients who'd been prescribed the waters. It had no strategic value. One hundred twenty American journalists and diplomats from Berlin had already been sent there and were settling in at a summer resort called the Grand Hotel. It didn't sound so bad.

Two black taxis that looked like hearses pulled up outside Mielle's hotel on rue Gabrielle. The men's suitcases hung out the back. Harl and Whitcomb had been snatched away from their families, awakened before dawn by a knock at the door, then told to pack. Their wives and kids were all French and had been told to stay put, so they sat stuffed against the passenger doors in misery.

Mielle brought only two sets of clothes and few belongings. She wore her only hat (the one given to her by Jane) and her only coat, the butcher's smock. She packed a few press passes, as souvenirs; the beret most correspondents had worn in solidarity with the French in '39; the brass artillery shell, the trench art, she'd taken from Jane's apartment that hungover morning in '38.

As the car waited for her, the old women who'd kept Mielle alive when she first moved to Paris came to the curb to say farewell. Half her height, wrapped in shawls and capes, they patted her on her hips and said to take care of herself. "Adieu. Adieu," they said somberly. She said to them, "À bientôt"—meaning "See you soon"—but they corrected her: "Non, notre ingénue. C'est adieu."

It began snowing once the taxis arrived at Gare de l'Est. Mielle heard a rumble inside from train cars coupling. She stopped herself on the plaza to see one last time, perhaps, how beautiful the station looked in falling snow. The marble arches, the massive half-moon of glass in front that reminded her of Notre-Dame. The glass of the atrium packed white with snow so that everything glowed a little pinkish underneath.

The five of them sat close on wooden benches in the same third-class coach, mostly in silence. There was no heat. Before long they were moving out from under the canopy, then cutting up to the warehouse buildings, then out to the suburbs, then all the fallow fields that stretched forever in the east of France. Nobody spoke. It was too loud with the wheel trucks hitting splices in the rails, the glass rattling in the sashes. Mielle faced the window, her eyes tracking in soft focus the rise and fall of power lines that ran alongside in the ditch.

With the loud rocking of the train, in the exhaustion of their misery, Harl, Haffell, and Whitcomb were soon asleep, slouched in their berths with overcoat lapels up over their cheeks. The older two hadn't slept an hour straight the past three weeks, thinking what it would mean to leave behind their wives and children in occupied Paris and what it might mean for them if they tried to stay. Mielle watched them sleep a long time. Hugged to themselves, legs crossed at the ankles, swaying with the train car.

"It's too bad for them," she said to Alden. "What if they never see their kids again?"

"Don't worry. They could have it a lot worse. We're going to a hotel, are we not? Not a concentration camp."

She and Alden spoke barely above a whisper, shoulder to shoulder, almost chin to chin. It was freezing cold on the train. It was the coldest winter that century.

Mielle felt something in her stomach as she sat next to Alden on the train. She was grateful to have him watching out for her.

He'd made sure all her papers were in order, had squared things away with the American embassy so her parents would be notified that she was being held at Bad Nauheim. (They still wouldn't have known that she had even left Iowa. Mielle would have given a lot to see the shock on her parents' faces when they read that letter from the U.S. State Department.) Alden had been her closest friend that whole year. It was a comfort to lean into his shoulder and breathe from his twilled wool jacket the fruitish scent of pipe tobacco and cologne. Alden made her feel safe. He was unshaken. Even on the platform as gestapo tore through their bags to search for radios, even on the train as a soldier stood at the door of their car smoking, watching them, Alden didn't flinch. He sat up straight with a smug look on his face like none of this mattered to him. Like all along he'd been wanting to get over to Germany for Christmas Eve, and how convenient it was to have the trip arranged for him.

"Listen," he whispered to her under the noise of the tracks. He looked to make sure the others were still asleep. There were nerves in his voice. Not bad nerves, but gravity. "I have something to tell you before we change trains in Frankfurt."

"What is it?" Mielle asked.

She half expected him to propose to her. She didn't know why—that's just the feeling she had, her head on his shoulder, rocking on the train through the fog of a dark winter morning. Her whole life, she'd never thought a man would propose to her. In that moment, if Alden asked, she would have said yes.

"It's Jane Anderson," he said. "If I helped you get in touch, do you think you could get close to her?"

She felt silly, smelling his collar, his neck. Thinking Alden might propose marriage. Only for him to bring Jane back into her life.

"Yes," Mielle whispered. "Jane would see me. She sends letters every few months, asks me to join her wherever she is at the moment. In Berlin, mostly."

"Good." Alden let out his breath. "In those letters, Jane asked if you would come and *join* her. That's the word she used? *Join?*"

"She tries to persuade me to her way of seeing things."

"Persuade you of the Fascist cause, that's what you mean. But she didn't...you don't..."

"No." Mielle spoke louder, her voice deepening at the word, the *no* rising out of her. "I wish they would leave everyone alone. I wish the Fascist poison would be erased from the face of the Earth. I told you before. That's what I stand for."

Mielle liked saying those words. That old feeling of her destiny rolled over in her gut.

"That's good," Alden said. "I needed to hear you say that."

She leaned closer to touch his neck with her cheek. "You already knew about the letters, didn't you?"

"That's why we're talking right now, do you understand? When we get to Nauheim, the Gestapo might take me away at the station. It is very important that you listen closely."

"What?"

"It is a simple job," he said, flashing his eyes toward the soldier who guarded the door at the end of the coach.

"What is it?"

"I wouldn't mention this if I didn't believe you were capable. It is a simple job."

"What job?"

"Quiet," he whispered. The guard was watching, his cloth hat tilted back on the top of his head. There was no way the guard could hear over the noise of the train, but he looked like he might approach them because they were acting too grave.

Alden turned to Mielle, touched a hand to her face, and kissed her.

She felt something stir in her abdomen at the clove smell of his aftershave, the feel of his lips on hers.

"I am sorry for that," Alden said. His cheeks were red. "Did he stop looking?"

"What?"

"*Him.*"

He had. The guard struck a match off the steel door then stared out a window to smoke.

"The job is simple," Alden told her. "Memorize who is there and what they say."

Her lips felt so swollen, bursting. She had trouble following what he said. His skin was glowing from the kiss. His heart must have been pumping just as hard as hers, his cheeks were so red.

"The army needs good people like you, someone who can move without suspicion."

Mielle wanted him to explain everything, but she knew he couldn't. She lay her head back on his shoulder. His lips nearly grazed her ear as he spoke.

"If you get the chance to go to Berlin, you must get close to Jane," he said. "They will try to convert more of us at some point. I am certain of that. There will be pressure to say sympathetic things about the Nazis."

Mielle glanced at the guard—very ugly in his gray uniform—then back to Alden. She knew it was important, what they were talking about. And she wanted to help. That was her destiny, wasn't it? That vision God had sent her. She had tried to forget all that, hadn't even responded to Jane's letters. But here she was nodding along with what Alden said, her lips moving near his, saying, *Yes, yes.*

What Alden proposed reignited the spirit of that vision within Mielle, the presentiment she'd felt when she was face to face with Jane in the washroom at Lilas. She felt the echo of that vision again—her eyes aching—this time face to face with Alden.

"But why do you want me to kill Jane?" she asked. "I will do it if I must, if she deserves to die."

Alden's face went white.

"*Kill Jane?*" He couldn't seem to swallow the words once they were in his mouth. "Did someone tell you that? That you should kill Jane Anderson?"

"No," Mielle said. "I…isn't that what you want?"

Alden still couldn't believe she'd said it. The glow was all gone from his face.

"*Find* Jane. That's what you will do. Get the names of every American who is working for the Nazis. Then get out of Berlin unharmed. That's what I meant. And *only* if she invites you there."

Alden leaned back to eye her, to see her entire face at once.

"You are not an assassin," he said. "You are not to kill anyone. Say it."

"I am not an assassin."

Mielle said it only because he made her. The words felt false as they passed over her lips. Inside, she felt like she had been chosen to be an assassin. That was what her vision told her.

Out of the corner of her eye, she noticed that the guard had moved into the aisle and was walking toward them.

This time it was Mielle who rushed a hand to Alden's cheek, then put her lips on his. They stared into each other's eyes, kissing, until the guard kicked against the steel frame of their bench with the hobnails of his boot.

"*Aufhören!*" he shouted at them. "Enough with that."

THE GRAND HOTEL

It was dusk by the time they arrived.

There would be six of them soon. A notorious foreign correspondent named Bob Best was due ten minutes after them on a train from Vienna. They decided to wait for him.

"It *is* you," Ed Haffell said as Best stumbled onto the platform. "What a surprise!"

The rest of them stood back and either nodded or muttered "Bob" to greet him. Originally from South Carolina, the son of a Methodist minister, he was well over two hundred pounds, square-jawed and square-shouldered, balding, and he cut a figure like the sales manager of a department store. Best had been in Europe a long time; he was married to an Austrian, and he also happened to be sympathetic to the Fascists. He hadn't been very popular with the other American correspondents for some time by then.

"What are you doing here?" Haffell asked. "I thought you'd never leave Vienna."

Best looked exhausted, his face pale, the tendons showing in his neck. "I woke up this morning with the Gestapo at my door, probably the same as you." He sounded exhausted. "A knock at four in the morning and they tell you to get a suitcase packed. Those guys...they sure have a way of making up your mind for you, don't they."

"And your wife? Is Erna on the train?"

"They wouldn't let her come. Said she belongs in the Reich because she's Austrian."

"Well, shit, Bob," Harl said. He and Whitcomb stood back,

leaning against the white station wall. "Me and Philip. They wouldn't let us bring our families because they're French."

Two plainclothes gestapos ordered them down the platform stairs and out through the small station into the night. There were sixteen hours of darkness each day in the German winter. With the blackouts and fog, you couldn't see farther than ten feet in front of you most nights. At least snow was on the ground here, which amplified the moonlight enough that they didn't bump into one another on the half-mile walk to the hotel.

The gestapos stuck behind them the whole way. Eight of them in the column, two by two down the middle of the street past the Sprudelhof bathhouses. They walked in silence. Before the war, Bad Nauheim would have been too chichi for any of them save Alden if he was traveling with his father. Most of the buildings were made of white and tan blocks, with baroque touches on all the doorways and scrollwork at the parapets. A bubbling stream cut through the center of town. Hearst had summered here only three years before. FDR himself spent many summers running through inhalatoriums as a boy because his father had a heart condition. But Bad Nauheim was an elegant ghost town when Mielle arrived. All the restaurants were boarded up. The same with the bath buildings that had signs that said GESCHLOSSEN nailed to the doors. The whitewash was fading and the stucco falling loose in patches. None of the streets had been cleared of snow.

"What do you think?" Mielle asked Alden.

He laughed. "You have to love what the Nazis have done with the place."

Alden was the only one to laugh—though he deserved some good cheer, since the Gestapo didn't nab him at the station like he'd feared. It made Mielle sad to see a town done wrong like this. To hear no singing or laughing, no one even frying a piece of meat by an open window to let the smell out. This was a place that could have been making people happy, but it wasn't because of the bad intentions of some higher-ups who had ambition.

Mielle could see the Grand Hotel from far off. It was big, made of sandstone blocks, and seemed to fit its pretentious name. The building was six stories with dozens of windows on each side that were buttressed with balconies and iron gates, and a roof of black slate.

She'd forgotten it was Christmas Eve until she saw the strings of lights inside the hotel. Once the door was open, once they were allowed to drop their bags in the ice-cold lobby, Mielle heard singing. She smelled roasting meat, saw a little pine tree, less than four feet tall, with a white paper star stabbed onto its top.

All the internees were packed into the ballroom to observe the holiday. Mielle and the other newcomers watched from the lobby like they had never seen such a thing. It had been a long time since any of them saw a celebration like this. All the cane tables covered with white linen and set with china. Mielle's jaw dropped when she walked into this death throe of old-gentry Europe. It seemed like a dream. The bright white room, the tall windows. Everyone in their best clothes. Suits and ties and formal dresses, no matter how frayed. A crew of gangly waiters wearing monocles rushed around the ballroom with bottles of bubbly—the Rhine version from the hotel cellar, but at least the bottles looked right, and they made a sudsy *pop* that filled the room when you whacked the cork with a knife. There was a roaring fire in the hearth. At every setting was a bowl of Hessian stew, a gift from the local gauleiter, with actual chunks of beef served over roasted potatoes. The aroma of onions and caraway seeds played on the roof of her mouth and the back of her throat in a way that reminded Mielle of her mother.

The newcomers were noticed then by the waiters, pulled over to a table, and given their own bowls of stew. It had been a day since they'd last eaten. All around the room, the others watched them devour the stew. Mielle peeked back at them. She felt like she was crashing a wedding. She didn't recognize anyone. They were mostly young men, but not all of them. About a third were in advanced middle age, gray and balding, with broad shoulders and spines so erect, they might have never grazed a chair back. These men were military attachés from the embassy in Berlin. There were a dozen women. Half a dozen children. They had all been here for more than a week.

Mielle kept eating. A second bowl of stew. Two hunks of dark bread soaked with the tomato and onion sauce. Potatoes finished with melted butter and paprika. Red cabbage baked with apples, cloves, and cinnamon. The last year in occupied Paris, Mielle had been forced to put great restraint on her hunger. But there was plenty that night. She remembered her appetite. Even when two men came over with a bottle of the Rhine bubbly to introduce themselves, Mielle kept eating.

"You're the Paris delegation, I take it," one of them said. "I'm Jack Fleischer. United Press, formerly of Berlin."

He looked like a junior partner at a Chicago accounting firm: fresh-faced with short dark hair, in a black suit with a striped necktie in a double Windsor knot, wearing too much cologne. His wire-frame glasses hooked behind his big ears. He wasn't small but was slightly built, with long arms and short stubby fingers. Fleischer looked very serious, but there was a sarcastic cramp to his voice.

"Welcome to the Grand Icebox," he said, grinning. "Believe it or not, all of us are *hoping* to get coal in our stockings tonight." He reached across the table to shake hands and get names. Mielle said hers with her mouth full.

"We met before," Alden said. "Don't you remember me? I'm pals with Howard Smith."

"Howard? That jerk was my roommate for two years in Berlin."

"I know that. I was hoping he'd be an inmate with us here. Where is he?"

"*Switzerland.*" Fleischer said the word slowly, jealous and miserable. "It's unbelievable. The guy takes a train out of Germany on December sixth. *The sixth!* As Pearl Harbor bursts into flames, he's sleeping off a steak dinner in a feather bed in Bern."

"What about Shirer?" Mielle asked. They hadn't met again after she blew him off in Paris. She'd been right, that night. A second invitation to Maxim's never came.

"He's in New York," the other man said. This was Eddie Shanke. "Bill left Germany a year ago, always a step ahead."

Shirer's fortunes were on a steep ascent since he'd left Europe. Alfred Knopf published his *Berlin Diary,* a firsthand account of the nationalists' rise to power in Europe. Every observation, every dirty secret that had been cut out of Shirer's radio scripts by German censors over the past decade was suddenly in print. It was a sensation and exactly the kind of shock to the senses all the correspondents had dreamed of publishing. Bill Shirer had done it. Now he had his own evening show on CBS. The book royalties made him rich and he was living on Cape Cod with his wife and kid. The Nazis went to great pains to keep any mention of *Berlin Diary* out of Fortress Europe. The book was a great personal embarrassment for Hitler.

Shanke reached around the table with the bottle to keep their glasses full. He was thirty-one, from Milwaukee, with a robust Midwestern neck that strained his collar when he smiled.

"Want to get up to speed about this place?" Shanke asked. "First, there's no heat upstairs."

"The Grand Icebox. I get it now," Alden said.

"This is a *summer* resort. Very beautiful and designed to let the breeze in. Second, the elevator is broken. Third, this meal is special. Don't get used to it. Meat only twice a week. And don't touch the lemon pudding."

Both Shanke and Fleischer made bitter faces.

Fleischer then tried to explain the German obsession with ersatz food products. They thought they could engineer everything. Fake coffee, fake butter, fake pudding, vitamin-enriched bread. It was all made of chemical extracts and hormones. Someday, if the futurists won, everyone would *drink* their daily bread instead of baking it.

"If you think this is bad," Fleischer said, "you should see what a German citizen gets now. It will turn you green."

There were one hundred twenty people for four hundred rooms, Fleischer told them. Most of them were from the diplomatic delegation in Berlin, but a dozen or more were journalists, and they were happy to see their clique expand.

"They're not bad chaps, though," Shanke said of the diplomats. "They're trying. It isn't an easy job to keep so many spoiled people happy."

"The place is okay too," Fleischer admitted. "It's just that none of us want to be here."

They did try to make the best of strange circumstances. Singing and dancing and joking about the food. They sang "O Tannenbaum" and "Stille Nacht," the German versions, for some reason. The embassy leaders handed out grab-bag gifts that included hairpins, cigarettes, shoelaces, and soap. Not the most exciting gifts, but necessities the internees were all glad to get.

They were all feeling good, but Mielle, once she was full, felt pulled down by the weight of the day. She needed to lie down.

"If it isn't too much," she said, "could somebody show me to my room?"

"Oh!" Jack Fleischer shouted. "Of course, fräulein. How rude of us to forget. And your luggage just sitting there. Tsk-tsk."

Fleischer and Shanke split them up. Shanke took Haffell, Harl, and Whitcomb up the winding stairs to the second floor; Fleischer took Alden and Mielle to the third. He carried their bags the whole way, hustling to keep ahead like a bellhop. At the end of the hall, he pulled a key from his pocket, unlocked the door, and led them inside.

It was a beautiful room. Despite all the time Mielle had spent in press briefings at the Hôtel Continental, then at the Ritz-Carlton (where the Nazis held briefings during the Occupation), she'd never actually been up to a room in a luxury hotel.

A single large bed with a canopy was pushed against the wall. There was a mahogany writing desk, parquet floors, a set of French doors that led out to a balcony. Even in the dark, it was the most elegant room she had ever seen. Mielle went to flip on the light switch to see it better, but Jack slapped her hand.

"Sorry. Strict blackout."

"Even on Christmas Eve?"

"Nobody trusts nobody."

Mielle looked out the French doors. She had a nice view of the charming little town: the stone and stucco buildings, the dark steeple of a Catholic church across the way, the narrow Usa River fifty feet below, the bluffs that surrounded the city. Everything was either covered in snow or frosted white.

Jack stood behind her to check the streets. Nothing moved outside.

"All the best rooms are already taken, I'm afraid."

"Deevil. You mean this is one of the worst rooms? I'd be happy to be buried in a bed like this!"

"This would be a good one normally. But it's got a balcony. You're going to freeze. The best are interior rooms with fewer windows. They trap heat much better."

On cue, the French doors rattled from a gale blasting down from the frozen Alps three hundred miles away.

"Here's a trick," Fleischer said, leading them into the bathroom.

The bathroom was the nicest room yet, Mielle thought. A claw-foot bathtub on a black-and-white-checkerboard floor. A shaving mirror attached to the wall by an accordion mount, with a hook to hang leather strops. Even the porcelain faucets were the old decadent style.

Fleischer started running a bath.

"What's the big idea?" Alden said. He felt good and couldn't stop joking. "That is quite a tub. Large enough for two or three, maybe. But we hardly know each other."

"If you can get hot water, leave it filled, like a fifteen-gallon hot-water bottle."

"There's American ingenuity for you," Alden said.

"You can even drag your blankets in overnight, if you don't mind sleeping with your head in a bidet."

"Not me," Mielle said.

She backed into the main room and fell on the mattress with her arms above her head. Down feathers flew up around her. "If you need me, this is where I'll be until the war ends."

Alden and Fleischer laughed from the doorway as the down floated back to the bed.

"Let's go next door," Fleischer said. "I think she's claimed this one, old chap."

ON THE BALCONY

Mielle couldn't believe she got a room like this all to herself. Sure, the room was freezing, but she was mostly used to that by now—Paris was freezing too—and it wasn't half as bad as blizzards in Iowa, when her father had tied a rope between their back door and the barn so he didn't get lost in a whiteout. Mielle lay on the eiderdown in the dark to soak it in. The plaster molding, the brass lamps she wasn't allowed to turn on, the corner drafting table to answer letters in the evening.

After a moment, she rushed to undress and submerge herself in the bath Fleischer had drawn. There was no reason to let a warm bath go to waste. Mielle had never been in a bathtub this large, one where she could stretch her legs out full and let her whole body sink under the water. As her hair spread out from her head, eyes closed, the warm water seeping into her skin, she thought about that last kiss on the train. It was a good kiss. She'd felt something move in her stomach. Alden's lips had swelled, his mouth watered. It made her chest flutter when she felt his lips on hers. That's what a good kiss felt like.

Her stomach hadn't moved like that since Jane kissed her in Paris. But she didn't want to think about Jane. She opened her eyes under the water and closed them again twice to shake Jane from her thoughts, then remembered Alden's lips and what his lips had felt like on hers.

She didn't stay in the bath long. She knew nobody was watching (or didn't think anyone was watching; those years, you never knew who might be hiding in the walls), but she felt too aware of herself, thinking of the kiss, too aware of her naked body in this room where she had just been joking with Jack and Alden. She dressed in her other set of clothes, then washed the dirty ones in the bathwater and hung them above the cold radiator to dry.

Through the pipes, Mielle heard the others carry on in the ballroom. That group of old pros knew how to party on a sinking ship. The best ones raged while the city was burning; when the revelers had a mortal justification to try and forget the rest of the world; when there was no future to look forward to, only that boozy moment right in front of you; when any pleasure you could grasp, any indiscretion, was worth the fare. Mielle had gone to underground clubs in Paris twice during the Occupation. Both were the wildest fetes since Jane and Cienfuegos had left town. Dance floors packed hip to hip and heaving. All mouths opening. And why not? If at any minute the doors could be kicked down? If they could all be whisked away to a camp?

Mielle stepped out to the balcony to stare into the darkness.

Below her, two guards were on patrol outside the hotel, crunching snow with their boots along the little river, the Usa, that cut behind the baths. Back home they would have called it a crick. The Usa was narrow, half frozen over.

After a moment she heard something beside her. Alden was on his balcony too, slouched against the stone-block building, drawing on a pipe. He looked amused because he'd startled her. Their balconies were only a few feet apart.

"There aren't any stars out tonight," he said.

"Not even the Christmas star?"

"None." He drew again on his pipe, then blew the smoke out the side of his mouth.

All the young correspondents bought brown ceramic pipes from a Swiss tabac two years before when they saw Shirer smoking one. Of all the fads they picked up on—Hemingway's absinthe, Joyce's obstinacy, Henry Miller's carousing with painted women—Mielle liked this one the best. The rustling of cut tobacco as it burned orange inside the pipe bowl, the aroma of cherrywood and cloves and ancient herbs.

"Why aren't you downstairs?" she asked.

"I'm not one for Christmas. Never have been."

"Oh, deevil. Right."

"Do you think my not singing carols with them will give me away?"

"I hope not," Mielle said. "They will just see that you're a snob."

"It is best to square that away straight off. The both of us, you and I. Incurable snobs."

Alden sat there joking like always. That easy smile of his. His stooped shoulders and square jaw, his way of hiding his body inside of itself. He made it seem like the kiss on the train, what he'd told her, that they'd been driven out of Paris by the Gestapo, that all of that was a dream. The kiss had evaporated, but Mielle didn't want it to evaporate.

"Should we say something about what happened on the train?"

"Yes," Alden said. Smoke rose above him where he sat puffing on his pipe. "If you ask me, Bob is the one to watch. If the Germans ask who wants to go say nice things about Fascism on the radio, there is no doubt in my mind that Bob says yes."

"Bob?"

"Yes. Bob Best." He stared at her so earnestly, like he had no idea that she could be thinking something other than what he was thinking. "You have to prepare yourself. They are going to come here looking for help with the propaganda war. You did well on the train today. I am sure you could get to Jane if they invite you to Berlin. There is no doubt."

Mielle sucked her lips into her mouth. Her eyes watered, but she wouldn't cry. She couldn't remember the last time she'd cried.

Alden stood and leaned over to her balcony. When he saw Mielle's face, he froze. "Is that not what you meant?"

"On the train today," Mielle said, "when you kissed me."

"Oh." Alden sat back down. He rubbed his hair to think about that. "You kissed me too, you know."

"Why did you apologize, the first time?"

"I'm sorry about that."

"Don't apologize."

"When we first met, things were different," he said. "Now that we're in this—well, I haven't thought about things like romance for a long time."

"You haven't?"

"Well, it hasn't been eons."

They watched out of the corners of their eyes to see what would happen, who would step first. If Mielle leaned over the railing, she could have kissed him again. She wanted to kiss him. But her mind kept pestering her. *Does he mean it?*

Alden leaned back against the building. They felt very far apart again.

"It was a good kiss, wasn't it?" he asked.

But does he mean it?

"Good night, Alden. Merry Christmas."

"Yes. Merry Christmas."

CHRISTMAS DAY

She could have slept until lunch if it weren't for the cold. She woke shivering, fully dressed under the eiderdown, her jaw sore from her teeth chattering as white morning streamed in the windows.

There were children rushing down the hallway to the tree to see if there was anything for them. Then it really felt like Christmas.

Mielle went to the end of the hall, where a winding staircase opened all the way down to the lobby. She watched from the balustrade. The gasps of the children, their weeping from relief: Santa Claus had found them after all. They surely felt forgotten most of the time, these children of important parents, parents whose main worry was keeping them all out of a concentration camp, with the holiday an afterthought. There were only a handful of children at the Grand Hotel, all of them with long, straight hair, in white cotton pajamas, their faces pink in the cold as they rooted under the pine branches for gifts. A package of chocolate wafers from Switzerland. A can of sardines from Portugal. A few sheets of paper to draw on. An empty bottle of bubbly, which was not a gift but had rolled there after midnight and been forgotten. The gifts were just as pitiful as the tree, but the children had been remembered. That's all that mattered.

The lobby looked very different during the day. The hotel had been opened on short notice—if you wanted to sit, you had to pull a white sheet off a wicker chair—and had last been decorated with a tropical theme. Palm trees sagged limp in pots around the bar and lobby, though the trees had dried up and died a long time ago.

A large portrait of Hitler was the only picture on the wall. One from the knees up, where his body was angled to the side and he had to twist to stare at you. That pugnacious glare he had in portraits, like an annoyed boy having to stand still, his chin sucked in.

There were bread rolls and ersatz coffee in the dining room. Half the guests came up and introduced themselves to Mielle. The undersecretary from the Berlin embassy and his wife. The naval attaché. Father Herman, the chaplain, told her when services would be that day if she was interested. She was not, but she thanked him anyway. All of them were upright Protestants in suits and ties and sleeved dresses, with comb rows marked in their hair. Mielle was the only female correspondent apparently, but there were half a dozen wives and another half a dozen girls in Scotch-plaid dresses from the embassy's typing and filing department.

Mielle learned that the dining room was always heated. As a result, you could find people sipping coffee there anytime, day or night.

Even trapped inside the hotel, the diplomats were relieved to be out of Berlin. A rumor was going around that they were to be returned to America soon after the New Year. (The rumor was grossly inaccurate, but they didn't know that then.) Mielle's heart jumped. She could feel the color rise in her cheeks, like it rose in all their cheeks at the thought of getting out of the war. They chattered on about people they'd met in Berlin and what a great thing it was to see the history they had seen, and to survive, and what a dream it would be to go back home to New York or Pennsylvania or Texas to see Mother again. They all gave up a lot to serve in Germany. Funerals. Weddings. The good years with their children. The last years with their parents.

But they didn't like to talk about all that. What they talked about were the comforts they could enjoy again when they made it back home.

"Fresh oranges."

"Bananas."

"Real coffee."

"Pancakes."

"A porterhouse steak with a glass of whiskey, served neat."

"Iced tea and real lemonade."

"Hollywood pictures."

"Carolina tobacco."

"Miss," one of them said to Mielle. "What are you looking forward to the most once you get home?"

She smiled and glanced around at their kindly faces in a way that must have made her look coy. But she wasn't playing; she really didn't know what to say. "The truth is…" She started to say that she wasn't allowed to return home, not the same way they all meant home. She didn't know where she would go if they sent her to America. "The truth is," she said, "what you all said sounds so perfect. That's what I want, what you all said."

"But which part?"

"All of it. I want it all."

"Ha! You're funny." One woman laughed, then they all did. "You can tell we're all Americans," the woman said. "Wanting everything, but nothing that's attainable at the moment."

They went on wanting: Turkey sandwiches. Fried eggs and bacon. Sweet corn. Baseball.

Did they miss apple pie? Yes, they missed apple pie.

TO BE REMEMBERED

Alden was the first to point out to her, two weeks after their arrival, that Britain was making bomb runs on Frankfurt and Stuttgart. Small ones at first, only two to ten planes that chipped away at strategic targets. Nothing like the five-hundred-bomber runs that would stream overhead in formation for hours and hours once the American war machine had been turned to full throttle. But even a single bomber could fill a town with the sound of roaring pistons and propellers.

"Listen," Alden said. There was buzzing above the clouds. "It's the Brits."

Bad Nauheim was close enough to Frankfurt that they could hear the 8,8 antiaircraft guns fire. They could see searchlights probe the clouds. Soot-black flak drifted over them. Then the baritone, hollow crackling over the horizon as the payloads took root.

Alden's face expressed a morbid enjoyment, watching the bomb runs.

Every night at the Grand Hotel, Mielle invited Alden through her room—past her unmade bed, past the steam that crept along the floor beneath the bathroom door—out to her balcony. It was January and still very cold, but there wasn't much else to do in the evenings besides play gin rummy in the dining room. Sitting outside was the only remedy for the claustrophobics. Mielle and Alden wrapped themselves in spare blankets and leaned against the building to stare out into the black sky as their breath fogged the air. The balcony was just big enough for the two of them.

"Do you think you will miss the war," Alden asked her, "once they send you stateside?"

She hmphed. It was a ridiculous question. Alden said things like this all the time—like when he urged Mielle to report on Hitler in person or to be there when the French surrendered at Compiègne—in a tone that insisted these were the sorts of things she'd want to tell her grandchildren someday. Mielle didn't have thoughts like that because she didn't think she'd ever have children, much less grandchildren. She'd left all that behind.

"No," she said. "I won't miss this. I wouldn't even know how to describe the war if somebody asked me to. Whenever I leave this place, I will forget. If that's possible."

"It is difficult to describe. You are right about that. That is why war reporting is so dull most of the time."

"It's so *big*. The sound of it. Not even that. The feeling when the sound hits your chest from this far away and what that means for anyone who got hit."

In Paris they had listened to Ed Murrow's nightly reports of the London Blitz. His catchphrase, *This is London,* followed by his descriptions of the ruined buildings, the sirens, the fires, the bloodied bodies. Even then, through the radio, you couldn't feel the shock waves. You felt the terror through Murrow's voice.

Alden took out his pipe and packed it. He was loud, how he went about it, to change the subject. Smacking the bowl against his palm and scraping its inside with an ebony pipe cleaner.

Mielle asked him, "How did you end up being a correspondent anyway? Some girl broke your heart in New Haven? Is that it?"

"Oh," he said. He became even more involved with his pipe and his little leather pouch of tobacco, his brass tamper, his box of matches. "You mean Evelyn," he said, puffing.

"She had a thing for boxers? Then you followed her across the ocean?"

He smiled, his features hard. There was a look of disappointment in his eyes. "There's only a little truth in that story," he said.

"She didn't dump you?"

"Unfortunately, *that* is the true part." He breathed deep, let the smile fall from his face. "But it was the war that brought me, even before it was a war. I have a job to do here. I knew that from the start."

"How dramatic."

"Yes. Very."

Alden told her how it had been for him at Yale. He'd thought this was an enlightened age when he started, but it wasn't easy for him there as a Jew. He still had only one name then: Alden Cohn. Even though he was tall and played end on the football team and was an officer in training, there were still plenty of people who would never accept him there, or anywhere, and who would think of him only as a Cohn and nothing else. That's when he started calling himself Alden Linden Elder. He drank a lot junior year and made friends with the kind of chums who thought it was very clever that the new monogram on his sweaters read ALE. At least he had some friends his last two years. That was when he met Evelyn, who had a thing for Jewish football players before she had a thing for French heavyweight boxers.

"Aren't you afraid someone might recognize you over here? That an old classmate might denounce you?"

"Why should I be afraid? I have a purpose for being here. That purpose is my north star."

"Your north star?"

"It is my *north star*."

Mielle thought she understood what Alden meant, that there was a reason he let slip that he'd been in officer training at Yale. By then it was fairly obvious that Alden worked for army intelligence in some capacity, in addition to doing the radio spots from Paris for Hearst. How else would he know so much about all the news correspondents in Europe? Why else would he have suggested he might have a job for Mielle to complete in Berlin? Alden hadn't come to Europe hoping to impress his ex-fiancée by being a foreign correspondent; he'd hoped to impress Evelyn by being a spy.

Mielle was proud of Alden for being so sly. She wouldn't have guessed he was capable of something like this when she first met him.

"What about yourself?" He nudged her leg with his leg, both of them wrapped bulky in blankets. "Who was your college sweetheart?"

She groaned. "Don't ask me that. You know the answer."

"The rumors *are* true? Good for you."

She had to laugh. He said that in a very earnest way.

It didn't bother Mielle anymore that the others had called her the Virgin—not after that long night of her spree in Paris. She kind of liked the nickname after she woke up across from the gigolo. She'd turned the joke around.

"Did you like college?" Alden asked her.

"I suppose I did," she said. Saying that surprised her. She'd never said it before, because college was very difficult for her. "College was a new world. Not many people get a chance to live two completely different lives. That's how I look at it. I was supposed to live my whole life inside the boundaries of a single county in Iowa. If I didn't go to college, I wouldn't have ever left that county. I would have had to die first."

"How dramatic."

"Yes. Well..." She shrugged and smiled and leaned her head on his shoulder. It felt good to tell someone this small bit about leaving the assembly, even if it was only half the truth. "What are you going to do when you get back to America?" Mielle asked him.

Alden said he would try to return to Europe, or, more likely, go to Africa as soon as it was feasible. By that November there would be American soldiers in Libya, he said, which meant there would be American reporters there as well. He wanted to be in the first wave. For now, he was content to stay at his post in Germany.

"What about you? Will you go home?"

Mielle regretted bringing this up. She stared into the black of the night, watched a flicker of orange on the horizon where Frankfurt had been hit. She didn't have an answer, of course, beyond returning to her old paper in Cedar Rapids for fifteen dollars a week, which she would never do.

"The last time I went home was four years ago," she said. "This was when American Plains Wire decided they needed someone in Europe to feed their Sunday magazines. Shirer recommended me somehow, and I offered to do the work for half as much as anybody else. They said, 'Go get on a boat,' so I found an apple freighter to work my way over on. I would have done anything to get here. My little sister—we called her Dolly—she came out when she saw me the last time I was at the assembly. I stood by the taxi ten minutes, up at the road, waiting for someone to come say hello. I was scared to return, seeing the old place, but I had to tell somebody I was leaving the United States. So I told Dolly. She looked like I'd just cursed Menno Simons. She was only ten."

"Had she heard of France?"

Mielle shoved an elbow in his ribs. "Don't be rude."

"What did your parents say?"

"I didn't tell them. I didn't come any closer to the house. I wanted to. It cost half a month's salary to take a taxi all the way out there. But seeing the hills and the farm and the milking barn took the wind out of me."

Mielle glanced up. Alden was listening, sucking on the mouthpiece of his pipe as he tried to understand what all this meant for her.

"When I left," she said, "I didn't really believe that they would never let me come back. My parents would make an exception for me—that's what I thought. You hold the vapor of these things in your heart, the things you can't admit to yourself. But I couldn't ignore the truth anymore, standing there on the dirt road with Dolly."

Mielle gasped, shocked by what she'd said, unthinking. She hadn't uttered the name of anyone in her family for years. But now she'd done it. She'd said *Dolly* to Alden, three times. Despite the shock, she was fine. Her heart didn't stop. No lightning shot from the sky to smite her. It felt good to say her sister's name, to tell someone what had happened, to tell Alden.

Recovering, Mielle went on. "The farm was doing good. They didn't slow down a minute without me. And if I stepped back on their land, nobody would have said hello to me. They would have turned their backs to me. They'd have to. Dolly made a big mistake coming out and hugging me. They'd have had to whip her if they found out. I told her that my coming by was a secret we would keep between me and her."

"So you left?"

"I got back in the taxi and left."

Alden tapped the back of his pipe on his heel to clean out the ashes, then packed away his pouch.

"That is the coldest thing I have ever heard," he said.

"Na. Deevil, na. They would have roasted up a big supper for me if they could. I don't blame them. Not one bit. They were only following the law because of who I became. I'm an *English* to them now. An outsider."

"I disagree," Alden said. "It's immoral to follow an unjust law. That's what I believe."

"But you're a New Englander, like Thoreau. That's your tradition. This is ours."

Alden leaned away to stare at her, but she wouldn't return his stare. She wanted to tell him all the things she had never told anybody before. If she looked at him and saw his reaction, speaking would be too hard for her.

"Don't think poorly of them," she said. "My father, he sent payments against my college tuition. He must have worried that I might owe somebody money. And my mother, she mailed me a few dollars every month—to the administration building, because she didn't know my address. Mammi and Daadi could have got in trouble for doing this. They were supposed to forget me. But they are good people. I mailed them my diploma when I graduated, to thank them. I should have sent them my clippings from over here when I had the chance."

Alden lifted the edge of his blanket and they moved closer together underneath it.

"No argument. Yours is a sad story." He was whispering then, into her bobbed hair that barely covered her ears. "But there are plenty of places to go besides Iowa. If you want a job after all this, I can help. New York? San Francisco? Just say the word."

"They are going to send us to New York, aren't they? At first?"

The rumor about being sent home after the New Year had turned out to be false, but that kind of gossip refreshed endlessly. Now the rumor said they would be home by Valentine's Day.

"Yes," Alden said. "Ships from Europe usually go to port in New York."

"So you'll be going there too?"

"I imagine. For as short a time as possible."

She buried her head in his chest to smell the stale tobacco on him.

Mielle had let herself get used to the idea of being deported back to America. This wasn't a vision, like she'd had before. This was just dreaming, just desire, which was not advised for a woman like her.

She tried to see herself and Alden on the wooden seat of a third-class train berth like the one that brought them to Bad Nauheim, but this time it would take them to Biarritz and then to Lisbon. Then a week on a steam freighter, holding each other at a rusty railing in the sea mist, like at that moment they held each other. They would both find jobs in New York, get a little working-class place to live in Greenwich Village. She had read cheap novels from the hotel library where things like this happened.

Mielle knew it was not advised to dream like that, to make exotic plans that depended on another person feeling the exact same emotion as you, at the same frequency, at the same amplitude. But she was still new to this kind of human game.

There was so much time in every day at the Grand Hotel. She had nothing to do but dream about romance, rescue, salvation. Walking the frozen corridors, she saw it in the eyes of nearly everyone there. They all wanted the same things, and they wanted them soon. Love, escape, salvation.

LADY HAW-HAW: A ROYAL PAIN

(American Plains Wire)
As reported on January 22, 1942

Patriotic observers note that a grizzled American voice has turned up on shortwave signals from Europe. You can hear her four times a week speaking from Germany's powerful transmitter at Zeesen, cursing the United States for entering the war.

And what does this woman say about the country of her birth? If you have the stomach for both treason and balderdash, read for yourself:

"The Roosevelt brain trust, alien to and superimposed on the land of Old Glory, is but a branch of the International Secret Superstate, which holds equally Soviet Russia, plutocratic England, and Roosevelt's America in the hollow of its hybrid hand...

"Roosevelt pulled a brass band out of his pocket and a concentration camp from out of thin air. Aren't there prisons in the United States? Aren't there work gangs too—I saw many of them growing up in Georgia, modern slaves. And if this is true, as it certainly is true, then why isn't Germany entitled to have prisons? Why shouldn't Germans have work gangs too?

"The American people have gone to war to save Stalin and the globalist bankers. These are the people who want war. If it was up to Hitler, there would be peace. Just on fair terms."

Who is this woman who says these things over the airwaves?

The British call her Lady Haw-Haw. She calls herself the Georgia Peach. Folks in the know identify her as Jane Anderson.

Born in Atlanta, she has spent most of her adult life in Europe, attached to one dubious cause after another. Though once the young bride of famous composer Deems Taylor, she is now married to a Spaniard.

After she spent six weeks in a Madrid prison as a suspected double-agent for Franco's nationalist army, Anderson stumped nonstop in the States as part of a campaign to rally Catholic support to nationalist causes. In those days *Catholic Digest* was enamored with her, though they certainly regret it now. That rag once called her "the world's greatest orator in the fight against Communism." Monsignor Sheen of the national Catholic University gave her a memorable nickname. He said that Jane Anderson was "a living martyr."

That explains what the Nazis see in her.

But will anyone in the U.S. buy her claptrap now that the worm has turned?

We doubt so. We hope not.

XOXO JANE

A letter arrived from Jane in February. Mielle hadn't heard from her in over a year.

> *My woman! There is too much to say in too little time. You should know that Bob Best has written to my bosses here in hopes of getting a job. They are giving him an audition in Berlin in <u>two weeks</u>. I told them to give you one too. Some of the folks from up here are coming down to fetch you from Nauheim. Hear what they have to offer. Come visit me, at least. No reply needed. If you accept, they will let me know.*
>
> xoxo Jane

THE LIVING MARTYR

Of all the nights, that night Alden didn't come to her balcony.

Mielle carried around the letter from Jane all evening, not knowing what to do with it.

She said nothing at dinner. The letter stayed hidden in her jacket. She was going to give it to Alden later when they were alone because he had predicted that something like this would happen. It felt only right to show him first.

By protocol, Mielle should have gone straightaway to First Secretary George Kennan to make the leadership delegation aware. But there was nothing Kennan could have done about it. Even the embassy higher-ups had no direct contact with Washington. This was an internment camp, after all. Gestapos barged into the Grand Hotel all the time to issue edicts and conduct searches. No matter how soft the beds, the machine guns the guards held were real.

Mielle paced around her room waiting for Alden. She tried to keep busy doing her normal things. Combing out her hair, picking up her socks from the floor. Even abnormal things, like making her bed, fluffing the pillows. It was a nice evening for February, warm enough to sit outside without a blanket. There was a gray glow to everything because the sky was overcast with low, fast-moving clouds.

After thirty minutes Mielle went to find Alden.

She put her ear to his door. It was silent. She walked the hallway and listened for his voice. But it was eerily quiet that evening. Some echoes of singing came from the stairs, from a choir group that practiced in the lobby.

They had been here two months already. Half of them lay around in their rooms all day, either reading or staring at the wall. The dream of a quick rescue had died in early winter and a spiraling logic took over. If the American government let them stay locked up for two months, then they could be locked up for two years, or forever. The pessimistic meaning of the word *indeterminate* took over. The walls moved in.

Mielle slowly walked down the stairs to check the second floor. Suddenly she felt guilty that she hadn't mentioned the letter to the embassy staff at dinner. After all, the government knew she was friends with Jane Anderson. It wasn't like Mielle could get in trouble for receiving a letter. She hadn't even told Jane she was coming to Bad Nauheim, it happened so quickly, but Jane would have ways of knowing.

And now Mielle was sneaking around the stairwells, the letter hidden in the chest pocket of her black butcher's jacket.

She didn't have to do this. At any moment she could have walked down to the dining room and told a whole bunch of the others about the letter, and they would have been on her side. She could have knocked on Kennan's door on the fourth floor, handed him the envelope, and been done with it. She could have denounced Bob Best, let the others know that he was conspiring with Berlin.

But Mielle didn't do any of these things. That's what sealed her fate.

As she pulled her bad leg down the stairs to the second floor, that old surreptitious thrill of being a misfit crept into her heart. That idea from her vision in Paris; what she'd told Alden on the train; that she was linked inexorably to Jane Anderson until one of them died.

Mielle snuck door to door, listening at each one for Alden's voice.

That's when it happened. She put her hand to the wall and felt a vibration. She didn't know what it could be. A shudder spread through the plaster. A noise. Words. *The world-famous Catholic, twice condemned to death by firing squad in Spain.* Mielle's heart raced. Her mouth went dry. She heard Jane's voice very faintly through the wall, with a big band playing underneath. A rendition of "Scatter-Brain," the Glenn Miller song, faded out as Jane's voice swelled. *I left a prison in Madrid to enter the world of liberty.* Mielle couldn't believe it. She must have thought she'd lost her mind or that her second sight wanted to punish her again. But her eyes didn't hurt, there was no pain in her stomach, so what she heard must have been real. Jane's voice got louder and louder as Mielle inched down the hall.

I vowed to dedicate my life to the consecration of the New Order—the gateway by which poverty and suffering would be obliterated. That concept was to dominate not only my thoughts but also my deeds. Men should no longer be permitted to perish under capitalism and Communism but to come into their heritage. That is why we fight. For a world freed of Mammon.

It was Jane. It could be no other. Mielle found the door where the sound came from. Room 228.

Jane's voice strained to hit a high note in her speech, to be impassioned without hysterics.

Just like Moses, the führer will go forth from triumph to triumph, from strength to strength. He has reached to the stars, and the Lord's will would prevail.

The music swelled again underneath her voice. The studio orchestra reprised "Scatter-Brain" as Jane signed off.

Always remember. Progressive Americans eat Kellogg's Corn Flakes and listen to both sides of the story.

Then Jane's voice was gone. Just the swing band played. The dumbed-down version of a syncopated beat. A clarinet soloist struggling to hit a high C.

Mielle pushed open the door to room 228. There were five men huddled around a radio, their suit jackets off, crouched as if on milking stools, with their hands cupped over their jaws to listen. Alden was one of them.

"Come in and close the door," he said, annoyed.

Mielle gathered herself, took a deep breath, then walked in without limping. She sat lightly on the edge of the bed and leaned her head into the circle.

The room belonged to Eddie Shanke. He had a battery-operated RCA Victor radio made of brown Bakelite, the size of a cigar box, on his knees. The little dial glowed because it was turned on. Somehow Shanke had kept his American radio from being confiscated.

"What is it?" Mielle asked.

"You dope, it's a radio," Ed Haffell said.

Jack Fleischer and Louis Lochner, AP's Berlin chief, were there too.

"But the broadcast?" Mielle asked. "It's from Berlin?"

"Yes. This is a U.S.A. Zone program."

"That was Jane Anderson they had on," Mielle said.

"I think so too," Eddie Shanke agreed. "On the air, they refer to her only as 'Lady Haw-Haw' or 'the Georgia Peach.' Why do they have to be so goddamned funny about everything? Can't they just use their real names?"

"You might be cagey too if you were committing treason," Alden said.

The Berlin reporters had been listening to these programs for over a year. Most of them were aimed at Britain, but Goebbels had been building a team of American broadcasters for a while. At Zeesen, outside Berlin, there was a radio transmitter so powerful that its signal was easily received on the Eastern Seaboard of North America and could be picked up as far as Denver on clear nights.

These shows were broadcast on frequencies that weren't for German consumption. The Nazis had laws against listening to anything but domestic propaganda. Shanke didn't care. He flouted the rules with his verboten American set, so why not tune in a verboten frequency?

"Put on the BBC," Lochner said. "I get so tired of them. Lord Haw-Haw, Georgia Peach, Axis Sally, E. D. Ward. It's cartoon-ish. A bunch of political fantasy and dog Latin about the king that you'd laugh off if the Luftwaffe hadn't been firebombing London for the last eighteen months."

The BBC had less filtered updates on the war. Though you wouldn't hear about it in the German press, things weren't going so well for Hitler's Operation Barbarossa on the Russian steppes. He bet too heavily on the dream that Russia would crumble after a few months of blitzkrieg. The Wehrmacht was so confident of an immediate victory that they hadn't sent along blankets and winter coats for its soldiers, but the Soviets had held the line at Stalingrad and Moscow. What casualties Russian tanks didn't claim, the Russian winter would.

Listening to the BBC, the correspondents leaned forward with wrinkled brows and took notes on folded pieces of paper with the stubs of pencils. Catastrophic British surrender in Singapore; waning American defense at Bataan; siege of Leningrad. They all lacked a medium, but still they gathered news where they could find it, even if that meant only telling one another.

Mielle pulled on Alden's elbow. "Can't we get out of here?" she asked. "I have something important to show you. On the balcony."

She wanted to wait until they were back in her room, but Alden stopped her in the hall.

"What is it that's so damn important? I wanted to hear that."

She pulled the letter from her pocket and had him read it.

"At least we know who we are dealing with now." He watched her expression, as he refolded the letter and handed it to her, to see how Mielle felt about Jane's invitation. "Some Nazi radio big shot will be here in a few days to invite you to Berlin. Are you ready? Do you know what to tell them?"

"Yes," she said without thinking. "On the train, you said this would happen. I didn't forget."

He swallowed hard, put his hand on her shoulder. "About that, the train ride."

"Yes?"

"I don't want you to do anything rash."

Mielle didn't understand. She hadn't forgotten that kiss. She still didn't know if they'd meant it.

"This is something that has worried me a long time," Alden said. He did look worried. His eyes narrowed. He sucked in his lips. "You asked if you were supposed to *kill Jane*. Do you remember that?"

Mielle looked over Alden's shoulder to avoid his eyes. They were set to different frequencies again. "I'm not an assassin," she said.

"You are not. Go see what's going on up there at Zeesen. Obtain schedules, the names of everyone working for them. Plant a seed in Jane's mind that it is not too late for her to stop all this nonsense before she commits treason. That is not factual, but she doesn't need to know that. Then let the Nazis return you. You come back to Bad Nauheim."

She hugged him close so she didn't have to look at his face as he repeated that the operation would be very, very simple.

"You don't have to worry about me," she said. "The only reason I'm going to Berlin is because you asked me to."

"Don't say that. If it were up to me, I would go myself."

"But it doesn't sound like they will ask you."

"No. I don't believe they will. Even Alden Linden Elder is too connected for them to flip over to their side. They heard plenty from him when he saw Hitler in Munich."

"And Alden Cohn?" Mielle asked. "If you don't mind my saying, he has no business going that far into the lion's den. Getting himself trapped in Bad Nauheim was foolish enough."

He smiled at her, put his hands on her shoulders so she had to look him in the eye. His face glowed. He seemed to be enjoying this.

"I don't care about that," he said. "If they invite me, I will go. I just doubt they will. The propaganda ministry knows where I stand, but they haven't heard of you, aside from what Jane has told them."

"If it was up to me," Mielle said, "I'd stay here." She pulled herself close again, let her voice soften on his shirt collar. "Are you sure?" she asked. "Are you sure you want me to go?"

He didn't move, didn't look her in the eye. He just said, "Yes. You must go."

INVITATION TO GOMORRAH

It was after the first of March when two officials came from Berlin to fetch Bob Best. He and three of the American journalists who had come from Paris were summoned: Harl, Whitcomb, and, of course, Mielle. The Nazis wanted to speak only with those who were compromised—the three men who had families stuck in German territory, plus, at the invitation of Jane Anderson, her "good friend" Mielle. Alden and the other recalcitrant journalists were told to stay away.

One of the round tables in the dining room was set with real coffee and shortbread cookies on saucers. Two men were waiting when the Americans came in. Mielle didn't recognize either of them.

"I am Anton Winkelnkemper," the first said, with only a little accent. He was an SS man and newly in charge of foreign broadcasts for the state propaganda organ. He held his hand out, though only Best shook it.

"And I'm William Joyce," the other said. They all recognized his voice immediately. It was Lord Haw-Haw! Though he wasn't a large man, he had a deep baritone and spoke in a working-class cant. They'd heard his broadcasts dozens of times on the radio. Here was the most famous British traitor of the whole war, sitting across the table with a shortbread cookie pinched between his fingers.

Joyce had a so-called Glasgow smile etched on his face, a deep scar that stretched from one corner of his mouth to the ear on that side, from a razor slash twenty years earlier that he blamed on a Jewish Communist rioter. He was thin, pale, intense, with a face that looked a bit crooked, all the way from his severely bent nose to his cleft chin. His treason was something of a sensation in London those years because of the blasphemous things he said about the king and royal family. He portrayed himself as a proper English gentleman, but he had actually been born in Brooklyn and was Irish, as his last name would suggest. The English-gentry bit was an act. In person, he looked like a brawler.

"I hope you have guessed why we're here," he said. "My show has been such a success that our hosts in this country require a few copacetic personalities who could complement what already there is on the air. The U.S.A. Zone in particular."

"There will be auditions in Berlin, the end of this week," Winkelnkemper said. "The pay is generous. One thousand five hundred reichsmarks per week, plus an Unter den Linden flat, rent paid. If things work out, you get your own time slot, four nights a week. If it does not work out, you will be sent back here to Bad Nauheim. I promise."

"That's the bait, such as it is," Joyce said. "And, if you ask me, that's an awful lot of notoriety for small potatoes like you chaps, and miss."

"And what do you expect from us in return?" Whitcomb said. His voice shook as if his bow tie were choking him.

"All we ask is the same as the Reich has always asked," Winkelnkemper told him. "Report on affairs in Germany without attempting to interpret them. Tell your people at home what is inevitable, that history alone can evaluate what now takes place under Hitler."

"There's going to be a gala at the Hotel Adlon," Joyce added, a bit more jovially. "This weekend, put on by the Reich Ministry of Public Enlightenment and Propaganda."

"Will Jane be at the gala?" Mielle asked.

"Of course, miss. It was her idea." Winkelnkemper looked her over, turning in his seat to face her and her alone. "Actually, Jane told us a great deal about you, fräulein. She said you would be perfect for the job."

"She did?"

"You wrote the news from Paris under both regimes. You didn't make trouble with the censors like some of them correspondents did. Your commentary was evenhanded. You are fair. A voice of reconciliation and coming together, so to speak. This has all been noted."

Mielle didn't think this was her they were talking about. She didn't really mean her reporting to come off that way. She just wasn't as adept at torching Nazis as some of them—certainly not like Thompson or Shirer, who had earned spots on Hitler's personal revenge list. She hadn't thought that anyone was even paying attention to her and her little dispatches to the rural women of the Great Plains.

"Any of you may come if you want," Winkelnkemper said, "but we are here for only two of you. I am shooting straight."

"What two?" Harl asked. He was getting impatient.

"Your Mr. Best there," Joyce said, nodding to Bob. "He has expressed in writing a desire to stay in Austria, where he has lived for many years. So he is a yes."

Best shrugged, stuck in that petty-bourgeois way he had of holding himself, like this was just a transfer from a company store in Cleveland to another in Akron.

"My wife is there," he said. "She can't leave Vienna, so I'm going back."

"So," Winkelnkemper continued, "he will leave with us in the morning, then audition with RRG in Berlin. Also, Frau Jane suggests we give her friend from Paris the same chance. And since she knew you two men as well, what is the harm in asking the lot of you?"

Harl and Whitcomb leaned on their elbows with their mouths

agape. Mielle couldn't look either of them in the eye. She stared into her lap, chewed on her thumbnail.

"And if we stay here?" Harl asked. His mustache was shaking. "Is it all carrots or is there a stick to worry about?"

"If you stay, then you stay here," Winkelnkemper said. "There is no guarantee you will leave this hotel or where you will go if you do. That depends on what your Roosevelt does with the German correspondents and diplomats he is holding prisoner in West Virginia."

There had been some rumors lately that the Grand Hotel internees would be transferred to a concentration camp. You could forgive the correspondents if that made them think twice about staying. None of them knew when they'd be deported out of Germany, or if that would happen at all. Harl and Whitcomb glanced furiously at each other.

"So, lads, who is coming with?" Joyce asked.

Whitcomb was the first to speak. "No."

Then Harl's voice boomed from across the table three times, as if to speak for them all. "No. No. No," he repeated. "I want to see my kids. But this price is too high."

Mielle hesitated. They all turned to look at her. Joyce and Winkelnkemper in particular leaned forward. They had come down here looking for her.

"And the lady?" Winkelnkemper asked. "What does she say?"

She almost echoed with a *no* herself. She didn't want to go to Berlin. She wanted to stay here. But her second sight had told her what she would do, and she couldn't escape that. Alden had told her, and she didn't want to disappoint him. Jane Anderson had pushed back into Mielle's life and Jane couldn't be ignored.

Her head dropped. She stared at her hands, her long strong fingers that were beaten up and crooked and scarred from sharpening her father's knives.

"Yes," she said softly. "Yes. I will come too."

* * *

Alden and Ed Haffell were waiting in the hallway afterward to hear what had gone on. They'd been trying to listen through a crack in the door, without much luck.

Once he learned that two of them had agreed to the German entreaty and that Mielle was one of them, Haffell tried to talk her out of leaving.

"Why on *earth,* woman? Why would you join up with the Nazis at this point?"

"I'm going to Berlin to see my friend," she answered. "I didn't join the Fascists. I didn't say yes to that."

She tried to walk away, but Haffell stuck his arm against the wall to stop her. Except for Alden, they all glared at her with exasperation. Even Bob Best was baffled.

"You don't have to do this," Best told her. "If you remain here and stay quiet, they will leave you alone. It's different for me. I don't have a home anywhere but Vienna. No one but my Erna."

Harl and Whitcomb were both still shocked, but they pleaded with her too. "We each have families here, and still we're not turning traitor," Harl said. "They came here looking for you. It smells like a trap."

"I want to see my friend," Mielle said. "It's only for the weekend."

Haffell turned to Alden. "Why so quiet?" he asked. His hands shook. "God, this is strange. You're a couple peas in a pod usually. Now she's off to Berlin and you have nothing to say? Come on. Out with it! Tell her!"

"It is her choice," Alden said. "If she must go, she must go."

Mielle waited for Alden to elaborate, to defend her. Alden knew why she was going, of course. He could have said something, told the guys that there was maybe more going on here than met the eye. But Alden said nothing more. He sulked away to the lobby.

"You just don't sound all that *convinced*," Haffell said. "A trip for the weekend?"

"I don't have to explain anything," Mielle said.

She backed away and went upstairs to pack.

LAST NIGHT AT
THE GRAND HOTEL

Alden came to visit at the usual time. They went out to her balcony.

The evening was pleasant. At least, the weather was pleasant, well above freezing, damp. The fog that covered everything that morning had lifted completely. The sun came up earlier, for the first time since they arrived, and set later. It would be beautiful here soon, Mielle could tell. The crocus would bloom in a few days. All the buds would burst on the forsythia. She would have liked to see Bad Nauheim in May with everything in flowers, even if it meant as a prisoner.

The two of them sat on Mielle's balcony and listened for the guards stomping below. Neither looked at the other. Neither said anything for a long time, until Alden took a packet from inside his suit jacket and dropped it in her lap.

"You brought it up, remember? So here you go. Just in case it makes sense. Only if you need them."

"What is it?"

"Medicine. If they search you when you get on the train in the morning, you tell them these are for your menses. Do you understand?"

"Yes," Mielle said. "But what *is* it?"

"Two tablets. Be very careful. One is enough to kill a full-grown man and make it look like a heart attack. They are for emergencies only, for this kind of job. Only if you need them. Remember, you brought it up."

"Oh," she said. "Where did you get them?"

"If some key Nazi—Goebbels, most likely—if one of them asks to come up to your hotel room, let him. Then you have the tablets to put in his drink."

"Na, deevil. What are you saying?"

She felt washed over with disappointment, the packet in her lap. Suddenly Mielle felt like she couldn't go to Berlin.

"But what if we are meant to leave Nauheim soon?" she asked, turning the packet over in her hands. She still couldn't look at him. "Did you think about that? It could be next week. And if we leave Bad Nauheim soon, then we could live together in New York, couldn't we?"

Alden took out his pipe, his tobacco, but stuffed them back in his jacket without even opening the pouch. "The rumors are just rumors. You must go to Berlin." He breathed deep. "You know I would much rather it was *me* going. But the events are bigger than the two of us. You have a duty to go to Berlin, just as I have a duty as Alden Cohn to carry on as Mr. Linden Elder. Do you understand what I mean?"

"Tell me," she said. "Which Alden am I talking to now?"

He frowned, his eyes glassy. This was one of the few times Mielle ever saw Alden show that his feelings were hurt.

It occurred to Mielle that this could have been a nice night, that tender things could have happened between them, the best kind of things when you're saying goodbye—but there would be no kiss that night, no leading Alden by the hand to that large feather bed that floated in the middle of her room. This was the last night she would ever sleep there, and she would sleep alone. There were too many other feelings for something sweet to take her breath away.

"You know me," he said. "You know who you are talking to. I'm the one who got you here in the first place. I'm the one who got you settled in Paris and walked you through every morning just so you could make it one week there without pining for your father. That's the Alden you're talking to right now. And how clever I was to pull it all off, if I say so, to get you into Berlin—"

She cut him off. "This is my life you're joking about. To think that everything is arranged at the snap of your fingers, that you are so remarkable, Alden Cohn. No, excuse me. Alden Linden Elder. How *dare* you."

He looked like he'd been slapped. "I don't know what to say to that."

"No. You wouldn't. Not a fool like you."

She could hear it just faintly then, between her breaths. The buzzing of bomber planes above the hotel.

"Do you want me to go inside?" Alden asked.

"No. I want you to sit there and be quiet."

So he did. He leaned against the wall and pulled tight his jacket over his chest. Then he pulled open a lapel to retrieve his pipe and tobacco. He puffed and filled the air with the aroma of cherrywood and cloves. It was a still night. The smoke clouded bluish white above them. There was no noise except the drawing of his pipe and Mielle breathing through her nose, trying to calm down, and the noise of the bombers coming.

More and more bombers washed overhead. A third wave and then a fourth. Then a racket from the sky that didn't stop for thirty minutes. The tremendous hammering of motors in airplanes that were too high to be seen. English bombers nonstop, headed for Frankfurt.

"They're really giving it to Jerry tonight," Alden said.

"Yes."

"I wouldn't want to be a German right now."

"No."

"They had their chances."

"Yes. They did. They've been hitched to the wrong horse a long time. Even if they didn't realize it until now."

"Most of them still don't realize," he said.

After a while, the lip of the horizon lit orange in the direction of Frankfurt. To Mielle, this felt like an omen in itself.

The urge came over her to tell Alden about the vision she had—that she was meant to kill Jane. She shifted under the blanket, tilted her jaw as if she was going to speak, but the words didn't come out. She was embarrassed to tell him the truth about her ordeal, about what she had faced her whole life. If she had told him about her second sight, Alden might have believed her. That was possible. Then he might have told her to call off the trip to Berlin and stay right there in Bad Nauheim with him, if only because he would have been worried about her state of mind. But Mielle couldn't bring herself to explain why she should do everything in her power to avoid Jane, lest her vision come true. She didn't want to kill her friend. She didn't want to kill anyone. But she said none of this to Alden.

"Are you still going to Berlin?"

"Yes," Mielle said.

"I think you should go."

"I am going."

"Good," Alden said. "Whatever you think of me now, as a man, going to Berlin is the right thing to do. And you will bring the pills?"

"Alden."

"Only use them if you have to, if it's right, and you can get away."

"Alden. Shut up."

All night the horizon glowed orange in the south.

If only Mielle had said no when she was asked if she wanted to take a trip to Berlin. If she held on for two more months, she would have been freed with the others, put on a train to Lisbon with all of them from the Grand Hotel who were repatriated. Exchanged for the German delegation aboard a Swedish freighter and sailed to New York. Mielle could have shared that tale of escape with the friends she made during her internment, could have gotten jobs with them at stateside papers, normal beats, reporting on a mayor's new haircut or the keynote at a chamber of commerce luncheon or any dumb thing like that. If she had waited two more months, until it was nearly summer, and they were all sent home.

But that wasn't meant to be. She'd had that feeling that her destiny and Jane's destiny were intertwined. A person does strange things when she believes in ideas like that.

BERLIN

March 1942

THE GEORGIA PEACH

(Jane Anderson)
As reported on February 5, 1942

So the American people have gone to war to save Stalin and the international bankers. Joseph Stalin is that very same Red Antichrist who is beating Christian children black and blue for their religion. Don't forget!

Meanwhile it is Germany who gives the Church the strength of her sword, the weight of her wealth, and the protection of her law. Throughout National Social Germany no one, whatever his station of life, had an empty hearthstone, and no child went hungry this Christmastide, or was robbed of the treasures of Santa Claus.

This could not be in Russia where Stalin has killed the Christ child in the hearts of the people, nor in the Anglo-Saxon countries, where, in black tenements that rear their ugly heads to the stars, little children die of hunger because there is no bread.

Roosevelt and Churchill secretly arranged to declare war upon Japan just to help the Communist leaders who are now fleeing for their lives before the advancing power of the German armies.

When Roosevelt offered the wealth of the American nation to the support of Communism, he offered it as a footstool to Stalin, the mightiest murderer of modern history!

Always remember, darlings, that progressive Americans eat Kellogg's Corn Flakes and listen to both sides of the story.

THE ADLON GALA

The address of Hotel Adlon was Unter den Linden 1.

This meant that the Adlon was the building nearest to the Brandenburg Gate on that most elegant German boulevard, the Prussian facsimile of the Champs-Élysées. The Adlon featured a grand baroque facade and a graceful beige tone in its stone blocks, with a design modeled on the Waldorf Astoria. Lorenz Adlon had the hotel built in 1905, with the blessing of Wilhelm II, and the kaiser kept half the hotel's suites on retainer for his guests and concubines. This ensured the hotel turned a profit.

During the First War, the Adlon was the social center of Berlin, full of Austrian, Hungarian, and Prussian aristocrats in dazzling military uniforms. Lorenz Adlon remained a loyal monarchist to the conclusion of that war, even after Kaiser Willy abdicated and moved to Denmark. As a result, Adlon refused to acknowledge that auto traffic was then allowed to pass under the center Brandenburg Gate archway. By law, for the previous hundred years, only members of the Hohenzollern dynasty were allowed to pass under that middle sandstone arch as royal prerogative. Ever loyal, Lorenz refused to stop for cars at that spot when he walked to work in the morning, as a matter of principle. So he was struck by a car there, not far from his hotel, in 1918. Three years later, Lorenz still declined to look before he crossed in front of the archway that was to be penetrated only by the royal family. This time when Adlon was run over, he died.

* * *

Mielle and Bob Best wandered lost through the sprawling Adlon lobby, where the marble ceilings were vaulted like a Roman tomb. They had changed into borrowed formalwear in their rooms but couldn't find the party until a bellhop directed them up a velvet-carpeted staircase, then through a labyrinthine palm tree court, then a solarium tearoom. This was a very nice hotel. The bellhop's patronizing expression and erect carriage told them this, that the Adlon was very large, very nice. He was an old man, dressed like a bellhop should be dressed, and he pulled them along in silence from majestic room to majestic room, nodding at the plush details of the furnishings, as if Best and Mielle were a father and daughter shopping for a wedding hall instead of two foreign correspondents trying to locate the nationalist gala they were obligated to attend. Finally they arrived at a large ballroom with candelabra wall sconces and terra-cotta festoons. A brass quartet played the "Radetzky March" while perched on a Veronese balcony at the end of the hall. "Sehr schön," Mielle said, "very nice," nodding in agreement as the bellhop pushed her and Best on their way.

That Mielle had been invited to this party must have felt like a mistake to the young soldier who manned the guest table. Dolled up in a gown that was loaned to her on the train from Frankfurt—a calf-length little black dress with crepe draped over the hem and a matching clutch purse—she somehow looked even plainer for all her elegant clothes. Her arms longer. Flat where she should have had curves. Mielle thought the dress was a Chanel knockoff when she'd first opened the box, but the tag confirmed it was a genuine article, no doubt stolen from a Paris boutique. Her heart ached as she opened that perfumed box. Paris came to her in a flash. Women parading under chestnut trees; lined around murmuring fountains; tossing bread crusts to fatten the geese. But both she and this dress were in Fascist Berlin. Both had been loaned out for a party.

The boy who barred the door hardly believed her credentials, even after Best vouched for her. She didn't look like a journalist, the boy said, so Mielle told him in German (more Pennsylvania Dutch than society Berlinese) that she worked for American Plains Wire as a fashion reporter. "Die Mode? Fashion?" He looked her over three times, this blond boy, before he let her in.

She felt so forgettable, sliding through the door with no announcement, then splitting from Best so she could make for the buffet instead of the bar. But she wasn't here to be remembered. In fact, Mielle preferred to be overlooked by everyone who saw her in Berlin. She was only there to find Jane.

The party itself was no great shakes. Lots of food, lots of booze, but the hall was only half filled, and the noise from the four-piece kept echoing over itself in the empty space because they couldn't blow their horns soft enough while playing a march. It was easy to spot Jane. There she was across the ballroom.

Mielle remembered all at once why she had fallen for Jane so easily before. No matter what anyone else thought of Jane as a person, in Mielle's eyes, Jane was a remarkable creation. Her strawberry curls peeked out from under a felt cap as she chatted up the men who surrounded her. A sheer veil draped to her shoulders. Her eyes eagerly stared out through a gap in the veil, searching the faces of her admirers to ensnare them as the tendons of her neck slid under her skin. She seemed to talk and laugh in the same moment. The velvet of her Georgia accent, her debutante elocution, floated above the hard consonants as she told a joke in three languages about being a prisoner in Madrid. The Communist torture chambers in Madrid were her obsession, and it had made her a lot of money the past five years. Her sense of being was so light among the crowd of men—the black and silver-rimmed uniforms of the SS officials, the other radio traitors, some German journalists and radio celebrities, about a dozen young men in green and gray uniforms. Jane uncoupled her arm from the crooked elbow of a tuxedoed Cienfuegos as she slowly loosened the lace of her own Chanel dress from her neck, her chest rising with breath, her breasts, as the crowd of those men leaned in to look for white scratches of scars that were like elm branches in her skin.

Jane clapped her hands to break the spell she had the men under, then tugged her neckline back into place.

In that moment Mielle forgot why she had come to Berlin. That half-lidded way she had of seeing Jane took her over again in a flash. There was that something about Jane—the way she spoke from her throat, how she was always moving her arms and her hips, how those men were looking at her—that Mielle had always found appealing. Mielle didn't want to feel this. She knew she shouldn't. But she couldn't help herself.

Cienfuegos was the first of them to notice Mielle. He laughed along at the periphery in a Monte Carlo tuxedo with tails and white spats stretched over his shined black calfskin oxfords. He looked like a stuffed bird as he rushed to Mielle at the buffet.

"We been expecting you," he said, his hand on Mielle's shoulder to look her over.

The Chanel Mielle wore was more day dress than evening gown, more silhouette than textured layers. After what happened at the door, Mielle felt too shabby to do credit to her little black dress.

"Put that down," Cienfuegos snapped, trying to take the plate out of her hand. "Come see Jane. She been waiting."

Mielle didn't respond. She was starving. She hadn't eaten since breakfast, and that was just a bread roll with jam.

"Well, fine," Cienfuegos said. He looked her up and down. "Eat first. You look beautiful in that dress, but too skinny. Have you been starving yourself?"

"I lost twenty pounds on the Occupation diet," Mielle told him, inching away to fill her plate. "None of my clothes fit anymore, Eduardo. Not even as well as this."

Cienfuegos watched her a moment. It had been over three years since they'd seen each other. Mielle was twenty-seven that winter. Her uncertainty in the dress aside, she was still less a half-formed thing than she'd been when they met. It happens that way for most people. You first see them fresh-faced and disheveled, thoroughly daunted by what it takes to get by in the world on their own. Then, a year or two later, those same people have found their footing. Their skin cleared up. They are no longer hanging on by their fingernails. No longer merely hoping to stay in the room long enough to pay next month's rent.

"You look different," he said. "Not anymore like someone from Chicago. Not like a farmer woman."

Cienfuegos looked different too. From far away, he was the same, but up close he looked like he'd aged a decade since Mielle had seen him last. His skin was waxy, his pores enlarged and clogged black. Even his hands were dry with flaky white skin, his nails all chewed short.

"Eat," he told her, snapping back into his indignant, stately ways. "Don't be so skinny. Then come hurry to get some champagne while it lasts. The Germans always say you can drink your fill, but they never really mean it."

She didn't have to be told twice. The long tables were loaded with rich food. Pâté de foie gras; Finnish caviar; Danish butter; medallion-size Wiener schnitzels; Dutch chocolate that could be pumped hot into mugs from a tureen; Hungarian sponge torte topped with whipped cream and cocoa powder; Turkish cookies with marzipan; Greek olives stuffed with red peppers and garlic; goulash; kielbasa; latkes with applesauce; pickled herring; Bulgarian feta; little Lithuanian potato zeppelins covered in runny sour cream. Mielle had never seen such a spread before. She wanted it all, even if these robbed delicacies would rot in her stomach.

Cienfuegos waited at her elbow while she gorged. He was as excitable as ever, pointing out the radio personalities, the nationalist dignitaries, the recruits from Mexico, Argentina, India. The Goebbels propaganda ministry produced radio shows in thirty-one languages, with over two hundred people on the payroll, and broadcast them worldwide. There were quite a few Americans too. Fred Kaltenbach. "He's also from Chicago," Cienfuegos said. From *Iowa,* precisely. Kaltenbach was severe and gaunt with an arrogant air, his hair parted down the middle. He had received the boot from his teaching job after he set up a local chapter of Hitler Youth in a Dubuque high school. He found his way to Germany soon after and had a couple of recurring routines: *Letters to Iowa,* in which he addressed a real friend from his high school named Harry, and *Jim and Johnny,* with another American named Max Otto Koischwitz. Koischwitz had been a professor at Columbia. He went by the handle "Mr. OK." There was Constance Drexel of the aristocratic Drexels of Philadelphia. She'd reported on the League of Nations conference to great fanfare, but that was a very long time ago. By 1942 she was delirious and constantly sniffling. There was soap-opera actor Edward Delaney, who went by the pseudonym E. D. Ward during broadcasts. At least Delaney was handsome. There was Douglas Chandler, a silver-haired man who served in the U.S. Navy during the First War and performed a recurring radio bit as a Fascist Paul Revere during the Second. There was Mildred Gillars. She played a character named Axis Sally whose broadcasts were designed to make soldiers feel homesick. Her constant theme was the infidelity of American wives, particularly wives whose husbands were mutilated in battle.

Cienfuegos told Mielle all about these people while she ate. They were an odd mix. As she made mental notes about each radio traitor, remembering again what Alden had asked of her, she couldn't help but wonder why they made pacts with the Nazis. There was the money, but it wasn't all that much money. Most of them could have made as much at home—and they wouldn't have risked being sent to a concentration camp if they offended their boss. They actually believed what they were saying, Mielle figured. They were anti-Roosevelt, anti-Semitic, and so afraid that Communism would conquer the globe that they put their rooting interests behind Hitler in the hope that the Fascists would protect Christianity and corporations and a way of life that valued people like themselves above all others. It wasn't all that complicated. Mielle could almost have forgiven them if it was just about the money. But how grotesque they were. Their bulbous red noses dripping from mold and cocaine. Their bleached-to-platinum hair. Their uneven shoulders and humped backs and crooked fingers. They looked all the more deformed in the dress clothes that were stolen for this occasion. Pale and wrinkled in ill-fit finery. They resembled a Greek morality play. Their gray teeth and yellow eyes. Rooting on a grand murderer, then writing hackneyed jokes about it all.

"Who is that?" Mielle asked Cienfuegos.

A man who looked like Emil Jannings was making the rounds. It *was* Emil Jannings. Goebbels hooked the old silent-film star by the elbow to make a big entrance. On a Babelsberg film lot, Jannings was shooting a new picture about Bismarck with himself in the title role. He was fifty-nine and only somewhat resembled his younger self. He walked with a stylish wooden cane in his left hand, the one that wasn't clenched by the Nazi propaganda chief. He wore a gray three-button suit with black lapels and carved ebony buttons. He was very large, very commanding, though his hairline had receded to the very top of his ample skull. His shoulders slouched like an old, beaten football player's. At six foot even, he was a full six inches taller than the Reichsminister and looked embarrassed to have scrawny Goebbels lead him around like a pony.

Goebbels hushed the room to remind everyone that it was Jannings, a German, who had won the very first Academy

Award for Best Actor. This was when Jannings still belonged to Paramount Pictures. "Now he's ours," Goebbels said. "Hollywood will never get him back."

People lined up to shake the old legend's hand. And why not? He'd once been the best actor in the world. If it weren't for sound making its way into pictures and Jannings's heavy German accent, he could have been a titan. Instead, he was an ideal poster boy for nationalist grievance. Knocked off a Hollywood pedestal because he sounded too German.

While everyone else made a beeline for Jannings, Mielle sidled behind Jane.

Jane was in an eau de Nil dress, the pastel green a perfect complement to her tawny hair. Even with the Jannings distraction, two men remained at Jane's side. One was Anton Winkelnkemper in his drab gray dress uniform, all the black piping and silver patches along its stiff collar. The other one Mielle hadn't met. He was just as squatty and bulldog-thick as Winkelnkemper, though a few years older and bald. The skin of his scalp was shiny, plastic, smooth. This one wore the black and silver uniform of the SS. Twin lightning bolts adorned his neck.

Mielle hugged her clutch tighter under her left arm as she snuck behind Jane. Inside that matching clutch, among other sundries, were two white powder tablets in a wax-paper packet. Mielle could feel the tablets vibrating. Or was it her arm that trembled? She remembered suddenly what her second sight had shown her—that she was meant to kill this woman standing there holding a half-empty champagne glass.

Without even moving her head, Jane spotted her.

"There you are, Mielle. Come where we all can see you." The three of them turned.

"Look at her, boys. Didn't I tell you she was the picture of Teutonic American youth? Mielle was practically raised by

Germans on a commune that reminds one of the Palatinate meadows of the Reich."

"Frau Jane?" Winkelnkemper asked. "Have you seen these communes yourself?"

"I would like to, one day. I think they would be very friendly to our cause. There are good people there. They would treat us very well."

Jane looked different up close. Her voice had taken on a husky quality. The cracks in her face showed. When she leaned back to smile at Mielle, her chin doubled. But Mielle hardly saw this Jane at all—not the wrinkles, not her battered voice, not her doubled chin, these things most people saw when they looked at Jane. The spell Mielle was under was so strong that she only glimpsed this reality in flashes.

"Look at her! Still so virginal," Jane exclaimed, her hands on Mielle's bare arms. "The war hasn't aged you a day, Mielle. You boys should have seen her when we met, such a brooding, provincial thing. Within a month she was getting us thrown out of cafés, once she loosened up an ounce. She will fit in brilliantly with this crowd too. I know it. Her perspective on German-American culture will be a great asset."

"But Frau," Winkelnkemper objected, "what about her voice? This is radio!"

"Funny. You know, I've never actually heard her speak."

She had the two men laughing.

Mielle felt like she was thirteen again, the way Jane spoke about her. She'd forgotten how Jane was, teasing and judgmental. Mielle grasped for the lapels of her canvas jacket to cover herself, but of course she wasn't wearing her jacket. She felt their eyes on her bare arms, neck, and shoulders, assessing her, ranking her against the other women in the room.

The other man spoke. "Mielle is an odd name."

"That's because it isn't her real name," Jane explained. "I gave her the name Mielle as a play on words. You know the French word *miel,* for 'honey,' because she is sweet. Then *mi-elle,* because she is my woman."

Mielle introduced herself to the officer. "My name is Marthe Hess. They only called me Mielle in Paris because Jane insisted. I don't really care for that name, to tell the truth. Not anymore."

Mielle and Jane exchanged an odd look. Both seemed baffled at why Mielle had pushed back like that. Mielle actually did still like the name—it sounded dangerous to her, mysterious, like she was a spy, like she was an assassin. Even though it was Jane who gave her the name, almost everyone called her Mielle, even Alden, and she never insisted they do otherwise because it made her uncomfortable to hear the name Marthe Hess said out loud. That was the name her family gave her. But she was different in Europe. That was how she felt about it. She was Mielle.

"You should be proud of the name Hess," Winkelnkemper said. "That could be your radio persona. Marthe in Hesse. Not that French kind of dog name like what Jane calls you."

Winkelnkemper laughed to himself, pleased, but only for a moment. Then he reconsidered.

"Now that I think about it, the name Marthe Hess brings to mind that unfortunate episode with the madman *Rudolf* Hess. He claimed to have supernatural visions that appeared to him in his dreams."

That Rudolf Hess had become a lunatic was in all the German news the year prior, when the deputy führer parachuted into a Scottish field on a clandestine mission to negotiate peace with Britain.

While the other two nodded, saddened and shamed at the memory of the Hess episode, a shocked sort of giggle came from Mielle's throat. Her eyes widened as far as they could. She stepped closer, mouth open, to ask Winkelnkemper what he meant. "Did you say *supernatural visions*? Like a second sight? That's what you mean? A spirit telling him what he must do?"

"Na ja. That is what Hess claimed. He told me himself one night over schnapps."

"Deevil," Mielle said. "How strange."

She had often regretted that she and Rudi Hess shared a last name, so it was amusing to have something else in common aside from their surname, something so peculiar.

"I do prefer calling you Mielle," Jane insisted, pulling closer at Mielle's elbow, her voice soft. This was the low voice she used when she tried to make herself endearing—though it came off as too motherly then, overbearing. "Mielle is a singular name. Just like you are perfectly singular. Perfectly unique."

Jane slid her hand down to Mielle's hand. Mielle looked away to the other officer, but she squeezed Jane's hand, then laced her fingers with Jane's fingers.

"Call me Mielle," she said to the officer. "I don't mind."

He looked her over again in a way that made her feel cheap.

"I am Oberst Nilo Steffen," he said, apparently uninterested in these minor theatrics about what to call the young woman. "Frau Marquesa Jane has convinced me to be your host and protector during your stay. But you are a large woman. Skinny but sturdy. I don't think you need protection, but rather for you to be watched for our own safety, yes?"

Steffen glowered over Mielle until she looked away. And even then, he was still staring at her when she glanced back.

"Nilo has a sense of humor that takes some getting used to," Winkelnkemper said, laughing.

It was uncanny how much the two of them resembled each other, like brothers, one with hair, one without. The only other way you could tell them apart was from the slight difference in their uniforms: oak leaves on Winkelnkemper's collar, lightning bolts on Steffen's. As with everything they did, Nazis were over the top with their fashion. The hyperbolic style of officers, effete in its offending way. Khaki versus stone. Boots versus oxfords. Mielle tended to think of Nazis in terms of the nationalist thugs she saw in Paris before the war—when they were mostly street gangs and farmyard bullies—but this was a cocktail party attended by lawyers, doctors, professionals, complete with a washed-up celebrity. All of them playing army.

"Si, ja," Cienfuegos said, sidling closer with an autographed photo of Jannings in hand. "That famous SS jocularity. What can one say?"

"Oberst Steffen lives right next to us," Jane said. "You will come visit while you're here, maybe find an open flat for yourself if all goes well. It isn't far, just on the West End. Steffen has a room on the same floor as mine. Our bedrooms practically adjoin."

Cienfuegos turned gray, hearing his wife phrase it like that.

Surely he was used to Jane disgracing him by then. Her dalliances and odd parochial passions. But he didn't have to stay in Berlin to watch if he didn't want to watch. He could have returned to his estate in Extremadura at any time. Cienfuegos must have found the idea of returning home to Spain without his wife too unsavory to consider. That would have been more shameful in Catholic honor culture than what he saw playing out in Berlin. And he loved her. This was obvious. He would wait out whatever Jane was doing here.

Across the room, Goebbels was tinking a champagne glass with a spoon. As others joined in, he climbed up onto a chair to make a speech. Goebbels needed the chair to be seen in the crowd.

"I hope every one of you has eaten and drunk very much, so therefore you will see the fruits of our labor these years and the prosperity we will bring to your countries in time, very soon. The new world order means great things for your homelands. That is why you have been brought here, to see and then to tell your people. It is not too late for the American people to throw off the shackles of über-Jew Roosevelt—nor for the people of all Americas to be free of both U.S. imperialism and Communist deception. What is it that our Mexican friends say? 'So near the United States, so far from God.'"

Goebbels stopped to let the laughter swell. He lived up to his reputation as a gifted speaker. His voice was deeper than you'd think, coming from a man as sickly thin as he was; he slipped easily from gentility to an ethnic slur to a banal joke. The Reichsminister was almost too charming for a Nazi—his showman's reptilian smile, the half-lidded way he glanced around a room.

"So eat. Drink. Take your fill, but quick. We have a surprise. You have been told there is a rally at the Sportpalast. But the surprise? Today the führer returned from the front to cheer up everyone here in Berlin. And, yes, yes"—shouting over the murmurs, his voice swelling—"und you get to come too, as guests of the Reich! You will see him in the flesh. A treat!"

It felt to the guests like only a moment, stuffing bites of potato zeppelins in their mouths, swigging the last of the champagne, before they were rushed out of the ballroom, out of the hotel, and into four impossibly long black Mercedes-Benz 770 cabriolets.

THE COMIC OPERA

At the end of Potsdamerstrasse was the massive Berlin Sportpalast. The arena was six stories high and squatted on an entire city block. Newly encased in clean white stucco, it looked baroque in that gleaming German way, like a stone block dropped from the heavens.

The Americans rushed through big red doors and up a set of stairs that led to private boxes on the middle level. Inside, the Sportpalast half resembled a symphony hall (with the loge boxes, the flourishes of flags, and a gallery deck that swooped out over the lower level) and half a high-school gymnasium. Hanging by wires a hundred feet above the crowd were 10,000-watt radium-filament light bulbs that glowed brighter than the sun.

It was strange to be only a spectator at a rally, with no little notebook in hand, without trying to chase down any man-on-the-street for a quote. Mielle's eyes scanned the crowd; her ears listened; she waited to see what would happen and how the crowd would react. The old habits of a reporter. But it was more than that. If the nationalist mania had waned after the Germans' first tastes of defeat to the Russians that winter, that would be useful information to tell Alden when she returned to Bad Nauheim. She suspected that the thrill must have dampened, at least for the bystander citizens, the complicit majorities. Even if people saw through Hitler or disagreed with him on principle, it was understandable that they might be convinced by the thralled masses at Nuremberg and the string of dominance won by blitzkrieg. There were benefits to being part of a crowd when it was winning. A simple Bürger caught up in the myth, the promises of unending victory, the Thousand-Year Reich. But after defeat, wouldn't that same Bürger have doubts? Wouldn't the cracks be too much to ignore?

Apparently not.

The ten thousand of them at the rally sat erect with their chests puffed. They were happy to be there, the white dots of their smiling faces like the pins on a bed of nails.

Their perfect columns and rows faced a stage where a skinny chrome microphone and a raised white lectern waited. A gigantic effigy of a Prussian eagle, gilded and graven, loomed over the stage. The party symbol was draped everywhere. On his radio show, years before, William Shirer said that Hitler was successful here because he restored *pageantry* and *color* and *mysticism* to the drab lives of Germans. This was on display inside the Sportpalast. The hypermasculine military fashions. The dolled-up middle-aged women beaming with gratitude. Nazism had become the national sport. Nationalism had displaced theater and opera and God.

A brass band began to play its program. The smell of roasting bratwurst leached out from the concourse. Then slowly the stage began to fill with functionaries who sat at long white tables on either side of the lectern. They wore jet-black uniforms with overlarge military hats perched on their small heads, their chests pinned with medals. There was a certain type who came to power in this crowd. The receding hairline. The gray teeth, yellow eyes, waxy skin. They all looked jaundiced, like their livers were about to fail. Some of them looked like they might fall from their chairs if it weren't for the brass band behind them blasting out Rheinische marches. Those in the crowd, in the box seats, weren't much better off. Maybe this is how it always is, everywhere. Mielle didn't know. She had lived quarantined from American society for almost her entire life. Even in Paris, she hated going to speeches and soccer matches and bicycle races—anywhere people massed to shout in unison. Maybe it was the same in London, in Washington, that those who held themselves up as the pillars of society, when you actually saw them in the flesh, looked like they were rotting from the inside out, and not slowly.

It was the same for the radio traitors. They were falling apart. All the drinking and little white pills, the injections of pharmaceutical masterworks. Pervitin and Eukadol. Mielle knew they had made grave errors just by looking at them. Their skin glazed with sticky sweat. They had chosen the wrong team. No matter what brought them here to wait for Hitler to take the stage. No matter how aggrieved. They had chosen wrong.

Suddenly the flutes and snare drums took flight with the opening notes of "The Badenweiler-Marsch." Everyone jumped to their feet; this was Hitler's entrance music. The crowd cheered and rushed to sort into sharper rows and columns. The movie cameras began to roll.

Goebbels had changed costume, walking out all in black, including a glistening vinyl coat. He was into death-squad chic that year. They all were. Göring in his clunking boots and double-breasted dove-gray uniform that he designed himself. They were in the fever dream of Nazism and couldn't see how awful they looked. And why would they? With the crowd cheering. The brass coming up behind the flutes and snares to announce the arrival of the emperor.

At last he came, a little off-balance as he pulled the curtain to the side, as if blown in by a wind from the east. There he was. The little dark man with his comic-opera mustache.

Unsmiling. His left hand raised to display the meat of his palm. Thousands of arms shot up in the crowd, but Hitler did not salute back. He was the victor, the leader. He only showed you his palm in blessing.

A little bug fluttered in Mielle's chest as she watched Hitler pace to stage left, then stage right, before he took his seat behind the microphone. Hitler in black leather boots, bloused trousers, a green military coat. Mielle couldn't help herself. Her heart raced. She strained taller to see him. The man sitting there was the most famous person in the world. She wanted to see for herself if he was really as short as people said or if he had inexplicably shaved off his mustache. It was him, all right. The mustache was in place. He sat on a folding chair, tilted off kilter, one bouncing leg crossed over the other, waiting for his theme song to end.

When he stood and walked up to the microphone, the crowd sat and went silent. Only when he commanded did they shout, *Sieg heil! Sieg heil!* But nothing else.

The essence of nature is that people are created and are stamped out. When he spoke, Mielle again looked close to make sure it was him. That voice from the radio one heard thousands of times before, but then there, in front of her. *One must take care that a continuous stream of fresh blood rises from below toward the top and that everything above, which is lazy because it is sluggish, should die. Because it must die. Because it is ready to die.*

Hearing his voice was surreal. There were little accents he made with his tongue. The cymbal crashes of his voice cracking when he mocked Churchill for being fat and greedy. The embellished aggressiveness of the Bavarian dialect broke through.

Whoever joined this movement in the early years had to be a boundless idealist. He was just speaking. Almost wistful, back home in the Reich. *Any other kind of man would only say: "He is an utter fool. He wants to build a new people, to found a new state, to organize a new Wehrmacht, to make the Germans free again—and he hasn't even a name, no money, no press, no political clique, nothing. The man is mad." They had to be boundless idealists who came to me then, for we had nothing at all to gain, but always only to lose, always to sacrifice. And how much have they all lost for my sake.*

His voice was calmer than Mielle thought it would be, a deeper pitch. His tongue trilled his *r*'s. He wasn't constantly shouting like he was in newsreels, so his German was easy for Mielle to understand. This was a long speech with many grievances to indulge. He took his time to enumerate every memory that popped into his head, every slight. Like they say, a Bavarian never forgets an injury. He kept looking down to his hand, where he palmed some notes. In the newsreels, he didn't need notes. But Hitler wasn't the same man, after all, as he was a decade before. He was stooped over. The pressure of the war was bending him in half. He coughed between paragraphs. Paused for water so often that a second glass pitcher had to be brought to soothe him.

The irony became even more apparent, once Mielle saw him, that the Fascist movement was being led by a man who railed constantly about the master race but was an absurd physical specimen himself. It was too much to ignore, too much to bear, once you saw it for what it was. No wonder Alden and the other green reporters had wanted to see Hitler in person. This was the most baffling part of the entire movement. Maybe you could buy all the claptrap about the master race if all you saw were Leni Riefenstahl pictures and propaganda posters that resembled Charles Atlas comic-book ads. But then you saw in person these men who claimed to be the cream of the cream. All the party figures were grotesque. The bullfroggish double chin of Göring. Goebbels such an obvious sleaze, chinless and grinning. Himmler a dorkish featherweight. Mussolini in Rome with his bald, vein-rivered head, massive in proportion to his body. And Hitler—where to go on? His pear-shaped torso, the soullessness in his beady eyes except when spewing spittle. His crooked little grin. No wonder so many mediocre slugs took these ridiculous men for their idols. If *this* was the master race, then why not you too? No wonder so many people wanted to believe the Fascist fiction. These were the same lies they had told themselves all along: that they were the best, that they deserved everything. The nationalists' defects weren't defects at all in their eyes. Being grotesque was the whole point!

If only the Nazis didn't breathe fire. If only they hadn't built the strongest army in the world. The joke wasn't funny then. These grotesque, ugly men—they had too much power to laugh at anymore.

No one in the crowd knew it then, but those men lined up on the stage had met in the Wannsee Lake district of Berlin less than two months before to adopt what they agreed to call the Final Solution of the Jewish Question. The men on stage must have still tremored with the thrill of the venture they had decided to undertake. The systematic disposal of an entire people, of an entire religion. At Wannsee they had even seen to the details. What factories could produce x chemicals. The logistics required to move y canisters of Zyklon B to Poland. At the rally, they smiled and laughed at their führer's jokes. They crossed their legs, folded handkerchiefs into neat squares on their laps, bent slowly to tighten a loose shoelace. They still wore their goofy uniforms with pride, still swaggered like geeks, all the time knowing what they had set in motion. Each moment pleased, in their own eyes, with how audacious they could be.

Hitler spoke almost calmly at the microphone, nearly monotone, citing figures about tanks and factory power and progress that would be made on the Eastern Front. All he talked about was defeating Russia. The speech was getting long, but he still had a peculiar charm that held nationalists in sway. He cracked jokes about Churchill's waistline and Stalin's failing health. In a pinch, Hitler snapped them to attention with chants and insults and threats, or let loose a *Sieg heil!* Those perfect rows and columns rose out of their seats. Shouts rattled around the arena like claps of thunder. If he pulled out the tried-and-true slogans—*Freedom and bread; Blood and soil*—the galleries were on their feet to shout along. That was what they were all waiting for. The chance to chant together with the führer god as the world's largest skating rink vibrated under their feet.

Lord God, give us the strength that we may retain our liberty for our

children and our children's children, not only for ourselves but also for the
other peoples of Europe, for this is a war which we all wage, this time, not
for our German people alone, it is a war for all of Europe and with it, in
the long run, for all of mankind.

Mielle had wondered if he still held such power over them.
There was so much pain and suffering, and so many people had
been done wrong. It was no shock that an injured party wanted to
be repaired. That was fair. But how it ends up being manifested is
just more shots fired, more suffering. At a certain point, nobody
lives free. She had wondered, but now she saw. Maybe they had
been bored with the details, the minutiae, but when it came to
shouting *Sieg heil, sieg heil, sieg heil,* they were right there with him.

Mielle looked at Jane's rapt body as the little man ranted. Each
word was a bolt shunting into a rifle. Mielle could smell the excitement coming off Jane. The aroma of Jane's perfume sickening,
like pear blossoms. The little dictator was rounding toward home,
and Mielle could almost hear Jane's heart thumping within her rib
cage. Jane's blood was pumping so hard that the freckles had come
out on her cheeks.

Something strange happened in Mielle's eyes then. When
Mielle looked back, Jane had changed. Jane wore the same green
gown, but all the glamour had leached from her, like when her
cracks showed in Paris. Her hair was flat and bobbed, plain orange.
Her top lip thin. Her face so fleshy it looked like a mask she wore
over the face Mielle normally saw, so Jane's once prominent eyes
were beady and black. Her eyebrows painted on. Her nostrils
dilated to match her racing heart. This must be how Jane actually
looked, Mielle realized. This was how other people saw Jane and
had all along. This Jane was battered. She had been led lame and
limping to this point, where her heartbeat quickened, her blood
pumped hard, just to be in the presence of a dictator.

Mielle didn't want to look at Jane. Didn't want to smell the
sickly pear of her perfume. But she couldn't look away. Jane stood

tall when she jumped from her seat to applaud (something Mielle had never seen a reporter do, but all the radio traitors did it that night) and shouted out, *Heil, heil, heil.* Jane grabbed Mielle by the elbow to make her stand, to exhort her to "clap, honey, clap!"

So she did. Mielle stood. She would never forget the numb feeling in her hands as she slapped them together, when her feeble noise joined with the roar of the masses that evening in Berlin as that man walked from stage right, then from stage left, to show them the flesh of his palm.

Heil. Heil. Heil.

Then it was over. The stage cleared. The crowds shouldered together toward the exits. The brass band rushed through its closing numbers. The microphone cords were rolled and stowed. All the air had gone out in the vacuum.

"What do you think?" Jane asked.

Mielle was speechless. She didn't believe she was actually there. She had seen it.

"That was something," she replied. Her mouth hung open. Jane and Oberst Steffen stared at her. "Something that I will never forget."

"It was unforgettable. Yes," Jane said. "Well put. *He* is unforgettable."

"And if anyone asks you, you will tell them that?" Steffen asked.

"Yes. I will tell them that I was here, and tell them what I saw."

Jane and Steffen seemed satisfied. Still buzzing after having witnessed the little dictator in the flesh. Mielle could have said almost anything, no matter how banal (that she thought the lighting was well done, that the bratwurst were perfectly grilled), and they would have approved. They were feeling too high to be brought down. They would hear what they wanted to hear.

As the group shuffled out of the box into the concourse, Mielle grabbed Jane by the arm.

"Where are you going tonight?" she asked. "Is there a party? Or a bar we could hit?"

Mielle felt the two tablets vibrating in her clutch. Behind her eyes, the feeling started to rise again. Mielle felt capable just then, empowered by Hitler's speech, but in the opposite direction. She even looked like an assassin in her little black dress. That's what she thought, what she felt. She should stay close to Jane and she could be done with all this.

But it couldn't be that easy.

"Oh, Mielle, not tonight," Jane said. "If only I didn't have to work at the studio. I put off recording all day to get the gala ready, and now duty calls."

They were rushing out the door, back to the cars. Mielle held Jane's arm so she could keep up without limping.

"What about after?" she asked. "We have so much to catch up on. So much I want to tell you. Do you remember all the brandy we used to drink together in Paris? I want to have a brandy with you!"

"Tomorrow," Jane said. "We will show you the town. You have your audition to rest up for. This is a great opportunity for you. You wouldn't want to sound froggy, Mielle, would you?"

"About that," Mielle said, lowering her voice. She pulled Jane close. "Do I really have to audition? Honestly, I didn't come to Berlin for that. I only came for you."

That was the truth, of course. But they all expected her to play along.

"You want to eat, don't you?" Jane asked. She didn't bother to whisper. "You've got to have a job that pays real money. This one does."

"Yes, but the very idea—"

"It's already been settled," Jane told her. "It's too late to back out now. We will take you there and you will audition. You will do your best."

Mielle got in the same Mercedes-Benz as Jane, Steffen, and Cienfuegos. They took her back to the Adlon to rest up for her audition in the morning. They would come for her.

"You will do great tomorrow. You have a beautiful voice, no matter what anyone might have told you before," Jane said. "Then, tomorrow night, we will go out on the town. I feel it coming on already. I'm ready for a party."

BETWEEN GRIEF AND NOTHING

Mielle couldn't sleep that night. She felt trapped in the room. There was no balcony. The windows had been bolted shut and covered tight with blackout curtains. The room was nicer than the one she had at the Grand Hotel yet even more like a prison. At least the heat worked.

She slipped out of the Chanel dress and returned it to its perfumed box. Her clothes were hanging in the armoire, along with half a dozen elegant blouses and skirts that had been left for her. Her own clothes looked so funny. Her wool sweater and black butcher's jacket. Her worn brogans with the stiff leather laces. The Nazis were baiting her. That was obvious.

As she stared into the armoire, seeing herself stripped down in the mirror, the truth hit her. No longer did she see Mielle the assassin, who wore a little black dress and was expected to spy, sabotage, murder, but Marthe Hess, with her men's shoes and workman's coat. The nude woman in the mirror was only Marthe, not Mielle.

The vision she'd had, the things Alden had asked her to do, would ruin her life if she followed through with them. What would be the point of any of this if she couldn't make it out of Germany alive? And how would she get out if she poisoned someone? She didn't know.

She said aloud: "My life is ruined."

Marthe didn't understand, again, why Alden had given her these pills. Just an hour before, she wanted to slip one of them to Jane. Now the idea paralyzed her. If she played along and did nothing, the Germans would return her to Bad Nauheim after the weekend. They had promised her that. Eventually she would be back home in America, then she could sell the pitches that rolled through her mind, about what life was like behind German lines that winter. But not if she poisoned Jane.

She stood over the toilet with the packet held over the bowl, that little half-cup of water at the front of German toilets. If she dropped in the pills, she wondered, would she be free from all these obligations?

"Will you release me?" She asked this out loud to God, or to her second sight. There was no answer for a moment. She watched as her hands unwrapped the packet over the toilet bowl to see if the pills would drop into the water. She was about to ask again could she be set free, but a wave of sharp pain shot through her eyes like electricity, down through her stomach to her curling toes, all her muscles in spasms, her hand clenched over the packet. The wave made her double over, she hurt so bad. And she understood. *No,* the vision, or God, had replied. She could not be released.

The vision came back to her, the second time it really came to her, with no nuance, no quarter. Jane was at one end of a blade and Marthe's own hands were at the other. A look of shock was on Jane's face. Jane was saying, *You betrayed me. You, my woman.* Marthe shook her head in response. She felt herself spinning. *No, no, no.* It was Jane who had betrayed. It was Jane who was the traitor.

Her life was something special as Mielle. So much depended on her. She was important, but only with a sword in her hands. That's what her vision told her.

She rewrapped the pills and put them in the breast pocket of her jacket.

It was ridiculous. She was no spy. She was no killer. Her whole life she had been told, she'd believed, that the only act for which God had no mercy was to take the life of another. It was better to die yourself than to kill.

But she had left Iowa, hadn't she? She was no longer a Mennonite, not really. She'd had that vision, and now she was here on German soil. There was no escape.

Maybe Marthe Hess was incapable of deception, sophistication, bloodshed. But not Mielle. She saw this, there in that mirror. Mielle could do anything.

She would audition in the morning and would flop. That should be easy. Then she would attach herself to Jane for the evening and wait for the moment to act. She had no choice. She was Mielle, she realized, fingering the silk of that little black dress as it hung in the armoire. Mielle was the name that Jane had given her.

RADIO ZEESEN

(Jane Anderson)
As reported on March 6, 1942

Let me tell you about my evening out in Berlin tonight.

My gentleman friend and I went to the bar at the Hotel Adlon. There, on silver platters, were sweets and cookies galore. I ate Turkish cookies with marzipan, a delicacy I happen to be very fond of. My friend ordered great goblets full of champagne, and into the champagne he put liberal shots of cognac to make it more lively. Sweets and cookies and champagne. Not bad!

When you hear of shortages and starvation inside Germany, don't fall for the lies. There is plenty of meat here. And cookies. And cake. And champagne.

Always remember, darlings, that progressive Americans eat Kellogg's Corn Flakes and listen to both sides of the story.

THE AUDITION

The overseas studios were located in a modern tan-brick building south of the city in Königs Wusterhausen, a wooded lake district that Frederick the Great had named the King's Desert Home
because it was so desolate compared to Berlin. It wasn't desolate
two hundred years after its naming and resembled a picturesque
suburban Berlin from postcards. A mix of Moorish and Bavarian
dollhouse architecture, punctuated every so often by Turkish
bathhouses with onion-shaped domes. The shore lined with sailboats, the beaches dotted with small dressing forts made of color-
ful striped canvas. Towering above everything was the apparatus
of the radio-transmission tower in nearby Zeesen.

Jane and Steffen collected Mielle at the hotel that morning and
brought her here in a Benz 770 for her audition. They made an
odd-looking couple. Steffen was in his uniform, with its careful
display of medals and insignias, the black stubble of hair on the
sides and back of his head, shaved weekly. Jane was even more
in costume. She wore the uniform of a Spanish Red Cross nurse
with long sleeves and a blue felt cape that buttoned at her neck and
draped to her waist. The two of them looked like a vaudeville duo,
a parody of what you would expect an intelligence officer and a
media tramp to look like.

"There's no time to change," Jane had said when Mielle came
out of the Adlon. They were both staring at her like she was the
ridiculous one in her own costume—the butcher's jacket, her
scuffed brogan shoes, her trousers. "You will have to wear those
things you have on."

In Königs Wusterhausen, Steffen had the car parked under the single tree that still stood near the new building, a towering Prussian pine that had been pruned up its shaft until only a tuft of needles remained at its top. The tree resembled a dandelion in seed. Steffen would wait in the car until it was time to go. He put his feet up on the seat and turned to face the lake. Every few moments there was the faint ripple of a bell clanging out on the water.

Anton Winkelnkemper was inside.

"We're waiting, we're waiting," he said, hustling them along. "Robert Best has already gone, and he did well."

"It's just a mike test," Jane explained. She had already said this twice in the car. By the third time, she was making Mielle nervous. "They want to hear what you'll sound like on radio. Almost everybody fails the first time. Sit straight. Speak up. Don't kick the table. Those are the key things to remember."

"We're not taking just anyone off the street, you know," Winkelnkemper said. "If you aren't good enough to be one of Murrow's Boys, we don't want you either."

They rushed her into a studio. This was the first time Mielle had seen one. It was a small office, more or less, with a table and wires coiled on the floor. On the table stood a chrome microphone top that was attached to what looked like a tear-gas canister.

"Have you used one of these before?"

"No," Mielle answered.

"This one is what's called a Neumann bottle. It's a condenser microphone. You're lucky. At the Wilhelmstrasse studio, they have to use a mouth mike."

Mielle didn't understand.

"You must place your lips right against the element because the design won't pick up sound waves from the air. That's how they keep the noise of the bombings out of the programs. It's genius, really. But disgusting."

"You can talk now," the engineer said to Mielle.

"What am I supposed to read?"

Winkelnkemper handed her a sheet of paper. "We wait outside while you do it."

With the door closed, the engineer motioned for her to start. Mielle tried to lean closer to the microphone, but she kicked the leg of the table. That was her first mistake, illustrated by the little hands of the machine gauges flicking back and forth. The engineer turned to glare at her.

"I read this?" He nodded. *Deevil,* she thought, glancing at what was printed on the page, *this is a trap.* But she read it anyway. She had to.

"Our führer gave the news straight to the people last night in a speech at the famed Berlin Sportpalast arena. The end is nigh for Stalin and his Red hordes. Once the war in the east is won, Hitler and his undefeated Wehrmacht will turn their total attention to the Allies in the west. Roosevelt had his chance. Now his fate is sealed. Though it isn't too late for the rest of our people back home in the good old U.S. of A. If any of my old friends out on the farm are listening, now is the time to resist before you find yourself on the wrong side of history."

It went on like that for an entire page.

Mielle knew the audition wasn't going well. Her voice was reedy, quiet. When she tried to speak up, somehow she sounded reedier, quieter, because she was so nervous. Her voice hardly even registered on the gauges. When they tried to turn up the volume, there was a squeal of feedback. She kept having to clear her throat, then she kicked a table leg again because she couldn't get comfortable. And the script was too much. Her voice rose at the end of every sentence as if each line were a question: "Roosevelt had

his *chance?*...If any of my old friends out on the farm are *listening?*...
The wrong side of *history?*"

She didn't care about any of this. The whole idea was to fail.

Winkelnkemper sat across the table when he returned, his jaw
set tight as he stared at her. "Tell the truth," he said. "Why are you
here?"

Mielle looked down at the sheet of paper. "To audition. I want
to be on the radio."

"You are not going to be on the radio," Winkelnkemper said.
He glared at her, visibly angry. "I hate your voice. No one could
enjoy the experience of hearing you speak."

"Toni," Jane said, nearly shrieking. "Everyone fails the first
microphone test."

"Robert Best didn't. He did fine."

"Oh, forget about Bob. We're talking about her." Jane squeezed
against Mielle until they sat on the same chair together. "There
are reasons she's here. First, she's fluent in a special German dialect. A kind of Plattdeutsch they speak on many farms across the
Midwest."

"I don't care if she speaks Deutsch! What matters is if she can
speak *American!*"

Winkelnkemper was getting worked up about sending Mielle
back to Bad Nauheim immediately. He gripped his pencil so tight
that his fist was nearly purple.

"That's what I'm trying to tell you, Toni. The Dutch she
speaks is a kind of *American* German. Tell him, honey! What's it
called?"

"Pennsylvania Dutch," Mielle said, nearly whispering. "We
call it Deitsch."

"There are many Amish and Mennonite people in America
who are ethnic Germans. And they're dissatisfied," Jane said. "They
hate American culture and still live in the old German ways."

Mielle felt her face turn red at the way Jane reinterpreted the

Anabaptist principles her family lived by—they had fled from Germany in the first place, Mielle wanted to say, because they couldn't stand the Germans—but she bit her tongue because Winkelnkemper looked intrigued. He loosened his grip, set his pencil on the table next to the microphone stand.

"I have not heard of this *American* German. Can she for me speak it? Here, read this."

From the small filing cabinet in the corner he pulled out another script.

Germany calling, Germany calling...In this matter, as in all others, the führer has been very patient. We wanted, and tried, to keep the war as clean as possible. That old satyr Churchill wanted to make it dirty, and he has succeeded. He is the culprit.

"Read this?" Mielle asked. "In Deitsch?"

She couldn't believe Winkelnkemper and Jane were nodding her on. It was the dumbest idea she'd ever heard. Radio broadcasts for Amish and Mennonite audiences? *What could go wrong?*

She didn't point out the obvious to them. She read as instructed into the microphone, translating into Pennsylvania Dutch as she went along.

"Louder this time," Jane urged her. "Make them hear you all the way out in Iowa."

"Es Deitschland rufe, es Deitschland rufe..."

Winkelnkemper pushed his glasses to the top of his head. His face contorted. "I can't understand much of it."

"It isn't for you," Jane told him. She grabbed Winkelnkemper by the hand so he would look at her. "Think what it means to have to flee the land where you were born, like this young lady had to. She left her family and friends and is now here in Berlin looking for a better life. Pushed out by her government because they don't respect her heritage. She is a refugee. An American refugee! Never to see her beloved Iowa again! That's a story worth telling."

Winkelnkemper swiveled back in his chair. He stared at Mielle, looked her up and down. All the color had drained from his face. He looked like the people she had seen at the rally. Pallid skin, gray teeth. The vitality draining out. Nothing was left but an urge to judge and sort people, to stamp documents and decide the course of lives with a flourish of a pen.

He cleared his throat. "She goes in the maybes."

"That's the spirit," Jane said. "All she's asking for is a chance."

Winkelnkemper straightened the papers and put them back in the filing cabinet.

"In the meantime," he said, "don't lose her, Frau Jane."

Jane squeezed Mielle tighter.

"I wouldn't dream of losing her. She is my darling. The only one who didn't turn on me in Paris a few years ago. She kept me going. Mielle, ma chérie de l'Iowa. Grâce au destin, nous sommes ensemble."

Winkelnkemper's face turned sour. "Drop the French," he said. "It is disgusting."

Jane looked baffled and hurt. She was proud of the Parisienne accent she had perfected and didn't like to have her tricks rebuked.

"Miss," Winkelnkemper said. "Please wait in the hall. It is time for Frau Jane's show."

Mielle left the door cracked ajar to eavesdrop. She could hear the venom in his voice.

"I have warned you about talking French," he said. "You will not be warned again."

"Oh, Toni. Live a little. What does it hurt?"

Winkelnkemper nearly ran over Mielle when he stormed out of the studio. His face was still red. He reddened more, tried to straighten himself taller, because Mielle and he were eye to eye when they were standing. It made him uncomfortable.

"Thank you for the audition," she said to him.

"Good," he said. She didn't back away. "You are in the maybes. But don't expect anything from us. I hate your voice."

"Yes, Herr Colonel Winkelnkemper. You mentioned that."

Mielle waited in the hall while Jane recorded her show. Even with the door closed tight, some of Jane's shouting slipped into the hall, muffled. *Hitler has reached to the stars! The Lord's will must prevail!*

The building buzzed with activity. Over sixty programs a day were broadcast from this facility. Each of those programs was supported with staff writers and secretaries and the dozens of layers of bureaucracy that were required to get anything done in Germany. Mielle took mental notes of everything she saw. What the building looked like. The names she heard repeated. In what office Lord Haw-Haw stopped after he returned from lunch. How long it had taken to drive to the studios and what roads they took. The proximity to the transmission towers in Zeesen. If she made it back to Bad Nauheim, she would tell all this to Alden. In many ways, this studio was like any other news organization. The self-important, handsome, but slightly odd-looking men in three-piece suits rushing around with dead cigars between their teeth. The army of young women in tan two-piece skirt suits, their arms laden with loose papers. The leaky drinking fountain down the hall. The smell of people unwrapping brown-bag lunches at their desks, pulling out a cold sausage squeezed into a bun, a large green apple.

Mielle had nothing to do but sit on that bench and wait. She wouldn't get the job. That was good. She didn't want to be associated with the nationalists in any way, even for pretend. And Jane had promised to take her out on the town in Berlin that night. Mielle would slip a pill into Jane's drink, then be sent back to Bad Nauheim somehow. That was all that mattered.

* * *

Less than an hour passed before Jane bounded out of the studio. "It's lunch," she said. "Time to go."

Mielle stopped her outside the building, where Steffen waited in his car.

"Why did you say those things in there? I'm very confused about all this. I'm just here to visit because you asked me to come."

"Well, what I said is the truth, isn't it? Didn't you have to run from home? Can't you not ever go back?"

"But Jane—the whole premise. Don't you know Mennonites can't *own* a radio? Nobody back home would ever hear a broadcast. It's not possible."

Jane's lips cracked open, but she didn't speak right away. Then: "I know that. No cars. No radios. No music except hymns, a cappella. That's the deal for Amish like you, yeah?"

"Then why? Why tell Winkelnkemper those things?"

"Just to get your foot in the door," Jane said, walking to the car. "Everybody lies to get a job. It's harder to force you out of the room once you're in than it is to keep you out in the first place."

Jane stopped with her hand on the car door handle.

"And it's true, what I said to Toni. You wouldn't be in Berlin unless it was to do something important. Right?"

Jane rested her hand on Mielle's shoulder and smiled. Jane believed every nice thing she said. She did. All of this. The audition, the introducing Mielle to important people. Jane was genuine. Jane was loyal. She wanted Mielle to get the job so they could work together, so they could live near each other and go out for dinner. Fascist or not, Jane truly wanted to help.

The oddity of the moment left Mielle dazed. Jane in that nurse's costume. The sailboats ringing their bells as they returned to shore. The smell of pine trees.

Jane slid into the car next to Steffen.

Mielle had no choice, then, but to follow.

PERSIL BLEIBT PERSIL

Something had changed by the time they came to fetch Mielle from the Adlon that evening.

Jane sat between Cienfuegos and Steffen in the back of the Benz 770. From the smell of her, Jane was already in her cups. Each of them looked numb, like someone had died.

Mielle stood in the open door.

"What happened?"

Jane recrossed her legs without changing her expression.

"I've been canned. Now climb in so we can get drunk some-place nice."

Mielle complied. The car pulled into Unter den Linden.

None of them explained what had happened, so Mielle asked. "Is it true?" Then: "Why?"

"American sabotage, that's why. My spot last night? American saboteurs broadcast a translation back into Germany this morning. That caused a lot of trouble."

Cienfuegos nodded at Jane's explanation, then looked back out the car window to watch as people lined up outside the shops.

"But why? I don't understand."

"You are so simple sometimes, Mielle."

Jane was wearing down, and it was more evident when she was dressed up like she was that night. Her jewels and the gold arrow she wore in her hair appeared gaudy now, tacky, even to Mielle. Jane looked inadvertently comic. A strung-out woman of some age holding on to a party that had ended decades before. She started to explain again but then looked at Steffen and stopped.

"Eduardo, do something useful. Tell her why I was fired so that I don't have to."

"Things, you see, here in Germany..." Cienfuegos kept glancing at Steffen, then biting his tongue. "I'll just say it. It's no secret that things are not so good in Germany right now. There are rations, you understand. Mostly Germans don't get much meat. Hardly any alcohol. No coffee. Not even torte, and this is Germans we're talking about. No torte is a crisis."

Mielle couldn't believe it. The Nazis had pillaged all of Europe. They'd stolen every choice morsel from Le Havre to Athens to Oslo. How could they be out of food? How could they have drunk every drop of booze?

"That can't be true," she objected. But the looks on their faces, even Steffen's indignant glare, showed that it was true.

Somehow the Nazis had mismanaged all their spoils. The prudent, miserly, conservative German had given way to a futurist who wanted to burn down the world. What else could have happened?

"So you see," Cienfuegos went on, "the people, they are not happy about this. To be starving is bad. Then to hear from my beautiful wife on the radio that we had a big Nazi party with champagne and candy and meat...they were not happy. Very much."

"Okay, husband. That will do."

It was cold at sunset. The gas flames were growing longer in the cellar shops. Mielle hadn't been in a real city for months. She missed the bustle of traffic, the double-decker buses and street trolleys, the people rushing everywhere. She'd forgotten how loud it was in a city. On some of the poshest blocks, entire streets were covered in a canopy of wire netting and leafy green bunches of cloth to make the boulevards look like park lawns to enemy bombers, with plumes of green gauze bunched to turn lampposts into trees. Underneath the canopy, neon signs advertised PERSIL

BLEIBT PERSIL. The cinemas showed revivals of *Triumph of the Will* to remind everyone of the salad days of national socialism.

The driver was taking them in circles, Mielle realized, because nobody had said where to go. They looped down Wilhelmstrasse, then back through the park onto Unter den Linden again. When Mielle looked up, she saw her hotel.

The others didn't seem to notice. They frowned glumly out the windows.

Cienfuegos sat up suddenly, his eyes stretched wide, his mouth grinning open. "This is the same. Exactament the same. The last time we were all together. Not you." He pointed at Steffen. "But us three. Me, my wife, and Mielle. When we were in Paris."

"No," Mielle said bluntly. She saw where Cienfuegos was headed. "Not the same."

"Exactament the same! My wife had got the ax, then we went out all night to celebrate."

"To commiserate, liebling. The word is *commiserate*," Jane corrected him.

"Ah, yes. To commingle with our misery. We will commiserate again, no?"

Mielle held her breath at the suggestion. She was still ashamed that she had gone on a Kristallnacht bar crawl. That wasn't a memory she wanted to revive, much less reenact.

She thought she was off the hook when she looked at Jane. Both Jane and Steffen leaned into the black leather seats. Steffen gazed out, expressionless, the skin of his scalp marble white. Jane thinned her lips, embarrassed by her husband. All the warmth from that afternoon was out of her.

Jane was in rough shape, but something changed as the car inched along Unter den Linden. She reached up to straighten the gold arrow in her hair—the one she wore the night J-G died, another thing that was the same—as if she could acquire some energy from the brooch.

"Liebling," she said, "I think you're correct. That's the ticket to revive our drowned spirits. What we need is a *proper* drowning."

Jane leaned forward to tell the driver an address. Then: "Geh!"

To the big Pschorr-Haus beer hall on Potsdamerplatz, a temple to the German art form of mass revelry. Jane pulled Mielle from the Benz up through the front doors into the main hall, to one of the long white wooden tables. A band played oom-pah music at the other end of the hall, though nobody danced (dancing was forbidden until the war in Russia was won, not that the ban needed enforcement here) and the place was more than half empty. Cienfuegos tracked down one of the beer matrons who wore peasant dirndls and aprons. He wanted to order for the table—"Vier Helles"—but the matron raised her palms between them and told him to sit. There was no beer, she explained, as curt as possible, because the grain rations made brewing difficult. What beer Pschorr could brew went to soldiers and party members.

"Look at us," Jane said. She pointed to Steffen in his SS blacks. "Party members. Dignitaries."

"How nice for *you,*" the matron said, her eyes narrow as a reptile's. "But we only got what we got here. You sit. I bring."

What she brought was a plate of fried mackerel, four beer steins filled with chemical-green lemonade, and four shots of grain ethanol. While they watched, the matron dropped a shot glass into each lemonade then shouted "Prost!" before she rushed back to the wings to hide.

"Don't bother," Jane said.

Cienfuegos had picked up a glass to toast, but he put it down. His face was in contortions, as if to say he'd drunk worse before.

Jane picked through her clutch and pulled out a blue and orange tube of Pervitin. "From my Hausapotheke," she said, dividing up four chalky white pills. One for each of them.

"These will get us started faster."

Mielle could feel herself sweat already. She remembered the little white pills and what they had done to her that night in Paris.

"I don't want any of that," she said. "Spiked lemonade is fine for me."

Jane pretended not to hear. She licked the powder from her fingers before she spoke, her voice deepening to contralto. "I thought we wanted to have fun. To commingle our misery. Wasn't that the idea?" In frustration, she snapped all the pills into halves, then quarters, until they were nearly pulverized to dust.

"Don't be like this," Cienfuegos begged her. Then: "How about just a little, yes? What do you think, Herr Colonel Steffen? A little can't hurt, yes?"

"Fine, good," Steffen said. Those were the first words Mielle had heard him speak all evening. "If you wish."

Steffen was short and plump and almost hairless. He was very white. All his emotions showed in his skin, Mielle had noticed, from his cheeks across his brow to the back of his skull. He'd sat watching until then, with his air of disgust. He picked up one of the pieces and set it on his tongue, then plucked another from the table, held it up to Jane until her lips parted, and set one on her tongue too.

Cienfuegos looked at Mielle. He was acting gregarious, the way he shrugged, then laughed, then picked out a fragment for himself.

"What can anyone do? These powders. They hardly even work anymore. Don't worry, Mielle. The first time it's a big punch. But after that? *Pff.*"

The other three watched Mielle to see what she would do. Jane told her, "Don't fall behind. You'll never catch up."

Mielle put a small piece between her lips, but as the others picked up their lemonades to wash down the fragments, Mielle secretly spit hers into the glass.

Jane and the men had drugged themselves. Their skin took on

a waxy texture again as they began to sweat. Their pupils dilated. They stared off at nothing, smiling to themselves.

"Let's go somewhere else," Mielle said. "This place smells like fish."

"Capital," Jane said. "Capital!"

They stomped out to the car without eating, without paying, and rushed to the next place.

To a joint Cienfuegos picked that was called Little Walter, the Soul-Comforter...this was the oddest, most apt name for a bar in Berlin, Mielle thought, though she wasn't entirely sure what it meant. The bar paired what it called the best cocktails in town with a unique spectator experience. In this case, it wasn't just the alcohol that soothed your ennui, but the owner (Walterchen himself) paced the floor nonstop, exchanging people from one table to another to facilitate the most amusing one-night stands. Walterchen was at an advanced age by then, with dark hair in a comb-over and square, black frames for his glasses. He was short and round. He swung his belly around the tables and chairs to examine his patrons, asking them to stand so he could get a better look, peeking at the table to see what they drank (and how much), to see if they were preening egoists or homely realists. He had a talent for matchmaking, at least back in his heyday. But in the winter of Zweiundvierzig there was no booze. All the bottles behind the bar were filled with colored water. The proprietor became too creative with his cocktails as scarcity took hold. What else was Walterchen to do? Garnish a drink with cubed turnip? Substitute beet juice for grenadine? He tried! The matches became suspicious of each other's merits without alcohol to grease the skids. Perhaps a war widow desperate enough for pleasure could find satisfaction here, but Mielle doubted it.

* * *

To Der Meisterverein…an old lokal pub with low ceilings where you had to push aside a leather curtain to get in, that was decorated in a theme of German military might. "How fun!" Jane shouted when they reached the bottom of the steps. She was desperate to make this work. She needed to have a spree, to shout and kick off her shoes and piss off the headwaiter. The walls in Der Meisterverein were papered with front pages that reported on blitzkrieg victories across Europe. Tschechien, Frankreich, Polen, Norwegen, Griechenland. From corner to corner, all around. Only marches played on the jukebox. The patrons bellowed along with twisted mouths when a new song came on: "In der Heimat, in der Heimat!" This place at least had some sour beer and pretzels, but all the other patrons were ancient First War veterans who hummed along with the brass or recent amputees back from the east or insufferable sycophants and jingoists whose skin was so pocked, who were so measly, so scrawny, that they had no recourse in life except to hang around a bar called the Champions Club. The whole place smelled damply of the beer they sweat from their pores. Mielle palmed the packet of tablets in her pocket, remembering how painful it was the night before when the vision of Jane's death came to her again, and how each reminder hurt more and more. She wanted her trials to end. But they didn't stay long at Der Meisterverein. They were moving again. "This is depressing," Jane said under her breath, glaring at Steffen because coming here was his idea.

So back to the Benz to see what else could be found in the night. Across the river toward Alexanderplatz.

To Die Geister von Weimar…the most bizarre place yet, somehow. They didn't have booze either. No Sister Euka, no cocaine, which was odd for a Weimar-themed bar. No. This wasn't a tribute to Weimar—that libertine era of experimentation—but a mock wake for Weimar, a cruel nationalist joke. The waiters, ostensibly all homosexuals, aped the worst stereotypes. A woman made up to look like Marlene Dietrich, in a tuxedo and top hat, swept peanut shells and cigarette butts off the floor. People spit at her. Jane sat sideways at the table, her legs crossed in a way that made her skirt hike up above her stocking line. She kept exhaling smoke up, so her bottom lip jutted out...there was so much to offend a person's goodwill here. A stage show with a fake guillotine appeared to lop the heads off a series of actors who dressed up like a whole chronology of Nazi boogeymen: Charlie Chaplin, Joseph Stalin, Hermann Müller, Napoleon. It was hard to watch, but Mielle couldn't take her eyes away. Luckily they didn't stay long. Die Geister von Weimar served only that chemical lemonade. That was one offense none of them could stomach.

Jane led them in circles, from one end of Mitte to the other and back. Cienfuegos turned green from all the U-turns. They couldn't find the release they were looking for. The hot tune. The long gaze with a stranger. The strong drink that let you destroy yourself in an instant. All they could find was lemonade. Only marches on old jukeboxes. Jane looked even more desperate than before. There was no escaping the fact that she had been fired by the Nazis for her misstep, because there was no escaping Nazis. They were everywhere. Their flags, their uniforms. Even the wallpaper. This was the heart of the world they had created. Jane was feeling then what many others had felt the past decade—*that threat:* If you weren't one of them, they were against you.

Mielle could see the panic in Jane's eyes now that she had been fired, now that she too was just an American in wartime Berlin without a job to protect her. Jane looked like a hunted animal in how she slumped in her seat in the Benz, how she rushed to the back booth before she could be seen too clearly in each club. They should have taken the weird energy in Berlin that night as a clue. Sometimes a party doesn't go off like it should. But none of them could say it. Cienfuegos ran to hold open every door. Pulled aside the headwaiter hopelessly to see if there was a bottle of Johnnie Walker secreted away under the kitchen sink or buried in the alley. He and Steffen were competing. They stuck to Jane's sides (like parentheses), desperate for her attention. If Jane asked for a glass of chicken's milk to drink, both of those fools would have rushed out to find a hen to milk.

All Jane wanted, though, was a good stiff drink and some charming atmosphere. That didn't seem like it should be so hard to obtain in the capital of the world's greatest empire, so they kept racing from bar to bar in Steffen's Benz to find a better place. A bar that still had booze. Where maybe a gypsy strummed a guitar in the corner, bending some phrase out of the strings.

They would never find this place. It was an impossible task. The Nazis had gotten rid of the gypsies. They had smashed the guitars. They had banned jazz. There was nothing Jane could find here that would soothe her like she wanted. All she could say was "Let's try someplace else," then trudge back out to Steffen's car. Steffen brooding the whole time. Steffen with an insect crawling over his bald skull. Each time the driver looked to Steffen until Steffen waved a hand and muttered, "Geh."

To the Golden Horseshoe…finally, a winner, where there was an open table, but only one. The club was packed, most likely because it somehow had a stocked bar that night with real Moselle and schnapps. At the middle of Der Goldener Hufeisen was a dirt track that looked a little like a circus ring. At one end were two white ponies in red leather saddles. For a fee, any patron could take a lap on a pony. It was fifty pfennigs to circle at a trot, seventy-five to go at a full gallop. Mostly it was women who rode. Their skirts flew up around their thighs as they circled the track. It was a great conceit for a club. Mielle was happy to see the ponies. They somehow hadn't been pulled away for the war effort or butchered in a back alley for their meat.

Cienfuegos ordered sparkling Moselle for the table. Their spirits quickly improved. Jane opened her purse, took out another white pill, and swallowed it. Jane was loud again with the boost. She handed her purse to Cienfuegos and pulled Mielle by the elbow.

"Let's show them," Jane said. "Come on. You can ride a horse." She pulled her to where a man dressed like a cowboy held the reins of the ponies. Jane handed the man some coins.

"We're both from the American West," Jane told him. She was much perkier in a packed club with a second dose. She stood taller, her shoulders back, her eyes wide, unblinking.

The riding master ignored her as he readied the ponies, so she kept talking. "Both of us. We grew up on horses. Chasing cowboys."

"There were no cowboys where I grew up," Mielle corrected. "More horses and buggies. Dairy farmers don't need to ride horses. We were butchers."

"Butcher?" The riding master was listening after all. "No, no, no. These mine. They for riding. Not for meat."

Mielle tried to explain but the man didn't trust her enough to listen.

"Look what you've done," Jane said. "Just get on."

They mounted the ponies. Scrawny little things, not much taller than the women. Mielle's pony shifted under its saddle to redistribute her weight, snorting twice. The animal seemed disagreeable, but then the cowboy cracked his whip and they were off at a gallop. The scrawny ponies could really move.

Mielle's long jacket trailed behind her as they breezed around the club once and then again. A cheer went through the crowd. Mielle looked behind her to see why.

Jane rode sidesaddle with her hair glowing in the stage lights, her scarf snapping behind her. Jane had brought along one of the champagne flutes and appeared to sip from the glass as she rode. The men all stood to whistle at her, to shout brava. She held the glass upside down to show it was empty, then tossed it into the crowd with a flourish.

They took a third, then a fourth lap, more than they had paid for. The cowboy didn't care. People were on their feet. Even the band stood to raise their steins as the drummer played along a gallop on his snare. Mielle felt drunk, her blood pumping, the tails of her jacket flapping in the breeze. Her mouth opened in a gaping smile. She didn't imagine the people were cheering for her, but they were. She and Jane made quite a pair. This young woman in her trousers and brogans on a midnight ride, looking vaguely like an outlaw, being chased by a lady with a golden arrow in her hair whose wild laughter rumbled through the whistles and catcalls.

This was the kind of thing Jane could do. The reason why Mielle had fallen for her in the first place—why anybody fell for Jane. It was just a moment, a solitary flash in an otherwise dull night, in a city that had made itself dull. But there she was with all that red-blond hair bouncing in the air. Jane. Her face glistening with sweat.

They would have ridden all night, but the ponies started to stumble. Mielle stopped hers and jumped off before the animal fell. Jane did the same, then waved to their admirers like she was a pageant queen.

Mielle threw her arms around Jane. She pulled Jane tight so there wasn't a millimeter of air between their bodies, then kissed Jane on the cheek with a loud smack. The men roared louder in approval of the two lady chums.

Their eyes met while they were in each other's arms. All the cheering white noise as Jane's green eyes held Mielle's. Mielle felt her stomach rise, as it rose on Jane's divan years before in Paris. She felt her blood rush away from her brain.

The sensation lasted only a moment this time before Mielle caught herself. She gasped to catch a breath, to coax her blood back into her head. She had no idea why she had kissed Jane in front of all these Berliners, these nationalists. She had no idea why she wanted to love Jane, only that she did. Her stomach turned over suddenly, making her gag. She shook her head violently to get the blood back in, as if she could erase the fact that she had embraced Jane, had just kissed Jane on the cheek, like it was Mielle who was Judas and Jane the one who would be crucified.

"Only speak German," Jane said into Mielle's ear, pulling her along to their table. "They like us. Don't let them find out who we *really* are. That would ruin the night now, I'm afraid."

They spoke German at the table. That was fine. They could all keep up except for Cienfuegos. He was lost in a bottle of schnapps anyway. Cockeyed in his chair, chin raised, one leg crossed over the other with Jane's purse held on his lap. He was someplace else.

Mielle was calming down out of whatever lunacy had gripped her. Her heart slowed. The sweat on her forehead cooled. Her legs started to go back into their cramps. With the band playing something slow, a waltz, people became docile after the excitement with the ponies. Everyone except Jane.

"Come to Stuttgart with me." She leaned over the table so her nose practically touched Mielle's nose. "It is prudent to get out of town for a couple weeks now that I'm unpopular at the ministry, so that's what I'm doing. Come with me. Nilo is tagging along. We'll have a blast."

Mielle hesitated. She hadn't known that Jane was leaving Berlin, though it made perfect sense. If Goebbels was upset with Jane, Berlin had become a very dangerous place for her.

"When would we go?" Mielle asked.

"The train leaves in the morning." Jane sat back so hard that her chair nearly toppled over. She hardly seemed to notice, as if her head were spinning. Her hair was wet with sweat. She still breathed heavy from the ride. In her eyes, you could almost see how her heart raced.

Neither of the men paid attention at all. Cienfuegos in his schnapps dream; Steffen still in his odd silence as he stared into one woman's eyes a moment, piercingly, then looked to the other without changing expression, without an apparent comprehension of what was actually being said. It was too bad for Jane that her safety depended on staying in Steffen's good graces. None of the Nazis had any use for her anymore—Jane had said this—except Steffen.

If Mielle went to Stuttgart, it would be impossible to free herself from Jane. Mielle could feel herself struggle to resist what her second sight told her would happen if she stayed too close to Jane.

"What about Bad Nauheim?" She took Jane by the wrists. "Aren't I supposed to go back there tomorrow? That's what Winkelnkemper told me before I auditioned. He will never hire me. So I go back to Nauheim. And you could come with me. You're still an American, after all."

A disappointed look took over Jane's face; her eyes narrowed. "The thing is, there's something we haven't told you."

Jane nudged Steffen in the ribs.

"It isn't Toni's decision anymore," he said. "It is my decision."

Steffen slouched in his seat, his chin doubling as he nodded. The whole night, he'd been eyeing Mielle, and now he wouldn't stop. "You have seen too much to go back to Bad Nauheim," he said. "You were in the radio studio. For more than an hour you sat there inspecting how everything works. Who goes where. Who says what. You could point out our transmission towers on a map. No. I thought it over. You know too much for us to put you back with the other Americans, ones we know are unfriendly to the nationalist cause. I am not dumb."

Mielle felt all the air go out of her. He was right, of course.

She *was* watching, she *was* taking notes. But to hear him say it. She couldn't stop her hands from shaking under the table.

"You can come with us to Stuttgart," Jane said.

"But only because Jane is your friend," Steffen added. "Only because she insisted. Otherwise—"

Jane nudged him in the ribs again, harder.

"Think it over a minute, then say yes," Jane said.

Mielle didn't really have a choice. She swallowed hard, her throat dry, and looked from Jane to Steffen and back. "The three of us?" she asked. Steffen's scalp had turned pink, was reddening. In her pocket she flipped over and over the pills that Alden had given her. And, again, that was her answer.

"Well, of course," Mielle finally said. "I'd be happy to come along."

Outside, the air-raid sirens started to wail. Nobody inside could hear until somebody propped the doors open. The band stopped playing and a dull plaintive whine echoed through the club. The party was over. Everyone threw money on the tabletops to settle up and get down to a shelter.

"What a stupid thing," Jane complained. "Where else would you rather ride out a bombing but drinking and dancing in a club? This is when we need them the most!"

Nobody listened to her.

"It is because of an order," Oberst Steffen explained. "To the shelters."

They stood to go with all the rest.

BOMBS OVER BERLIN

Though she shouldn't have been, Mielle was astonished at how easily Jane maneuvered the air-raid wardens on the Kurfürstendamm. Jane had made a career out of slipping by gatekeepers. That had always been her main talent as a journalist, to sneak in where she wasn't invited.

"Stick close," she said. She grabbed Mielle by the elbow.

The trick was a traditional sleight of hand. Jane and Mielle, arm in arm, walked straight toward the warden matron who herded people down to the train tunnels. Jane made eye contact with the matron, then she glanced furiously to her left, so the matron glanced too. Just at that moment, Jane darted right. By the time the matron noticed (or Steffen and Cienfuegos, for that matter), Jane and Mielle were rushing away halfway down the block.

Slipping by wasn't really all that difficult a trick, Mielle would realize later. The main thing was to keep walking when an authority told you to stop. When the matron blew her whistle, when she shouted *Halt!*, they did not halt. So they got away.

Jane had grabbed her and she'd followed, limping along. Then, once Mielle noticed that Steffen and Cienfuegos were stuck in line (the two of them drunk, looking around for Jane), she didn't care why they were running away from the shelter in the first place. She was happy to be rid of them.

Jane's apartment was around the corner.

"I can't stand a bomb shelter," Jane tried to explain, but once they were in the doorway it was almost impossible to hear. The antiaircraft batteries across the street in the Tiergarten began firing. "I'm claustrophobic," she shouted.

Mielle knew that.

Jane insisted they go upstairs to where she lived on the fourth floor so they could watch the show. She flung open the windows. There was a good view of the operation. The cannons firing in the park. The little pinpricks of light in the clouds when flak shells detonated. The window let in all the noise. It seemed to go on forever. Planes circling for a target. The wail of the sirens cycling over and over under everything.

This was Mielle's first experience in a real bombing. She froze up inside, standing at the window. All the racket. The streets empty except for the civil defense corps rushing around. It didn't feel real. She wasn't even afraid. It was exhilarating. Her arms numb. The whole city busy with its destruction, and Mielle with nothing to do but watch.

There wasn't much of a show, however, relative to other nights. The raid was a dud, as would be reported on the radio later. A formation of only five Russian bombers, one of which was shot down outside the city. The bombs they dropped landed on an inflatable decoy that floated in the middle of a lake.

"Aren't you lucky you followed me?" Jane asked. "You must have been born on a Sunday. Once they get you down there in those concrete tubes, they want you to stay there all night. No, thank you. We're better off here. I've been in hundreds of bombings. Not once has one ever dropped on my head. Not once!"

Jane fished around in a cabinet at the other end of that cool circular room. She pulled out a bottle of schnapps, one she apparently had hidden from her husband. The air raid with all its busyness and noise seemed to have cheered her up.

Mielle stood at the window and watched as the pinpricks of flak moved farther out into the night sky. It was a bright evening with all the searchlights playing on the clouds.

This was the first time Mielle had seen Berlin from this angle, as the windows in her hotel room were blacked out. She had a view of the elegant West End from here. Normally all the streets would be alive with theater lights and cinema marquees and variety houses and the gaslights of dozens of tiny lokal bars. The streets would echo with footsteps and taxicabs. But the lights were doused, of course. No light was allowed except searchlights. No sounds except the echoes of flak guns and bomber planes. The little boutiques on the West End were shuttered.

Across the road, in the massive Tiergarten, there were river birch trees and stout lindens everywhere. She would see it better in the morning, where bomb craters marred the park. All over the lawns were irregular ovals filled with rainwater and statues reduced to torsos.

At first Mielle didn't understand why anyone would bomb a park, but then she remembered that the biggest flak guns were in the Tiergarten. Four cannons mounted on a monstrous concrete platform, a hundred feet high, painted green to blend in with the Prussian pines and lindens and birch trees. The Germans had drawn fire there and in the process were reducing their monuments and trees to nothing but pebbles and cordwood.

Paris had been largely intact when Mielle left. Very few bombs fell on the French capital. And though it was just beginning here, the German capital already looked worse off. The Germans had given up so much. They sold their souls to the Austrian in order to finally win the war they lost in Flanders twenty years before. They would do anything to win this time.

Mielle's legs had her in agony by then. Her calves rock hard, in cramps. Luckily no one had been on the streets to see her limp. She sat under the window, in the dark, to rub the muscles of her legs.

Jane poured them both drinks.

"I was thinking about where you came from," Jane said. "All

you Amish live in communes. Isn't that right? In other words, you are socialists."

"We call them *assemblies*."

"You aren't a sozi anymore, are you? If you had to choose." Jane could hardly get the words out through her laughter.

"I don't like it when you tease me," Mielle said.

"Don't hold it against me. You're my little sister. I like having you around. Is that a bad thing?"

Jane drank fast. She refilled her cup. Mielle hadn't taken a sip yet, even a pretend sip. Jane was buzzing from her pills; now she was going to get drunk too. She kept standing to grab some memento she had laid out on a table or to pull her luggage out from the closets. The reality that Jane was leaving in the morning set in, and that Mielle would be going with her.

"Don't you like it here?" Mielle asked.

Jane started, like she'd forgotten Mielle was sitting under the window in the dark. "Yes," she said. "This is one of the nicest places I've ever lived."

"Is it expensive?"

"No, honey. The Nazis give you everything for free, as long as you say nice things about them. They threw out some unfortunate Jew, I'm sure, and then we moved in."

"Then it isn't for free."

Jane laughed her horse laugh. "I see what you mean. We women understand, don't we?"

Jane paced back and forth, trying to choose what to bring and what to leave behind. This life was ending for her. She didn't know where she would live if the Nazis didn't take care of her anymore. She looked pathetic. Her hair loose from where it had been pinned with the arrow of gold. Her clothes baggy and ill-fitting. She was exhausted, broken. Her nerves burned to stubs.

This was Mielle's chance. She felt it.

They were alone. Jane was in crisis. If she could get one of her pills into Jane's drink, then her chore would be over. If Jane was found dead in her apartment from pills, who would believe that she hadn't done it to herself?

Mielle reached into her jacket and felt for the pills. She had them. She pulled the packet out and set it on her lap.

"Come sit down," Mielle said. "Where is your cup?"

Jane came over, as directed. She picked the bottle from the floor and looked in at the liquid. But she didn't fill her cup like Mielle expected. Jane extended her arm and poured the rest of the schnapps out the open window. Then she dropped the bottle to let it, seconds later, shatter on the pavement.

Jane slouched against the wall, slid until she stopped, then patted the floor for her cigarette case.

Mielle covered the pills on her lap with her hands. "Deevil." She cursed under her breath. Why had Jane dropped the bottle out the window? How could she slip Jane the pills now?

"I'm happy you're coming with me, Mielle. We will go to Stuttgart for this thing. Some hospital there, if they even want me to speak to the boys anymore. If I'm not too old and ugly. If they don't want me, then I don't know. Munich. Austria. Italy. They're sending me far away from Berlin. That's all I know."

Jane's face was half in shadows, half in moonlight.

"Why does Steffen have to come?" Mielle asked. "Can't it just be the two of us?"

Jane laughed. "Eduardo is going back to Madrid, at his own request. But Nilo, he comes in handy. Better to have a friend in the SS than not. Don't learn that one the hard way."

Jane's head flipped back. Blue smoke rose from between her teeth.

Mielle saw again how she was tied to Jane. If Jane died that night, there would be no one to protect her. Steffen wouldn't bother to get Mielle out of Berlin. She was stuck even worse than before. Her situation was hopeless. But, still, inside her, that needling behind her eyes remained. Mielle was here for a reason. She was the scales and the sword.

"You have to tell me the truth, Jane. Do you really believe those things you said on the radio? All that about Roosevelt and the Jews?"

Jane stubbed out her cigarette. She clicked open and shut her case repeatedly, open and closed, without taking out another cigarette to light.

"Not all of it," Jane admitted. "I believe in the future. I believe in destroying Communists. I don't believe in all of it, no. Not that stuff about Jews having horns. And Roosevelt? If his people had been nicer to me, I don't know, we could have been friends. But they treated me very poorly when I came back from Spain. They called me all sorts of mean names. It sounds idiotic to say out loud, but it's true."

"Then why say those things on the radio?" Mielle asked. "What's the point of telling lies?"

"You can't throw out the baby with the bathwater, honey. The broadcasts advance the bigger cause. What does a little lie hurt?"

Jane clicked her cigarette case open and closed and open. There were so many people who genuinely believed the most ridiculous lies. Jane was somewhere in between, with her little lies, her concessions to gain power. Still: *What did it hurt?* A whole continent had been swallowed up because of the people who could have but didn't stand up to the little lies.

The cracks showed in Jane's face again. More and more Mielle saw Jane like this—as Jane really was. Jowly and stiff. The sound of Jane's voice not gravelly and seductive but grating, gauche.

"You look ugly," Mielle told her. This as much impulse as the kiss was before.

Jane didn't seem to hear. She stared out the window.

"What did you say? Can you speak up?"

"You look so *ugly* to me."

Jane gasped when she heard. Then she breathed heavy. She could have been crying.

"I haven't felt beautiful in a long, long time. That's the truth," Jane confessed. "It isn't easy being me. They expect so much—"

"That's not why."

"—so very, very much. I can't sleep. Not even Sundays. They make me work Sundays, which is my day of rest. You remember that. I used to sleep all day on Sunday."

"That's not why you're ugly."

Jane's mouth gaped open. She searched for Mielle's eyes in the dark.

"I don't like it when you say *that*. A friend wouldn't say such words."

Mielle shook with anger. That's why she said what she said. She was trapped. She couldn't get back to Nauheim. Of course she was angry. She felt for a moment that she was strong enough to lift Jane from the floor and force her out the window. She could end this. Jane would break, like the bottle of schnapps broke, when she hit the pavement.

This was not a vision. This was just what Mielle wanted in that moment.

"Tell me something nice," Jane demanded. "Compliment one of my good features."

Mielle slid up against the wall until she was standing, her legs pulsing with blood. She put the pills back in her pocket. She didn't want to be here anymore. She wanted to go back to Nauheim, back to the Paris from before the war. But these people wouldn't let her. They had pushed her into this corner.

"How does my hair look tonight?" Jane asked. "That's an easy one."

"I don't want to. You are a Fascist. You are ugly."

She stepped closer to Jane. She put her hands on Jane's shoulders.

"Come on. How about my legs? *Your skirt...your long legs...not bad*. Say it just like that. *Not bad*."

"You were the most beautiful woman in the world. An important journalist. Smart. Daring. I admired you," Mielle said. "Not that long ago, you were beautiful."

A wave of pleasure washed over Jane's face. Her whole body rose up in its carriage in a flash of delight.

"The *most* beautiful. That's what they always told me."

"And then what happened?" Mielle asked. "Did it go away all at once? Or so slowly that you didn't even notice?"

"Don't *say* these things to me!" Jane pleaded. Her face drooped in an instant, like Mielle was killing her with these words. "I don't understand what has come over you. I am at your mercy."

And it was true. Mielle felt the same way. Maybe she was a little drunk, but she could feel it, that she had Jane. But not yet. If she took Jane at that moment, if she pushed Jane out the window, there would be no chance of escape for herself. And her vision had showed her, when she took Jane, it would be with a sword.

Down in the streets, there was the sound of people coming home. The wardens blew their whistles again. The tunnels would soon be empty and the streets would be full. The two of them were still alone, but not for long. Rushing behind the wardens, indignant and enraged, were Cienfuegos and Steffen.

Mielle knew why she called Jane ugly. It was clear in that moment. Jane had chosen wrong, and people died as a result. All the radio traitors. They were such cowards. There was no point in calling Jane ugly, except that Mielle wanted to hurt Jane. So she did.

Mielle had to go to Stuttgart. There was no other way.

SWEETS AND COOKIES

(American Plains Wire)
As reported on March 24, 1942

Renegade broadcaster Jane Anderson spent the past year as the star of Nazi Germany's foreign propaganda arm, which transmitted her vile perspective across the Atlantic four times a week.

Note the past tense in that statement. Her show has been abruptly canceled.

Anderson being defrocked can be chalked up as a victory for U.S. intelligence operations.

American officers did the trick by sending back into Germany a translation of one of her recent broadcasts.

The offending commentary was intended to set the record straight on what she called "false reports" of food shortages in her latest adopted nation. On the air, she spun an indulgent tale about enjoying a Berlin gala with her Nazi friends, then stopping for cocktails at the famed Hotel Adlon.

"There, on silver platters, were sweets and cookies galore. I ate Turkish cookies with marzipan, a delicacy I happen to be very fond of. My friend ordered great goblets full of champagne, and into the champagne he put liberal shots of cognac to make it more lively. Sweets and cookies and champagne. Not bad!"

Miss Anderson went off the air soon thereafter and hasn't been heard from since. Each night an announcer offers her regrets: "We are sorry that Jane Anderson is still not able to speak to you tonight." Apparently her whereabouts are unknown.

"Not bad"? That depends on your perspective. For us, we say: Not bad at all!

STUTTGART

March 1942

LIKE CLOCKWORK

The grand pavilion of the massive Friedrichstrasse Station, all red brick and glass and copper oxidized green, was a striking sight in how it straddled one shore of the Spree.

Cienfuegos was there early the next morning to see them off at the platform. Once the train left, he would go to the Tempelhof aerodrome and catch a flight bound for Madrid. He stuffed his hands deep in his pockets and looked annoyed at everything. His wife was going south with Oberst Steffen instead of crossing the border west with him. The Germans had told Jane she was forbidden to leave the Reich—so for her, Spain was out of the question—but that didn't make Cienfuegos any less aggrieved. He screwed a cigarette into an ivory holder, then puffed only enough to make the cherry smolder. Smoke curled from his lips. He looked like he hadn't slept a wink after the air raid.

"Just go," Jane told him. She wore her Spanish Red Cross uniform again. With its cape and brightly colored felt, it looked like a stage costume in the train station. "What if you miss your flight? You want to get stuck alone in Berlin when you could be home in Spain?"

Cienfuegos looked between the idle train and a clock that hung from wires above them.

"I want to see for myself you get aboard this train. I don't trust *them*." He winced in the direction of Steffen. "All your sneaking around. Like last night, trapping me in a bomb shelter with him. That was low, very low. Who knows what else you have planned?"

"Don't be paranoid. We will board when it's time. Sometimes trains are late." She moved close, put her hand on his shoulder. "Pouting in Germany will stop nothing. Whatever happens while you're in Spain is exactly what will happen if you stay here. Go. Don't miss your flight."

Cienfuegos looked at her out of the corner of his eye, smiled, then said, "If that's all, my wife, then good luck."

He kissed Jane on one cheek and, without a word to Steffen or Mielle, strolled down the platform into the station hall.

Jane didn't seem to care. She paced back and forth, checking the tags on her luggage. They had to wait almost two hours on the platform. The train was late because there wasn't enough diesel to fuel the first engine, and the lone porter (an old man who looked ridiculous in his boyish costume) wouldn't put any bags on the train until he was convinced they weren't going to again change tracks. Who could blame him? He looked like he'd retired from a job like this twenty years ago, but the Reich required him to return to service. He couldn't move the bags twice.

"This country is a morass," Jane complained, a bit too loud. Her face flushed, her teeth clenched. "How does anyone function with no beer in the beer halls? No diesel in the engines?"

She had a point. All anyone heard about through the terror of the thirties was German efficiency. Along with everything else that came with the Nazis being in charge, at least the trains ran on time! Now the Nazis had conquered most of Europe, but there was only dysfunction. Half the engines on the Continent had been requisitioned to take the fight to Russia. There were only four trains in the station that morning. If everything was going to feed the war, then there wasn't much left for anyone else.

"If only they would let us sit in our compartment. If they brought us fresh coffee and today's papers, this delay would be bearable, at least." Jane lifted the bags and reordered them in a straight line. It wasn't like her to care about banal things like luggage. When she'd left Paris, she abandoned half her clothes in her apartment and relied on the landlady to straighten things out. Now her hair was heavy with sweat because she paced with an overstuffed suitcase at the end of each arm, as if someone would grab them out from under her if she wasn't careful.

"German precision." She spit. "Ha! Like clockwork! Ha!"

"Be still!" Steffen stomped his bootheels on the platform. "You are still a foreigner here, Marquesa. One who is free only at our pleasure."

"Free?" A burst of air erupted from Jane's mouth. "I grew up motherless in the Arizona Territory, buddy. Don't try to explain to me what it means to be *free*."

"I did not have to bring you. I did not have to bring your friend." His scalp was as pink as a steamed shrimp. His voice came from the back of his throat. "You're lucky I like you. If it weren't for me, you would be in a camp by now."

Jane stopped pacing and dropped the bags to the platform. She was in shock, it appeared, for a moment. She looked defeated until she heaved up her old gumption to rally. She and Mielle glanced at each other. Jane seemed to laugh at their situation. Then she smiled at Steffen so she resembled herself, so her blood flowed. "So you say, liebling." The charm rising in her voice. "If it's true, I suppose we do need each other after all."

Steffen's expression remained stony, but the color of his scalp cooled to white, then, in another moment, went back to his natural gray.

Jane slid her feet a step closer to him.

"Tell me, darling. Is it lovely in Stuttgart this time of year?"

"Ja," he told her. "The cherry trees will soon bloom. Then the apples."

That was the end of their fighting for a while.

253

This whole time, Mielle sat doubled over on a bench and held her gut, envious that Cienfuegos had escaped this trap where she and Jane were still stuck. Now her arrogance from the night before was waning too. Ever since Jane had told her that she was no longer allowed to return to Bad Nauheim, Mielle felt like she couldn't catch her breath. What a mistake it was to come to Berlin.

Mielle was covered in grime after all the running during the bombing, followed by the rush to the station in the morning. Her hair was greasy, longer than it had been since she was a girl. Her legs were stiff because she'd slept on a sofa.

At least Jane and Steffen were silent until the train was ready to depart.

There was a private cabin reserved for the three of them. The train was mostly empty except for a few women who carried picnic baskets and had matching sets of straw-haired children trailing behind them for Sunday outings in the country. No one else appeared to be ticketed for an eight-hour ride cross-country, with a transfer in Nuremberg, like Mielle, Jane, and Steffen were. At each stop, the train shed a few sets of the incomplete little families, until it felt like only the three of them were on the train.

There wasn't much to do but read and smoke cigarettes and stare out the window at livestock. Forsythia glowed on the railroad embankments. Storks circled low over the marshes. Every so often there was the burned-out carcass of a fighter jet that had crashed and exploded in a field. Even those were boring after a while. You could tally up the flags on the tail fins of these corpses, but such tallies meant nothing in the grand scheme of things. The Soviet Union, it seemed, had an infinite number of planes to hurl at Berlin.

Mielle was so nervous she could hardly breathe. The pills kept vibrating in her pocket, begging to be used, like they were a bomb whose timer had rung. She had a cup of coffee once the cart was wheeled around just to keep her hands busy. It was good, but it gave her the jitters. She had to urinate so bad, her belly button was going numb, though she didn't dare stand while the train swayed and rocked at full speed. Her legs gave her a lot of trouble on trains. She might fall over, then she'd have to explain herself to the officer. Steffen had eyed her the whole trip. When she caught him glaring, Mielle bent her lips into a prim smile, met his eyes, then looked down quickly to throw him off, like she had done growing up when the wolfish men in their assembly fixated on her and her limp. But after a while, she simply had to go, whether Steffen was eyeing her or not. She gathered herself, took a deep breath, and stood to exit the cabin without limping. To Jane, she said, "I got to pee."

By the time she returned, Jane and Steffen were at it again. They hardly noticed her as she stumbled into the compartment.

Jane stood with her arms crossed on top of a window sash. Steffen sat stiff on the upholstered bench across from Mielle.

"Honey. Settle a debate." Neither of them looked at her. "I was telling Nilo what a *blunder* it was to drag the U.S. into this war."

"The West is conquered," Steffen said. "Maybe two years ago it would have mattered, before we built the Atlantic Wall. Where will now the Allies land? There is no breach. Only machine-gun nests and land mines."

Jane lamented that things had turned out this way. If only Hitler hadn't declared war first, he could have kept the U.S. in the Pacific. "I worked so hard to get America in on the right side of this," she cried. "Now all that work will mean nothing."

"At least you picked the winner," Steffen said. "If you take your medicine now, go away with me for a little while, you will have earned a spot in the new world order."

"You really think they will forget how I misspoke on the radio?"

"Goebbels? The führer? No. A nationalist never forgets."

"Then what's the point, Nilo?"

"The point is, once the Allies are defeated, you will return to Washington, DC, to rebuild it in the image of Berlin."

"I wouldn't be so sure." Jane spoke bitterly. She had seen the First War up close, she explained. America entering that war made German victory impossible. "America is too big. There are too many of us. I saw it from the trenches, Nilo. I saw it! You were not in the trenches like I was. A woman!" Steffen instantly turned red. "If America doesn't matter, then why was the propaganda war so important? Why worry at all what side the Yanks are on if it doesn't matter?"

"It was timing," Steffen said. "To fight them one at a time. Poland, Norway, France, Britain, Soviet Union—"

"Well, they're all coming for you now. I wish it weren't so, but trust me. You're going to see what an American is made of before you know it."

He laughed again, puffed on his cigar. "And here is one of your Americans." Steffen pointed his cigar at Mielle. "Is she our prototype? Quiet. Nothing to say. Strains when she walks to keep herself upright." He raised his eyebrows as he said that. "If this is what's coming for us, I'm not quaking in my boots."

"Mielle?" Jane said. "She wouldn't hurt a fly! Would you, honey?"

She went stiff on the bench. Suddenly she couldn't catch her breath.

Jane leaned down to kiss Steffen on the top of his head. She whispered to him, "Leave Mielle alone, would you?"

The officer kept eyeing her. Mielle felt like crawling out the window to be anywhere other than with Nilo Steffen in a train compartment.

Steffen was a Prussian name. He held his carriage stiff

and aggressive; he wore his medals every day to live up to his Prussian blood. Yet, as Jane pointed out, Nilo Steffen was not a military man. He hadn't fought during the First War but was an apprentice clerk in the Karlsruhe city hall. He had hoped to attend the Kriegsakademie, the great Prussian war academy, once he came of age, but the quirk of his birth year, along with the Treaty of Versailles, made that impossible. He studied law instead. Like so many of the Brown-, Black-, and Grayshirts who took Germany by force in the thirties, his was a revolution of clerks and expedient pencil pushers who rose rapidly as those around them were arrested, denounced, disappeared. He was a professional cynic, an anti-humanist, a fat-faced rat. He'd built a career out of resculpting facts and making his masters' enemies look stupid. Did it matter if Nilo Steffen really hated Jews and socialists? No. He could demonize anyone—Catholic priests, Romani gypsies, the marauding accountants of Manhattan, the Bedouin of North Africa—if that helped along the cause. But Steffen, like so many others in politics, became bloated and inflamed. Too many grievances are as bad for the body as they are for the soul. Veins bulged over his skull. His gut strained against the brass buttons of his coat, full of enough gas that he could be punctured like a balloon. He was only thirty-six years old. All the alcohol and Pervitin he required to alternately numb and stimulate his soul into submission were taking their toll. As Jane bent to again kiss the top of his head, he looked half fetus and half crone, like a deformed man-child being doted on by his still wild, twice-married aunt.

Mielle's skin crawled, but she couldn't look away.

Jane wrapped her arms around his neck and collapsed into his lap with the swaying rhythm of the train, then rested her head on his shoulder.

"Whatever happens, you will protect me. We have been

through too much, haven't we, to let one measly Roosevelt come between us?"

Jane's eyes closed as she laughed.

Steffen didn't laugh at all, Jane whispering in his ear. His gray eyes stared across the compartment. Steffen kept both eyes on Mielle.

STATION PLATFORM IN NUREMBERG

They had to transfer at Nuremberg Hauptbahnhof.

Mielle had never been to Nuremberg, though she'd seen it on film, of course. Nuremberg was the setting of *Triumph of the Will*, so Mielle recognized the city and its medieval flourishes, all the turrets and spires, the pocked stone buildings draped with Nazi standards.

With the fog, the ancient stone station in Nuremberg was submerged in a white glow, which produced an eerie light on the platform.

Jane paced again once they hopped off the train.

"How long is the wait? Twenty minutes? Thirty?" she asked Steffen. "That's enough time to hit the bar, wouldn't you say?"

"Go without me," Mielle told them. Her legs became so swollen on the train that she felt like she had dropsy. She felt strange. She still couldn't fully catch her breath. She needed to stay upright until the feeling in her feet came back.

"Of course, honey. I'll down a shot on your behalf."

Once she was alone, Mielle held to a steel column and raised her heels up and down to stretch her calves. It had been a long time since her legs were this stiff. All the walking last night on Jane's worthless bar crawl, then waiting for the train, the stress of having Steffen stare at her for hours in the private compartment. Mielle could hardly stumble along, her calves were so tight. Pinpricks spiked along the soles of her feet.

She did not stop to catch her breath. She did not gather herself.

She could not help but limp. Yet the more Mielle allowed herself to lurch along the platform, the more feeling came back into her legs. Only her right calf still seized when she asked it to move. Ten more minutes of limping along the platform and her legs would have been stretched out. Then she would have really felt better. Then she would have been able to breathe.

Of course, Mielle shouldn't have let herself slip like this. She should have seen it coming. But she didn't spot them until they had already spotted her.

When she turned, two local police and a plainclothes gestapo were inspecting the luggage. The police were nearly the same age as her but with gaunt faces. One was very tall. Her legs seized when she saw them walking straight for her.

"Fräulein, haben Sie einen Pass?"

"What is it? I'm waiting for a connecting train."

She responded in English for some reason. She couldn't think what to do. They had seen her limping and now she had spoken English to them.

"Your *pass,*" the gestapo said. He looked even younger than the other two, in a new gray suit that still had its creases. "Do you have a passport?"

"Jawohl!" Switching back to German felt like she was hiding something. Of course, she was. She put her hands in her pockets and clutched the packet that held the pills. That too was a stupid thing to do.

They asked her again. "Haben Sie einen Pass?"

"Ja, bitte schön. Here it is."

Mielle pulled her hands from her pockets, careful to not dislodge the pills, then took out her papers from inside her jacket. The gestapo looked shocked when he saw the special pass she carried, with the red foil seal of the ProMi propaganda ministry, paired with her foreign passport.

"Amerikaner?"

"Natürlich. Of course."

The cops looked her over. She could see it turning inside their heads. What were they going to do with her?

"Why are you in Nuremberg?" the gestapo asked. "I thought they got rid of all the Americans." He picked with a fingernail at the foil seal on her travel papers. "How did you get a pass like this?"

"This is a goodwill tour," Mielle said. "Have you heard of the U.S.A. Zone? It's radio broadcasts. I'm a journalist. I don't understand everything that's going on, but it's on the ticket. See? We're going to Stuttgart. Myself along with a famous writer from the United States. Jane Anderson, the living martyr. Have you heard of her? And a colonel with the SS."

Mielle didn't know what to say. She kept glancing at the stairs, hoping to see Jane rushing over to explain things. Every time she looked, the steps were empty.

"How did you get stuck on this detail anyway?" she asked them. She had to charm them somehow. "It can't be very exciting patrolling station platforms. And on a Sunday! Don't they think you'd rather be home?"

"All this luggage belongs to you?" the gestapo asked her.

"No," she said, quiet. Her chest was tight. She could hardly speak. "Check the tags. Only that bag is mine."

"Grab it, then. Follow us."

"What do you mean? My train leaves in five minutes."

"That isn't our problem," one of the kripos said. He picked up her bag by its strings and locked elbows to drag her along.

"Wait," Mielle pleaded with them. "I'm with him."

Oberst Steffen came down the stairway just then, the top of his uniform unbuttoned. His cheeks had turned rosy from the schnapps he drank at the bar.

"Do you know this woman?"

"Her? Not very well," Steffen said.

The gestapo explained how they came across a woman acting strange on the platform. There was something wrong with her. Her legs malfunctioned. She abandoned quite a lot of luggage. So they looked into the matter. The gestapo asked if Steffen knew that Mielle was an American. If he knew she claimed to be a journalist.

Steffen knew.

"It is okay with me," Steffen told them, "if you men do your jobs. Search her."

"But the connection?" Mielle said.

"Strip her here on the spot if she will not go to the office."

The two kripos shrugged at each other, then one of them grabbed Mielle's jacket by the collar and pulled it off her shoulder. As he forced her arms out to her sides to expose her middle, the other kripo knelt and rubbed his hands along her legs from the tops of her brogans to the tops of her thighs.

Mielle gasped each time he squeezed the top of her legs, left, then right.

The first tossed her jacket to the platform, untucked her shirt, and felt inside her waistband. He pressed against her stomach, her ribs, then clutched her breasts. His hands were cold and dry. They tore through her little bag to fish through her extra pairs of underwear and socks.

"Nothing?" the gestapo asked.

The kripos shook their heads.

The young gestapo put his hands on his hips. He glanced at Steffen. Steffen nodded for him to go on.

"Why do you wear men's shoes?" he asked. "And this jacket? A man's jacket?"

The jacket lay there in a clump. Inside one of its pockets were the tablets, but the gestapo didn't search the pockets, less interested after the other two had felt her up. He kicked around the jacket with the tip of his shoe.

"These clothes remind me of home," she mumbled, almost

whispering. Her clothes hung loose, untucked away from her body, so she felt the cool damp of the fog on her skin. "My father wore a jacket like this when he worked," she explained. "He was a butcher—"

Steffen spoke up to interrupt her. "If you must detain her, officers, that is within your rights. We in the SS ask for no special treatment. If she misses the transfer, she can catch the next train tomorrow. Or the day after that, if necessary."

He smiled like a crocodile as he said this, staring at Mielle, his scalp pink with joy.

"Na ja," the junior gestapo said, trying to come up with a reason to continue. "But she is with you? She showed us a pass."

"What the hell is this, Nilo?"

It was Jane, finally, striding across the platform in her Spanish Red Cross uniform like she had just stepped off a film set instead of a train station toilet, her tawny hair flowing behind her, until she was right in the middle of them.

"Are they searching our bags?"

"Just hers," Steffen said, flipping a thumb at Mielle. "She raised suspicion. They will detain her to sort some things out."

"No, they will not keep her. Not one minute." Jane turned to the officers. "Don't you boys understand how train schedules work? If she misses this one, another doesn't come for a long, long time. Isn't that right?"

"Not until tomorrow," the taller kripo said.

"Tomorrow?" Jane shrieked. Her eyes rolled into the back of her head. Since she was a girl, she'd always had Jane-the-debutante at the ready. "Well, me and her are old friends. We both have travel passes that were approved personally by Dr. Goebbels." She pulled out her own pass with the red foil emboss at the top. "And we have plans to get reacquainted tonight. If you keep her here in Nuremberg, that means I have to stay here too. I don't want to stay in Nuremberg. I want to go to Stuttgart."

Steffen laughed so loud that his voice echoed off the platform roof.

Mielle heard the train approaching the station, saw the black diesel smoke rise from its engine as it pulled straight in. She stuffed her socks and panties back in her bag and drew tight the string. She picked up her jacket from where it lay in a clump and pulled it back over her shoulders.

She didn't notice at first, none of them did, but a little wax-paper packet had fallen from her pocket and landed on the pavement.

There were others rushing from inside the station hall to board the train. Porters striding out to pick up bags and toss them aboard.

Jane stood tall, her chest out, between Mielle and the officers. She smiled at them without laughing.

"You win," Steffen said. "We go, Marquesa. Get on the train."

The junior gestapo nodded, said, "Of course. Good voyage." He folded up Mielle's papers with her passport and handed them back to her.

"Thank you," she said, like a fool, like they hadn't just forced their hands under her clothes.

When she bent to pick up her bag, she noticed the pills. She almost collapsed onto them, almost jumped. But her body was so stiff she could only jerk in that direction, as if she'd lost her balance, to slap a hand over the packet and snatch it off the ground.

"Get up now," Jane said. She reached to help Mielle stand upright. "Here we go."

They got on the train.

PALACE SOLITUDE

Steffen had arranged for them to stay on the grounds of a retreat palace outside Stuttgart.

A car collected them from the Hauptbahnhof station and drove them up the winding hills and dormant vineyards that surround the city. The palace was painted the same ivory shade as elephant tusk and was situated at the edge of a forest, atop what was known as Der Talkessel, the Cauldron. This was Schloss Solitude. All soft edges and elegant stone steps that spiraled up to a gilded ballroom. Solitude, ironically, was built to host parties. Inside were blind nooks perfect for the surreptitious lifting of skirts and secret rooms everywhere to sneak off for bumps of cocaine snorted from the thumb webs of the crown princes of Württemberg.

Most of the palace was boarded up by then. The grounds had last been used as a retreat for the Reich's labor service. Apparently the shovel corps didn't require those illicit nooks and secret rooms.

Two detached residential wings were open, however, which was where the shovel corps had made camp before they were called off to build bunkers in Normandy and repair runways in Ukraine. In Weimar times, a Jewish family had owned and operated a hotel out of these once posh quarters, but the Fascist government had Aryanized the property during the intervening decade.

"Have you ever slept in a castle?" Jane asked Mielle. Mielle just laughed. "It isn't the bohème life you had in Montmartre, certainly. But castles do have their advantages."

Mielle and Jane paced the rough cobblestones while Steffen saw to things inside. They were to stay here at least two days, Jane said, before moving on. Jane had called it a goodwill tour, but she didn't seem to know what that actually meant any more than Mielle did. All she could say was that she expected to entertain a platoon of reservists, perhaps visit a hospital. Steffen was handling all the details. He was to be in charge of their every movement from then on. He'd told the women this in the car.

"We have no obligations this evening," Jane said. She unclasped the cape of her Red Cross uniform and draped the felt over her head like it was a habit. "Doesn't that sound wonderful? It's been ages since I've truly had a night off. All this radio! All these speeches! There's only so much one woman can give before she runs out of steam. Those foul politicians don't see how *boring* it is to tell the same story over and over and over. I'd be glad to be done with it, if only one didn't need a job. It's unfortunate. The Cienfuegos clan has lots of land—loads of rolling country-side, Merino sheep, cork oak. But when it comes to money..." She sighed, then eased herself onto the steps outside the office. "Nothing can ever be easy. Not for women like us. That's the sad truth."

Mielle nodded, only pretending to listen. The long trip and all its drama had exhausted her. She didn't feel like consoling Jane.

It was late afternoon. Mielle had thought the fog might lift as the sun set, but the blanket was growing even thicker. That was good. If the fog was thick, the English couldn't bomb.

Something had changed in the war after Christmas. England began thumping industrial cities like Stuttgart with four-pound thermite sticks and incendiary bombs. Not just factories and dock-yards, but populated areas too. On March 4, the night before Mielle traveled from Bad Nauheim to Berlin, a Bosch factory in the Bad Cannstatt area of Stuttgart was hit by more than a hun-dred twenty English bombers. Things would only get worse.

Mielle sat next to Jane on the stone steps that led to the office door.

"You know, it was very stupid to let them see you limp at the train station. If I hadn't been there to save you, those men would have had you locked in a small room with them."

Mielle didn't know what to say. She knew she had erred.

"Don't you understand?" Jane asked, listing so her shoulder knocked Mielle's shoulder. "I will spell it for you: S-t-u-p-i-d."

Mielle didn't react at all. Even her eyes unfocused; she let the fog blur into nothing except a solid white haze.

"I had to save you, Mielle. You're special to me. Even after you called me that word last night. I can call you bad words too, you see. Stupid. Ah. We've both done it. We can feel better now."

A door slammed inside. Steffen emerged.

"I got us Duke Eugen's personal quarters," he boasted, his voice inflated. "The best room—the caretaker said so. We're lucky they still have it. Every other room has been closed up for some time. All the labor workers are away at the war."

Upstairs, the rooms smelled of Lysol and the damp, decaying aroma of spring. One side of the parlor was wall-to-wall windows that opened to either a courtyard garden or the palace. There was a separate bedroom plus a kitchenette that was really just a wet bar with a dumbwaiter that must have dropped down to the kitchen when this was a hotel. The bookshelves all displayed fishing rods and shotguns with dull gray barrels. Gilt-framed landscape paintings were tacked to the whitewashed walls here and there. In the middle of the floor were two corduroy upholstered sofas facing each other, both turned gray from the dust that covered them. Other pieces of furniture around the room—cabinets and high-backed chairs—were under white sheets.

At the foggy, half-lit conclusion of the day, the covered pieces looked like ghosts who hesitated in the corners. The Jewish hoteliers had lived here, Mielle realized. These were all their things that had been draped with sheets.

The caretaker delivered some slices of ham and a hunk of

crumbling orange cheese. Mielle stood at the window and ate most of the ham herself. She didn't want to turn around, or she would have had to look Jane and Steffen in the eye. The thought of spending a night in the same room as them turned her stomach. Steffen explained that they were here because, as a boy, he had come to Solitude with his father to camp and hunt and scamper around the palace grounds. All that German obsession with nature. But it still didn't make sense to stay in an empty palace. There were hotels in the city; Steffen could have visited Solitude in the morning. To be isolated, in this ivory palace, in the fog... Mielle's insides clenched as she imagined what Steffen might have planned.

"What is this goodwill tour?" she asked. "I don't know what that means."

Jane fell back into one of the uncovered sofas, her arms outstretched, and let the dust rise around her.

"I had very much hoped, Mielle, that you wouldn't point out that particular elephant in the room. But now you have."

Jane glowered like she expected Mielle to do something about the awkwardness, like it was Mielle who caused the awkwardness in the first place.

Steffen swatted at the furniture with a broom, then went around opening all the windows to let out the dust. Instead of dust going out, wisps of fog sneaked in.

"I am here for meetings in the city tomorrow," he said. "My closest contemporaries in the Gestapo are here, so we will visit. One man, my friend Klaas, we grew up together not far from here. We are to meet in the morning. I look forward to seeing him."

"And me, liebling? Mielle was asking about me."

Steffen took off his jacket and unbuttoned his sleeves. Underneath, his shirt was dark because he'd sweat through the fabric.

"For you? Your friend is right. There is no goodwill tour. No German troops want to meet you, Frau Georgia Peach."

"*Not now* is what you mean," Jane said. "Not after my mistake on the radio."

"Yes. That is one reason." He turned to swing futilely at the fog with the broom. "You will be safe here. Then I will take you to Austria, where it is even safer. Berlin is not a good place for Frau Marquesa right now, you understand."

"And me?" Mielle asked.

Steffen let the broom rattle to the floor. He leaned against one of the high-backed chairs, rested an elbow on top of the sheet. "I have not decided about you."

It looked like the sheets had surrounded him.

"Oh," Jane wailed. "That Schwob sense of humor. You will stay with me. We girls are responsible to only each other, after all."

THE SCALES

There wasn't much to eat for dinner, but the bar was half stocked.

They took turns making cocktails and snacks with what they could find in the wet bar. Jane went first. She presented snifters of Goldwasser and knäckebrot crackers on a Bakelite tray. It tasted okay. The Goldwasser was stale. Steffen was next. He made something like a Manhattan with Asbach Uralt brandy paired with limp sweet pickles dipped in gritty peanut butter. It was disgusting, but they reveled in every nauseating bite. That was part of the game.

They were getting loose. Jane went to the bedroom to change into her kimono and emerged barefoot and barelegged. Steffen leaned back into the sofa with a glass resting on his thigh. The room filled with cigarette smoke. Finally the two of them stopped picking at each other. Mielle felt the liquor too, in the fog and smoke, in the room lit by golden-yellow candles stuck into green beer bottles. She didn't know what to do with herself. There was a deck of playing cards on the table, so she asked if they should play skat. "Sure," Jane said. They sat on two sofas around the low table.

Mielle dealt the cards. None of them reached to pick up their hands.

"My glass is dry," Jane said. Then: "Mielle, isn't it your turn to play bartender?"

She went to pick through the bottles. Schlumberger Brut, some green wines that had surely gone bad. A crumpled box of Palmin coconut cooking fat. Some Persil powdered soap.

She hadn't shed her jacket because of the damp air spilling in through the windows. In her breast pocket were still wrapped two little white pills. She opened the wax-paper packet. One of the pills was split and one was crushed. She brushed the powder into a glass. Into another, she dropped the halves. In a sagging damp box, she found saccharine. She pulverized the clumping crystals with the bottom of a glass and added that to the powders.

She hardly realized what she was doing as she stirred the drinks so it all dissolved together. Time raced. Her eyes pulsed so hard, she could hardly see. Her whole body surged with electricity. This was her chance, she hoped. That was the only thought she let tumble through her mind. There was no sword, like her vision told, but the spirit was the same. This was her chance. She would give the drinks to Jane and Steffen, they would die, and she would be free.

Mielle glanced up as her hands worked, and no one was watching her. They were lost in those first rushes of a drunk when everything feels easy. Jane swayed around at the edges of the parlor to lift the sheets off furniture. Steffen sat with his head resting on the back of the sofa to stare at the ceiling. "Will you hurry?" he said, suddenly irritated. "We're thirsty."

"Oh, look!" Jane shouted. "A phonograph! Records!"

Mielle kept working. Her hands shook as she poured in some brandy, some synthetic honey.

"I haven't seen these in years," Jane cooed. "Oh, you won't like it, Nilo. Race records…jazz…who knew you could still find Bessie Smith in Germany? Under a sheet in Stuttgart, of all places. That's where!"

"Don't play them. They are forbidden."

"What's that, Nilo?" Jane didn't look up.

"I say, don't play them."

Steffen was standing, his shoulders aimed at Jane. She held up one of the records.

"They're real oldies. Gershwin, Irving Berlin, a bunch of Tin Pan Alley stuff. Here's a Jelly Roll Morton. I met him once in Harlem, back when I had a thing for piano players. He was a

Creole, and he could really play. My first husband introduced me to a bunch of musicians when I lived in New York."

"I said don't!"

His scalp was red. All the tension of the day rushed back in a flash, his temper set off, like earlier on the platform, like on the train, when he felt that Jane had undermined him.

"Fine, liebling. Fine." Jane kept looking through the cabinet to see what else was there, but she wasn't really looking. She glanced up, then again, to see if Steffen had sat down. He hadn't. The way Jane spoke about the records triggered some switch inside him.

Mielle had finished making the drinks. She only made two of them, she was so nervous, both with the powder in them. Nobody noticed. Jane's whole arms tremored. Steffen's skull pulsed dark red. He moved his hand to feel for the pistol at his hip. Jane noticed that, glancing up from the records, then watched his hand so intently, eyes wide, that Mielle saw too.

"Why don't you set those drinks on the table," Jane said to Mielle, "and come over here next to me. Don't spill, honey. We're all being real careful right now."

Mielle complied. She felt numb with terror, a foot away from Steffen as she put both highball glasses on the table. She felt heat come off him. His hand rested on the butt of his gun.

"You don't mind if we look, do you, liebling? Come here, Mielle. Tell me again the name of that Iowa trumpeter. You told me once, when we first met. I remember everything except his name. These are real oldies. I bet there's a record of his here. If there's one anywhere, there's one in Stuttgart."

Mielle took a deep breath, straightened, and walked to Jane. She limped. She couldn't help it.

"Bix," she said. "Bix Beiderbecke."

"Beiderbecke! That's it! A good German American boy from Kenosha."

"From Davenport."

"That's it. Davenport! Sure!" Jane whispered in Mielle's ear. "Don't move. Look here at the records and he will calm down soon. They're all like this. Every man reaches for a gun at some point."

Mielle stared at the top of the record cabinet. Her back was to Nilo Steffen. She kept her eyes down and didn't even look at the records as Jane recited their titles. "The Sheik of Araby." "Black and Blue." "Bye Bye Blackbird." Jane was barefoot, Mielle saw. Her feet were edged black with dirt where they met the parquet floor. She had white scars between her toes, red spots where rats had bit her.

When Mielle turned to look, Nilo Steffen sat on the sofa with his back to her. Both highball glasses on the low table were empty. He'd slammed them both down.

All the color was gone from him. He sat perfectly still.

"Good gracious," Jane said. "That should calm your nerves, if anything can."

Jane closed the phonograph cabinet, then covered it with a dusty white sheet.

"Can you make two more just like those?" she asked Mielle. "They must be brilliant cocktails for Nilo to swill them both."

Mielle couldn't respond, couldn't move. She didn't even shake anymore. She gaped at the two empty glasses in shock.

Jane took her by the elbow. "Come on. We can't let him get too far ahead of us. Make us two more of what he had, won't you?"

Mielle let herself be pulled across the room to the bar. As she passed Steffen, she saw the look on his face. The same blank stare he always had.

"Jane," he said. "I feel very odd. My stomach, Jane."

"Two drinks in one swallow! What did you expect?"

Mielle stood at the bar with the two empty glasses in her hands. All at once it hit her. Nilo Steffen was going to die because she had poisoned him.

Both glasses fell from her hands and shattered on the floor.

"Good God," Jane said. "What's gotten into you two?"

"Where is the phone?" Steffen asked. "I want to call someone. A doctor. My stomach is very bad."

"Wouldn't you rather lie down?" Jane said. "It's rotgut. The pain will pass."

Steffen stumbled away from the sofa and started lifting sheets to find a telephone.

Mielle awoke. She rushed across the room to stop him. She didn't want Steffen to die—she didn't want to be the one who killed him—but she couldn't let him survive. If he managed to find a doctor, she might be caught. The blood pulsed behind her eyes. Her shoulders inflated. She had never felt so scared before, or so *exhilarated*. She couldn't help it—she felt the ghosts in the room moving, the spirit inside herself rise up and vibrate. She was smiling. Even her own movements felt like they were out of her control.

Steffen pushed her out of the way. He found a telephone under one of the sheets, grabbed it, but doubled over before he could lift the receiver to his ear.

"Give me that." Jane took the receiver from him, hung it up, and flipped the sheet back over the phone. "Those drinks are too sweet, that's the problem. A man your age drinking that much sweetener all at once. Go lie down."

Steffen nearly collapsed. He made it to the sofa, then lay on his side, moaning. Jane made him lie on his back with his feet up.

"Have another drink," Mielle suggested. "If only there was beer. Or water!"

She found the last glass and filled it at the sink.

"Here's an idea," Jane said. "Can't you make him a poultice, a sedative? Something with herbs from the garden?"

"I think so," Mielle said.

"Like when you grew up on the farm. Some Mennonite potion. You people are so resourceful."

Steffen could hardly speak. He kept doubling over to clutch his stomach. His skin was maroon. The thought kept racing through Mielle's head that he could be saved if a doctor was summoned to pump his stomach. But nobody was getting a doctor.

Jane dumped out the water from the last clean glass, filled it with brandy, then wandered the room. "I love a good potion. Hiccup cures. That's what I mean." A smoldering cigarette in her other hand. "Concocting a good hiccup cure is an invaluable skill."

Jane kept winking at Mielle like she was in on what was happening to Steffen. Like they were doing this together. Like they were killing this man to save themselves—though this was impossible. If Jane knew that Steffen had been poisoned, then she must know that Mielle had tried to poison her as well. But Jane showed no indication of that. She sipped brandy as she folded the sheet back off the phonograph to flip through the records, rambling to herself the whole time. Steffen moaning on the sofa.

Mielle could see what was going to happen. They were going to let him die.

She rushed down the back stairs to the garden. Mielle felt the spirit inside her, and she hoped as hard as she could that Steffen dying might satisfy the vision that haunted her. It was one thing for Nilo Steffen to drink the poison, but another if the vision demanded more. Mielle prayed to God that it was over, that she wouldn't have to kill Jane.

She waited for her second sight to come back to her, gazing up into the foggy sky as she stood in the garden. But she saw nothing. Her eyes didn't ache. Nothing stabbed her stomach. Her second sight said nothing.

In that silence, Mielle thought of running. She could have limped into the night and left Jane with the mess. Alden had told her that one pill would kill a man and make it look like a heart attack. But what if a person took two? What if he foamed at the mouth and had a hole burned in his stomach? Still, with her legs, she couldn't run far, not if the Germans suspected her of murdering an officer. Running would be the worst thing to do in that case. It was too late to turn back.

There was hardly anything growing in the garden that early in the season. Mielle fell to her knees in the muck of black leaves to look for shoots of chives, some baby sprigs of mint, some horehound or valerian. It could be anything. Edelweiss and crocus would do. The bright yellow flowers of forsythia. She didn't need the mixture to work, of course. Mielle muddied the knees of her trousers, her hands full of various herbs and shoots.

She had gone this far with murder—the very worst thing, she had always been told that to take a life was the worst thing one could ever do—but the earth didn't open up and swallow her. No lightning bolt shot from the dark foggy sky to strike her down as she rose to her feet in the garden. The only ones who could object were the ghosts, and they were on her side. And Jane, of course. Jane was the wild card.

Mielle had to keep Jane drinking and talking all night so that she wouldn't notice what was happening to Steffen. Upstairs, Mielle heard a jazz record playing.

Jane sat cross-legged on the floor, leaning forward to roll cigarettes, across from the sofa. Steffen lay with his back to her.

"Some party this turned out to be. He's asleep," Jane said. She didn't look at Mielle but at Steffen.

His back swelled with shallow breaths. He hardly breathed at all.

"What do I do with these?" Mielle held up the shoots she'd picked.

Jane looked over, swaying.

"Oh, the medicine. Put that on the bar. If he wakes up, we'll make him a potion." Jane turned back to Steffen. "Look at him. Asleep like a baby."

Jane was more her old self in her black kimono. She almost resembled the Jane whom Mielle had met in Paris four years before. Jane got up from the floor and sat down on the other couch, sliding her legs underneath her, a highball in one hand and a cigarette in the other. Her hair was shorter now, and curled, the color dull. She had put on weight. From all appearances, she was in distress. But the look in her eyes, the energy she gave off, Mielle recognized her. Jane was not so broken that she didn't still lust after chaos.

"Can I confess a little something to you?" Jane asked. Mielle sat next to her on the sofa. They began to drink from the same glass. Mielle turned the glass to put her lips on the same spot where Jane's lipstick had smudged the rim. "All things considered, I'm glad they didn't send me back to Spain. Is that stupid of me? Oh, I know we're in danger. If it weren't for Steffen, the Germans would have me in a concentration camp, and who knows what happens if the Russians break through to get their hands on me. But after all that I went through in Madrid, just to be banished out on a farm with Eduardo. How horrible would that be? How horrible?"

"You make more sense in the middle of a war. That's what I think." Mielle handed back the brandy.

"I know you're humoring me. But *don't* I? There's nowhere else in the world where I belong except in the middle of a big, fiery fight."

Jane turned and looked Mielle over, from her face to her lap and back, as if Jane had never seen Mielle before with her mussy hair, with her butcher's jacket pooled underneath her bent legs.

"But you, you're very different from me. You make more sense on a farm, don't you? You are a strange creature in a city." Jane laughed long and hard. "Like when I met you in Paris. A strange creature, Mielle. Out in Iowa, I bet you made more sense."

"I was different, if that's what you mean. They didn't really like me either. I was a stranger there too. But I liked the farm. I would have stayed there forever if I could have."

Jane slid back to the armrest to stare into Mielle's eyes. "I don't believe that for a second. Nobody accidentally ends up moving from Kalona, Iowa, to Paris, France."

"But it's true," Mielle objected.

Steffen gagged on the other sofa. Like he choked on his tongue. Sweat poured off his head. His back hardly rose at all except when he gagged.

Jane didn't notice. Her eyes drifted shut. The edges of her robe fell open. She pulled her legs up to the cushion and showed how dirty the bottoms of her feet were.

Mielle kept talking to distract Jane. She went across the room to fetch a bowl of warm water and a towel from the bar.

"Lie back and close your eyes," she told Jane. "You never take care of your feet, but you must. It's important."

It was thinking of Iowa again that made Mielle get the water and some soap to wash Jane's feet like she had in Paris. In the assembly where she grew up, they washed the feet of strangers who were traveling through. A traveler's feet were always in shambles. Swollen, dirty, bloody, wet. It was an act of charity to wash a stranger's feet.

"My father was the one who said I had to leave the assembly. That's the truth. I wasn't shunned by law until after I left for college, but, first, my father said I had to go. It was his wish."

"How awful," Jane said, the slow drawl back in her voice. "To be banned from a dinky farm, of all places. Why did he do it?"

Jane reached down and put her hand on Mielle's shoulder as Mielle washed her feet. Her eyes stayed closed; she breathed deeper through her nose.

"There was a man who caused trouble. A traveler."

Mielle couldn't believe she was saying this. She had never told anyone why she'd left the farm. Not when she was in college. Not

Alden. But the words were coming and she didn't try to stop. She wanted to tell someone. She had Jane's attention. Jane was listening, her eyes heavy-lidded.

Mielle filled the glass halfway with brandy and passed it back to Jane.

"Was he a young man? A wanderer?" Jane asked. Inside her robe, Jane's chest was blotched red. Her color was coming up. "There was a boy like that for me. Mine was eighteen and I was fourteen. If he wasn't Mexican, Pop might have let us get married. Instead, they kicked me out of school for depravity. Pop would have killed the boy if he'd married me."

"My story is nothing like that. He was thirty. I was sixteen. His name was Joubert. Mennonites used to all be wanderers, exiles. That's how anyone ends up in Iowa. The restless ones leave where they're from and start somewhere new. But it's hard to tell the difference between a good one and a bad one. Joubert had lived in Ohio and Indiana before he looked around Iowa. He knew how to help with the kind of work we did, so he stayed with us. My father was a butcher."

"A butcher? No wonder we are the kind of women we are. Both our fathers were butchers and murderers. Yours with a knife. Mine with a six-shooter."

Mielle kept talking. The sound of her hands rippling in the warm water soothed her. There was something noble in the stillness of the room. It was a strange peace. A disordered splendor. Her hands on Jane's feet. Steffen had stopped breathing.

"Joubert raped me. In the milking barn. That kind of thing, on a farm, you don't talk about it in an assembly, but it happens a lot. It was stupid of me to get caught alone in a barn with a man. I knew it would happen—I had seen it very clearly for months, even before Joubert arrived—but I didn't do nothing to stop it. If a girl tells an elder that she broke the rule about being alone with a man, more likely than not, they make *her* leave. Even the idea of a girl being alone with a man is enough. They say *she* tempted the man who raped her, that he was helpless against temptation."

"Yes. That's how they did it in Arizona too. In Texas. In Georgia. In London. In Spain."

"Things like that were never a problem for me. The men in our assembly were scared of me. I had the second sight. I saw things, then what I saw came true. That's how I knew the stranger would come for me. I didn't know then how dangerous it is to ignore my second sight. I told nobody what my vision told me. Not Mammi or Daadi. They could have helped, but before I said a word to them, he got me alone."

Jane had closed her eyes. Jane didn't flinch when Mielle said she had visions.

"Father walked in the second time Joubert trapped me in the barn. That's why I had to leave, after that."

Mielle told how it happened. The stranger on her back when her father grabbed him by the shoulder and held a knife to his throat. Her father in his butcher's coat, in the apron he wore that held his knives to his chest. The knives sharp as razors. Joubert stumbled back, smiling, in shock.

Then, as he had done countless times before, as was his custom when he slaughtered an animal, Mielle's father ordered her out of the barn before the cutting was done.

Mielle's father took care of the stranger with his butcher tools, then sank the meat into a privy. When anyone asked about him, the next week, they said that Joubert had moved on. The lie was accepted. That's how the commune worked. They weren't allowed to care about anyone except those who lived in their assembly. What happened outside those border lines might as well have happened in Shanghai, on Mars, in Hades. The only thing that mattered was what went on between a Mennonite, her family, and God.

"My parents wept the whole night. Father had committed the

worst sin, the only thing God could not forgive. To judge another man for his acts, when it is only God who can judge. He gave up his own soul to stop what Joubert was doing to me. He shouldn't have done it. Not for me, not for anyone. Do you understand?" she asked. "Do you see why I had no choice but to leave?"

The next day, her mother went to Kalona to see if the librarian could arrange for Mielle to go to college somewhere. The librarian could and did. Mielle was a gifted child. She was in dire straits. It wasn't so hard to find her a spot.

Mielle could have refused to leave. She could have tried to explain things to the deacons, but it wouldn't have made a difference. Telling the deacons would have only made things worse.

So maybe it was an accident that Mielle ended up in Paris, and maybe it wasn't. There was a chain of coincidences and reactions. Mielle had the capacity to succeed after she left, and she wanted to get as far away from Iowa as she could. She could never go home to where her family lived, where, still, the butchered body of a traveler named Joubert rotted in a latrine.

Mielle felt like that was too much to share, but she couldn't stop once she got going. There was too much at stake. She had to tell Jane everything.

"I saw something about me and you. Something very bad." Mielle swallowed hard. "Three years ago I saw that I will put a blade against your heart. I keep seeing it. It won't leave me alone."

Mielle twisted away as she spoke to look out the window into the foggy night, suddenly embarrassed after all that. It was quiet on the other side of the sofa. Jane had no response.

There was no noise at all from the other sofa. Steffen hadn't moved the whole time.

Mielle turned to look at Jane, but Jane had passed out, her neck curved over the top of the sofa, her mouth agape. Then Jane breathed deeply, gasping, as she began to snore.

Mielle didn't know how much Jane had heard of her

confession. It had taken a lot for her to say those words, to admit in her own mind that she had taken part in killing a man. When she thought of this, when she looked across the room and saw Steffen's body lying there, Mielle felt herself harden inside. She thought it was better that Jane didn't hear her confession. Mielle doubted it would make a difference. So much had conspired to bring her to this point that she believed she would never escape her vision. She had killed once. There was already that mark on her soul. What was there to stop it from happening again?

She stood and walked across the floor to the bedroom. There was only the one bed. She took it.

She couldn't sleep all night, but she lay there in the sound of Jane's soft snoring from the other room. She could have taken Steffen's pistol and killed Jane then too, and it wouldn't have changed the mark on her soul. But she hoped that she was done with killing, that the vision had been satisfied.

She prayed for hours, on her back, staring at the ceiling.

She asked for forgiveness.

She asked that all this struggle would end with the death of Nilo Steffen, that she never again be cursed with a vision like the one that prophesized she would kill Jane.

She asked, over and over, that she would finally be free of her darker instincts. That old Mennonite dream, that she could be left alone to be happy without having to hold another person's face in the mud to get what she wanted. So she prayed.

ONLY AN ANIMAL

The fog lifted by morning. Mielle opened her eyes to sunlight flooding the bedroom. She crawled across the room to look out the window. There wasn't a cloud in the sky. The sky was a perfect blue.

"Call a doctor," Jane shouted.

Mielle didn't move from the window. Mielle scarcely breathed herself, waiting, that moment.

She heard Jane slapping Steffen; Jane saying, "Nilo...Nilo." Then, as Mielle stood in the doorway, "What's the use? He's already cold."

Mielle was the one who went to find the caretaker in his office and ask him to phone a doctor. The caretaker was a short old man with glasses, a big nose, and a full head of dark curly hair. He looked like an eccentric, especially in Nazi Germany. After three months in this country, Mielle didn't believe there still existed men who smoked all day in small rooms while letting their hair grow long. This man was apparently an archivist, a sort that always was good at hiding themselves away. Boxes of papers and stacks of old books cluttered his office.

"Did you say doctor?" he asked. "Or police? He is dead. That's what you said."

"Only doctor," Mielle replied as calm as she could manage. "Isn't that the right way? Wouldn't the Polizei only make trouble for all of us? My friend, the lady upstairs, she is already very distressed. Inviting the Gestapo..." Mielle shook her head slowly. "Who needs that?"

The caretaker looked even more thoughtful, glancing around

at his dozens of crates and folders and notebooks. It wouldn't do, he seemed to think, to have to sort all those boxes again if the Gestapo upturned them.

"I will call the SS office," he said, "and have them send a staff doctor. That is all."

The doctor came in his own car, a red cabriolet roadster, followed by two female orderlies in an ambulance. He was a very old man, much older than even the caretaker. (It was something Mielle noticed. All the German pensioners had been pulled out of retirement to fill in for the missing men.) The doctor was short and stooped, wore a white coat, carried a black bag that rattled with his instruments as he waddled up the stairs. The two young women slicked back their hair and wore white slacks and white shirts, like they were milkmen. The doctor had them lug Steffen's stiff body to the bed, where the doctor examined him. He checked under each eyelid, under the tongue, down the throat. Lifted the hands to see the cuticles up close. Undid the trousers to peek below the waistband. Took off the shoes and socks to see the soles of the feet. Took the body's temperature.

Then that was all. The doctor said nothing. He went to the window and stared across the courtyard at the palace. He lit a cigarette, smoked it slowly while staring out the window, then lit another.

Mielle stood in the doorway next to Jane. They'd been with Steffen's body for over an hour by then (Mielle had known all night, of course), and it was hard to remember that he was alive just twelve hours before. The body was stiff and gray, his mouth stuck in a rictus after the doctor forced open his jaw. Mielle had seen so many animals die—saw them bled and disemboweled and dissected into edible bits—that she could convince herself that Nilo Steffen was only an animal, and that all animals eventually die and are dissected.

Jane shook as she smoked a cigarette to the nub before snuffing it out under her slipper. She still wore her black kimono. How strange it would have been if she'd changed into her Red Cross costume, only to stand by chain-smoking, helpless. Though that's all the doctor was doing at that moment.

"So what is it?" Jane finally asked. "What's the verdict?"

The doctor shrugged. "A sudden lack of oxygen, but his heart stopped first."

"A heart attack?"

"Ja. Very simply."

"We were boozing," Jane admitted. She paced along the length of the bed, her fingertips skimming over the black wool of Steffen's rumpled uniform. "Do you believe that's what did it? Something he drank?"

Mielle had to grab the doorframe so she didn't jump. *"Oh, deevil!"* The words erupted from her throat.

They turned to her. "Miss?"

"He had two drinks at once. Strong cocktails. That's when he got sick."

"That will do it." The doctor turned back to the window, his face ivory white in the reflection of the white palace. "A heart attack. That's all."

He produced a death certificate from his leather bag and signed it. *Heart failure* was given as the cause of death. He stood by the window another fifteen minutes to fill out the form, then left. The orderlies put the body on a board and carried it down to their wagon.

The oddity of this put Jane in an even worse state. The explanation was too simple.

"How strange this is! Do you think he could have been poisoned?"

"No," Mielle said. "Absolutely not."

"Sure he could have!" Jane dropped the kimono from her shoulders and rifled through her bags naked. "Communists on the train! A porter! That caretaker downstairs. Doesn't he look eccentric to you?"

"No," Mielle lied. "He looks normal."

"What if that caretaker poisoned the glasses before we came up here?"

"But we drank out of them too," Mielle reminded her. "And we're fine, aren't we?"

Jane stretched her Red Cross smock over her head in one piece and straightened the skirt over her hips. She didn't look well. Her skin sagged under her eyes. The strain of the past few days had not been good for her.

A familiar feeling returned to Mielle in that moment. Steffen's dying had not made it go away after all. Mielle felt sick to her stomach, her eyes began to ache at the first rumbling of that vision in her mind—her holding a blade, and at the other end of the blade, Jane.

Jane walked across the room because Mielle was crying. Mielle didn't even realize she was crying until Jane brushed away the tears with her fingers.

"You are bad luck for me." Jane kissed Mielle on the forehead. "So much trouble finds us when we're together."

"It does."

"And will it get better?"

"It will not."

"Or will it get worse?"

"It will get worse. I have seen it."

If it weren't for Steffen having a close friend in the Gestapo, his death certificate wouldn't have been questioned. But Steffen was supposed to meet with an inspector named Alfons Klaas that morning. Inspector Klaas knew that his old friend was traveling with two American women, and he wasn't going to let that drop.

A message came for them before lunch, not even an hour after the doctor left. Jane and Mielle must present themselves for an interview that afternoon at Hotel Silber, headquarters of the Gestapo in Stuttgart.

HOTEL SILBER

A car collected them at Solitude after lunch and drove them down through the dormant vineyards into the Cauldron of the city.

Hotel Silber was at nos. 2–4 Dorotheenstrasse. The locals still called it a hotel, though for the thirty years prior, its five floors housed police headquarters. Now the Gestapo had taken it. Mielle thought Silber was a strange building as she and Jane hesitated on the front steps. It stretched an entire city block but was only two rooms wide with an endless, straight hallway cut through its middle. At the end was a tapered terra-cotta facade that added another forty feet in height, with pennant-bearing cupolas and belfries popping up every six windows to add to the illusion. All the buildings were majestic behind the Württembergisch palaces on this wide airy avenue that was blocked on the end by Altes Schloss, the old medieval fortress, and then the sprawling new castle that opened up on the grand imperial square. Dorotheenstrasse had been the bureaucratic back room for the old monarchy. Across the street on one side was the Foreign Institute. On the other was the Interior Ministry. You couldn't move ten feet without a red flag hanging over your head.

Mielle would have been inclined to like the place if she were visiting under different circumstances. These glimpses into Old Europe, the medieval touches to the buildings. The chestnut trees. The audacity, the sense of purpose. Though all that represented something so different the past decade.

Inside Hotel Silber, to the left, was a restaurant, but a dour woman at the reception desk told them to go straight to the fourth floor. Mielle took a deep breath, gathered herself, and climbed the central staircase next to Jane.

In the car, Jane had told Mielle what to expect, the two of them conspiring in the back seat. This was far from the first time Jane had been brought in by police. It had happened all over the front when she covered the First War. It had happened many times in Paris. There was Madrid. "Only admit to the most basic facts," Jane had said. "Generally, cops know next to nothing. Don't make it worse for yourself by volunteering new information." She spoke soft so the driver didn't hear. "We didn't do anything, and we will stick together. Keep telling yourself these two things. We didn't do anything. We will stick together. Two orphans like us, we only have each other."

When they reached the second floor, the idea of a hotel turned headquarters for the political police began to make sense to Mielle. Those endless halls of cramped rooms were perfect for the interrogations the Gestapo used to keep tabs on local citizens. They kept climbing. The third floor was where the Gestapo administered the Nazis' foreign-worker operation, those millions of enslaved Poles and Russians who kept German factories humming while the Germans focused on war.

The entire fourth floor was devoted to the Department for Espionage, Sabotage, and Defense. Counterintelligence. Foreign spies.

A man in a black suit waited for them at the landing. Mielle and Jane startled when they saw him. They glanced at each other to check if they both saw the same thing. The man looked like an exact double of Nilo Steffen, except this man had blond stubble on his jaw and skull, and he wore a double-breasted suit instead of an SS uniform. He had that same stalking heft, the long arms and short legs. The prominent Roman nose and square jaw. It could have been Nilo Steffen standing before them, except they had just spent that morning with his corpse.

"I am Alfons Klaas," the man said. Then: "This way, come," because the two women had frozen stiff on the stairs in disbelief.

Jane and Mielle whispered as they followed Inspector Klaas down the hall.

"Nilo said they grew up together. They were close."

"But friends, right? Not brothers."

Inspector Klaas led them to a corner room. He told them to sit, then left the door open and settled at the small table across from them.

Up close, the resemblance held. The blue eyes, that suspicious German way. Alfons Klaas had studied law with Steffen in Karlsruhe, then used his status as a party member to rise fast in the state police. The Gestapo was largely composed of young lawyers and statisticians. There was a lot of money to be made under the Nazi regime for those in logistics, accounting, human resources. After the war, very few of them would admit to being true believers; they were just functionaries. But what did it matter if they were real wolves or just pretending to be wolves?

"Tell me what you are doing in Stuttgart."

"Nilo Steffen brought us here," Jane said. "In fact, he was here to meet you."

"But your papers…my understanding is that you are supposed to stay in Berlin and environs. For the radio."

"I'm on leave from the radio."

"And her?"

"She was never hired." With her eyes, Jane told Mielle to stay quiet. "And if you look again at our papers, you will see we are permitted to travel south for the next four weeks. The ministry is, I believe, intending to resettle me in Austria. We are attached, with express permission from Dr. Goebbels…that is, we *were* attached to Nilo Steffen for the duration."

"But Nilo Steffen has been killed." Klaas looked amused by all this. He pulled on his sleeves to straighten his suit jacket. "So you are attached to a dead man, yes? That is a not so good situation for you."

This was an ordinary sort of room, with some resemblance to a hotel room. The tall windows and pert rectangular shape of the room with a cutout where a high-backed velvet chair could have once perched. But the energy was changed by then. The smell of sweat and urine and testosterone. Dozens of deep gouges in the floor where the desk had been dragged from one end to the other. The walls were yellowed, the plaster dented and scuffed and smoke-stained. There was sadness in every corner.

"Herr Klaas, you are correct," Jane said. "No doubt about that. A smart man like you. But the papers are still valid for both of us, regardless of whether Nilo is alive or if he expired. Nilo did not sign the passes. Herr Doktor Goebbels did. So, Herr Klaas, what we require is not new passes but rather a new oberst to show us the way south."

The look of amusement vanished from Klaas's face. "Nilo was a dear friend," he said.

"My condolences." Jane inched forward on her seat. "He was my friend too."

Jane reached her hands across the table. Klaas pulled away like the gesture sickened him.

"How did he die?" Klaas asked. "Tell me the details. Step by step."

"We traveled all day by train. He was aggravated the whole time. Prone to argument. We settled in at Solitude, up in the hills, and had a few drinks. Nilo, the silly fool, boozed heavily. He drank too much and fell ill. The doctor said it was a heart attack. I'm inclined to agree."

"What did you argue about?"

"I don't remember."

"Come, Frau Cienfuegos. I am not a fool."

Klaas shifted his gaze to Mielle, and his eyes crossing over her body tripped something inside that made her speak.

"It was the war," she said, rising halfway from her seat. Her voice cracked, sounded reedy. Jane slid a hand onto Mielle's lap to push her back into her seat, but she was too late. Klaas motioned for Mielle to go on.

"Herr Oberst Steffen claimed the war would be over before Christmas for certain. But Jane disagreed."

"She did?"

"Yes. Jane insisted that it wouldn't last even that long. It would be over by All Saints' Day."

"All Saints'?"

"Yes," Mielle told him. "That's in November."

Klaas snorted. "Is that correct, Frau Cienfuegos?"

"Yeah, of course. November first, every year."

Somehow Jane kept a straight face. She looked like she was enjoying this.

"Who made the drinks?" Klaas asked. "You two were alone with Nilo in the room when he died. Who mixed the drinks?"

"I don't remember," Jane said. Then: "We all made some, didn't we?"

"That's right," Mielle said. "We turned it into a competition to see who could make the best one."

"Do you think," Jane asked, "that he got some bad liquor? That the bottles had been poisoned before we arrived? That thought occurred to me this morning. It could be. We only drank what we found in the room. That is not typically my custom. We were making do—"

"My belief," Klaas cut in, "is that Nilo did not drop dead. A man of his stock does not simply die. There must be something that killed him. Then, ergo, someone."

"And the doctor disagrees, yes?"

"The corpse is being examined again by a Gestapo doctor as we speak. A chemical analysis of his blood will tell the tale. That is my belief."

That was the last thing Mielle wanted to hear. She had to focus to keep from shaking.

"Nilo took all sorts of chemicals. That analysis will tell a lot of tales." Jane laughed, but Mielle noticed Jane's legs, they too were shaking. "Pervitin, all sorts of hormones. Nicotine, alcohol. There's always cocaine in Berlin. You know that, I'm sure. It's something of a Berliner tradition. Jelly doughnuts and cocaine!"

Klaas held up a hand to stop her.

"Would you stand and follow me," he said. "Come. This way."

"Both of us?" Jane asked.

"Of course."

Klaas stood and ushered them with an open palm to the hall, Jane first. But once Jane was through the door, Klaas stepped between the women and put his hand against Mielle's chest.

"Not you, fräulein. Go sits."

He followed Jane, then closed the door behind them.

Mielle was alone. She had no idea what to do. She sat in the chair, as Klaas had told her, but then she stood, paced to the windows, then to the door. Jane had said the most important thing was to stick together. Klaas had tricked them.

At the door Mielle could hear Jane object to something vociferously, in her way, but the voices of several other men in addition to Klaas's talked over her. It wasn't often that anyone could shout over Jane Anderson. But the Nazis had battered her for weeks in Berlin. Through the door, Mielle could tell Jane was ceding ground. They all went quiet. Then the bunch of footfalls led her away.

Mielle jumped when she heard a hand turn the doorknob. She rushed back to the chair so she was sitting, waiting, when Klaas came in and locked the door behind him.

He looked at her with perverse appetite. He must have seen her as the weak one.

She gripped the wooden seat of her chair with both hands to stop shaking. She was scared. Her legs were numb. She felt locked inside her fragile body, vulnerable to any kind of torment. That her life would end in a small room like this one had felt inevitable, from the moment she decided to stay in Paris during the invasion, then the Occupation; from the moment she left Bad Nauheim for Berlin. She'd had that vision, that idea she could be an assassin. But this was the most likely outcome all along, wasn't it? She would push her luck too far. A cannibal Nazi would see her weakness, lock her up, eliminate her. This was always her most likely fate.

"Who are your friends here in Germany?"

"I don't have any friends in Germany. Only Jane."

"You must now talk," Klaas said. "Do you realize that? There is nobody to protect you. Nobody can save you from this room. Not your government. Not your newspaper. Not Jane. No one. We can do anything we want. You will never leave. Do you understand?"

Mielle said she understood very well.

"Who do you know in Germany?"

"Nobody," she said again. It was the truth. She tried doing as Jane had instructed in the car—to tell herself that she'd done nothing wrong. *We didn't do anything.* In her thoughts. *We didn't do anything.* But Mielle knew this wasn't true. She had killed Nilo Steffen. That was the truth.

"Do you think I did it?" she asked. She was shaking so hard, she couldn't control her mouth. She kept talking. "Am I under arrest?"

His lips curled inward into something like a grin. Klaas waited a moment to let her tremble, then he opened a drawer, said, "Arms at your side. Sits still."

He handcuffed her, then connected the handcuffs to two iron rings that were screwed to the floor, moving deliberately to make sure she was held tight to her seat. He took two short pieces of rope from the desk drawer and tied her ankles to the legs of the chair so she couldn't move at all.

Klaas asked again who her friends were in Germany, who she had spoken to, who had told her to travel to Berlin. A string of names came from her mouth: William Joyce, Toni Winkelnkemper, Eduardo de Cienfuegos, Eddie Haffell, Alden Linden Elder. Inspector Klaas looked bored. Told her to go on. "Wer sonst? Who else?" So she did. She was so terrified she couldn't help herself. Fred Kaltenbach, Bob Best, Louis Lochner, Joseph Goebbels, Emil Jannings.

At the name Jannings, Klaas smacked her across the face. It was the first time Mielle had been smacked since she was a little girl. It felt the same as it had then: like she would die.

"Are you going to tell me the truth? Who are your friends? What Germans have you met?"

"I met Emil Jannings at the Adlon Hotel," she explained. "I'm not lying."

Klaas closed his hand into a fist and punched her in the jaw.

He said again that Nilo Steffen was his friend. "So I am going to get to the bottom of this."

"It was a heart attack. The doctor said so."

"I don't believe it. Not Steffen. Not a brother officer."

Klaas looked deranged. He couldn't control the shape of his eyes, his mouth. His hands rubbed the inside of his thighs.

"How did she do it?"

"Who are you talking about?"

"The old bitch! The other American. Anderson."

"His heart—"

"Don't lie to me!" He slapped her across the face once, three times, until her head snapped down. She slumped into herself.

Klaas forced her to look up. His face right next to hers.

"Tell me. How did Anderson do it? Did she slip something into his drink?"

"She didn't," Mielle said. His breath was sour in her mouth. His hand inched up her calf to between her knees. "It was me," she admitted. She was so scared, the words just came out of her. "I did it."

She could barely speak. If he pushed his hand farther, she would die.

"Look at you. Your knees are shaking." He put his hands on her kneecaps, one on each. "I don't believe it was you. You are not capable of killing a man like Nilo. Tell me the truth. Or you will never leave this room."

"It was me," she whispered. "Me."

Klaas looked like he wanted to kill her. He could have done anything to her and would have been within his rights, because she had none. She was crying, her face swollen, her lips bleeding. His hands were on her.

But Mielle wouldn't die in that room. She looked into herself to see the future—if she had a future—and what she saw was herself holding a blade. Not Klaas, not anyone else. Just Mielle.

"No more lies," Klaas said. His lips touched her ear. "It was that woman who did it. She has been plotting this from the start."

"No. It was me."

"Nilo told me about her. Jane. He loved her, the pig, but he didn't trust her."

Klaas stood then, wiped his fingers with a handkerchief, straightened his clothes, and left the room without another word.

ONE STEP, THEN ANOTHER

Mielle stayed bound to the chair another hour. Every so often she heard footsteps in the hall, clapping wingtips that stopped outside the door. But then the person turned and walked away.

She cried and wished she were still in Iowa. Then she could have lived and let live. What did it matter that she killed one Nazi? What would it matter if she could kill two or twenty or two hundred, if she had to give up her own life in exchange? If she had stayed on the farm, if she'd never let herself get trapped by the stranger in the barn in the first place, then she wouldn't have ended up here.

She stopped crying by the time the footsteps returned and the door was opened. It wasn't Klaas but a guard in a blue wool uniform who untied her from the chair.

"Get up," he said. She tried but couldn't. Her legs had seized. "Geh!"

"Wait! Stop that!" Jane rushed into the room. "What is it, Mielle? Your legs?"

Jane was panicked. Her eyes searched Mielle's face, darted from Mielle's swollen lips and eyes to where the handcuffs had rubbed her wrists raw.

Jane whispered in Mielle's ear, her green eyes big and imploring. "We can go. But only if you stand up. So take a breath. Yes? You must do this. Take a breath and walk without limping."

Mielle let Jane take her by the hand and lift her. They moved slow into the hall.

"Eduardo is coming. He's flying back from Madrid. That's very good," Jane kept whispering. "If Eduardo is with us, they

297

can't kill us. He's Spanish royalty, a dignitary. That protects all of us." They made it to the stairs and were inching down. "We can't leave the city until Nilo's autopsy is done. Apparently they think we weren't friends with Nilo." Jane raised her voice so everyone on the stairway could hear. "We were all good friends. Nilo was my pal. Everyone in Berlin will say the same, and this sham will end."

Murky light bathed the city when they stepped outside. The sun was behind the government buildings. They'd been inside longer than Mielle thought.

They went slow down the steps, heads bowed to make sure their feet stayed under them. Jane whispered in Mielle's ear the whole time, her words the only thing keeping them upright.

"One step, then another. Eduardo is coming. He has powerful friends. El Jefe. That's what he will tell the Germans. *El Jefe says no!*"

They stopped at the curb to look for the car, but there was no car, only the large Old Castle at the end of the street with its dark turrets. Jane's face contorted. She asked, "Where's the driver?"

Mielle noticed before Jane did. Fifteen feet behind them, on the steps of Hotel Silber, Alfons Klaas stood watching. He stared at them, expressionless.

Mielle nudged Jane so she saw him.

"Well, yeah." Jane turned back to the street. "No car is coming. Have you got any money for a taxi? Never mind."

Jane dragged Mielle around the corner. In another two blocks, the avenue opened up to a busy square where the mass of people swept them along with the current. This was Marktplatz. Once Jane saw gigantic City Hall, she knew where they were. "Turn, turn. This way." Mielle had never been here before. She had no idea where she was.

They huddled on a corner across from City Hall. They should keep walking, but it wasn't that easy. Mielle wanted to crumple to the pavement. And in what direction should they go? All those medieval spires and granary towers on the buildings were giving Mielle the creeps. That massive Rathaus with its stained glass and slate shingles, the big clock in its tower the only thing that didn't make it look like a cathedral.

Behind them, Klaas followed. Mielle didn't care. She was out of that building, that room, that chair. This was all that mattered. Let him follow.

"I didn't want to tell you when we were inside. We must go back in the morning," Jane said.

Mielle shook her head no, violently. "I won't. They can shoot me in the street first."

"Don't be dramatic, honey. If you say things like that, those Nazis will take you up on the offer." Jane slipped her arm farther under Mielle's shoulders to help her walk faster. "God, look at what they did to you."

People rushed everywhere and there were few taxis. Mielle and Jane were too slow to grab one. It unnerved her to be among so many ordinary people, in their suits and skirts, who were worried only about hailing a cab to get home for dinner, while two feet away she was being pursued. Her blood was still wet on her lips. Mielle felt naked every time she and Jane lunged to a curb only to have the car pull away.

Klaas kept his distance, following behind in the same half-steps as Mielle and Jane.

Mielle would have tried to run if she could, but her legs were weak. The whole city swayed and swirled. People jumped out of doorways and rushed to the streetcar.

"I want to go to Nauheim," Mielle said.

"That's impossible." Jane tried to explain. If they ran, they'd look guilty. If they looked guilty, they were as good as dead.

"We must stick together. That's our best chance to make it out of a jam like this. Eduardo is coming. We have friends in Madrid.

Trust me. We will wrap ourselves in the Spanish flag, and the Gestapo will get bored with us after a few days, a week. We won't be worth the trouble."

"If we got a car. We could drive to Nauheim tonight."

"No, Mielle. Trust me. I've squeezed out of tighter spots than this."

Mielle noticed how much Jane's hands shook. There was a spot on her cheek that had started to bruise.

Over Jane's shoulder, Mielle again saw Klaas stalking them. He waited to see if a car got them or if they ducked into a building. He wanted to discover who they were working with, who they had conspired with, but he was wrong. There was no one. Only Jane and Mielle.

Jane breathed too hard, her chest rising and rising to bursting. They had to stop or the both of them were going to collapse in the street.

"Hotel Silber. That's what Madrid was like." Jane was rambling. Her face lit up, her eyes and mouth stretched open to shout. "The Rojos always came at five in the morning to wake you up. Don't answer your door before sunrise, that's what people said, but how can you not? God. That, today, that's *just* what it was like when they took me in Madrid. The Reds say to not bring nothing when they take you. *Don't pack a bag, you will be home for lunch.* But once they have you, you can see it in their eyes, they will never let you go. You will never be free again. Even if your body escapes, they keep your soul."

A cold breeze passed over them, one that grew into a gust and blew their hair to the other sides of their heads.

Mielle noticed the ripples of chaos before she heard the motors roaring. Air wardens ran by them in the street, blowing whistles. Then the sirens. Then, from far away, Mielle could hear them. Bombers.

THE SWORD

The big flak guns roared on the other side of the castles.

All at once, cars disappeared from the square. Air-raid wardens rushed everywhere with their whistles to corral panicked stragglers toward a shelter. The sirens wailing. Mielle saw two dozen four-engine airplanes at first, their wings marked by yellow and blue circles with a red dot in the middle of the insignia. But then there were more and more. A whole swarm. One hundred twenty-one RAF bombers were coming.

Mielle and Jane stood, shocked. What were they supposed to do? They were damaged. They were being followed. Smack in front of City Hall was a bad place to freeze, but they froze.

"Damen, Damen." One of the wardens tried to usher them along, but Jane shrugged her off. That awakened something in Jane. They needed a safe spot—but Jane would go mad in a shelter. She took off, the sound of her heels adding to the cacophony. The matron chased her a few steps, blew her whistle in protest, then gave up. She wouldn't bother with one crazy woman. So Mielle ran past her too. The matron wouldn't bother with two crazy women when there were all the city workers to save.

Mielle's legs were stiff and weak, but she willed herself to chase Jane. Around the corner off Marktplatz to Bärenstrasse. Jane's hair bounced off her shoulders to reveal her neck. She ran blind to get away, turning at every corner.

Mielle looked behind her for Klaas, but he had vanished.

They ran to Kirchstrasse below the towering steeple of the Stiftskirche cathedral. Under the sirens, the church bells tolled. Mielle could almost reach Jane. Both of them running. The twin thumps of the 8,8 flak guns drumming off the buildings like the heartbeat of a Titan.

To Schillerplatz, where stood a massive green statue of Schiller in a long robe with a laurel wreath on his head, where Mielle reached out to grab Jane and spun her by an elbow.

Jane still ranted.

"Every day they tell you it is execution day. They put twenty of you out in the square. When the rifles fire, you don't know. You don't know! Not until the woman next to you drops. Every day they will tell you: Today, it is execution day."

From the square Mielle could see down Dorotheenstrasse and, at the end of the block, Hotel Silber. Jane was leading her in circles.

Mielle put Jane's arm over her own shoulder and carried her to the only way inside the Old Castle, its open iron gates. All that stone and its towering granaries made the fortress look insuperable—except the courtyard was open to the sky. She could see the bombers circling. The hammering engines, the drumming eight-comma-eights. The orchestra at full swell. All of it to terrorize you. To make your heart thump so hard it might burst.

Dozens of old oak and iron doors spread out under the arches of the courtyard. "If this door doesn't open..." she said, trailing off. And it didn't. She carried on to the next one. It didn't open either. None of these doors would be unlocked—she knew that—but she had to try. She had to find a place for Jane to sit down, to hide.

The whole time, running, she couldn't see Alfons Klaas following them, but suddenly she heard his shoes slapping the cobblestones behind her, back around the corner. When they ran, he followed like a dog. Mielle had to keep trying doors. A third, a fourth.

The planes circled lower and lower, flames erupting from the wings of one. The planes dived with a terrible shriek to drop their whistling cargo. Then the sound of the bombing melted and molded together like a thunderstorm.

When Mielle tried the iron handle on the fourth, it turned. They burst through the door and collapsed inside.

The corridor was dark, but Mielle didn't care. She carried along Jane. Jane ranting, "Every day they will tell you! Today! It is execution day!" Still through the walls bled the *thump-thump* of the flak guns.

Mielle knew Klaas had followed them inside. She felt someone behind them in the corridor. So she started over again trying doors, dragging along Jane, until she found one that opened.

"In here," she cried. She couldn't hear her own voice, the swells of thunder were so loud.

The room was dark, but not completely dark like the corridor had been. This room had windows. It was a storage room. Full of wooden crates and furniture covered in white sheets.

She pulled Jane inside, then shut a metal bar across the door.

Mielle had to make Jane be quiet, but Jane was still ranting. Mielle put her hand over Jane's mouth. That only made her worse. Jane couldn't stand to be touched. She was desperate to get out of the room. She stood and tried to lift the bar from the door.

"What are you doing?" Mielle grabbed Jane by the wrists, pulled her away. "Be quiet!"

"I want to go!"

"If you open the door, he will kill us."

The bombs were landing closer.

Only a moment passed before Klaas found them. "You women!" He threw his whole body against the door. *"Open!"* The planks splintered and cracked. The hinges began to bend.

Mielle had to do something.

She saw glints of reflected bomb light that shone to her across the room. Sparks off gilded hilts and blades. The light came from the blade of a sword. She was certain.

She acted without thinking, without worry. This was meant

to happen. Her head hurt so much behind her eyes. All she wanted was to make the pain go away. All she wanted was to be free.

She let go of Jane's wrists and let the vision pull her across the room to where sabers hung from stiff leather knobs. She grabbed one by the hilt. In that instant, she heard, she saw, she smelled everything that was alive in the world. The light of the fires outside, the whistling bombs, the shape of the room, even herself, as if she stood at a distance to watch her body pull down a saber and let its point clang to the floor. She dragged the blade across the room.

Jane still ranted. "Every day they will tell you: *Today!*"

Jane stood and removed the bar from the door. She pulled the door open herself.

Klaas was there. He struck Jane across the face with the back of his hand, once, three times, until Jane collapsed to her knees.

The room flashed with strobe blasts from outside. The whistling filled Mielle's ears, the groaning of engines as the bombers climbed. She circled behind Klaas.

He didn't notice her. He stood over Jane, unsnapped the top of his holster, and drew his pistol. He shouted something, a sentence to condemn the woman, as he put the gun to Jane's head.

Mielle couldn't hear what he said. She was going to make her own pronouncement with the saber. He didn't count on her.

In a flash of light she pushed forward the blade.

Mielle saw Klaas in the reflection of Jane's eyes. The look of Jane's shock as a point ran through the officer's gut, then withdrew, then ran through his chest. Jane's mouth froze as Klaas dropped to the floor—the two women revealed to each other over the gasping heap of his body. Jane's eyes flashed green in the bomb light at Mielle holding the bloody saber.

"Mielle. My God. What have you done?"

Jane raised a hand for help. Her eyes searched Mielle's for a clue of what would happen next. Mielle still held the blade.

She took Jane's hand. With the other, she lifted the point of the saber and held it to Jane's chest.

"Mielle. My God, Mielle."

It was too late to stop. She only had to push. With the bombshells screaming, she closed her eyes to shove the blade in.

THE CAULDRON

She would never forget the instant before the two great flashes filled the world with white. She pushed forward. She had. Her arm extended to its length.

The white flashes were so bright, she couldn't even hear their detonations.

Some awesome power pulled her by her shoulders, as if by the back of her neck, and whipped her across the room. Then the world went silent, dark.

Part of the wall was gone when she opened her eyes. Then she could see, but she couldn't hear. The dust settled slowly. She looked down and saw her whole body covered gray with dust. She looked out and could see the evening sky darkened with black clouds of flak.

By some miracle she could stand. Whatever it was that pulled her by the scruff of her neck had saved her legs. She was in a corner of the room that didn't collapse.

All at once she came out of the fever—like she'd been shocked out of a drunken haze with a bucket of water. The gravity of what she'd done hit her.

She had to get out of there at once. Somehow, she had to get out of Germany.

She could walk. She couldn't hear, but she could see. So she stumbled forward, shouted deaf (*"Jane!"*) into the settling dust. *"Jane!"* But the room was empty. All the swords, the old furniture and artifacts, even Alfons Klaas's lifeless body, had been sucked out and strewn along the street. Mielle checked the other corners. She tried to lift the stone blocks that had been blown loose in the blast. But it was no use. Jane wasn't there.

Mielle gathered herself. She took a deep breath, turned her face away from Klaas, and limped away from the Old Castle. The upper rooms were on fire. The clouds of smoke burned orange a hundred feet into the sky.

Crowds of people streamed out of buildings, away from the fires, to the main treeless drag of Königstrasse. A web of streetcar wires hung limp over their heads. There were miles of broken glass. Dining sets and mattresses littered the streets where they had been sucked through windows whole by the vacuum of the explosions. Police stood outside damaged buildings to shout *"Raus!"* until everyone alive came out. A truck with a camera in the bed inched along to film a newsreel.

The people's faces were red, their mouths open to wail. Mielle couldn't hear their laments, just as she couldn't hear her own. Her mouth stretched open. Her jaw moved. She felt the strain in her throat, but couldn't hear her voice. *"Jane! Jane!"*

She wondered if she had done it. She had tried to push the blade in.

She moved in the crowd away from burning Mitte, away from the sword room in the Old Castle, away from Hotel Silber. All of them limping without shame over broken glass where the pavement had buckled in a flash of heat. Where chestnut trees stood amputated down to stumps.

She looked for Jane but wouldn't find her. Jane was gone.

Mielle knew to keep walking. That was the idea that pushed her as she limped up the hills to get up and out of Stuttgart. She had to get out of Germany before they caught her again.

TWO SISTERS

Mielle joined the column of people climbing out of the Cauldron to the countryside. All those whose homes had been destroyed, or who were stranded, had to find some place to go. Mielle blended in with the frantic and desperate as they limped up long banks of stone steps that were strung together from plateau to plateau in the side of vineyard hills, near the same winding roads she came down that afternoon. The hills graded steeper and steeper until she reached the top of the valley. She was out of the city and headed into the trees.

At first Mielle thought she should return to Schloss Solitude to see if Jane was alive and had gone there. But then she remembered Alfons Klaas. If the Gestapo was looking for her, going back to Solitude would make it too easy for them. So she climbed up and out of the hills into the middle of the night. She knew how to navigate by the stars. She had learned that in Iowa. She headed south, sticking to small roads in the woods. Dirt lanes that cut through the forests like branches of a stream.

When she looked back, orange columns of smoke rose in the sky. She wondered if Alden watched Stuttgart burn from his balcony in Bad Nauheim, if it was possible that he saw the particular orange cloud that had erupted over her head. The thought of returning to Bad Nauheim occurred to her too, a brief fantasy of waiting out extradition with Alden and her friends at the Grand Hotel. But, again, that would put her in the hands of the Gestapo. Her only choice was to walk south to Switzerland. The idea was an impossible one, but she had no other hope.

She limped along all night on those roads. She ducked behind stands of spindly tree trunks when she heard a motor approaching. Dozens of people did the same thing. People who had enough with living in a manufacturing hub, a principal cog in the German war machine, a prime target, too, and were heading out to live in the hinterlands. Hiding out the rest of the war in a cousin's barn was better than having a bomb dropped in your lap. All these people limped along. They carried nothing. Maybe they were Jews sneaking out, among the last free Jews in Germany, who picked this moment to leave their hiding spots and make a break for it.

Mielle had no idea what had become of Jane. If she had escaped the bombing unscathed. If she too had been pulled out of harm's way by the scruff of her neck. If she had been obliterated, and that's why there was no trace of her body. Maybe, if Mielle had only hurt her, if the blade did go in, Jane was waiting at Solitude.

Mielle couldn't care about that anymore. She forgot about her vision; finally, the vision had forgotten her.

Mielle had pushed forward the blade—she had done that, she was certain. That was all the vision had demanded of her, wasn't it? And if not, what else could she give?

Mielle surprised herself that night. She hadn't slept. She'd been beaten. A bomb had been dropped on her. She was still deaf from the ringing in her ears. Yet she persisted.

The past two years, she had waited for her life to come to an unnatural end. She assumed she would die in the war, with only the manner of death a mystery. Would she be killed at the whim of a nationalist? In a firebombing? A garden-variety execution? She didn't know. There were so many ways to die. What she had known, what she had believed, was that she wouldn't resist. She would welcome death when the time came, whatever the circumstance.

But on the forest roads south of Stuttgart, she kept going. The idea popped into her head that she must walk to Switzerland. So, yes, she must.

The grass was gray and snow-trampled in the pastures when she had to cross one, with hard, sticky mud at that time of year. Everywhere the ground was a sponge under her feet. She wished the grass was thigh-high and dry instead of there being hoarfrost in the meadows. Mud clumped around her brogans until the cuffs of her slacks were stained too. The walking was very slow then. Her feet too heavy. She had to rest after each open acre she rushed across—pasture by pasture—trying to stick close to a stream she found that wandered south. She felt safer, more hidden, when she stuck to the forest roads, but the farther she got from Stuttgart, the narrower the way forward became, until it was only foot-paths through a woods that connected one cottage to another. Then there weren't pastures at all, only damp woods so thick with branches that it was hard to pass, and there was still plenty of mud. She drank from the stream. She ate moss from grown-over tree trunks until it made her sick. She used sticks to scrape mud from her shoes, then learned how to stay on top of the dry leaves to keep the mud from caking. She had no way of knowing exactly how lost she was. As a girl she'd learned to orient herself by the sun and stars—but that assumed she would be able to see the sky. A good assumption on an American prairie. Not so good near the Black Forest. All she could do was note where the sun rose and set a general course south.

After the first twenty-four hours, she decided to walk only at night. She still couldn't hear because of the ringing in her ears. Stumbling deaf and night-blind through the woods was safer than having to explain herself if she was stopped by a farmer or sheriff or soldiers on patrol. There was no fighting here. That helped. Farmers still left their barns open—their eggs and horse oats were unguarded, their orchards hadn't yet been denuded of even the rotten fruit. But something bad was coming for these people. Mielle could feel that.

She hid in half-frozen ditches to sleep, her body numb with exhaustion. When awake, she licked the dew from leaves. She spotted small hopping birds and mice and foxes. At night she saw above her the fluttering webbed wings of bats and could feel the displaced air as they buzzed by her hair, but she still couldn't hear them.

The ringing in her ears wouldn't go away. She was frightened nearly to death having to walk through the forest deaf, alone, but she kept going. Her feet were numb even as her legs kept moving. Her face was still swollen and aching from where Klaas hit her. There were times when she wished she still had just one of those white-powder pills that had killed Nilo Steffen so she could swallow one herself and put an end to her suffering.

But still she walked. Still she wondered if each sneaking creature she spotted was edible; still she knelt to puddles and drank sulfur-tinged water from cupped hands.

She had to laugh. A person could fight so hard to survive while, at the same time, she wanted so much to die.

She wandered in circles for three days. One morning before dawn she came upon two women near the entrance of a barn. The women were shorter than Mielle but not short; stouter but not stout. Between them they swung a hog carcass to load into a truck. Blood soaked the dirt in the barn where other hogs hung by their toes. None of this bothered Mielle in the least.

Just like her, the two women wore black canvas butcher's coats. She saw that as a good omen.

Mielle stood watching the two women until they spotted her. It was still dark. Spotting a strange person stumbling out of the woods would stop your heart.

Mielle couldn't hear what they said to each other when she approached them. She hardly knew what she was saying herself in her old German dialect or if she made any sense at all.

The two women looked like they could be sisters. Their small upturned noses and broad, thin lips. One's hair had been chopped short, but the other had hers in braids. They looked rough and wary. The long scimitar knives from the slaughter still hung from leather straps, only a few feet away. The two women didn't shrink back to summon a man from the barn for help. They didn't tremble or run or shriek.

Mielle asked if they lived by themselves. They both nodded.

They spoke to her but Mielle couldn't hear their voices as more than a distant murmur. She couldn't read what German words their lips formed, especially not in the dim lamplight of the barnyard. She told them this.

"My ears," she said. "I can't hear."

She was desperate. Her lips swollen, her clothes covered in mud, spotted in blood. She had a black eye. She had to trust them.

The one with braids ran into the house a moment and returned with a pencil nub and a brown envelope. She wrote the name *Gerda* on the flap and tapped her chest with her thumb, then looked at the other woman, but this one shook her head. She wouldn't write.

Mielle said her own name out loud in response. She said her real name: Marthe. The feel of it was unnatural in her mouth, on her lips. How perplexing to say your name out loud and not be able to hear it.

Something switched inside with her name on her tongue. She didn't feel like she was Mielle any longer. She felt like herself. Saying her name to these butcher women changed her. "I am Marthe," she said again. "Marthe Hess."

The first one, Gerda, wrote on the envelope, *Wohin fahren Sie? Where are you headed?*

Marthe said, "In die Schweiz."

They looked her over. They saw she wore the same kind of coat.

This doesn't bother you? Gerda wrote on the envelope. She gestured around them. *Knives? Blood?*

"No."

Marthe explained as best she could that her father had been a butcher.

They looked one another in the eye and understood. Marthe couldn't say what it was, what deeper thing, but they were the same people. She could trust these women.

"Hilf mir," she said. She tried to whisper but her voice was a mess. She could feel her throat tearing like she was shouting. She said it again. "Help me."

All three worked together to load the truck as quickly as they could. The back of the truck was wrapped in canvas to protect the track where the hogs hung.

Once the truck was loaded, the sisters ran inside. They brought Marthe a jug of water and food wrapped in a wax-paper package, then helped her into the back where she could sit against the cab and be hidden by the hogs. The hogs didn't bother her.

There was quite a lot of food in the wrapper. Cold ham with gherkin sweet pickles and dark bread. Marthe ate and ate as the truck lurched forward. She tried not to worry about what would happen to her. She didn't know these women. For all she knew, they could be driving her back to the Hotel Silber at 2–4 Dorotheenstrasse. Marthe had to trust them.

She ate mechanically. The entire package. Every crumb. Each pickle, including the stems. The hog carcasses swayed on their hooks as she chewed and swallowed.

* * *

They drove for over an hour. Marthe had made it only twenty miles south of Stuttgart. They were driving farther south, Marthe thought, though she wasn't certain because it was still dark. They passed no one on the roads.

Marthe shivered in the back. Blocks of ice lined the truck bed. She thought they were going downhill the last mile, from the downshifting of the motor. They could have been winding down the roads into the Cauldron of Stuttgart. There was nothing Marthe could have done to keep this from happening.

When the truck stopped, Gerda peeked in through the hogs and motioned Marthe out.

The air was different here than it was in the forest. It was cooler, damper, the sky still dark when Marthe stood to stretch her back. They were at the shore of an immense lake. She didn't know it yet, but the two sisters had taken her to Lake Constance. Across the water, on a shore just visible through the fog, was Switzerland.

The other sister left, and they waited for her a long time, Marthe and Gerda, sitting silent on the flat bumper of the truck. Gerda pulled on the ends of her braids to flatten them. The sky started to blue just slightly over the water. Dozens of swans floated along the shore, the tips of their wings smeared black from the estuary mud. This too was a good omen, Marthe knew. A few people emerged at the shore to fiddle with boats. In the distance, small dogs were chasing seagulls.

Then the other sister returned with a small old man who wore a thick wool sweater and a longshoreman's beanie. Marthe had the impression that she wasn't the first refugee the sisters had brought here. They asked her for nothing.

She was so lucky. She tried to tell them this, but they waved her on.

The old man led her down to where his boat was lashed to the shore and loaded her in beside his fishing kits and nets.

He rowed them out, then started the motor.

They skipped atop the waves as the sun rose over the water.

Somehow it seemed too easy. All the towns along the far shore were just waking up, with thin tails of smoke rising from chimneys. That was Switzerland.

Marthe still had her passport and half a dozen expired press passes and credentials that said she could report the news from France, Italy, Germany, Monaco. All the places she'd been.

She was still a foreign correspondent, in addition to everything else she now was, and that would help her on this side of the border. They would let her in. She could walk into a wire office in one of those towns and send off a cable, collect, to her chief back in Jefferson City—he was the only person she could think of who could and would receive a cable from her at that moment—just to tell someone she was alive.

She had made it out of Germany.

She was alive.

Full stop.

SALZBURG

October 1947

A FLOOD OF DISPLACED PERSONS

(Marthe Hess)
As reported on April 12, 1945

No American who visited Germany over the last decade would recognize the place now. When traveling by jeep, as the U.S. press corps is now, one finds that the Teutonic landscape turns more and more desolate the farther north one goes.

The little villages and places like Constance, just over the border from Switzerland, appear mostly untouched. But the closer one gets to manufacturing hubs like Stuttgart and Frankfurt, less and less remains of what was once there. There are reports that Hamburg is even worse off, and one can only speculate about Berlin and Munich. When one hears such stories, one wonders if those cities will exist at all after the bombing the Allies are giving them.

If you loved Germany before the Nazis took over, it's probably best not to know that there is little left except charred rubble now.

Following behind Allied troops, the press encounters all sorts of refugees. That's another thing that has changed since I was in Germany three years ago. So many French, Russian, Czech, Yugoslav, and Polish peoples were enslaved in factories back then. They were in Germany, no doubt, but you never saw them. You can see them now.

There are at least 10,000 freed laborers wandering around Frankfurt, with thousands more filling the roads in all directions. It has become an unreasonable task to gather all of them into one of the massive displaced persons centers that were established in the wake of 3rd and 7th Army advances.

The refugees are bewildered and so thin you can see bones through their skin. Yet many appear cheerful despite what they have gone through. The French, who haven't seen home in five years, shout in celebration at the sight of American jeeps. These are the people strong enough to walk home. They have taken to the task with gusto, looting German wine cellars along the way to keep their spirits high.

Outside Stuttgart we saw liberated Russians and Poles raid the food stores of Germans. It is a delicate situation for American soldiers. Protocol bars theft, even if our boys would like to see a starving Polish slave fatten her bones at the expense of her German slave driver. "Rules are rules," the guards say, then they look the other way while the Poles make off with condensed milk, canned mackerel, and saltines.

Many refugees stay in the factories after they have been liberated. They know not where else to go.

"Do they really still remember us at home?" one refugee asked a group of reporters. "Does my village still exist?"

These are impossible questions to answer.

To hear some German citizens talk, you might think that no one supported the Nazis, that none of them who remain bought what Hitler was selling. Maybe in Munich, they say. Maybe in Berlin. But not here.

This is another thing that has changed in Germany, they would like you to believe. Somehow all the real Nazis have vanished. All the brown shirts and red flags have been burned with the garden rubbish. The Germans who remain are the good ones, they tell us. All this time, they were only waiting to be liberated.

You shouldn't believe them. I was here. I saw them. There were Nazis everywhere.

On some walls, the ones that still stand, posters can be seen that urge the German people to keep their mouths shut. *Schweigen hilft siegen*, these posters read. "Silence helps us to victory." The Nazi authorities put these up before fleeing. Even after defeat, the Fascist threats will still carry a lot of weight with these people.

But where are the Jews?

Reporters ask this of everyone in German villages. In the late thirties, there were hundreds of thousands of Jewish refugees, plus maybe triple that number who were already in camps. Now they are gone.

Not many Jews lived here in the first place, we are told. All the Germans we meet say the same thing. "I hid a Jew." "I'm half Jewish myself." "Jews never lived here. They lived one village over."

These too are lies. Our interpreters are German Jews who used to live in this region. They tell a different tale. But knowing that someone is missing isn't the same as knowing where they have gone.

Every day reporters learn more about this new Germany and the atrocities that occurred here. A sense of dread has filled each and every one of us because we realize that we know only half of what went on inside the Third Reich. We may never learn it all, but we are retelling the stories as best as we're able.

FOR MOST OF IT I HAVE NO WORDS

(Edward R. Murrow)
As reported on April 15, 1945

Dr. Heller, the Czech, asked if I would care to see the crematorium. He said it wouldn't be very interesting because the Germans had run out of coke some days ago and had taken to dumping the bodies into a great hole nearby. Professor Richer said perhaps I would care to see the small courtyard. I said yes. He turned and told the children to stay behind...The wall was about eight feet high; it adjoined what had been a stable or garage. We entered. It was floored with concrete. There were two rows of bodies stacked up like cordwood. They were thin and very white. Some of the bodies were terribly bruised, though there seemed to be little flesh to bruise. Some had been shot through the head, but they bled but little. All except two were naked. I tried to count them as best I could and arrived at the conclusion that all that was mortal of more than five hundred men and boys lay there in two neat piles.

The clothing was piled in a heap against the wall. It appeared that most of the men and boys had died of starvation; they had not been executed. But the manner of death seemed unimportant. Murder had been done at Buchenwald. God alone knows how many men and boys died there during the last twelve years. Thursday I was told that there were more than twenty thousand in the camp. There had been as many as sixty thousand. Where are they now?

I pray you to believe what I have said about Buchenwald. I have reported what I saw and heard, but only part of it. If I've offended you by this rather mild account of Buchenwald, I'm not in the least sorry.

LET IT DIE

She wrote next to nothing the first three months she was in Switzerland. A few telegrams to collect her back wages; a whole other series of telegrams to the U.S. embassy in Bern to establish a visa and her residency. She wasn't a combatant, as far as anyone knew, so she wasn't moved to a Swiss holding camp like downed pilots and AWOL soldiers were. Other than that, she did next to nothing at all.

Mostly she slept. She ate. She recovered.

She thought a lot about what she had become and if she could live with the result.

After a month she wrote a letter to her mother and father. Without knowing if they would ever read what she sent, she told them that she was alive, in Switzerland, and had escaped from Germany. That was all she mentioned about that. What she really wanted them to know was that she was doing fine, that she'd found friendship and love and felt she belonged in the world. If they ever wondered if she was lost, they should know she was fine. She was fallen, she had to wander, but she was a survivor.

What she really wanted them to know was that she was at peace with the fact that she would never see them again in this world. She forgave them for everything that happened. And she knew that they forgave her too.

She hoped with her whole heart that the letter reached them.

Two weeks later she wrote another letter. This one was much shorter. It would have fit on a postcard with room to spare. *Dear*

Jane, it read. *Are you there?* She had it sent to the Georgia Peach, c/o the Reich Broadcasting studios in Berlin. A week later she sent another one to Schloss Solitude in Stuttgart.

She never received a response.

Marthe didn't know if the blade had gone in during the bombing, only that she had pushed it forward toward Jane's heart. But she wished that the blade didn't go in. That she'd missed Jane's heart. That she had been pulled back by the scruff of her neck before she pushed forward the blade, so that Jane wasn't killed, so that Jane wasn't even nicked.

By the end of May she saw the news that the Grand Hotel internees had been released from Bad Nauheim. They'd been sent by train to Lisbon, then by boat to New York. She and Bob Best had departed prematurely; Louis Harl and Philip Whitcomb decided to remain in Lisbon in the hope of reuniting with their families in France. All the rest made it safe to New York.

Marthe wrote a third letter once she read that news in *Time* magazine. This one was to Alden Cohn, c/o Mr. Linden Elder, International News Service, New York, New York.

> *Dearest Alden, if you haven't heard yet through your clandestine channels, I made it out of Berlin alive. Currently I reside in Zurich, at 21 Bahnhofstrasse. If you can make it here, I would do anything to see you. I don't have the faintest idea if that is possible on your end or on mine. But I can imagine that YOU might have an idea or two on how to drop in. There are many things we left unsaid. I would like to say them. xoxo, yours, etc.*

* * *

Before the end of the war, Alden did find a way to join her in Switzerland. She would tell him about everything she had seen and done.

But this is the story of two women.

One found her moment in the limelight. The other was stuck in Germany and nearly forgotten.

Marthe Hess was twenty-seven when she got her first major byline as a foreign correspondent, a series of syndicated columns about life behind the curtain in the Third Reich. What she had seen in Berlin, the degraded state of their once-famous night-life; what she had seen in Stuttgart—at least, in a general way. She didn't include many personal details. She named few names in her columns. Her report for U.S. military intelligence was more complete, but for the public it was just what kinds of foods they could get in Berlin, how gaunt the faces of the women were, and what it was like to be on the receiving end of an English bomber campaign.

It was believed among people in the know that Marthe sat out the rest of the war in Switzerland. It's true she remained in Zürich until the summer of 1945, when she found consistent work reporting on the roundup of Nazi war criminals in Austria and Germany.

From the outside looking in, people would think Marthe had it easy the rest of the war. She stayed in a Zürich hotel room. She had friends. She knew people and was known. She published well, but she didn't make the big time. She was more than fine with that.

She still walked with a limp but wasn't much changed. She still wore her hair short, still wore the black canvas butcher's jacket she bought in Ornano that reminded her of her father. Nobody remembered her in Germany. She was on no secret lists. She certainly wasn't a public enemy, besides being an American.

There were many rumors about what happened to Jane Anderson, that other woman.

That she had been executed by the Nazis, shot in the head, when they took her off the air in 1942. Marthe knew this rumor wasn't true.

Other rumors claimed Jane had been sent to a concentration camp as a criminal and died there. Or that she survived until the final days of the war but then perished in a Berlin air raid at the hands of American tonnage. Marthe was almost happy when she heard these rumors, because it meant Jane was alive after Stuttgart.

The truth is that Jane Anderson lived in Baden-Baden until 1944. After she disappeared during the bombing of Stuttgart, she stayed in southern Germany with her husband. Later, a Belgian man named Charles Hennus joined them. The three tried on numerous occasions to enter Switzerland. Hennus and Cienfuegos were often successful in crossing the border. Jane was not.

Jane and Cienfuegos lived in Austria, at Ehrwald, until April 1945. Jane moved briefly to Reutte, alone, then went to nearby Garmisch-Partenkirchen in Germany.

She wore her Spanish Red Cross uniform all the time after the war ended. Something she hadn't done in years, since getting kicked off the air. For a while she traveled with a man named Erik Kuem, until he was arrested by U.S. forces. Then Jane went back to Austria. She slept with a woman named Johanna Mayer in Innsbruck, in an apartment at 7 Beethovenstrasse.

In 1947 Jane and her husband were under surveillance in a Bregenzerwald village. This was in the French zone of occupation. She had known for a long time that the Americans were looking for her. They had charged her with treason in a federal court in Washington, DC, four years earlier.

She and Cienfuegos requested that the French allow them to travel to Spain. They renewed appeals for asylum to Switzerland.

Marthe had once felt so lit up inside to have a wild friend like Jane Anderson. But Jane was hardly recognizable to people who knew her before. Half starved, her skin loose around her neck and arms. She was only weeks away from turning sixty, but she looked much older than that. If she claimed to be only sixty, you wouldn't have believed her. Her hair dull and thin, cut short. She wore a felt chrysanthemum on her lapel. She wore no makeup. There was none.

Her green eyes were panicked, unnerving when they darted from underneath the mask of her face.

The French wouldn't have arrested her if she didn't tell them who she was. She needed everyone, anyone, to know that she was wanted, that she had been considered the most beautiful woman in the world once. If they didn't believe that, then she would tell them that she'd published articles in the *London Daily Mail, New York Times, Harper's Magazine;* she had three novels. She'd list off the titles for you: *The Happiest Man in the World. Down to the Depths.* If that didn't move the needle, then she would tell you how she once had her own radio show, one that was broadcast worldwide on shortwave. Yes, and OSS, FBI, Interpol, wouldn't they like to get their hands on her. And her name? She had a few. Foster Jane Anderson, Marquesa Cienfuegos, Lady Haw-Haw, the Georgia Peach. She *was* wanted, as it turned out.

Jane was arrested at Innsbruck, in the French zone, on April 2, 1947. Since the end of the war, she and her husband, the Marqués Álvarez de Cienfuegos, had been living in impoverished conditions under assumed names in the village of Egg.

She was three inches shorter than the description attached to her dossier.

She spoke impeccable French—so perfect a Parisian accent that her arresting gendarmes doubted she could really be an American.

She was almost happy to be arrested. She said she wanted to clear her name.

But her hands shook uncontrollably when she was in custody. She habitually asked for Pervitin, then for any white or red pill, but there were none. She begged soldiers for cigarettes. She was partial to Gitanes, but Lucky Strikes would do.

The Cienfuegoses were kept under town arrest in Salzburg after they were handed over to the Americans. That was fine. There was nowhere good to run at that point except Madrid. Jane would never have made it to Spain under her own power.

Salzburg, the city of Mozart's birth, held together through the war. Hohensalzburg Fortress still perched high on the hill. The church bells still rang. (Jane said she loved hearing bells ring because it meant she was surrounded by Catholics; she would refer to herself as a living martyr until the day she died.) Boys still crouched along the Salzach River to catch brown and rainbow trout, and the trout had not been poisoned, they were good to eat, with bright red gills and glistening tail fins.

GIs in olive-drab uniforms and cloth hats sped everywhere in open jeeps.

Jane and Cienfuegos stayed on a middle floor of a tall yellow building not far from the river. The building sagged a few degrees to the left, but it stood and would stay standing a long time. There were even lace curtains in some of the windows that billowed out in the breeze. It was a cheerful building, despite its wear, in that whimsical European way. Two GIs were stationed in the entry-way. Like concierges, but with machine guns. They made sure Marthe's name was on their list before they let her up. The whole building, they told her, was full of war criminals who were waiting to go on trial.

A hangman's scaffold had been put up in the courtyards of one of the government buildings. Everyone knew that.

The stairways smelled like cabbage and urine and stale cigarette smoke. Someone had spilled dry oatmeal in the hallway then let it grind into the soggy carpet.

Jane answered the door when Marthe knocked, like she had been waiting for a visitor or pacing the floorboards. She invited Marthe in, cleared off space on the sofa. "Sits, sits," she said. She looked Marthe in the face several times without knowing her. Neither introduced herself. It had been five years since they last saw each other.

Even with a breeze coming through the open window, the room smelled the same as the hallway had. The carpet and the upholstery of the sofa were sticky. White powder covered every stationary object, though there wasn't much furniture to dust. A round dining table had only one chair. Strewn across the floor were dozens of magazines and copies of *Stars and Stripes*.

Marthe held her breath, realizing that Jane didn't recognize her. She hadn't anticipated that. For a second she doubted that she had the right room, but only for a second. The woman must have been Jane. The vaguely tawny hair butched short. The green eyes. The woman rushed back and forth between the kitchen and the sitting room. Her hands shook when she came back with a porcelain mug.

"How do you like Salzburg?" the woman asked. Her voice smoky, battered, warm. "So much music normally. Did you ever like Mozart? I did. As a girl." She was rambling. She rushed back to the kitchen.

"Is Eduardo here too?" Marthe asked. "The tribunal told me he didn't return to Spain."

Jane was trying to make coffee for them, without much luck.

She poked her head in from the other room, fumbling two components of an electric kettle in her hands.

"Eduardo? Do you know my husband?"

Jane stooped over to inspect Marthe closer. She was at a loss, her green eyes begging for help, for any clue.

Marthe wore a khaki uniform that was given to members of the American press corps so they fit in amid the military. But otherwise she looked the same, she thought. Her hair kept short. She wore untied brogans. Maybe her face had lost the round-cheeked hints of girlishness, if she'd ever had them. She was thirty-two by then.

It was hard to believe that either could forget the other. But the war changed people. Noses grew longer. Skin hardened. Backs bent. Even the color of an iris faded. It was rare to see anyone with a twinkle in her eye. The two women froze to stare at the other, to see if they had once known each other and if they could trust what each saw in the other's eyes.

Marthe recognized Jane at once then, because of those green eyes, her long limbs. Marthe had rarely seen Jane as she actually was before—instead seeing Jane as she wanted to see her.

She reached out and took Jane by the wrists, the real Jane who was stooping there. Then Jane could see her too.

"Mielle? Is that you?" Jane dropped the kettle parts to the floor. "You haven't changed a bit, have you? You look beautiful without makeup. But then, did you ever wear any?"

"No," Marthe said. She released Jane's wrists, then leaned back to recross her legs. She took a deep breath. She could breathe now that Jane had remembered her.

"Mielle," Jane said. Her face twisted, like she couldn't believe what was happening. "It is you. God Almighty. I thought you had died."

Jane reached over and touched the sleeve of Marthe's jacket. "You aren't a *ghost*, are you? *Ha!*"

Jane's manic voice was recognizable, that contralto of her laugh.

"What on earth are you doing here?" Jane asked.

"I'm a correspondent," Marthe explained. "Wire stuff. Arrests and trials, mostly. There aren't so many fashion shows right now."

"Ha! No, I expect not. Good for you!"

A sparrow flew in through the open window. Jane followed the bird, called to it, *"Birdie, birdie,"* but made no real effort to shoo it back out. The bird flitted from corner to corner of the room, then sat on a burned-out sconce.

Jane came back to the sofa and sat to face Marthe. She took Marthe's hands in her own.

"I thought the English had killed you," Jane said again. "I looked for you after the bombing. Without any luck. Were you trapped under a wall?"

"No. I was covered in dust. The explosion knocked my lights out for a while. I don't know how long. You were gone when I woke out of it. And I was deaf. I couldn't hear anything for days after."

"I knew it had to be something. I was calling for you. *Mielle! Mielle!* What a mess. No wonder. You couldn't hear me. Ha!" Jane's fingers inched from Marthe's hands to her wrists. "But you escaped? The Gestapo didn't get you? Good. I'm glad to hear it."

The sparrow watched from the old sconce across the room. It considered them out of one eye for a moment, then turned its head to watch with the other.

"The Nazis never did decide what killed Nilo Steffen," Jane said. "Didn't you wonder? It had to be a heart attack. And that horrid Inspector Klaas was dead too. I doubt anybody cared one way or the other by then. Not that it helped my cause with the Germans. They sure had a way of blaming other people when… wasn't it their own fault? Don't you think? Poor Nilo. Nazis like him, from the start of it all, they were all destined to die in some horrible way. There was no other possibility. Goebbels, Nilo, even the führer. It's too bad. Especially that maniac Klaas. How could someone like him hope to survive? He had it coming, what you did to him."

Jane's eyes opened wide, remembering.

"I never told a soul what you did to him, because you and I are friends. I would never spoil a friendship like that."

Marthe shifted in her seat, leaned closer to Jane to get her attention. She wanted to change the subject, but Jane was quicker.

"Did you like it? Doing that. Killing a man. Did it make you feel good?"

Marthe startled back. She opened her mouth to shout *No,* but nothing came out.

"You butchered him," Jane said. "You are the sword and the scales, I told you that, years ago. You're a Libra, just like my dad. I see it in your eyes."

Marthe was speechless so Jane pushed further.

"Is there only one notch on your blade? I bet not. A person doesn't take joy in killing like that and then just stop."

Her fingers inched up Marthe's forearms.

"Do you regret it? Or is your conscience clear because he was only a Fascist? And it made you feel good to kill a Fascist, didn't it?"

Marthe pulled away.

"Listen, Jane." Her voice stretching. "You are to go on trial in the morning. Are you aware of that?"

"Yes, yes. I'm aware."

"Do you have an attorney to defend you? When you are convicted, you could be hanged."

"They wouldn't hang me. There won't even be a trial, dear. You'll see. This whole thing is just politics. I'm a political prisoner. I don't like it, but that's all there is to it. They want to drag my name through the mud for a while to make themselves feel better.

All the elites. All the pointy-heads and hook-noses in Washington. They never liked me, but they can't make me go away." Jane's face filled with indignation. "A doctor once told me that I was made to last forever. What do you think of that? I think he was right. He was exactly right."

Jane stood and walked around the room. Her limbs jerked awkwardly, detached from each other, like her brain had short-circuited. Marthe didn't know how she could even talk to Jane. Jane jumped from subject to subject. Jane's eyes roamed around the room without focus.

"You were crazy when we were in Stuttgart." Jane knelt to the carpet and picked up the pieces of the electric kettle. "You tried to kill me. Remember?"

"I had a dream that I was supposed to kill you," Marthe said. "So I tried."

"But you're better now? You don't still have that dream?"

"No, I don't." Marthe shifted in her seat. She recrossed her legs. "But it isn't up to me. It never was."

Jane marched to where the sparrow perched. She and the bird looked each other in the eye. "If it wasn't up to you, that means we can be friends when they let me out."

"They're not going to do that," Marthe said. "They're going to make you pay for the things you said on the radio."

"No, no. Stop talking like that."

Marthe didn't know why she told Jane they were hanging traitors. She thought she had come to peace with what happened in Stuttgart a long time ago. She had shoved forward the saber, no doubt. Even if that invisible hand pulled her away, she had still pushed forward the blade. She couldn't take that back. She wouldn't even have tried to ask for forgiveness until she was in that room. But looking at Jane, and Jane's trembling hands, how Jane was doubled over, three inches shorter, Marthe felt compelled to speak.

"I hope you get what's coming to you," she said. "But I'm also sorry. Sorry for what I've done, or tried to do."

"Everyone gets mixed up in a war, honey."

"It's important to me. I must ask for forgiveness."

Jane dropped the kettle again to hold her arms out from her body, her head thrown back, like she was being crucified.

The sparrow, spooked, fluttered from the sconce and flew out the window.

"Is that all? All you need is forgiveness?"

Jane touched her middle finger to her thumb, like she was Christ, and held out her hand toward Marthe.

"I forgive you. You are clean. All your sins have been paid for. You are redeemed. I redeemed you."

THE TRIAL

They held the trials in a post office on Franziskanergasse, near the old Franciscan cloister that had been used as the local Gestapo headquarters in Salzburg for the previous decade. The Posthof was a classic Austrian building in the center of town, not far from where Marthe and Alden were staying. A tan stucco building with an Italian campanile rising from its center that was made of corroded green copper. Over the shoulders of its peaked roof, you could see the white bricks of the fortress, behind that the rolling hills that led to the Alps.

Marthe woke with the sun the next morning and ate breakfast at the hotel. She hadn't slept all night after she spoke with Jane. She had been there only half an hour. Cienfuegos hadn't come back. Yet in that time, Jane had managed to upend her again.

Marthe hoped that Jane would get what was coming to her. Her second sight didn't tell her what would happen. That was how she felt. She would have visions the rest of her life, but the vision of Jane's death stopped after what happened in Stuttgart. Marthe had peace in that way, at least.

She dressed and ate and walked across the street to the post office with the intention of providing a sworn affidavit with firsthand knowledge that Jane Anderson had in fact lived in Berlin as a collaborator during the war. This would give her peace too, she hoped, if she could close the book on Jane.

She had heard that Jane claimed there was no evidence against her. That nobody could prove she was the same woman who'd played the roles of Lady Haw-Haw and the Georgia Peach on the radio. That it was impossible to tell one woman's voice from another on a transcript. There were no living witnesses.

Marthe intended to be that witness.

She walked into an office on the first floor. A young GI sat behind a Smith Corona typewriter at the desk.

Marthe had it all squared away. She had the case number for Jane's trial. She wrote out all the dates for when she was in Berlin in 1942 and had seen Jane at the RRG transmitter station. The GI took her statement and typed it out. Every detail. How and when she met Jane Anderson in Paris. What she was doing in Germany in 1942. Who among the Nazis had she seen Jane fraternize with. Why the Georgia Peach could be no other woman in the world than Jane Anderson. They spent a lot of time together in that small post-office room amid the smell of ink and brass rollers and sweat. The GI time-stamped each of the four pages he had typed out, then stapled them all together. He opened a metal filing cabinet in an adjacent room, added Marthe's statement, then slammed shut the drawer. He thanked Marthe and told her she could leave.

"I'm willing to say it all again in person. At the trial today," she said.

"No, ma'am. That won't be necessary," the GI said. He was pudgy and square. He hardly looked old enough to drive a car. Marthe would remember how young the GI looked, that he had probably still been in grammar school when the war began. His voice was reedy. He had an accent like he was from Minnesota. There were a million boys like this one back on the northern plains. This one had something important to tell Mielle, but he didn't understand it was important.

"The lady you mean, she has been released," he said, sitting down behind a bottle of 7 Up. "The charges were dropped. On account of her being a Spanish citizen."

Marthe didn't believe him. "Say that again," she told him. She moved her chair closer and stared at his lips as he repeated himself. "I'm prepared to testify right now," she said.

"You don't understand, miss. Both the lady and her husband were on the first plane out this morning, headed for Spain. She's already gone. There will be no trial. The charges got dropped. She's been forgiven."

"Forgiven? On whose authority?"

"On the authority of the United States Department of Justice. That's who!"

The GI swiveled back in his creaky office chair, put his feet up on the desk, and sipped his soda pop. He filed all the orders from this court, he explained, so he knew. That morning at five, Jane Cienfuegos and the Marqués Álvarez de Cienfuegos were escorted from their apartment by two MPs and put on an airplane that was bound for Madrid. They had no possessions with them.

"Nothing," the clerk said. "Maybe she got off easy for a traitor. But at least she left empty-handed."

Marthe wandered out of the post office, across a narrow bridge over the river, and then into Mirabellgarten. Her left leg dragged a little in a limp. The heel on that foot wore down faster than the one on her right. She didn't think about it at all. She didn't know what to think.

In the garden, an old man raked the pea gravel smooth over a path.

Alden was waiting for her. She just had to find him. The air was clear and clean, but an odor lingered here and there, something similar to the sulfur of tank exhaust. Marthe thought, for no reason, because of the sulfur, that in fields everywhere surrounding them, all over the world, still, bodies rotted.

She had no trouble finding Alden. He waited alone on a bench, a lilac hedge behind him, and watched the old man rake smooth the gravel paths. Alden had taken to wearing white suits.

His hair was very thin, fine, and light, which made him more attractive, Marthe thought, more dignified.

He smiled when she sat next to him. Put his arm around her. Asked her how it went. If she was required to return later for the trial or if they could go to lunch together.

Marthe explained what happened. Alden wasn't surprised. The war had been over two years already. Even the trials at Nuremberg were over. There were lots of people like Jane who slipped between the widening cracks in the denazification program.

"It's kind of funny," Alden said. "Her American citizenship saved her during the Spanish Civil War, and her Spanish citizenship saved her from the Americans now."

Marthe wasn't amused. She didn't feel like this was over.

"Jane put the screws to me yesterday," she said. Her heart beat hard as she remembered. "Now she's vanished. What kind of person is she? To ask me in one breath if I regret putting a blade through a man's chest, if it's okay because he was a Fascist. And the implication that I felt no shame over killing. That I *enjoyed* killing! The gall. To ask me if I regret it."

"Well," Alden asked, "is she right?"

Marthe didn't want to answer. She wanted to point out that she was only doing what she had to, only what was asked of her. But that's what all the Germans said after the war. They only did what they had to do to survive.

Marthe didn't care if it was true or not. She wanted to be better than the deniers, the capitulators. Her second sight had led her to that moment, and it wouldn't relent. She didn't want to feel pain like that ever again. Her visions demanded that she lift a sword to Jane's heart, and she had done that. She had answered the demand, and the vision left her alone about Jane.

"I do regret it," she admitted to Alden. "I wish none of that had to happen. Even the specks of dust I am responsible for in this landslide of suffering. I regret what I did, but I can only be who I am. I can do no other."

Alden uncrossed his legs, put his hands on his knees.

"You are thinking too much about this. The situation made us all who we are. We had to react." He breathed deep. "People like us have a duty to do what is right, to protect other people, to be the best, the strongest. We are Americans. That is our north star, what guides us to do right—"

"Oh, shut up."

Marthe lay her head on his shoulder and closed her eyes. She was very tired. Somewhere not far away, someone started tuning a violin.

"We don't have to remember everything, do we?"

"No, we do not."

"People like us. We're allowed to forget."

The air was clean and cool that morning, with just a slight tincture of ozone and spoiled eggs, just here and there.

An old man smoothed gravel paths.

Someone was tuning a violin inside the conservatory, near an open window.

A woman and a man sat close on a bench in Salzburg. Sunning themselves. Their eyes closed to take it all in. The air from the mountains cool on their skin.

An old man knocked bits of gravel back and forth.

The woman and the man closed their eyes to listen.

Somewhere close, a violin was coming into tune.

ACKNOWLEDGMENTS

First, and always, thank you to Nicole, Madeleine, Clara, and my family.

The early stages of this book received significant institutional support in the form of fellowships from the National Endowment for the Arts and the Nebraska Arts Council. Thank you to the judges who advocated for my project in its early days and to the administrators who enabled me to see this book to fruition.

Thanks to the runners at Creighton University's Reinert Alumni Memorial Library and the University of Nebraska at Omaha's Criss Library for keeping me surrounded by books even when the buildings were closed during the COVID lockdown year. I would have been lost without them. The staff at the Hotel Silber museum in Stuttgart and the numerous research specialists who kept pointing me in the right direction at the National Archives are indispensable. Anita Carey-Yard, archivist at Akademie Schloss Solitude, helped plant the seed for this project almost a decade ago by finding me a stack of books about Stuttgart during the war.

It has been a heartening experience to work with my publishing family on a third straight novel.

Vivian Lee is a dream of an editor. Immensely bright; generous; the kind of reader who always sees a book on its best terms. To find a kindred spirit for an editor feels like more than anyone deserves.

ACKNOWLEDGMENTS

I can't imagine what misfortune befell me in a past life to have led me to an agent like Stephanie Delman in this one. Stephanie worked with me on this novel from the beginning, kept my focus straight during early drafts, never let my spirits dry up during the depths of a pandemic, and then helped push the book beyond its original conception as we saw the other side. This book wouldn't exist without her.

Thanks as well to Khalid McCalla, Morgan Wu, Karen Landry, Danielle Finnegan, Katharine Myers, Tracy Roe, and all the unheralded heroes at Little, Brown and Trellis Literary Management for helping to get this book out into the world in the best shape possible.

A special thanks to Nicole Wheeler, Kassandra Montag, and Amy O'Reilly for being my first (and always best) readers. And to Bonodji Nako, Steve Schoening, Anne Gustafson, Ryan Norris, and Sam Slaughter for their eyes as well. Thanks to Ada, Ella, Maddie, Tom, Emily, and Chloe for holding down the fort at the bookshop so I could write.

So much of this story was inspired by the writing and lives of my journalist forebears, many of whom are fictionalized in these pages. Maybe it's too obvious to state, but without their books, broadcasts, and articles, there couldn't be this book. You should know their names. You should read their work. William L. Shirer, Dorothy Thompson, Virginia Cowles, Sigrid Schultz, A. J. Liebling, Edward R. Murrow, Howard K. Smith, Martha Gellhorn, and Rebecca West, to name just a few.

Thanks to all my readers. Not that long ago it felt too audacious to believe I could publish one book. Now, here is my fourth. Every day I sat down to write this story I thought about you. It makes a huge difference to know there is an audience here for the performance. Thank you.

ABOUT THE AUTHOR

Theodore Wheeler is the author of four books, including the novels *Kings of Broken Things* and *In Our Other Lives*. He has won fellowships from the National Endowment for the Arts, the Nebraska Arts Council, and Akademie Schloss Solitude in Stuttgart, Germany. Wheeler worked for fourteen years as a journalist covering law and politics, but he now operates Dundee Book Company, an independent neighborhood bookshop, and is a professor in the English Department at Creighton University. A native Iowan, he now lives in Omaha, Nebraska.